Martin Clark

The Legal Limit

Martin Clark's first novel, *The Many Aspects of Mobile Home Living*, was a *New York Times* Notable Book and a finalist for the Stephen Crane First Fiction Award. His second novel, *Plain Heathen Mischief*, prompted *The Charlotte Observer* to call him "a rising star in American Letters." A circuit court judge, he lives in Stuart, Virginia, with his wife, Deana.

www.martinclark.com

The Legal Limit

Martin Clark

The Legal Limit

VINTAGE CONTEMPORARIES

Vintage Books

A Division of Random House, Inc.

New York

FIRST VINTAGE CONTEMPORARIES EDITION, JUNE 2009

The Library of Congress has cataloged the Knopf edition as follows:
Clark, Martin, 1959–
The legal limit / Martin Clark.—1st ed.
p. cm.
1. Brothers—Fiction 2. Murder—Fiction 3. Ethics—Fiction I. Title.
PS3553.L2865L44 2008
813'54—dc22 2007042861

VINTAGE ISBN: 978-0-307-38866-7

www.vintagebooks.com

Printed in the United States of America
10 9 8 7 6 5 4 3 2 1

FOR MY WIFE, DEANA

So we look for a message and we search in our souls
As we sift through the wreckage like we're shoveling coal.

—ROBERT EARL KEEN, "Train Trek"

In any prosecution for a violation of driving under the influence, the amount of alcohol in the blood of the accused at the time of the alleged offense as indicated by a chemical analysis of a sample of the accused's blood or breath shall give rise to the following rebuttable presumption: If there was at the time of the alleged offense .08 grams or more per 210 liters of the accused's breath, it shall be presumed that the accused was under the influence of alcohol intoxicants at the time of the alleged offense.

—Section 18.2-269 of the 1950 Code of Virginia, as amended

Part One

I became a judge when I was thirty-two years old, and my first novel, The Many Aspects of Mobile Home Living, was published when I was forty. Given my interest in both law and writing, people have frequently encouraged me to put together a nonfiction, insider's book about the legal system, a temptation I've always avoided for two main reasons. Most notably, I very much value the business of the courts and the importance of what we do as judges, and I believe that parting our velvet curtains to offer the world a wholesale view of the cogs, cranks, belts, braces, booms, and pulleys deep behind the stage is not necessarily a wise idea. Courts need a certain measure of dignity—and, yes, mystique—to function at their best. The Great and Powerful Oz was never the same after the dog embarrassed him, and without his mask the Lone Ranger would be a run-of-the-mill do-gooder, just another guy on a fancy horse.

Moreover, and at the risk of eroding that dignity and mystique, it's fair to say that day-to-day jurisprudence is a numbing, flat, repetitive affair, leavened with occasional spells of predictable farce and eye-rolling nonsense. On probation-violation afternoons, for instance, the officers and clerks usually bet on which criminal with a dirty drug screen will be the first to claim—his right hand raised extra high for emphasis—he's the victim of "some dude" slipping cocaine into his coffee. "Dudes are bad about giving their dope away as a prank," I always respond with a straight face, while a five-dollar bill discreetly switches owners in the periphery. As an author, I've never seen where it would be worth the effort to chronicle such as this for three hundred pages.

My thoughts on not mixing law and literature lasted until 2003, when I changed my mind and decided to write about one of my cases and turn it into this book. At quitting time on a drab Thursday in November of that year, a deputy at the Patrick County jail phoned and informed me there was someone who hoped to speak with me, someone I knew. This call led to three lengthy meetings during which I became privy to a remarkable history, a narrative that was far more compelling than anything I could ever dream up, and it gradually occurred to me there might be a novel in the story I'd been told. I was convinced I'd gotten the truth in these meetings, but I nevertheless spent the next few weeks quietly nosing around and checking the particulars. I talked with a couple of the people involved, read old files, studied transcripts, and took a trip to state police headquarters. Everything jibed.

The Legal Limit, *then*, is not a literal diary of what I do as a circuit court judge—it's not quite the undertaking that has been suggested to me—but it is at its core a reasonably accurate account of lives and happenings I discovered only because of my job and wouldn't have come across otherwise. In terms of perspective and the angles I see from where I sit, this story should also give folks a taste of how it feels to make hard decisions, stick them in a lonely black robe and situate them so they can understand how the correct answer, the right ruling, sometimes brings along its own tricks and complications.

That having been said, this book is done as fiction. I cut several scenes from whole cloth, portions of dialogue are an educated guess as to the actual conversations and names are tweaked or rearranged in places, although my friends here in Stuart, Virginia, won't have any problem deciphering who's who. A few parts are inverted, sort of written backward. Much of the small detail, however, is reproduced exactly, with only a minimum of writer's gloss. I was amazed by what people could recall two decades removed from events: a missing section of plaster in a room, a sound, a scent, an odd phrase, even the luckless kamikaze bird that introduces the first chapter. Simply put, there are plenty of facts in these pages, but I've definitely retooled them to serve the story I wanted to tell.

Finally, I suspect many people will find my choices in this matter troubling and disagree with how I determined to finish things, since my attempt at an act of conscience arguably doesn't square with the familiar, black-and-white dictates of the law. Perhaps I made a mistake. Still, my predecessor on the bench, Frank Richardson, once advised me that a smart judge always has a little juju up his sleeve, even if the rules don't contemplate it and the parties don't see it coming. "Every now and then you're entitled to play the wild card" was how he explained it. "Justice can occasionally be a fickle, blind bitch, and somebody has to keep her honest."

Part Two

Chapter One

The shooting came in October 1984, abrupt and rash, a quicksilver *bang*.

The day it happened, Mason Hunt had spent most of his morning settled into the afghan-covered recliner at his mother's house, watching a nondescript black and brown and white thrush fly against the big den window again and again as it tried to punch through the glass, the bird evidently sickly or a bona fide lunatic, remaining behind while its kin abandoned Virginia and migrated farther south. Despite the suicidal thumps and flutters that gained it nothing and left it pitifully outside its hope, the misguided bird never learned a lesson or gave up on its headlong, full-steam shortcut to sanctuary, never stopped, kept at the foolishness for hours. Mason was home from his final year of law school, visiting his mother and enjoying her flapjacks and rich casseroles for a weekend, waiting for his older brother, Gates, to arrive so they could saw up a maple tree that had blown over in the front yard and stack it into winter firewood. By the time Gates pulled in the gravel drive at eleven thirty, Mason had finished two cups of coffee, napped, read three issues of the *Stuart*

nterprise and carted the kerosene heater from the basement to its
spot near the couch, even though there was no fuel in it and the
weather wouldn't turn cold for another month or so. Soon after he
heard Gates cut his Corvette's ignition, Mason noticed that the bird
had quit its sallies and was stuck in a holly bush next to the window,
one wing draped across a run of green, prickly leaves, its beak
gapped, its head listing and its feet dangling, unable to take hold of
anything.

Gates opened the mudroom door but didn't move too far past
the threshold, let out his neck like a terrapin leaving its armor to get
a better view of Mason and his mother. "Hello, Mama," he said in a
voice a few notches above normal.

"Gates," she said, not looking up from her kitchen work. She was
peeling green baking apples, circling off the skin in deft turns and
cuts that went from stem to bottom without a hitch.

"What're you cooking?" he asked, leaning against the doorjamb.

"A pie." The two words were absolutely neutral, ciphers. "The
phone not workin' where you were at last night?"

"I'm sorry; I know I promised I'd call when I can't make it home.
You forgive me?"

"It's common courtesy, Gates—if you're living under my roof you
could at least let me know where you are. Twenty-seven years old,
and it's the only thing I ask from you."

"It won't happen again."

"Perhaps you should ground him or take away TV privileges,"
Mason joked, trying to lighten the mood.

"There you go," Gates said. "That'll keep me on the straight and
narrow."

"You ready to get started?" Mason asked, bending over to retie
his shoes.

"Sure. Yep. Ready, ready, ready. Ready as can be." Gates was
wearing a Washington Redskins jersey with the name "Hunt" stenciled across the back in gold block letters. Five inches over six feet
tall, he didn't fit well into the doorframe. "Mason, man, I need you
to run an errand with me before we take care of the tree, and then

we're right back here lickety-split." He glanced at their mother. She still didn't look in his direction.

"An errand?" Mason repeated.

"You boys be careful with the saw," Sadie Grace Hunt said from the kitchen. "Chain saws are dangerous, Gates." She finally made eye contact with him.

"Yes, ma'am," Gates answered. "You don't need to worry about us."

"And if you're goin' somewhere with Mason"—she held the paring knife in front of her, pointing it at the ceiling—"you let him drive, you hear?"

"If it'll make you happy, then I'd be delighted to have my little brother chauffeur me around." He winked at Mason, promised his mom he'd be back for a piece of warm pie and headed out the door.

Mason was a large man as well, two inches shorter than his brother and not as thick through the shoulders and trunk, but substantial enough that the Corvette's passenger seat was uncomfortable. The shape hit him all wrong, and he had trouble with his knees. He didn't attempt the safety belt. "Damn, Gates, what—you just start distilling the hooch in your car, cut out the middleman? It smells like a speakeasy in here." There was a plastic Star Wars cup—a faded fast-food giveaway—resting on the console; the contents were yellowish green, SunDrop and vodka without any ice to dilute the potency.

"I'll roll the windows down and drive real fast." Gates nudged a cassette with his index finger and a mechanism eased it from sight, inhaling it into the dash. He had recorded a Huey Lewis and the News album onto the tape, and "I Want a New Drug" came on mid-refrain. "While we're on the subject, can I offer you a little nip?" he asked. "I've got vodka and a bottle of Wild Turkey Denny gave me for my birthday."

"I'll pass," Mason said. "Thanks just the same. It's a bit early, isn't it?" The question didn't have any bite in it, wasn't a rebuke. He grinned at his brother.

"I'm grandfathered in for the entire day, a carryover from last night. So long as you don't stop, it's just a continuation, not the same as drinking for breakfast or somethin' pathetic and alcoholic." Remarkably, besides the odor and a few aggravated blood vessels in his eyes, Gates seemed fairly level. An occasional syllable was spit-heavy, but that was about it. "Our pal Robbie Hanes is leavin' for the Navy, so we had a throwdown yesterday for him at the Woolwine Ruritan building. That's why I'm behind schedule—the party took us hostage and wouldn't let us go."

"I'd have never pegged Robbie for duty on the high seas."

Gates reached under his seat and located a Crown Royal bag, a deep-purple felt sack with bold yellow stitching and matching yellow drawstrings. He set the bag in his lap and took out a vial of cocaine and an elaborate spoon, the spoon either silver or pewter, in the shape of a mermaid, her hair serving as a grip, her toes clutching a tiny scoop. "I need to boost my shit, brother. I'm assuming you're still not interested?"

"If I tried it, I'd probably like it way too much. In no time at all, I'd be pissing myself and scavenging butts from ashtrays at the bus terminal. Quoting Timmy Leary at the homeless shelter. Thanks just the same." Mason turned down the music. "Perhaps we'd be wise to get out of Mom's sight before you start doing that."

"Only take a sec." Gates dipped the spoon into the powder, raised it to his nose and snorted—hard—three times.

"By the way, why does everyone I know carry his dope in a Crown Royal bag? Or the cassette cover for an Allman Brothers tape? Can you explain that to me? I think the Supreme Court's decided the cops have probable cause to search whenever they spot either of those in a car, regardless of the circumstances."

"You have a better suggestion?" Gates wiped his nose, then sipped his drink. "The bag's a pretty damn fine creation."

"True. Can't argue with you there."

"You like the album?" Gates asked. "Huey Lewis and the News?"

"Yeah. It's okay, though it's a shame they don't get any more air-time than they do. And I always feel like Huey might be sort of pulling our leg musically."

"Too much schoolin', I'm sorry to say, has made you into a boring smart-ass." Gates fired the engine and they crept down the gravel drive, the car chugging and straining in first gear, the tachometer barely registering because Gates didn't want to risk nicking the paint with kicked-up rocks.

"Where're we going?" Mason asked. "What kind of mischief are you dragging me into?"

"Nothing too tough, I promise. Robbie's leavin' behind a nice dresser, and he said I could have it. You and me are going to meet Claude and him in Woolwine, load the dresser onto Claude's pickup and haul it to Denise's trailer."

"How are you two doing? You and Denise, I mean?"

"Everything's cool. She got a promotion at work—off the floor and into the office—and she finally finished her associate's degree. Looks like a million bucks, still crazy about me." He made a goofy face after the last declaration. "We're thinkin' about maybe considering buying a house together. The old Mabe home is for sale. I love that place—it's on five acres, has a nice pond and a humongous porch for cookouts and warm-weather drinkin'. Man, you could just put the speakers in the windows, grill a steak, invite friends by. Only problem is that I need my luck to improve so I can pull my part, you know? I'm hopin' this insurance job with State Farm comes through, so I can quit living fuckin' hand to mouth."

"Good for you. I think the world of her."

"Me too."

Mason wanted to maneuver more space for his knees and shins, but the seat was at its limit, had no play in it. "It'll take us two hours to drive to Woolwine, load the dresser, then drive to Denise's and unload, don't you figure?" He wriggled into a new position.

"Close to it. You can call Mom from Robbie's and give her an update." Gates sniffed and touched his nostrils with the back of his hand. "So long as we have the tree done by dark, we should be okay."

"We have all morning tomorrow if we need it," Mason said, flashing his brother a wry smile.

It took them several minutes to cover the half mile of dirt and stone that led to the blacktop, but Gates slammed the accelerator the moment the wheels touched the asphalt, causing the car's tires to spin and the rear end to break traction.

They met their friends and wrapped the piece of furniture in an old quilt and laid it in the bed of Claude's pickup. Before they started to Denise's, Robbie warmed barbecued pig and baked beans, left over from his party. He placed the food on the tailgate of the truck, and they all dug it straight out of tinfoil tubs with plastic forks and wiped their hands and faces on paper towels. Gates poured himself another mixed drink, and the other three men popped cold Miller beers. The truck's doors were open, the radio playing, the hardwood trees in southside Virginia turning crimson, yellow and fire-orange, an occasional dry, brownish leaf sifting through the air on its way to the ground.

Denise's mobile home was in Five Forks on a small parcel of land she was buying from her uncle. She was a hard worker and a smart, solid woman with restraint and sensible tastes uncommon for her circumstances, and she kept her yard and dwelling neat. Mums and azaleas and other flowers and bushes that Mason couldn't identify were planted here and there, the grass was still green and nicely trimmed, and the property was free of birdbaths, kitschy cement animals, busted lawn chairs, junked Monte Carlos and matted cur dogs chained to a rusted post. Gates had helped her build and stain a covered deck; a single dragonfly wind chime hung from the four-by-four that supported the tacked-on roof, a friendly jack-o'-lantern welcomed visitors from the top step. Denise's white Celica was parked in the drive, a Mazda RX-7 behind it, and the moment Gates saw the Mazda he became angry.

"Damn," he snapped.

"What?" Mason peered across the interior at his brother. "What's wrong?"

"That's Wayne Thompson's car."

As Mason understood it, there had been a period when Gates and Denise, romantic since high school, had separated for a number of months. After Gates walked away from Virginia Tech, and after he failed to catch on with the Redskins, and after he declined a plum job at Masonite—human resources, a gig with dress shoes and a coffee mug, for heaven's sakes—and after he barely squirmed out of a DWI over in North Carolina, and after Denise allowed as to how—six years removed from his graduation—he needed to find work, quit freeloading at his mother's house and stop lollygagging around in the Corvette for hours on end, and after she finally gave him a deadline he spitefully ignored, after all this considerable forbearance, she sent him packing and began dating Wayne Thompson. Gates quickly enrolled in real estate school and signed a lease at the Dorn Williams apartment complex, begrudged measures that lasted just long enough to tamp down Denise's ire but were sufficient to spark their reconciliation. At least he'd *tried*, she told friends who poor-mouthed her boyfriend and suggested she was making a mistake by offering him yet another chance.

There was also small-town scuttlebutt that Denise had slipped a time or two or three or five since reconciling with Gates, talk that she'd been spotted at the Tanglewood Beach Music Festival with Wayne or gotten hooted with her girlfriends and mentioned him favorably or been seen picking up her car—early in the morning— from the elementary school parking lot not far from his house. And who could blame her, given what Gates had to offer and his headstrong, good-for-nothing nature?

Wayne was a paradoxical fellow, a handsome boy who'd moved from Georgia to Stuart with his parents in the middle of his ninthgrade year and finished Patrick County High School with Gates's class. Quiet but tightly wound, Wayne had been in a vicious, bloody fistfight in the school hallway and tended to turn scarlet around his jawline when a teacher called on him with a math problem he was unable to solve or a treaty date he couldn't remember. Yet he was polite to the point of shyness, a whiz with an arc welder, a volunteer at the old-folks home, the treasurer of the Spanish Club. He'd begun a minimumwage, part-time job with the highway department while he was still in school, and nine years after earning his diploma, he was employed at the same place, now an assistant foreman with a few night classes at Patrick Henry Community College to his credit, drawing a steady state check, cruising the roads in a bright orange VDOT truck, keeping tabs on bridge repairs, potholes and vandalized traffic signs.

He'd fathered a child out of wedlock but never hemmed and hawed about paternity. He let the lad take the name Wayne Jr., paid for the baby's delivery at the hospital and made arrangements to have child support deducted from his check and forwarded to the mother in Roanoke. By all accounts he generally attempted to do right by his son, keeping him every other weekend and treating him to dirt-track races, Santa photos at the Martinsville Kmart, a Myrtle Beach vacation and trips to the Patrick County fair, even though the boy was too young to ride most of the attractions or win prizes on his own. It was widely known that Wayne had once sucker punched Harley Stevens at the Old Dominion roadhouse and then kicked him in the ribs when he was flat on the floor, but if anyone had it coming, it was Harley, a lout and a loudmouth, so the law was never notified and nothing more came of it.

The brothers were still in the Corvette, the engine idling, Huey Lewis and the News playing, when Wayne appeared on the deck. He was wearing a snug leather jacket scarred by asymmetrical silver zippers and black jeans rolled into chunky cuffs. Gates erupted from the car without turning it off. "What the hell do you think you're doin'?" he demanded, striding for the trailer, Mason instinctively falling in beside him. Claude saw the Hunts sail out in a hurry, and he jogged a few steps from his pickup to join them.

"It's a free country, Gates." Wayne was walking guardedly toward his RX-7, careful not to act cowed or to blink too much.

Denise stepped onto the deck and told Gates to calm down. She was a shapely, graceful woman with a striking face, and she pushed her hair back with both hands after she spoke.

Wayne made it to his car, where he opened the door but didn't get in. Gates and Mason halted at the bottom of the wooden deck steps. Their friend Claude, a beanpole of a man with a sketchy mustache, was beside them. "How many times do I have to tell you to stay away from Denise?" Gates shouted. "Huh? Am I just goin' to have to beat your ass to a pulp so you'll understand?"

"This is Denise's property, not yours, Gates. You ain't got any control over how she uses it or who she sees."

Denise didn't hesitate. "Wayne, I've asked you before not to come around. You're a good guy, but right now you're just making things bad for all of us."

Wayne put his hands on his hips and squared off toward Gates. "I'd be embarrassed if I was you, Gates. Damn right I would. A grown man and you don't even have a pot to piss in. Livin' off your mama and your girlfriend."

Mason had a fast grip on his brother's biceps, but surprisingly, Gates didn't attempt to pull free or rush Wayne or ape through a frenetic, piss-and-vinegar, hold-me-back charade in an attempt to impress Denise. Instead, he half-smiled and chuckled, stared at the closest step and kicked the ground next to a bright yellow mum. "Yeah, Wayne, you're the man," he said in a mocking tone, pausing to look up. "King of the road, ridin' around and shoveling dead possums and dogs off the highway. We all want to be you."

"Nice jacket," Mason chimed in gratuitously, making certain there was no doubt where his allegiance lay. "Part of the *Knight Rider* collection?" He released Gates's arm.

"Opossum Boy," Claude added.

Wayne seemed relieved that this was the extent of the confrontation and that the brothers were keeping their distance, content to insult him from across the yard. "You all can kiss my ass," he said as he was sliding into his car, but the words didn't have much vigor in them. He drove to the main road, stuck his middle finger out the window in their direction, turned left and disappeared on the other side of a severe curve.

Agitated again, Gates stared up at Denise, who was bent over the porch railing, a small crook in her back, her arms stiff and supporting her weight. "What the fuck was he doin' here?" Gates asked, his voice sharp. "In your house?"

"He came by and said he needed to talk to me, claimed it was important and wouldn't wait."

"And you said, 'Sure, come on in and I'll chill the champagne and put on something low-cut?' "

The Corvette was still running, and Claude scurried toward it, eager to be occupied. He took a seat on the driver's side and switched off the engine, staying put after the car went quiet.

"It's not like that at all, Gates," Denise protested. "I haven't even seen him in months, and he shows up on my porch with no warning, hell-bent and beggin' me for five minutes. I told him you were on the way, but he was bound and determined to speak his piece, so I let him. I can't help it if he shows up out of the blue, now can I? I was as surprised as you."

"So why can't he do his important talkin' on the porch?" Gates asked.

"Listen, Gates," she said, her voice gaining an edge, "if you want to pick a fight about this, fine. But I'm not going to stand here and listen to you cuss me and accuse me of crap I didn't do, okay?" She straightened up from the railing. "He caught me by surprise, and when he asked if he could come in I said yes. Anyone would. I'm sorry if that's a sin. I told him you and me were together, and you and Mason were due any second."

"You heard her, Gates," Mason said, touching his brother's shoulder. "You heard her tell him how things are."

"What'd he say?" Gates demanded. "Why'd he drive out here in such a lather? Why today? All of a sudden?"

"Just stuff, Gates. It's not worth repeatin'." She was looking directly at him. Her hands had shifted to her hips, but her tone was more plaintive now, conciliatory.

"You want me to move the truck closer?" Claude asked from the Corvette. "I think I will."

Gates ignored him. "He was walking on the very deck I built, talkin' shit about me and hittin' on you, right? That pretty well sums it up, doesn't it?"

"Yes, Gates, but like I said, I told him to forget it. You could've knocked me over with a feather when I opened the door and he was standin' there. I don't know what in the world made him come out here all torn up after . . . Well, you know, I haven't said more than hello to him since forever, and the last time we discussed the situation I was crystal clear about me and you, and him not fittin' into the picture."

"Pretty exceptional circumstances," Mason said. "And she handled them with class, as well as could be expected." He focused on Gates, trying to make him see reason.

"He's a piece of shit," Gates said, but he wasn't looking at anyone, instead was staring at the curve where the RX-7 had driven out of sight. "I could snap him in two if I wanted," he muttered, still locked onto the road.

"Just forget it, Gates," Mason encouraged him.

"I think he's gone for good," Denise said. "Come on, Gates, let's not ruin the day."

"If he ever says another word to you or even so much as drives by here, I want you to tell me." Gates twisted his head so he could glare at his girlfriend above him. Two creases met and formed a "V" between his eyebrows. His mouth was a peeved slit. "We understand each other?"

"Yes, Gates," she said.

"I'm heart-attack serious," he warned her.

"*Okay*, Gates. So now can we just put it behind us, please?"

"Fine advice," Mason told him. "Let's see about unloading the dresser."

"Yeah . . . well . . . well, first let's see about a stout drink to celebrate how ol' Wayne tucked tail and ran," Gates suggested, his tone brightening.

"Count me in," Claude said.

"The bottle's under the seat, Claude." Gates started up the steps. "You got any mixer, baby?"

"Probably," Denise answered.

"You gonna have one with us?" He walked to where she was and put his arm around her. "It's the weekend and a pretty day and we have a special guest appearance by Mason, the boy wonder."

"I might," she said.

"How about you, Mason?" Gates asked. "You gotta bend an elbow with me, no more than we see each other."

"Sure, a beer would be great."

Denise spoke almost before he finished the sentence. "I'm fresh out, Mason. I knew you were going to say that's what you wanted.

I've only got a few wine coolers and a dab of vodka Gates left in my car. I'll be glad to drive to the store—what kind do you like?"

"Don't worry about it. There's no need to go to any trouble. I'm happy with whatever's here."

"I need to get some cigarettes anyway," she said. "It's not a problem."

"I'll drink a wine cooler or some vodka. No big deal. I'm okay."

Despite his protests, Mason's simple beer request was soon made the mainspring for a slice of the improvised, freewheeling, low-wattage hedonism that Gates could scare up from the barest of surroundings, and just like that the men were checking their wallets and Denise was contributing a ten from her purse, and since Claude and Mason were going to buy beer they might as well grab burgers, buns and charcoal and another bottle of vodka, and while they were taking care of business in town Gates and Denise would pick out some excellent tunes and roll a joint from the reserve she kept hidden in a tampon box, and she would call her friend Shannon to see if she wanted to come to a cookout, and the dresser stayed put, draped in patchwork while the party took root around it.

The quarrel with Wayne Thompson was forgotten by the time Shannon arrived at three o'clock with her cousin Suzi from Florida. The women brought chips and snacks, but it was left to Claude to cook the hamburgers, and it was growing dark before they ate supper, everyone except Mason buzzed off the pot and beer and vodka and peach wine coolers, and even Mason drank four Budweisers, more than normal for him. Goosed by the alcohol, he was probably too long with his explanation when he phoned their mom to let her know they were delayed at Denise's trailer, helping her move heavy furniture. "Don't bother waiting up for us," he sheepishly told Sadie Grace.

After the Blue Ridge Mountains completely stamped out the sun, the six of them sat on the porch wrapped in jackets or blankets, watching the orange briquettes fade to ash, talking nonsense, swapping stories and singing and howling along with "Werewolves of London." They moved on to drinking games with a deck of cards—Mason didn't play—and Claude entertained everyone with his impressions: Nixon, Reagan and John Wayne at a bordello. Gates was stoned, relaxed, happy to be with his girlfriend and delighted to have his brother home for a visit. All afternoon, he'd teased Mason about his prissy diction and tight-ass habits, but encouraged by a shotgunned beer, he finally broke down and encircled Mason in a headlock and told him how proud he was, and there was no doubt he was sincere, meant every word. When he turned loose of his brother, none of the others said anything, just sat there with dopey grins and starched eyes, the women and Claude wholly taken in by the men's affection for each other. A dog barked somewhere close by, a car whooshed past, the cassette finished and the portable stereo clicked off.

Shannon broke the silence, sweetly blurting that she loved Herb Alpert and the Tijuana Brass, having heard them as a kid on an eight-track her folks owned, and her Florida cousin suddenly left for the car and returned with a spiral-bound notebook and volunteered to read some of her poems. Mason politely noted he'd be glad to listen but warned her he didn't much care for poetry: it was a fine trick, but what in the world to do with it. "It's like a party favor or a Matchbox car or those stunted trees and shrubs people carve all tiny and precious, kind of literary bonsai." For several mute moments, they all looked at him as if he'd solved Stonehenge or translated the Dead Sea Scrolls, then Gates began giggling and said, "What the fuck are you talkin' about?" and Claude snorted and snickered and the women began cutting up also, and the lot of them went on a laughing jag that didn't end until Denise announced she needed to pee and wobbled off the porch.

Around ten thirty, after the dope, food, alcohol and cigs had been exhausted, Mason mentioned the firewood tree and his four-hour trip back to Richmond the next day. The men finally carried the dresser from the truck into Denise's bedroom, and when they'd situated it in the space she'd cleared, Gates stood back, folded his arms, cocked his head and said with silly, exaggerated satisfaction, "Now *that,* gentlemen, is an excellent effort. Mission accomplished." He debated staying the night with Denise, especially since Shannon and Suzi were making noises about traveling to the Dutch

Inn Lounge in Martinsville for dancing and Fuzzy Navels, but he decided to kiss his girlfriend good night, biting her neck and squeezing her rear before letting her alone. He and Mason thanked Claude for the help, shook his hand and left him talking to the women about what to do next.

Like always, Gates—drunk, stoned—insisted he was going to drive, and Mason—sober, clearheaded—agreed he could, thus avoiding a skirmish over the keys and a pointless, profane give-and-take that would end with Gates even more determined to have his way and result in his speeding and ripping through the gears so as to demonstrate that he and his liquored-up self were beholden to nobody: it was *his* fuckin' car and *he* would drive it and the hell with the police and the rest of them who wanted to tell *him* how to live *his* life. It helped that the rural roads to their mom's house wouldn't be busy, Gates was an old hand at drunk driving and there were ordinarily only two county deputies on duty, most likely lenient sorts who'd know both brothers and Sadie Grace and could be counted on to sigh and make the brothers change seats, or at worst, shake a finger at Gates and swear to him this was his last break.

They'd gotten to the crossroads at Five Forks, and Gates had just fished a cigarette butt from the ashtray and clicked fire to the last hint of tobacco when headlights zoomed in behind them, aggressive high beams, fierce illumination that made the knobs, gauges and numbers in the Corvette starkly apparent and lit the side of Gates's face, his neck, his arm as it angled toward the shifter. They quickly identified the car as Wayne Thompson's—"it's friggin' Wayne," Gates said, his eyes rolled up toward the rearview mirror—and for the rest of their days, neither of them would know whether it was happenstance that Wayne had discovered them or whether he'd come looking, still brooding about his ill treatment at Denise's trailer and determined to prove a point where she was concerned.

For reasons that seemed sound to a drunkard behind the wheel of a Corvette, a drunkard who was also frustrated and at war over a woman, Gates punched the gas, shot across the main highway and barreled down a two-lane side road, Wayne and the RX-7 right on his ass. Mason shouted at him to stop it, told him to quit acting like a moron, but Gates didn't pay him any attention, and for two miles of narrow shoulders, blind curves and spotty, patched blacktop, Gates and Wayne performed reckless, pea-brained stunts, the Corvette accelerating to eighty and then screeching as Gates jammed on the brakes, the RX-7 filling the lane beside the brothers so the two cars were racing down a country road door-to-door, neither of them yielding, neither of them giving the slightest thought to precisely what they were accomplishing.

Mason told Gates to slow down or he would jerk the car out of gear and let him worry with what happened after that. "I mean it, Gates. You better fucking quit it. You two can kill yourselves, but you're sure not taking me with you." He put his hand on Gates's wrist and squeezed. "What the hell do you think this is proving?" Wayne had dropped behind them again but was still giving no quarter.

They zipped past a field of cattle and a lopsided barn. "Asshole," Gates muttered, alternating his gaze between the mirror and the road. The word was slightly slurred, stuck to his tongue.

Mason leaned closer to the driver's side and ratcheted up the pressure on Gates's wrist. "I don't know how you're planning to pay for a blown engine or a new transmission."

"I've had enough of this shit," Gates said, his voice without inflection. He began slowing, gradually, and Wayne mimicked him, sixty to fifty to forty, the RX-7 following suit, its lights continuing to burn on high, thirty, twenty, ten, nothing, and the two cars were stopped dead in the road. A lackadaisical moon and a pasture with large round hay rolls at one corner were to their right, a tangle of woods, mostly pines, was on the left.

Gates turned off the car, set the brake and stretched across to the glove compartment. He was quick, efficient, and Mason could see him clearly, the light pouring in from behind them unnatural and loud. Gates removed a gun. Silver, unholstered, a brief barrel, a .38, and before Mason could utter a word—warn his brother not to do something crazy—Gates was standing in the night, the driver's door swung open, tucking the pistol into his pants at the small of his back.

"Easy now," Mason said, stepping from the passenger seat onto the side of the road, but at least the weapon wasn't pointed at Wayne and with any luck it would stay put, right where it was, no more than a dangerous precaution.

Peering over the car's roof, Mason saw Wayne advance on Gates, closing the distance with uneven, choppy steps, a small club, maybe a foot long, at his hip. He halted at the rear of the Corvette and cursed Gates. "You sonofabitch," he said.

Gates didn't respond, simply stood there with his arms folded across his chest.

"Why were you tryin' to run me off the road? Wreck me?" Wayne demanded, obviously torturing the truth, ginning up a reason to fight. "Huh?"

"That's hardly what happened," Mason said, his forearm resting on the Corvette's top. Wayne was far more boisterous than usual; Mason assumed he'd been drinking. "Why don't you," Mason continued, "just forget this and drive away before Gates hurts you?"

"Fuck the both of you."

"Wayne," Gates said, "that pitiful little stick you're holdin' ain't goin' to help you when I come back there and whip your ass. Either leave right now or take a beatin'."

"Oh, don't worry, you ain't gonna have to come to me." He took a step closer, then another, so that he was almost within Gates's reach. "I damn sure ain't afraid of you."

To Mason, who well knew his brother's moods and inclinations, Gates seemed irritated but not irrational, anxious in the manner of someone who had the upper hand and was eager to use it, like a sixteen-year-old poised above a yellow jacket nest with matches and a gallon of gasoline at twilight. "This has been a long time in the makin'," Gates said.

"You need your baby brother to help you?" It had become clear Wayne wasn't planning to leave without taking on Gates, who was considerably taller and a hundred pounds heavier. "Think you might could handle somethin' by yourself for a change?"

"I won't need any help with a pissant like you," Gates told him.

"You're so worthless, Gates. Sorry as a dog. How's it feel to go downhill every single day after high school? Huh?" Wayne still had the club, but it was at his side, flat against his thigh. His voice was shrill, the words rushed. "Big football star, ready to shake up the world and now you're livin' with your mommy, probably stealin' beer money outta her purse." He bobbed his head up and down in agreement with himself. "Never done nothin' 'cept sponge off your momma and Denise, and never will do nothin'."

Gates licked his lips and started to speak, but the thought was stillborn, arrived dead and gurgled. His mouth remained open, and he took a stride away from Wayne, creating more space between them. The retreat was slightly off kilter, unbalanced, and Mason realized that his brother probably hadn't slept the night before and was chock-full of dope and alcohol, but still figured he would maul Wayne. And if he couldn't, Mason would pitch in to make sure Wayne received a good thrashing, fair or not.

"I want you to think about where I've been whenever you're kissin' her. You think about that, Gates."

"You goin' to drop that billy club?" Gates's voice was empty, dull.

"A loser, that's what you are. Me, I'd take welfare before I hung myself around my mother's neck. It's just a matter of time before Denise sees the truth and dumps your ass. Me and her are goin' to be together—you know that, don't you?" The club didn't stir.

Mason—concerned with the blackjack—never saw his brother take the gun from his pants and aim it, but he heard the shot, saw a whitish-orange burst at the end of the muzzle. He looked directly at Gates . . . and the scene stalled right there for an instant, seized up while the report from the pistol took issue with the trees and hills and anything else the least bit solid and doubled back on them. The Corvette's interior light and the high beams from the Mazda overran Gates's face, made it seem as if he'd been plugged into a socket and flooded with current, his skin electrified chalk, the artificial glow clinging to his features, turning them out eerie and pronounced: an etched, viperish mouth; a raised, crescent-shaped scar near his temple; a brace of violent lines cutting through his forehead. His eyes, though, remained dark, sequestered, two black gouges in the midst of all the shocking white.

When Mason glanced away from his brother, Wayne was gone,

shot, out of view on the ground, partially hidden by the tail end of the Corvette. Dumbfounded, Mason hurried around to where Wayne lay on the road, his head split and soggy, the awful damage barely skimmed by the bottom of the RX-7's beams. Mason looked at the dead man, then at his brother, so stunned and unhinged that his first words were trite, lacking, the stale scold of a stick-in-the-mud spinster aunt: "Now you've gone and done it, Gates."

Gates appeared horrified, was actually holding the gun at arm's length, examining it as if it had mysteriously arrived and latched on to him. "I . . . I . . . damn . . . I didn't mean to do it." He continued to puzzle over the .38.

I didn't mean to do it: a peculiar, last-ditch mantra that Mason Hunt would hear many times over the years, from many lips, in many courtrooms, though it rarely, if ever, had any application to the genuine truth of the matter. His brother had stopped the car, reached across to the glove compartment, armed himself, left the vehicle with the pistol, considered his choices, removed the gun from his trousers, aimed, fired—hardly an accident or fluke. No, what he really meant was *I wish I hadn't done it.* Peering at his brother's spooky face and regaining a trace of clarity himself, Mason realized that the violence had issued from Gates in a spasm long in the making, like an accumulation of tinder hit with heat. The shooting was not so much malicious as hardwired and visceral, a copperhead's strike, a third cousin to the impulse that causes an owner to kick a pet at the end of a crummy week, or a spouse to scream wild threats and slam down a receiver. Feckless, thwarted, angry and left behind, his world gone to naught because of his own weaknesses, Gates Hunt shot and killed a man for no good reason.

At first, acting on adrenaline and brute instinct, Mason didn't question what he should do, never really considered anything beyond helping his brother. "Let's go, Gates. Get in the car, and let's go before someone drives by."

"Damn, Mason. Shit. I can't believe this." Gates was anguished, on the verge of tears.

"Go! Go! Drive." Mason was scrambling for the door.

"We . . . wait . . . wait . . . we need to hide him or somethin'." His voice quavered. "We can't leave him here."

"No way. We can't move him—the body will be found sooner or later anyway, and we're in this stupid Corvette with no room, and there'll be blood and hair and all kinds of evidence if we use his car. And we damn sure don't want to be seen driving a dead man's ride."

"Then we should take money or his wallet, right, make it seem like a robbery?"

"Only if you want to get sent to the chair—that would make it a capital crime." Mason was standing beside the door, about to duck down. "I'm the lawyer, okay? Come the hell on. There's nothing to tie you to this. Nothing. The more you try to do now, the more you give the cops later on."

"You mean just leave him here?" he asked, slowly gaining composure, his voice stabilizing.

"Exactly. Now come on. Somebody probably heard the shot. And don't spin the tires when you pull off."

Gates glanced at the dead man bleeding out onto the pavement. "Jeez, I can't believe this." He dashed into the car, cranked the engine and babied the gas. "Lord, Mason, what're we goin' to do? Huh? I didn't mean to shoot him . . . It . . . it just freakin' *happened.*"

"Listen to me, Gates. There are two people in the world who know the truth. You and me. Don't ever say anything to anyone about this." Mason was staring right at his brother. His voice was stern. "No matter how drunk or stoned or mad or boastful you become, never, ever say a word. Not a peep. Never. Do you understand me?"

"Yeah, yeah. I wouldn't anyway."

"You know you can trust me, right? I'll take this to my grave for you—you know that. It's always been you and me, Mason and Gates, taking care of each other."

"I'm so sorry to drag you into this," Gates said. "It just came over me. I swear I barely remember shooting him." He shifted gears and was clumsy with the clutch, causing the car to lurch.

"Yeah, well, I only have a toe wet, Gates. You're the one who fucked up and shot the guy. I'm not *into* this at all. This is your alba-tross, not mine."

"What about self-defense? We could say he was threatenin' me with that blackjack. Tell the police—"

"Sure, great idea. Let's see: there are two of us, he's drunk, you're twice his size, he has a pathetic little stick and you have a gun. Brilliant plan."

"It's better than nothin'."

"No, Gates, it's not," Mason said emphatically. "Nothing, in this case, is the least shitty choice where you're concerned. They'll have a body on the side of the road, no witnesses, no forensic evidence, no leads, no confession. We last saw Wayne hours ago, and you laughed him off, didn't jump him when you had the chance and all grades of provocation. So what we're going to do now," he stated, his voice dropping, "is travel to Martinsville, stop by Peter's Lounge, get lost in the bar, flirt with the girls, act normal and pay for our drinks with my credit card when we leave. If Claude and those two women aren't there—and it's a cinch they won't be—you'll call Denise's collect, to check on them. Short term, you need to find a safe place to stop so I can drive us; it would be nice to get there without wrecking. We'll take the back roads to the gravel pile, then haul ass to Martinsville."

"Claude said they were goin' to the Dutch Inn, not—"

Mason interrupted him. "Exactly, Gates. And on the outside chance they've shaken themselves free of the Doritos and Pink Floyd, we damn sure don't want to run into them, now do we? Arrive there *after* they do?" He shook his head. "I'm positive they said Peter's."

"Yeah. Okay. I'm with you." Gates paused to look at his brother. "Should I go over shit with Denise? Or Claude? Rehearse what happened and so forth when Wayne was there?"

"Absolutely not. Just let it unfold and act surprised. We don't need any of them to have suspicions. You and I left, thought about missing a good time with our friends, went to Peter's Lounge, didn't see anyone, called to check on Claude and what'shername, stayed till closing, then drove home. That's the story. It'll be the truth minus the problem with Wayne. You clear?"

"We left Denise's, you mentioned maybe extendin' the night, I'd been partying right smart, so you drove us to Martinsville, then home."

"Correct. Say I started driving at Town and Country Market." They passed a vehicle, a pickup judging from the lights and silhouette, the first one they'd met since the confrontation with Wayne. They'd traveled four or five miles past the shooting scene. "Maybe it'll turn before it gets there," Mason said anxiously. "Buy you some more time and make it harder to establish when he was shot." He peered over his shoulder, following the truck until it vanished. "Find a pull-off and let's switch. And then we're actually going to have the entire conversation, give it a couple run-throughs so we're consistent about who said what, that sort of thing. Oh—wash your hands and face as soon as we arrive at Peter's, and we'll need to check your clothes before we go in, then burn them after we get back to Mom's, just to be safe."

"Okay. Yeah. I will." Gates seemed distracted.

Mason rubbed his eyes with his thumb and forefinger. "I'll take care of the gun. We'll hide it tonight temporarily, and I'll carry it with me tomorrow and destroy it as best I can and dump it somewhere." He sighed. "I hate to do it, but I'm worried you'll screw it up, and for damn sure it doesn't need to surface around here. Neither of us is going to be well served if the police discover the gun, you especially." Even though it entangled him more than he would have preferred, would make him less than passive in Wayne's killing, Mason concluded that disposing of the pistol himself was his only option if he planned to protect his brother.

Gates nodded but didn't say anything.

"Understood?" Mason demanded.

"Fine with me," Gates said, still distant.

"What's wrong?" Mason asked.

"You know, that prick pretty much got what was comin' to him," Gates remarked, trying to sell himself on the notion, no more than minutes removed from the killing, his fear and conscience already elbowed aside by a scoundrel's brazen denial. "Hell, he chased us down, called me out, pulled a bat on me, attacked Denise's character—what'd he expect?" Gates stopped the car.

The sudden lack of remorse and crude rationalizing pissed Mason off. Before changing seats, he put his hand on Gates's arm and glared at him in the dark. "Shut your frigging mouth, Gates. There's no need to make it worse than it already is—quit acting like a punk." He resisted an urge to punch Gates, to draw back and knock him cockeyed and show him what he thought about his craven, unrepentant behavior, maybe bust his nose or loosen a tooth, punish him for the dreadful mess he'd pinned to them both. Mason formed a fist but kept it in his lap, just squinted and breathed deep, and as he was exiting the Corvette, he took another pass at Gates, spoke with one foot on the floorboard, the other in weeds and unruly grass: "At least he had a job, Gates. And it wouldn't hurt you to shape up, would it? Mom's too old for you to be constantly disappointing her. Don't you dare say another word about how anyone's to blame except you."

He didn't mention it, but he considered reporting Gates to the police—he could call and leave an anonymous tip, and it was manslaughter and not murder so they wouldn't jail him and discard the key forever. Besides, Gates was thoroughly guilty, very much deserving of consequences, if not for the shooting, then for living his life as a wastrel and weighing down so many of the people around him.

"I'm sorry, man," Gates mumbled as they hustled past each other at the front of the car. To Mason's ear, he didn't sound contrite, merely tired, drugged and in a bind, willing to mouth whatever it took.

"A damn tar baby," Mason said, more to himself than his brother, as the deed began to tattoo itself into his mind and gut and he imagined the shape of things to come, the pangs and complications that would always companion the poorly lit image of Wayne Thompson lying there with his head bored through.

Chapter Two

In a certain fashion, Stuart, Virginia, was the same in 1984 as it was in 1994 or 2004, and the same as it will be into perpetuity.

The county seat, Stuart is a village of 971 people, and Patrick County itself contains 19,000 or so residents scattered over a chunk of the Blue Ridge Mountains and the spread of flatlands below. It's a part of the world where people wave as they meet on the highway, take baked goods to a neighbor after a funeral service, organize fire-department fund-raisers for families with unexpected afflictions and call firstborn boys by their daddy's name, always with a "Junior" or "Little" affixed—a five-year-old Harold becomes Little Duane until he grows big enough to make his own mark, a young Terry is Mike Junior until Big Mike passes on and Terry respectfully cor-rects an elder and asks to be called by his given name. There's a weekly newspaper, the *Enterprise,* and a radio station with a signal that doesn't quite reach the county line. Sixth-generation Rorrers, Heaths, Halls, Beasleys and Turners eat ample portions of fair-priced, straightforward meals at the local cafés and talk about the board of supervisors or the proper mixture for a hummingbird feeder or deer hunting or gospel singing or kids gone away to college, the parents hoping their children won't land too far from home when they finish their studies at Radford or Virginia Tech.

The citizens frequently carry tales and trade rumors, but the gossip is never sneaky or sub rosa in Patrick, instead takes place for all to hear and see at the Coffee Break counter or in the grocery store aisles, as people are fond of blunt speech no matter what the subject. Predictably, the area has always had its fair share of crackpots and mugwumps, the usual naysayers and malcontents who bitch about how LBJ ruined the country and dispatch poorly spelled screeds to the newspaper decrying their high property taxes or the influx of know-it-all newcomers. On balance, though, it is—and has been for decades—a splendid, serene, no-frills spot where the population is satisfied to be on the banks of the mainstream, clear of the current, passed by. Great old customs may have vanished in other communities, but Patrick County merchants still seal agreements with a handshake, and local gents politely touch the bills of their hats when a lady approaches on the sidewalk.

In this staid place, Wayne Thompson's murder was extraordinary. His corpse was discovered not long after midnight by a carload of teenagers aimlessly riding the country roads, five kids who stopped simply because they thought the RX-7 might have broken down. WHEO didn't broadcast the incident until its Monday-morning news program, and the *Enterprise* ran it as a headline article on Wednesday, but the convenience stores and breakfast tables were abuzz well before that, and the story picked up distortions and colorful speculation during its race through the area early Sunday morning. A deputy's wife told her Bible study class at Stuart Baptist that marijuana was found in Wayne's car and the police were exploring the possibility of a drug deal turned sour. Before he learned of the shooting, Claude had recounted—and much embellished—the dispute at Denise's to his rabbit-hunting buddies, the four of them sipping coffee laced with moonshine at dawn while their beagles yelped and squalled and gleefully chased smells into the bramble. When he contacted them later and swore them to secrecy, it was too late—word was out and Gates Hunt's name was circulating. Wayne had been drinking at the Old Dominion for several hours on Saturday evening, and he'd raised a ruckus with Allen Roberts about a ten-dollar pool bet, so the cops were knocking on Allen's door early enough after sunrise that he appeared in his undershorts, half-asleep.

Denise received the report from her sister's husband's nephew, who volunteered on the rescue squad and had helped deliver the body to the hospital. When she phoned Sadie Grace's house a few minutes past nine on Sunday morning, Gates answered and did a credible job of acting surprised, foggy. "No shit," he said, his voice freighted with disbelief. "Dead?" He stretched the black spiral cord from the wall phone as far as it would go and leaned against the edge of the kitchen table. "Do they know what happened?" he asked. Then: "Well, I can't say I liked him, but you hate to see anyone wind up killed." Next came a series of grunts and huh's. Finally, he barked an indignant, insulted "No!" He glanced at Mason, who had been standing beside him, eavesdropping. "If I'd wanted to do somethin' to his worthless ass, I could've done it at your place, Denise. Mason and me left your trailer and went straight to Martinsville. That's where we were when I called lookin' for Claude." He told her not to worry, to just tell the truth, exactly what had been said. "Hell, I was with Mason the whole time, and we were at Peter's Lounge. I don't have anything to hide, babe. Here—Mason just came in. Talk to him. He's the lawyer in the family."

Mason took the receiver and asked Denise why Gates was so out of sorts. "I only heard the tail end of the conversation," he fibbed.

She told him Wayne had been murdered. "Don't take this the wrong way, Mason, but I was, you know, worried about Gates because of Wayne bein' here yesterday and the two of them arguing. It was the first thing that went through my mind."

"Well, we left your house and drove straight to Martinsville. Gates said he called you, looking for Claude."

"Yeah. He did."

"I'm sorry to hear about Wayne," Mason told her. "Do you know any details?"

"Just that they found him shot over on Russell Creek Road." Her voice cracked and Mason could tell she was crying. "What should I tell the police if they ask me questions?"

"Everyone needs to tell the truth, okay? Don't try to lie or cover for Gates. There's absolutely no reason to—we were either with you guys or at the bar or at home. We never saw Wayne again. Don't worry."

She sucked a cigarette so hard the sound came over the line. "It's awful close to my house, where it happened. I was scared to death."

"Don't be."

She lowered her voice. "What if they ask me about, well, about me and Wayne? Our relationship?"

"Listen." Mason did his best to sound reassuring. "No one blames you for anything. Gates can be a handful." He looked Gates in the eye and kept talking. "Tell the truth, all the way around."

"This is terrible," she said, her voice trailing off. "So sad."

"You hang in there," Mason offered, continuing his stare.

"Mason, I know how much you think of Gates and what you two have been through with your father and the tons of bad stuff. I mean, you're his brother, and I understand that. Who could pick between helpin' the police and helpin' your family, no matter what they did? The problem is . . . is, to be honest, half the time I don't know what to believe with Gates. But you're different, Mason, okay? Everybody says so—and you're promising me, givin' me your word he was with you and had nothing to do with this?"

"You have my word," he lied. He averted his eyes, quit drilling his brother.

Mason wanted to be present when the police first interviewed Gates, so they paced themselves working on their mother's uprooted tree, taking more rest than they needed. Twice, they practiced their stories again. Sadie Grace returned home from church and, with her apron over her Sunday clothes, prepared a heavy meal for the three of them, topped off by the fresh pie. She mentioned Wayne's death, having heard about it at Sunday school. "That's what happens when you start running the roads drinkin' and druggin'," she pointedly noted, directing the comment at Gates.

"Yes, ma'am," he agreed. "Mason and me were talkin' last night.

I really am going to fly right and scale down on my bad habits." He laid his fork across the rim of his mother's old china plate. "I'm sorry to be such a chore for you," he said softly.

Their mother nodded, dabbed her mouth with a paper napkin and didn't linger on the topic. "Another piece of pie?" she asked them. She'd heard apologies and promises before and would wait to see if this one was any different, might actually amount to something.

A uniformed deputy and a sheriff's department investigator arrived in the middle of the afternoon. Gates and Mason were sitting in the den, watching an NFL game, and their mother was napping in the recliner, the *Parade* magazine from the Sunday *Roanoke Times* resting on her lap, turned to a story she'd not finished. The afghan—full of orange squares and red diamonds—was draped over her legs. She woke when the cops knocked on the door, and she went to greet them, fiddling with her hair as she walked across the small room, still in her best clothes. Standing at the entrance to her home, holding the screen door partially open, she was polite and respectful to the officers, even inquired about coffee or a cold soda. She didn't presume to ask what had brought them there, but she had her ideas, and her free hand was fidgety and her smile and hospitality were unnaturally fragile.

Danny Owen had worked with the sheriff's office for twenty-three years, the last eight as an investigator. In his fifties, he was trim and easygoing, a pipe smoker whose one vice had discolored his teeth and yellowed the nail of his index finger. He wore glasses with silver metal frames and was dressed in slacks, a knit tie and a blue sport coat. The second officer was stocky and muscular, younger, his hat in his hand, his surname—Williams—announced on a shiny plate above his shirt pocket. Owen carried the conversation; he was gentle with Sadie Grace, and courteous. She and his sister pulled the same shift at United Elastic, and he mentioned the connection, made pleasant small talk, declined the coffee and eventually asked if Gates happened to be there, although the Corvette was parked in the drive and the answer was obvious. "He and Mason are watchin' the ball game," she said. "You sure you don't want to come in?"

"We appreciate it, Mrs. Hunt, but we'll wait here. Maybe you could ask him to step out and join us." Owen gave her a tight, professional smile. He had brown eyes and black hair weeded with strands of gray.

Gates and Mason could hear the exchange, and they went to the door and met their mother. "Go on inside, Mom," Mason urged, bending near to her when he spoke, hoping his size and closeness would bolster her, not letting on that her resignation and weary expression made him heartsick. She left for the kitchen and started with the dirty lunch dishes, and they all could see her through the window after Mason shut the door and the four men were gathered in the drive. She kept to her work and didn't check on them, never so much as peeked to see how her sons were faring.

"I thought you'd be headed back to law school," Owen said to Mason after they'd shaken hands and talked about the game on TV.

"I'll probably leave around seven. Try to entice one more good meal out of my mom."

Owen and the deputy forced a laugh. "Don't blame you," Owen said. He hesitated and took his pipe from the inside pocket of his jacket. "Mason, you mind if we talk to Gates alone?"

"About what?" Mason asked. He narrowed his eyes.

"A police matter," Owen answered.

"Why can't you talk to me right here and now?" Gates demanded. He was beside his brother, facing the two policemen.

"We'd rather speak to you in private," Owen said. "We could talk in the car." He motioned with his pipe toward their unmarked Ford.

"Mr. Owen, I don't mean to be rude or interfere with your job," Mason butted in, "but I think we're entitled to know why you're here. And if Gates wants me with him, that's his prerogative."

Owen produced a slick plastic bag of cherry-flavored drugstore tobacco. He dipped the pipe into the bag. "Fair enough, Mason. You don't have to call me 'mister,' by the way."

"Thanks," Mason answered.

"Yeah, I definitely want Mason to stick around," Gates said. "Not often a man gets free legal advice."

"So, you gentlemen have any guess why we're here?" Owen

inquired. He'd packed the tobacco and was lighting it, eyeing the two Hunts while he puffed and shook a match dead and teased out sweet smoke.

Mason didn't hesitate. "I assume we do. We've heard Wayne Thompson was killed last night."

"How'd you hear such as that, if you don't mind my asking?" The pipe smoke was wafting toward Officer Williams, who moved to avoid it.

"Mom heard it at church, and Denise called Gates this morning," Mason said.

Owen focused on Gates. "I hear you and Wayne had a little row yesterday."

"Yep," Gates replied. "We sure did. He was at Denise's when Mason and me and Claude stopped by, and I let him know I didn't appreciate it."

"I see," Owen said.

"But that was it," Gates added. "He hit the road and that was the last we had to do with him."

"Disagreement over the girl, right?"

"Yeah, basically."

"Okay." Owen glanced at Mason. "Y'all mind if I take a few notes—help an old man remember things better later on?"

"Be my guest," Mason said.

"So what happened after he left your girlfriend's?" Owen now had a pen and small notebook in hand.

"Well," Gates began, "we, uh, stayed at Denise's, had a couple drinks, grilled burgers and whatnot, listened to music, just an ordinary day." Gates hadn't shaved in a while, and his face was covered with black stubble. He sawed the whiskers on his chin with his thumb, shrugged. "Nothing more than that, Danny."

"How 'bout when you left?" the deputy interrupted, and Mason noticed Danny Owen frown before catching himself.

"We drove to Martinsville—Mason and me. Well, you know, Mason drove. I'd been drinking."

"What time you figure you took off from Denise's?" Owen asked.

Gates scratched his head. "Wow. Ten, maybe ten thirty."

"That's fairly accurate," Mason said, looking thoughtfully upward and twisting his lips.

"No stops? Direct to Martinsville?" Owen was writing something on his pad.

"We stopped once, for a couple minutes, at Town and Country—"

"To change drivers," Gates finished his brother's sentence. "Like I said, I'd had a beer or two." He grinned. "Or fifteen."

"What in the world took you to Martinsville at that hour of the night?" Owen pressed.

"Prime party time," Gates answered, and he proceeded to disgorge the altered, rehearsed version of events in which he and Mason had decided to track down their friends and keep the fun rolling. He stuck to the script, managing to seem carefree and helpful. He finished by admitting he didn't have any use for Wayne Thompson—"there's no need to lie about it," he remarked—but he certainly wouldn't wish this on anyone, even a guy as disagreeable as Wayne.

Mason held up his hand and volunteered the name of a girl who'd written her phone number on his palm, then went into the house and returned with a crumpled credit card receipt from Peter's Lounge. "I realize it makes sense for you to interview us, Mr. Owen," he said, still not using the detective's familiar name, "but the bottom line is we didn't see the guy after he left, and Gates could've taken care of his gripe at Denise's if he'd had those kinds of intentions."

"I suppose so," Owen said. He perused his notes. "So you boys see the deceased at Denise Puckett's trailer around one or so, have some hot words and he drives off. Correct?"

"Yes, sir," Mason said.

"Then you two, Denise, Claude Whitlow, Shannon Stone and her cousin, lady by the name of Suzi, are at Denise's until ten or ten thirty? Mason and Gates go to Martinsville, remain till closing at Peter's Lounge. Then straight home." The policeman appeared to be reciting his own notes.

"Yeah," Gates answered. "But write down that the time we left is just approximate. We didn't have any reason to tie it to the second, you know?"

"Oh—Claude and I went to the liquor store not long after Wayne left," Mason volunteered. "Just so you have the full details. We also stopped by Alexander's to buy cookout supplies."

"I already talked to Claude." Owen took a drag from his pipe, exhaled the smoke. "He filled me in on who was there and what happened. Anything else I should be aware of?"

"Well, I mean, if you have a doubt that we were at Peter's Lounge in spite of everything we've provided you, I know Gates called Denise's from there trying to locate Claude and the girls." Mason's nerves were beginning to vex him. His saliva felt as if it were thickening, and the tension was pinching his belly. He licked his lips, rearranged his feet.

"If you tell me you were there, I'm takin' it you were. Although Claude told me y'all discussed the Dutch Inn, not this other place." Owen flipped through several pages while holding the pipe clamped in his teeth. "Dutch Inn is what he mentioned to me," he said from the side of his mouth. "Least that's what I wrote."

"Did he also tell you they all were fairly impaired? I was sober, and I recall Peter's, but hey, you know, maybe I'm wrong. I can't see what difference it makes." Mason tacked on an ad-lib to demonstrate how in the dark he was: "Was Wayne at the Dutch Inn or something? Is that why you're asking?"

"Not that we know of. It's a difference in the accounts, so I'm supposed to see about it."

"You have any leads or an idea who did it?" Gates inquired, patting his pockets, searching for his cigarettes. "Damn, left 'em inside. You got me wantin' a smoke," he said good-naturedly to Owen.

"None to speak of," Owen answered, his tone revealing nothing of what he'd actually learned.

"We couldn't discuss it with other people even if we did," Officer Williams informed them. He appeared pleased with himself and his contribution.

"You own a gun?" Owen asked abruptly, addressing Gates.

"A .22 rifle that our sorry dad left here," Gates said. He'd pur-chased the pistol from a greasy survivalist with a mouthful of dental neglect at a South Carolina flea market, spurning the man's invita-tion to join the Aryan Brotherhood and declining the opportunity to acquire more lethal weapons, such as grenades, assault rifles and mortars. A cash transaction, definitely no paper trail.

"That it? Only one rifle?"

"That's it." Gates sounded almost cheerful. The pistol was deep in the woods behind their mother's, buried there for the time being. They'd soaked his pants, shirt, socks and shoes with lawn mower gasoline and burned them first thing that morning, when the sun was muscling its way over the horizon line, raking a few leaves and setting them on fire afterward in case someone was curious about the smoke.

Owen shifted his weight. "Would you give us permission to look through the house? Conduct a search? It would protect us all later on if there are any questions." Owen had drawn a bead on Gates and was trying to gauge his reaction.

"Hey, fine with me." Gates didn't miss a beat.

Mason reflexively put his hands on his hips and asserted his chest. "Well, gentlemen, I think we should ask my mom before we make any plans concerning her home, don't you? Show her a little respect? Not to mention the legal issues."

"Absolutely," Owen replied.

"Absolutely," the deputy echoed.

"How about the car?" Owen asked. "Gates, you care if we look in there while y'all talk with your mom?"

"Help yourself," Gates said. "Door's open." At Mason's prompt-ing, they'd removed the velvet contraband sack and scoured the interior for roaches and cocaine detritus, but they'd left the trash, beer cans and empty vodka bottles, lest the Corvette seem suspi-ciously clean for someone of Gates's notorious habits.

Owen gestured to Officer Williams. "How 'bout gettin' me one of them consent forms from the trunk?"

Gates signed a document granting the police permission to search his vehicle, and the two cops began examining the Corvette. As

Mason watched them, it appeared to him the effort was on the desultory side, and he took it as a positive sign that there didn't seem to be much enthusiasm.

Their mother was in the kitchen when they returned, facing away from the police and her sons, preoccupied by a cup of black coffee she was reheating in the balky microwave with its spinning glass carousel. The oven stopped its huffing and rotating and let out an alert, but Sadie Grace didn't remove the coffee. "What is it?" she asked. She had been a beautiful girl and a comely younger woman, but at forty-eight her attractiveness had long ago been swallowed whole, replaced by sags and pallor and veins popped by punch-clock days on unforgiving factory floors. There was still a hint of what once was, but her blue eyes were tapped out, her high spirits gone to seed amidst hard knocks and serial betrayals. She was tall like her boys, battle-tested, resourceful, and had maintained a single vanity since her teenage years—a head full of lustrous, dark hair that seemed impervious to age and disappointment.

"The police want to search the house," Mason announced. "They're here about Wayne Thompson." He paused and took her hand, engulfing it in both of his. "Wayne and Gates had a disagreement yesterday afternoon, so the police are chasing down every possible lead. They're just doing their job."

"Lord, Lord," she said. "Tell me Gates hasn't gone and done somethin'."

"Gates was with me and a bunch of other people. He has an absolute alibi. We were at Denise's, then at a lounge in Martinsville. Gates is fine on this. The police simply have to dot their *i*'s and cross their *t*'s. Their being here is routine. Once Gates is eliminated, they'll move on."

She was looking at the floor, on the verge of tears. "Why would they come if he wasn't in trouble?"

Mason drew her closer, releasing her hand and sliding his arm around her waist. "Mom, they're just checking things. It's nothing serious."

She snapped her head up and nailed Gates with a furious stare. "Gates, certainly you aren't part of a killin'? The drinkin' and lyin' and sorriness I can take—I'm used to them—but you better tell me right now you had nothing to do with what happened."

"Goodness, Mom, you know me better than that. I've done some stupid things and let you down, okay? I sure have. But you know I wouldn't cause you this kind of grief. I—"

"Hush," she said, not allowing him to finish even though she'd demanded an answer. "I don't want to hear your same old pitiful apology again." She turned to Mason. "He was with you?"

"All day, Mom. I promise." He was relieved to utter a few literally honest words.

She blinked and brushed her eye with the back of her wrist. "There's some family I would lie for, Mason, 'cause that's what blood does. Some I would lie for even if they don't deserve it. And some I wouldn't no matter what. You're almost free of this place, Mason, so close to bein' a success."

The words pained Gates, causing his mouth to shrink and his posture to lose shape. He didn't speak, though.

"I understand," Mason said. "Gates couldn't have done this. A lot of people besides me will stand up for him. I don't know when Wayne was killed, but we were with a group of people who will vouch for Gates's whereabouts, then at a bar miles away." He continued to keep his arm wrapped around his mother.

"I trust you on what we ought to do," she said to Mason. A tear broke loose on her cheek, but her voice was steady. "You decide."

"I think we should tell them they can search, so long as they don't go into your room. Everywhere else is fine."

"There you go," Gates chimed in. "That's a good solution."

"Whatever you think is best, Mason. I'm puttin' this in your hands."

Mason removed his arm from around her. "Let's go tell the police they're free to search on those terms. I'll stay with you. You don't need to worry. I'll be right here until they're gone."

"If that's how you see it, then that's what we'll do," she said.

The two officers both thanked Sadie Grace for her cooperation, and Owen told her he very much regretted the inconvenience, leav-

THE LEGAL LIMIT • 41

ing everyone with the impression he truly felt bad about rummaging through her home and handling her property. They found nothing, and Mason and Gates allowed them to take the .22 rifle with them when they departed, along with a pair of substituted jeans and a shirt Gates dug from a hamper and identified as Saturday's dress. "You can look at my shoes, but I ain't gonna let you have 'em," he informed Owen, helpfully raising a foot.

"Think they'll be back?" Gates asked as he and Mason stood at the threshold to the mudroom, watching the police car and its long, thin antenna tail poke toward the main highway.

"I don't know," Mason replied. "Keep me up to speed if they do. And try to stay sober, huh? It would help the odds of your remaining quiet."

"I'm not stupid, Mason, contrary to what you and Mom might want to think."

"I never suggested you were. That's why I know you recognize it's your ass on the line if there's a slipup. You'll be the one wearing the colorful jumpsuit, pleading for cigs and extra shower privileges, not me, not Mom. Try to remember that."

They ate a somber supper together, silent except for requests to pass a dish and the scrapes and squeaks of silverware on plates as they cut through hamburger steak and arranged bites of vegetables. Sadie Grace packed a full meal for Mason to take with him, and Gates accompanied him to his clunker Chevy Monza. They hugged and backslapped, but Mason was on edge as he drove away with the pistol hidden in his trunk, trained as he was to always anticipate every possibility and worst-case scenario: he could wreck and the damn gun be discovered, or the cops might just have a search warrant ready to go, waiting at the foot of the drive to bust him with the .38 in his possession—pretty difficult to explain, especially since he didn't envision his brother charging in to accept responsibility.

He traveled cautiously, keeping to the right lane on the divided highway, lights dimmed regardless of traffic. In South Boston, he stopped at a Burger King and placed a drive-through order. He parked in a far corner, popped the trunk, pretended to search his suitcase and laundry bag, removed the cylinder they'd separated from the .38, palmed it with a napkin, pulled on his jean jacket, then sat in his car and made a show of eating his chicken sandwich and fries. Every time a vehicle circled past, his pulse would surge and the food would turn to sawdust in his mouth. A teenager in a uniform and paper hat appeared at the rear of the business, taking a cigarette break, another worry. Mason and Gates had cleaned and wiped the gun before burying it, and they'd used needle-nose pliers to damage the firing pin. The barrel had been scratched and pitted with a Phillips-head screwdriver, so that if the weapon did somehow turn up and was reassembled, its firing patterns would be useless to the forensic lab and couldn't be traced to Wayne Thompson's shooting.

When the smoker returned to work, Mason placed the napkin and cylinder in the sandwich carton, bagged the carton and, wearing a baseball cap so low it hit his eyebrows, walked to a Dumpster and tossed in the sack. The remains of the sandwich, fries, and large drink and the lump of metal landed without complaint, didn't strike bottom or clash with anything too solid. Paranoid and jittery, Mason left the parking lot and worried all the way to Richmond that a tramp or Dumpster bum would discover the pistol piece or—his luck—it would turn up miraculously wedged onto a tomcat's nose, the perfect kind of filler for the local news broadcast.

He went out of his way to Petersburg, where he ditched the gun frame, concealed in a *Richmond Times-Dispatch*, at a public green-box site. It was late when he returned to his apartment on Hanover Avenue, and his two roommates were asleep, although they'd left the TV playing and most of the lights burning. Mason lay in his bed with his clothes still on, his shoes, socks, jeans and jacket, unable to rest, his conscience flogging him, his thoughts ragged and horrific. For several nights that followed, his sleep was tenuous, fitful, just beneath a translucent surface, never either completely here or there. He'd done nothing but watch, slack-jawed, as his brother slew another man, and yet the turn of events had left him morally hog-tied, an accessory after the fact, the entire damnable bundle laid at his feet by someone he loved dearly, and that visceral, epic connection to Gates, unfortunately, was the alpha and omega, trumping everything and everybody.

As it happened, Mason had no need to be concerned about Gates incriminating himself—he was far too narcissistic and egotistical to do or say anything that might bring him hardship. He proved to have a rascal's capacity to write off his crime and a gift for absolute self-preservation that kept him from ever mentioning the killing, no matter how drunk or high he became. In early November, he even found a job as a floor supervisor at a textile plant in Martinsville, and he announced to Denise he was cutting back to only beer and pot— no more coke and hard liquor and three-day binges. He lost the job after six weeks, showed up for work with the giggles, sunglasses and rum tainting his breath, then packed off his dismissal on his boss, claiming the guy had it in for him for no legitimate reason. In the months after his firing, there were sporadic trips to church basements for AA meetings, a monstrous blowout with Denise that prompted her to call Mason and hotheaded feuds with his mom followed by the usual fulsome apologies and vows to shape up. In other words, typical Gates.

The police worked diligently to solve Wayne Thompson's murder, but they had no leads, no witnesses and no worthwhile evidence. The shooting had occurred on a rural stretch of road, and the occupants of the closest house a mile away didn't hear a thing, or if they did, it didn't register in an area where most people owned guns and there was frequent hunting and target practice and carrying-on that occasionally included firing a few Jack Daniel's rounds at a stump or the wide-open sky. Danny Owen visited Gates a second time, and Gates frowned and sighed and told the officer he simply didn't know what else to say—they last saw Wayne at Denise's and never saw him again. Owen flew to Florida and interviewed Cousin Suzi, hounded Allen Roberts about his alibi after the pool game, contacted Mason's credit card company and the girl he'd met at Peter's Lounge, took a trip to Charlotte to question a drug dealer who'd been arrested with a .38 and obtained statements from Wayne's coworkers and family as well as the owner of the Old Dominion. According to the laboratory, there was marijuana and a small amount of methamphetamine in Wayne's car, but the RX-7 was devoid of anything helpful in the murder investigation. Toxicology revealed he was legally drunk; the small club next to him suggested a confrontation. Owen and an older deputy returned the .22 rifle to Gates in March and futzed around with a few more questions, but it was apparent they had nothing fresh or important to quiz him about.

The file went from Danny Owen's desk to the very front of a cabinet drawer to a thick collection of papers tucked behind ten or fifteen other baffling problems to a case number on a computer disk of unsolved crimes to a statistic that showed up every year on the report the local office sent to the state. Letters were written to the paper highlighting the sheriff's department's failure to solve a cold-blooded murder, the sheriff himself had to hear about his inability to bring the case to a conclusion when he stood for reelection in 1987, the family offered a reward and there were fits and starts and false leads and flashes of effort until there was eventually nothing left but inertia, lore and a rubber-banded old folder with a battered tab and a case number from an obsolete system. When Danny Owen retired in 1991, he didn't even mention the Thompson murder to his successor, instead spent most of his time briefing him on an undercover drug operation and a theft ring that was targeting vacation homes in Kibler Valley. Even the gossips and busybodies lost interest, as they generally do the moment there's something new to excite their tongues.

While the death of Wayne Thompson would always trouble Mason, the raw, punishing anguish started to recede after a couple months—it became permanent in him but less acute, a submerged shame that would occasionally be roused and set his palms to sweating or cause a bolt of adrenaline to burn across his abdomen. He'd see a cop show or hear the name Wayne or hit some catalyst—an RX-7 always did the trick—that would send him through a rabbit hole of speeding thoughts and blurs and fragments and return him to the side of Russell Creek Road and the sight of his brother holding the gun, his arm fully extended.

Near the end of the year at law school, Mason's guilt and concern were unexpectedly piqued when he received a brass-tacks assessment of his brother's situation during an advanced criminal law seminar. The professor had organized a panel discussion on how to properly defend a murder case, advertising the event throughout the university. With a single exception, the panel contained the usual collection of academics who'd never set foot in a courtroom and habitually filed tedious, sixty-page amicus briefs in high-profile appeals so they could see their names in the newspaper or snag an appearance on a Sunday talk show. For most of the presentation, the guy everyone in the class wanted to hear from had very little to say, and when the moderator solicited student questions, the peacock professors jumped in with clever answers and grand, drawing-room circumlocutions.

Jim "Bulldog" Young was one of the best criminal trial lawyers in Virginia, a charming, robust man whose genuine decency never failed to influence a jury and whose capacity to take a witness apart and not seem like a showboat had served him well for thirty years of practice. He was wearing a brown suede jacket and an ordinary tie, a white shirt. He was quick to smile, listened with a gentleman's interest to what was being said, and seemed satisfied to let his fellow panelists dominate the show while he scribbled notes, sipped water and fingered the point of his tie. At last a questioner called him by name and asked for advice: "Mr. Young, what's the most important thing to consider when you try a murder case? If you had to give us one insight?"

Without any flair or preening or affect, Young rocked back in his chair. "Only thing that matters in a murder case is did the fellow who's dead need to be killed, and did the right sonofabitch do the job."

The class roared and laughed and stood for an ovation, Mason along with everyone else. As he was leaving the lecture, though, he became pensive when he replayed the lawyer's response. If the police ever located enough evidence to take Gates to trial, his prospects were not too sound when judged by Young's standard, and Mason understood there was a chance he could be dragged into the bog right behind his brother. He stopped suddenly in the hallway outside the classroom, causing the woman behind him to veer off and graze him with her backpack. He repeated Young's test, mouthing it quietly while a stream of yapping law students washed through the hall. "Zero for two," he said out loud. "Damn."

Chapter Three

By early 1990, Gates had journeyed around the bend. His mother, with Mason's blessing, had evicted him from her house, the Corvette was a two-hundred-thousand-mile heap of scarred fiberglass, bungee cords, duct tape and leaky gaskets, Denise had served him with a no-trespass notice and was engaged to an algebra teacher at Patrick County High School, and he was residing with a twenty-year-old feckless skank and her illegitimate toddler, living off her food stamps and welfare check and what he could earn peddling small amounts of pot and cocaine. On rare occasions, he'd do some logging or help in a hayfield or get paid under the table for a week of warm-weather construction work. Patrick County being what it was, most people greeted him with a word or two and a stony expression or simply acknowledged him with a stiff nod when they saw him in town. His hair was too long, his clothes unkempt, his conversations laden with hustle and excuses and get-rich-quick schemes. He'd spent a month in jail in 1989, after he busted out the windows of a girlfriend's car and was dumb enough to hang around making threats—an eight ball of coke in his pocket—until the police arrived to arrest him.

To no one's great shock, it was a failed, inept attempt to sell drugs that ultimately did him in. Very few people aspire to a job retailing baggies of marijuana or carefully build toward a career in powdered cocaine, but for Gates, it just seemed to be an inevitable fit as time went by, a hey-why-not vocation that promised easy money, scarcely any labor and a business inventory of his favorite drugs, a layabout's tri-fecta. He started in the mid-eighties by selling from his own pot stash, then bought a quarter extra on credit, which he mixed with oregano and sold to his buddies in the Old Dominion's bathroom or at the parking lot of Moody's Funeral Home. A biker from Greensboro who went by the name Kong hooked him up with a steady supply of coke, and at first Gates simply took his payment in kind, distributing in exchange for free dope. Given the size of the community, it didn't take long for the police to get wind of what Gates was up to, though for sev-eral years he avoided the authorities by sticking to nickel-and-dime transactions and dealing with the same people, friends he'd known since grade school and the regulars at the roadhouse.

The serious trouble arrived in the summer of 1990. By June, Gates and his girlfriend, Sandra, were beset with difficulties. Their trailer rent was in arrears, and the landlord had seen enough, wanted them gone. The Corvette had completely given up the ghost and was parked at a haphazard angle in the yard, the grass the push mower didn't catch outlining the car in a shaggy fringe. Social services had sent legal papers seeking "custody of the infant known as Jade Bon Jovi Bowman," and Gates and Sandra didn't like that plan one bit, hell no, vowed to fight the state tooth and nail and ranted about the injustice of it all, the *idea* that a bunch of meddling bastards thought they could take Jade away from a parent who loved her so unconditionally. "They're tryin' to claim I'm a bad mother?" Sandra indignantly demanded of the poor deputy who'd delivered the paperwork to her. The fact that they would lose a monthly check, rental assistance, Medicaid and free food wasn't important. It was the principle. The *principle*. Wanting only what was best for sweet Jade, they realized they'd need money for a lawyer, since Gates's uppity brother in Richmond was no help whatsoever.

In an effort to raise cash, Gates agreed to unload the Corvette, which would leave them only a single vehicle, Sandra's ragtag Chevette with its mismatched, primer-colored fender. He'd received the car after graduation from high school, obtained it from a Christiansburg auto dealer who supported Virginia Tech and wanted to do all he could to ensure that the talented freshman linebacker from Patrick County understood just how welcome he was in this new world. Gates was . . . uh . . . employed by the dealership, and he drove the car home for the first time during August of 1975, in an era when the NCAA wasn't so nosy and draconian. His friends in Patrick were proud of him and didn't begrudge him the flashy red reward, believed he'd more than earned it, what with his daddy absent for years and he and his brother struggling to stretch Sadie Grace's meager paycheck from the plant. Right off the bat, Gates took his mom for a joyride, kicking it up to eighty through Spoon Creek bottom, both the windows open so the warm, whipping air could add to the thrill. She squealed at him to stop but was laughing when she called him down, delighted with her boy and what he'd accomplished.

Sandra looked up the number and Gates called Clyde Turner, who bought and sold used cars out near Fairy Stone State Park. Gates invited him to drop by the trailer and price the Corvette, claiming they weren't that anxious to make a deal but really didn't need two vehicles. A day later, Clyde arrived and walked around the car and stuck his head in for a peek at the interior, checked the engine. Chewing on a toothpick, he offered Gates nine hundred dollars.

"No fuckin' way," Gates snapped. "What the hell's wrong with you, Clyde? It's a collector's item."

"Well, it might be if you was Fred or Lamont Sanford," Clyde drawled. "I'm interested in cars I can sell. Cars that run. This one's in awful shape, and it ain't runnin'."

"Nope. Not a chance. I gotta have ten thousand, minimum."

"I ain't here to offend you, Gates. No, sir. I'm just tellin' you what she's worth to me. If we can do business, fine. If not, we'll shake hands and leave with no bad feelings. You might do better to try in the paper or with another person 'sides me."

"Give me eighty-five hundred, Clyde."

"Gates, friend, listen. She's been beat to death. She's old. You're lucky I ain't chargin' you to hook to her and drag her off."

"Hell, Clyde, a coat of paint, a little body work, a few parts, the car's mint again."

Clyde arched his eyebrows. "Friend, I'm gonna take her for salvage. You want to put her in shape and call me back, we'll discuss a higher price. I'm thinkin' of this thing for scrap. You're lookin' at serious jack to restore this car—you know that. And you know a '75 ain't no big deal to a collector these days. I'll go a hundred more, but that's my limit."

In the end, after ten minutes of haranguing and foot stomping, Gates relented, gave Clyde Turner the title to the Corvette and watched him tow it away to be stripped down and sold piece by piece, a worn-out hulk, its luster diminished, its low-to-the-ground sleek speed crippled, its engine spent and gummed up for good, the hoses dry-rotting, the wires brittle and unpredictable.

For months, Kong had been after Gates to increase his productivity, and he agreed a few weeks after the sad Corvette transfer, accepting an advance of five hundred dollars, which he and Sandra paid to a lawyer—together with two hundred and fifty dollars of the car money—to partially finance the custody battle for Jade. Of course, as soon as Gates walked through the mobile home door with a big ol' bag of Kong's powder, they phoned Sandra's mom to babysit for the night and dove into the coke, drinking beer and listening to "Living on a Prayer" at top decibel until Sandra turned blue and melodramatic and they fell into an argument that ended with her chucking an ashtray at Gates, then threatening to leave him for Jade's daddy, who'd written her from the penitentiary and was eager to reconcile. Gates grabbed her by the collar and slapped the hell out of her, leaving elongated red marks across her cheek. They made up within an hour, had high, wallowing sex that they were unable to finish, and awakened at noon the next day with shredded nostrils and fractured recollections of the prior night.

Not long afterward on a stagnant July evening, Sandra and Gates stopped by the Old Dominion for a cold pitcher of beer and a small cheese pizza. Their pal Barry was already there, playing pinball, leaning into the machine, bumping it with his pelvis, rapid-firing the flipper buttons, a draft beside him on a table. An old friend and reliable client named Hank Lawless, Jr., had introduced Barry to Gates and vouched for his trustworthiness. As Gates understood it, Barry lived in Richmond, making a living as a long-distance truck driver, but he often showed up with Hank at barbecues and fiddlers' conventions in Stuart, a good guy who'd always let folks bum a cig or borrow his music. For nearly a year, Gates had been selling him fifty-dollar dabs of cocaine when he was in town.

Barry shouted hello, and Gates walked over to watch the game and chew the fat. Barry had most of the bonuses lit and a high score, and he earned two extra balls and thousands of points before his run ended. He and Gates talked about Hank and a trip Barry had made to Los Angeles to deliver a load of produce. Barry put another quarter in the machine and started with a new ball. "You able to do anything for me today?" he asked, his tone confidential and hushed.

"Yep," Gates answered. "I'm your man."

Barry pulled back the silver knob, adjusted his stance, then released it. *Chings* and *plunks* and wild caroms and skittering lights commenced again. "Weight?" he asked, watching his shot, not looking at Gates.

"I'm flush. You name it."

"Really?"

Gates checked the bar for Sandra. She was drinking a beer, chatting with another woman. "Oh yeah." He rolled out a braggart's smile.

"I've been thinkin' about tryin' to locate enough to hold me between trips up here." He glanced at Gates and the ball got away from him, clipping a flipper and disappearing. "And maybe get a little volume discount." He gave Gates his full attention.

"I'll work with you. You know that."

"An ounce?"

"Cool," Gates said. "Piece of cake."

Barry returned to the pinball game and hunched over the machine, launching his second shot. "How much?"

"For you, twelve."

"Shit, man, I ain't lookin' for no tourist price." He playfully jabbed Gates with his elbow. "You gotta do better than that."

"I'm giving it to you for what I have in it," Gates lied.

"A grand." This play wasn't productive; the ball was retired after only a handful of ricochets and a single trip through a spinning gate.

"Jeez, Barry. I'm not Goodwill. I'm already offerin' you a discount."

"Best I can do. A thousand." Barry winked at him. "And I'll pick up your tab for the pizza and beer."

"Man, you're torturing me here." Gates paused. "Shit, all right, but don't you tell a soul what you're payin'."

Barry pressed his thumb and forefinger together and drew them lengthwise across his lips. "Zipped, Gates. Not a word from me."

"Good."

"I'm goin' to have to go get the cash. I'm staying at Hank's, so where should I meet you?"

"Moody's?" Gates suggested. "Behind the funeral home?"

"Ouch. That's too creepy for me. Let's try somewhere else."

"How well do you know Stuart?"

"Okay, I guess. Pretty good. I can get Hank to come with me if need be. I'm sure once he hears what's up, he'll be happy to tag along and sponge off my bag."

Gates chuckled. "No doubt."

"What about the fairgrounds, down past the hospital? I'll just slip in next to the cinder-block building where you buy your ticket."

"Sure. Fine with me. How long?"

Barry rotated his wrist and checked his watch. "Hour?"

"Cool. I have to make a stop myself, so that's perfect."

Barry extended his hand for a quick shake, entwining his thumb with Gates's. "Treat me right. I'm expectin' some kick-ass shit from you."

It was twilight when Gates, folded into the Chevette, eased into the entrance road at the fairgrounds, the air still stale and sullen, the day's heat refusing to budge. He was dressed in a tank top and cutoff jeans, barefoot, drinking a Miller beer, the coke—diluted with a generous sprinkling of baby laxative—tucked beneath his seat, a .22 pistol lying on the console, just in case. Barry was already there, exactly where he said he'd be, and the large lot in front of the fairgrounds was empty. Gates liked the location; the exchange would take place in a spot that afforded them a thorough view in every direction, and a vehicle or two in the lot wasn't uncommon since people used the flat field inside the gate for Little League practice and pickup softball. He stopped his car so they were window-to-window, facing in opposite directions. Barry was listening to Metallica's "Enter Sandman," but he turned off the music when Gates pulled up.

"You been here long?" Gates asked.

"Nah. Five minutes, maybe."

"We good to go?" Gates set his beer between his legs. He scanned the lot, the road, the area behind the gate and the small, squat building that housed Rotary Club ticket takers when the fair was in residence.

"I've got the thousand if you're ready with the coke."

"No offense, Barry, but, ah, I need the dollars first."

"None taken. Just business, right?" Barry conducted his own quick, tense survey, then handed Gates ten hundred-dollar bills, thrusting them through the window, the cars so close that his arm stretched into the Chevette.

Gates counted the bills twice. "Awesome," he said. He knocked back the beer, reached under the seat, took another nervous look around, located the dope and passed it to Barry. "A pleasure doing business with you."

"You too, Gates." Barry opened the baggie of coke and studied it. "You're the man."

All hell broke loose.

A spotlight hit the cars. The wooden shutters on the ticket building crashed open. Vehicles with red and white lights strobing from their grills tore into the entrance, accelerating even as they made the sweeping turn toward Gates and Barry. Two men—cops, fucking cops—leapt out of the building, weapons drawn, crouched, screaming, "Your hands, show us your hands, Gates," their badges worn like necklaces, STATE POLICE emblazoned in yellow on the black vests protecting them from gunfire. Another officer was sprinting to the scene with a rifle. Barry surged forward in his Firebird, stopped. Spilling out, he aimed a pistol at Gates from behind the door: "State Police. Don't even think about it."

Gates ran. Bolted. A decision, he would later tell his brother, that was his biggest regret in the whole affair. Shoeless and desperate, he jackrabbited, not man enough to salvage even a speck of dignity by raising his hands and swallowing his medicine. As far as the cops were concerned, the futile escape attempt made him the absolute worst kind of coward, and when they gang-tackled him in the fairgrounds parking lot, skinning his knees and staining his shirt with red clay, a crew-cut special agent called him a pussy and bellowed what they all were thinking: "Where the hell you plan on going? Huh?" Two local deputies yanked him up, steered him to a cruiser and stuffed him inside.

Scared and panicked, with his knees throbbing and trickling blood and his hands cuffed behind him, Gates struggled to balance himself on the rear seat of the police car. He spoke for the first time as he and the cops swung through the serpentine curves that led into Stuart. "Guys, listen. Hey, I'm sorry, okay? Can't we work something out? I don't need this. How about a break, some slack?" The road went from left to right, causing his shoulder to hit the door. "Please. I got a mother to take care of and a little girl I'm raisin'. What about them?"

The officer on the passenger side half turned so that Gates saw him in profile. He was still wearing his bulletproof vest. "It's not up to us, Mr. Hunt. The courts make those decisions." The response sounded rote, practiced.

"Heck, right now, it's your call. You can do whatever you want."

"And we want to take you to the magistrate and charge you with felony distribution." He twisted a few more degrees in Gates's direction. "That's how it is."

"Man, there's no need to be so hard-nosed. Come on. Sir, I'm pleadin' with you."

"Nothing we can do." The cop fixed him with a cold stare, started to add something but didn't.

"This isn't fair. It isn't. Shit." He flicked his dry tongue over his lips. "Maybe I could give you, you know, a little help. Point you to the big fish. I'm not the guy you're after. I'm way down the line, barely even worth the effort."

The officer turned away, ignoring Gates.

"Hey, why are you actin' so rude? You could at least answer me."

The two policemen began talking to each other about how long it would take to process Gates and where they could find a meal on their way home.

"You can't hear me?"

They continued their conversation and didn't respond.

"Hey, okay, you know what, fuck both you guys. I tried to be cool about this, but you can both kiss my ass." He was crossing into irrational, cornered, dead-end rage.

They passed the bank, Main Street and the old brick courthouse. The driver flipped on his blinker, and the vehicle sat motionless for an instant while another car passed in the oncoming lane.

"You assholes will regret this day for the rest of your lives." Gates's words were amped and rabid. He began pulling against his cuffs, herky-jerking his shoulders. "My brother's a lawyer, and you clowns will be lookin' for work soon. That's a promise. You hear me? I'll fuckin' have your jobs for this. I want your badge number. " He flopped back violently against the seat. "I know my rights, mother-fuckers, and I want your names and numbers."

"Sure, yeah, you know your rights," said the driver. "You got us there, Mr. Hunt. I'm Bruce Wayne, millionaire Bruce Wayne, and this is my sidekick, Dick Grayson. We're badges number one and two. How's that? Anything else we can help you with?"

The response made him that much more incensed, and it took a total of five cops to drag him yelling and flailing into the magistrate's office, where they charged him with disorderly conduct and multiple counts of assaulting a police officer in addition to felony distribution of cocaine. The magistrate, whose house he threatened to burn, denied him bond, and he was incarcerated for the second time in his life, tossed in with the slugs and petty criminals to await his day in court.

"This is total bullshit, Mason," Gates railed as soon as the deputy shut the door to the interview room at the Patrick County jail. "Man, this is all so wrong. I'm innocent." He was wearing an orange canvas jumpsuit but, oddly enough, seemed to have a rekindled interest in his grooming and appearance: he was clean-shaven, his hair was orderly, his nails were trimmed and the short sleeves of his jail outfit were rolled into tight, smart bands at his biceps. It was the afternoon of the day following his arrest; Mason had driven to Stuart from Richmond, briefly visited their mom and then traveled into town to meet with his brother.

"Oh?"

"Absolutely." They were separated by a plain wooden table. Gates leaned forward, closer to Mason, gesturing manically. "This is a mistake." He widened his eyes, rounded his mouth. "I'm just hanging around at the fairgrounds, shootin' the breeze with Hank Lawless's friend Barry, and the damn cops swarm in like the Marines or somethin'. Crazy. They claim they found dope on Barry and they arrest me! How does that make any sense?" He waved his hands frenetically. "You need to set this straight, Mason. Apply some lawyer grease and get me out of here."

Mason put his elbows on the table and deliberately lowered his chin into his palms. "That's what you're telling me?"

"Absolutely. Look, I'm no Boy Scout, I've done stupid things, broken the law, but not this time. This is some messed-up shit. They didn't find any drugs on me. None. I can't help it if Barry's holdin' dope and I happen to be there."

"This is what you've come up with after a night of reflection?" Mason asked impassively.

"Meaning?"

"Meaning I don't know what's worse: the lack of creativity or the unconscionable lying." Mason withdrew his chin and sat back against the slatted support of his chair.

"Mason, I'm your brother, and I'm telling you the truth. I didn't have anything to do with it. My word on it."

"You were in the wrong place, wrong time?"

"Exactly." He vigorously bounced his head up and down.

Mason folded his arms over his chest and made certain his disdain was obvious when he spoke. "Here's the truth, Gates. Barry is a state police undercover officer who was working with your hopeless friend Hank Lawless. Hank found himself in a jam for buying a bunch of stolen heavy equipment and decided to polish up his junior deputy's badge and cast his lot with the cops. You're on tape demanding money for the dope, and two other cops watched from the ticket building while you sold an ounce of cocaine for profit. The bottom line is you are guilty as homemade sin and they can prove it. Lying only makes it worse. Hell, you have to know this fellow Barry was a cop—he helped arrest you."

"Have you heard this tape they supposedly made?"

"No. The sheriff was kind enough to give me an overview. And even if they didn't have the recording, there're three or four cops standing in line to say they saw you sell cocaine. A thousand dollars' worth. With a frigging gun in the car."

"I got that cash from the Corvette," Gates declared. "You can check with Clyde Turner."

"Yeah, well, Clyde must have copied down the serial numbers and marked the bills, because the money in your car was the same money Barry handed you for the dope."

"So you think I'm boxed in?"

"Yeah—a very precise box, like a coffin."

"And you believe them?" Gates asked.

"What's not to believe?"

Gates scooted his chair away from the table and stood. "Shit, Mason, it's entrapment then. They set me up." He flung his arms to each side and held them aloft, crucified on an invisible cross. "Pressured me into it. Tricked me, lied to me. That won't fly. The police can't operate like that."

"I thought you just told me you weren't involved? Gave me your word?"

"Well, shit, I guess we got a change of plans if what you say is true. Have to go with what'll work, right?" He dropped his arms. His palms slapped against his hips. "Entrapment. You know what? I asked that prick Barry, asked him if he was a cop, and he lied to me. I'll testify to it. They gotta tell you if you ask—the police can't lie."

Mason shook his head, sighed. "First," he said, nettled and glaring at Gates, "you never did any such thing. Second, even if you did, it doesn't matter—that's a damn urban myth. Nonsense. It's the Dillinger exhibit and bathtub kidney surgeons. They're working *undercover*—they're supposed to convince you they're not cops. They don't have to tell you diddly."

"Well, I've heard—"

"I don't give a damn what you've heard, Gates. It's not true."

"Then you are just goin' to have to come up with some lawyer tricks. You can do that, right? Clever as you are, you can get one over on these hicks any day of the week. 'Lawyers, guns and money,' like the song says. I need your help, Mason. I do. And I swear—I swear to God—I've learned my lesson. After this, I'm a changed man—nine-to-five, no drugs, no drinkin', church, the whole kit and caboodle."

"Peace Corps?"

"Say what?"

"What about the Peace Corps? Signing up to do your bit in impoverished countries?"

"Why're you being a dick, Mason? Huh? I'm facin' a world of hurt and you're crackin' jokes?" He'd started pacing.

"Gates, there comes a day when you've cashed all your chits and flat worn everybody out. You hit that mark a long time ago."

"I'm not arguing with you, okay? I've screwed up again, and I know I've promised to do better before, I know that, but you can't leave me danglin' in the wind. I swear on our mother's health this is it for me. If you'll just pull some legal strings and keep me out of jail, I . . ." He paused, swallowed. "I've truly learned my lesson. With God as my witness, I'll never cause you or anybody else a problem if you can please get me clear of this."

"Most people," Mason said solemnly, "would have learned their lesson years ago." He cut his eyes at his brother. "You catch my drift?"

"Yeah." Gates stood still, his breathing erratic, almost a pant. "At least help me fight it, Mason. Please. You're a lawyer—that's what you guys do, work the system and find loopholes. Twist words to make them different. There has to be a way. Somethin'." Sweat droplets were gathering at his hairline and dribbling down across his forehead.

"Gates, I'm not a criminal lawyer, but this much I can promise you: about the only people who could extricate you from this would be Sherman and Mr. Peabody operating the Wayback Machine. Lawyers aren't wizards or shamans. This isn't Tolkien—there's no spell we can cast to erase your voice from the tape or incantation we can recite to strike these police officers dumb. You need to come to terms with what you've done. The more you lie and caterwaul, the more you'll piss off the police and the commonwealth's attorney. I'll see what I can do, but your best hope is to plead guilty, tell the truth and walk into court meek, humble and hat in hand."

They studied each other for a moment, the room silent and stuffy. Above them was the antiquated county jail, and a thud and whooping curse penetrated the ceiling and dawdled there with them in the thick air. Gates closed his eyes and rocked back against the dingy green wall. A chunk of plaster was missing near his head, a white scab, and the wall's weak hue made him appear pale and watery, like he was dissolving. "How in the world did I wind up here?" he said, his voice faltering, his eyes still shut.

"I'll do my best," Mason offered. He went around the table to his brother and laid his hand on his shoulder, squeezed him through the rough cloth and then left him, didn't turn back even though— striding out of the room—he heard Gates call after him to please, please, please wait a minute.

Mason hadn't spent much time in Stuart since finishing law school and accepting a job in Richmond, and he wandered the roads without any purpose after departing the jail, listening to the local radio station and making a willy-nilly tour of the area: the elementary school, the bridge across the Mayo River where he and Gates usually fished on the opening day of trout season, the Staples house where they'd all—teenagers—smoked cigarettes in the basement and pored over a stolen *Playboy* and played pool until Eddie Staples died of leukemia and his parents moved to Norfolk, the ramshackle Chevrolet dealership, Gypsy Boaz's tobacco fields filled with row upon row of sticky green leaves, a Ford tractor and a flatbed trailer parked catty-corner to the curing barn.

The sights failed to stir Mason or set much loose in him. He was years removed from his hometown, and his recollections of Stuart had been refined into stylized, formal renderings, a scattershot collection of snippets and images without juice or vitality, like a series of petrified butterflies skull-pinned to a collector's board, far more husk than heart. Everything was familiar, nothing intimate. He was at arm's length with his brother as well, distant and low on empathy, and he switched the radio to an NPR broadcast, trying to find a distraction. A second-rate pair of sunglasses was in the glove compartment, and he put them on. He raised the air-conditioning fan a notch. He sprayed the windshield with blue cleaner and watched the wipers beat it away. He loosened his tie, went to work on a pack of gum. Adjusted his seat belt before releasing it altogether.

When he returned to his mother's house, she was sitting in the den, a square electric fan blowing on her, her hair gathered atop her head. A TV show was hopping from scene to scene, but she hadn't turned up the volume. Mason offered to treat her to the whitefish and popcorn shrimp plate at the seafood restaurant, but she claimed to be under the weather, not feeling so great, and said she'd rather slice a garden tomato and warm some corn bread and leftovers.

"Mom, you have to face people sooner or later," Mason encouraged her. "This isn't about you. Everybody understands that. No one could've asked more from a parent. Gates should be ashamed."

"I suppose you're right, honey. Gates is Gates. But I'd just like to take me a day off, you know?" Her lips quivered and she drew them determinedly taut and thin. "Just have one day when I don't feel like I'm drownin'."

Gates sulked and pouted and berated his mother and Mason when they refused to hire a private attorney for him and recommended he take advantage of the public defender's office. "Gates, there's nothing anyone can do," Mason insisted. "I've told you over and over." He and Sadie Grace were visiting on a Sunday, talking to Gates through the bars. "And I'll be with you every step of the way. I promise."

"Yeah, thanks. You and a guy the state's paying. You've never even done a criminal case, Mason. I'm real confident of my chances." Gates had been in jail for three weeks and continued to pretend he was entrapped. He'd called his mother and begged her to approach the commonwealth's attorney about a bond, written Mason a long, rambling letter to posit fantastical legal strategies, sent notes to his buddies asking for canteen cash and done his best to get in touch with Sandra, who'd already abandoned the trailer and wasn't responding to the messages and threats he'd left at her sister's. "Y'all are just turnin' your backs on me."

Their mother rarely talked much during visitation, normally sat silently after she said hello and asked a question or two, occasionally smiling wanly at one of Mason's corny stories or mumbling a thank-you when Gates complimented her appearance. Every Sunday, after the same nonsensical diatribe, she would agree to help find Sandra so Gates could have his leather jacket and "valuable" personal items returned, although it seemed obvious his girlfriend had skedaddled for good, not at all anxious to be on the margins of a felony drug trial. When Gates accused Mason and Sadie Grace of deserting him, her neck and face flushed, and she aimed a finger at Gates and jabbed him hard in the chest. "I wish I could reach my hands inside those bars and get at you. I do. You need to grow up and act like a man. I'm sick and tired of hearin' you complain. *I'm* the one who ought to be feelin' put upon, not you." Her voice was loud enough that another family halted their conversation to see what was causing the commotion. "You better watch what you say to me. I'm about fed up." She left after saying her piece, the low heels of her church pumps clacking on the concrete floor as she went, and she skipped two Sundays before resuming her visits.

Gates's court-appointed lawyer turned out to be a very capable man named Gary Cardwell. Cardwell was a former prosecutor, middle-aged, who'd quit the commonwealth attorney's office for the other side of the street. The senior public defender, he was bright, experienced in court, jolly, and from all accounts a fierce advocate for his clients. Mason was pleased when they met and reviewed Gates's case. Cardwell seemed both realistic and eager to do what he could, assuring Mason his brother was like a lot of other defendants who were reluctant to accept that they were in a legal bind and on the brink of a nasty prison stretch. "You don't try to force the unpleasant truth down their throats," he told Mason. "Nope. No more than a doctor would stroll in and announce to a patient, 'You're dying, there's nothing we can do and we're not planning to try.' They have to come to it in their own time. You listen to them, take them seriously and explain their prospects. Guys like your brother have to know they've tried every exit and exhausted every option. Most of them will see the light, usually when the trial gets close. It's not immediate enough for some people until they actually sit at the defendant's table or hear the indictment read. I've taken this case apart, and they have him cold. We'll try to swing a deal, and if we can't, we'll plead guilty and put on the dog for his sentencing."

"I told him exactly the same thing," Mason said.

"He'll reach that point. It's the only choice he'll have in the end. If he pleads not guilty, the commonwealth will demand a jury, and he'd be a damn fool to take his chances there. They'd eat him alive."

The jury trial began on a frigid January Tuesday, three days after an insistent snowstorm had pushed over the mountains and covered the county with five white inches that would linger for a week. Mason gripped his mother at the bend of her arm as they climbed the steep stone steps that rose to the courtroom, on guard for ice or a slick spot that hadn't been completely shoveled. The commonwealth's attorney had offered five years on the dope case, ninety days total for assaulting the police officers and a dismissal of the disorderly conduct charge, and after seating Sadie Grace, Mason met with his brother in the interview room and tried yet again to reason with him about his plea. A cig pinched between his thumb and forefinger, Gates sat there beside his lawyer and sneered and snorted and arrogantly, pigheadedly, rejected the deal, which both Mason and Gary Cardwell assured him was fair as could be.

"Fuck the commonwealth's attorney," Gates snarled. "I'll take time served and probation."

"You'll take what they suggest," Mason said. "You have no bargaining power."

"How about I tell them where the stuff came from?"

"They already know," Cardwell said. "They arrested your friend Kong the day after they caught you. We've been through that in detail. You're one slot too low in the pecking order because of it. They had his whole network in their sights. In fact, I'm pretty sure the cops followed you down to Greensboro a couple times when you were, shall we say, visiting him. So it's a no-go for any kind of cooperation arrangement."

"Damn," Gates carped. "There has to be something better than five years."

"I'm sorry," Cardwell told him. "But five and ninety is a pretty good outcome, given what we're facing. And if you plead on this, they're going to forget the other sales to Barry. Those cases are still possibilities."

"I'll take my chances," Gates said.

"Suit yourself," Cardwell replied. He removed his glasses and placed them on a table. Permanent red impressions from the plastic pads marked each side of his nose. "You're exposing yourself to a lot worse, okay? You understand? I'd take the deal. I wouldn't want to go in front of a Patrick County jury on a drug case."

"I'd accept the offer as well," Mason warned him.

"I can't" was all Gates said.

The jury listened attentively to the lawyers' opening remarks, and it seemed to Mason, watching with his mom from the first row of the gallery, they were an evenhanded group, committed to giving both sides a fair hearing. He saw their moods shift after the undercover cop described how Gates had eagerly sold an ounce of cocaine and another officer played a surveillance tape that ended with Gates hotfooting it away from the Chevette. They went from curious to convinced to angry, and by the time the commonwealth rested its case at two thirty, they were quietly livid, insulted because Gates had brought them to town and wasted their day when he was so remarkably guilty. And while they all had been sincere in taking the oath and declaring themselves objective and willing to decide the case on the courtroom evidence alone, this was Patrick County, and several panel members knew Gates or knew of him, and one man, Otis Cooper, had worked with Sadie Grace before retiring from the plant, and he realized that the clean-cut, coat-and-tie fellow at the defense table was an outright fraud—underneath the fancy suit was a boy who had leeched off his mama forever and was so lazy he wouldn't hit a tap at a snake.

The awakening that Cardwell had predicted never came for Gates. Cardwell did the best he could, chipping and scratching and finessing, but the facts incriminating Gates were powerfully simple. The brothers and the lawyer met in a side room after the commonwealth concluded its case, and Mason once again explained the wisdom of a guilty plea.

"Listen," he said. "I sat there and dispassionately heard the evidence and took stock of the people on the jury. They're going to set your ass on fire. You have to know that, Gates. You've got to plead and allow the judge to sentence you or let Mr. Cardwell see what the commonwealth's willing to offer. I'm telling you, don't do this to yourself."

Cardwell was sitting in a chair by a large window. The room was chilly, heated by a rattling steam radiator that had been painted the same color as the walls. "Gates, son, I did all I knew how to," he remarked, "but I have to side with your brother. This is a calamity waiting to happen."

"Easy for you guys to say," Gates complained. "Easy for you to deal away over five years of my life. I can pull this off. I can. I thought of somethin' when the undercover guy was testifyin'."

"Pardon?" Cardwell asked, incredulous. "I'm not sure I understand what you mean."

"You just follow my lead, okay? Put me on the stand and ask me what happened. I'll take it from there. And don't forget to mention the stuff about football, where I was all-state and my scholarship to Tech. People still respect me because of that, no matter what."

"You'll *take it from there*?" Mason mocked him. "Have you lost your mind? Have you? This isn't workshop day at the community college drama class. What're you planning to say?"

Gates was loud when he answered. "You don't have to be such a prick, Mason. Anyway, I'm old enough to make my own decisions without help from you. You think you can waltz in here from Richmond and tell me how to run my life, but you can't. I don't need you around if all you're gonna do is criticize me, okay? You're either with me or against me, and right now you seem mostly against me." He glanced at the floor for a moment and softened his tone. "Guys, five years or five hundred—it's all the same to me. I can't do it. That's what you two aren't understandin'. There comes a point where you get so screwed up and stir-crazy there's no chance of recoverin'. Any more time in here's gonna ruin me, if it doesn't kill me first. I know you think I'm bein' stubborn, but it's a chance I've got to take, even if it probably won't pan out." Another hesitation. "And I'm sorry I've been so short with you both. I truly am."

Mason drew a bead on him but didn't answer. He finally glanced at Cardwell. "Thanks for your help, Mr. Cardwell. Good luck." He left the room, not bothering to shut the door behind him, and took a seat beside his mother.

Cardwell brought Gates to the judge's office and explained, on the record, that his client wished to testify, against counsel's advice. "Unfortunately, Judge, I'm hearing certain details for the first time today and that puts me and my client at a disadvantage. I've told Mr. Hunt it's a bad idea." Cardwell cleared his throat. "So no one gets the wrong impression, his new statement is consistent with what I've been hearing all along. It's just an amplification, sort of an expansion, and while I believe him, I've warned him against presenting it to this jury."

Worried and nervous as he faced twelve men and women who anticipated he was about to tell them a fanciful lie, Gates still managed a certain amount of cheap charisma on the stand. He was large and handsome and seemed to know, at least initially, what to do with his hands, where to look, how to sit, when to say "sir." Cardwell led him through a series of basic questions and then approached the heart of the case, the cocaine sale at the fairgrounds. One of the jurors, a wiry woman from Meadows of Dan, inched forward and cocked her head. A man who'd been taking notes wrote something on his yellow sheet of paper. The courtroom was cavernously silent, sealed off by double walls of meticulously mortared red and brownish brick.

Cardwell walked to the witness stand and actually turned toward the jury, not Gates, when he asked his first question about the charge. "Mr. Hunt, did you in fact meet a man you knew as Barry at the fairgrounds?"

"Yes, sir, I did."

"How did you know Barry?"

"We were close friends, or so I thought. We were introduced by Hank Lawless, Jr."

"Of course, you realize as you sit here today he's an undercover police officer?" Cardwell was now focusing on Gates. The lawyer had both hands in his pockets, his suit coat open.

"Yes, sir. Obviously I didn't know it at the time." Gates bent the wire neck of the witness stand microphone, positioning it closer to him. "I truly believed he was a friend. Him and Hank both."

"Well, let's get to the question the jury wants answered. Did you give that cocaine to Barry for a thousand dollars, as the commonwealth's attorney is alleging?"

Gates bit his lip, dipped his head, playacted remorse. "I did, sir. Heck, it's on tape. I don't deny it. Everything the police have said is true."

"So you don't dispute that money and drugs changed hands?" Cardwell asked. "The commonwealth's case is accurate?"

"As far as it goes, yeah." Gates's face contracted. The single-syllable "yeah" leaked the first hint of deceit.

Cardwell was a savvy lawyer. He waited, didn't rush, allowed a confident silence before asking the tough, obvious question, and he posed it with a mixture of disbelief and astonishment that perfectly mirrored the sentiments of every juror. "What in the world were you thinking, Mr. Hunt? Can you tell these ladies and gentlemen what caused you to do what we all agree you did? Why were you swapping cocaine for money? Why in tarnation are you fighting this?"

"Sure. Yes, sir. Like I said, I don't dispute what's been proved so far—it's just not the whole story."

"Okay," Cardwell replied. "You tell us the parts that have been omitted."

Gates bored in on the jury, but his set jaw and earnest eyes were too aggressive, too dramatic, and when he spoke, he was antsy, pushy, a grifter with a valise and shiny shoes. "Here's what's not being told. See, Barry, or Agent Simpson—I'm not sure which to call him—gave me the drugs. Gave 'em to me days before the arrest to hold as collateral. We were close friends, and I ran into him one evening at the Old Dominion, and he tells me how he's up against it, in a jam because his kid's sick and needs medical care and begs me to let him borrow a thousand dollars. Well, I'd sold my Corvette to Clyde Turner—"

"Mr. Turner is here and prepared to testify, correct?" Cardwell interjected, helping as much as he was able.

"Right. And he'll confirm what I'm sayin'. So, you know, gee, he's a friend and he's down on his luck, so I loan him the money but, like anybody else, friend or not, I need to make sure I'm protected, so I asked for some collateral."

A juror in a coat and tie, the assistant manager of an oil company, was the first to anticipate the remainder of Gates's defense, and his expression soured. He folded his arms across his chest and tipped back in his seat, began gazing at the ceiling.

"What collateral did you receive?" the lawyer asked.

"I know this sounds horrible, and I know I never should've done it but, well, all he had, or so he claimed, was this cocaine. I mean, I asked about car titles or jewelry or guns or whatever, but he said he was broke and in hock and was plannin' to sell the drugs to help with his situation but needed the cash right then, pronto. So, stupid me, I took his coke and kept it, and a few days later he phoned and said he could repay me. We met at the fairgrounds, and I swear to every single person here today, I thought I was only returning his property and bein' repaid. It was dumb on my part, but I was only tryin' to help a friend. I realize I made a horrible mistake, and I apologize to the court and the citizens of our fine county and the police."

"This was a setup?" Cardwell emphasized.

"Yes, sir. I was entrapped. I wasn't in the habit of selling drugs."

Observing from the front row, Mason saw the commonwealth's attorney smile and whisper something to the detective beside him. Cardwell grimaced—his mouth twitched and his eyes nearly shut—before regaining his composure. He asked a couple more questions and sat down, buttoning his jacket once he'd settled in his chair.

The commonwealth's attorney, a tenacious lawyer named Tony Black, asked for a conference with the judge, and when court was called back into session, the jury soon learned—since Gates had carelessly introduced the subject, opening the evidentiary door—that he was indeed a drug dealer, and a relatively active one to boot. After Gates was eviscerated on cross-examination, and after a comically uncomfortable appearance by Clyde Turner, the defense rested, and Black was then allowed to present evidence of Gates's several other drug transactions, lining up baggie corners of coke on the railing in front of the jury box as he ticked off dates and places. To make matters worse, he'd managed to provoke Gates with his questions on cross, had gotten him riled and flustered, and Gates sat slumped and glowering during closing arguments, a pissy, ill-tempered churl misbehaving in front of the very people who were deciding his fate.

While they were waiting for the jury to return, the sheriff was kind enough to permit Gates a taste of liberty. He sat—shackled at the ankles—with Mason on the blustery courthouse porch and worked on a cigarette, the smoke reinforced by the winter air when he exhaled, a deputy watching him from a distance. "I know what you're thinking," he said to Mason between drags. "But if there was one lie standin' between you and jail, you'd damn sure tell it."

Mason checked to make sure the policeman wasn't within earshot before he answered. "Yeah, well, I think I'd be more careful in selecting my material. The whole thing had the ring of an eight-year-old's sandbox fantasy, kind of made up on the fly—'then Superman and the Hulk find a secret potion that makes them invisible and they enlist Batman and his rocket ship so they can travel to outer space to fight the Klingons.' That's how it came off."

Gates laughed, a raucous, unchecked burst of pure amusement that caught Mason by surprise. "Well," he said, giddy and frazzled, nothing left to lose, "I gave it a try. But I'm afraid you're probably right. Thanks for bein' with me and puttin' up with my shit. You take care of Mom." He tossed the cigarette onto the concrete and extinguished it with his heel. "You're okay with me, right? I don't want this to get us sideways with each other—we've been brothers too long for that."

"I'm fine," Mason said. "I just hate that you're in this mess."

"Not your fault, despite what I might've said when I was pissed off. Nobody could ask for a better brother. I appreciate it. And tell your beautiful wife I'm sorry I've kept you so tied up."

"Yeah." Much of Mason's aggravation had lifted. He leaned into his brother so their shoulders touched, bumped his knee with a fist. "Let's hope for the best. Who knows what a jury'll do."

"I'm ready to go inside," Gates hollered to the officer.

The jury sentenced him to a total of forty-four years, and as they filed back in to hear their verdict announced, every last one of them stared right at Gates, determined that he would see their mettle and what they thought of his lying and low behavior. Gates cursed when he heard the number, cursed out loud, and he vowed the men and women responsible for his sentence would most certainly pay a price when he was released, shouted it to them while the bailiff was clicking the cuffs around his wrists.

Gary Shelor raised dairy cattle and lived on a farm that had been in his family for generations. The foreman of the panel, he stepped away from the jury area and stood in front of Gates after they'd been threatened: "I wish you *would* come looking for me. One-oh-seven Harrell Ridge Road's where I'm at. I'll be waitin'." Almost every juror acknowledged Sadie Grace as they walked past her, and Justine Hiatt stopped and knelt and patted her on the arm.

"I'm sorry, honey," she said. "We just done what we thought was right. It isn't your fault your son sold drugs."

"I know," Sadie answered, weeping and gagging breaths, her hands trembling. "But why'd you have to take his whole life? It ain't as if he murdered someone."

Chapter Four

There's a meanness in certain men that is bestial and set apart. It's not the trite, commonplace variety born of an insult or a mouthy challenge, not the slap or fist or hasty knife that has its genesis in carousing and brown liquor and not the kind found in bullies, boyfriends who puncture their exes' car tires or the boss who trifles with employees for sport. Some men, as they say in Patrick County, are just plumb mean, mean without reason, mean without provocation. Gates and Mason's father, Curt Hunt, was such a man.

Curt was tall and stout like his sons, handsome in a commanding way, black-haired, dark-eyed, rawboned. Three years older than Sadie Grace, he married her the October following her graduation from high school. She was enrolled in college, studying to be a nurse, barely nineteen, away from home for the first time, and she wound up pregnant, steadfastly refusing to accept her condition until she was a full month late, praying and cutting deals with the Good Lord right up to the moment the infirmary doctor gave her the news. It was 1956. Belly-sick and clutching three white carnations, she discovered herself at the courthouse in Dobson, North Carolina, with her parents and a girlfriend, the ceremony, as it were, conducted by a skinny old clerk who switched her names around when he asked if she intended to take Curt as her lawfully wedded husband. They'd dated for over a year, so it wasn't the end of the world, but she confided to her happy-go-lucky aunt that she would miss school and the fun people and the life that was more seasoned and vital than the one she'd catch in Patrick County, a toddler on her jutted hip.

Curt never hit Sadie Grace. Instead, he raved and cursed and destroyed doors, plates and furniture to the point she almost wished he'd go ahead and be done with it, her tiptoeing dread as painful as any beating he could possibly deliver. They'd been married three months when he first showed himself, and the worst of it was how the outbursts would always catch her cold, their sneaky cat's feet. A year into the marriage, sitting at the dinner table, Gates napping in a playpen, eating the beans and weenies she'd prepared prior to leaving for a third-shift night at the plant, Sadie Grace inquired of Curt, who was saturating a slice of loaf bread in his buttermilk, whether he'd remembered to pay the light bill while he was in town. Curt stood and took his chair with both hands and broke it to pieces, first slamming it against the table—glasses shattering, the silverware airborne with each concussion—before finishing it off on the counter. Not content to quit there, he took a leg spindle and whipped it against the fridge until the wood finally splintered, the destruction, from beginning to end, steady and calculated rather than crazed. Then he snatched his coat and the car keys and stayed gone for two incommunicado days, stranding his wife and child since they owned only the single straight-shift Chevrolet.

And yet Sadie Grace stayed. She stayed because she didn't know what else to do, because she was afraid, because she was embarrassed, because she had no money and a dead-end job, because she was responsible for a baby boy, because it was an era before activists, vigils, shelters, Hollywood ribbons and laws worth a damn and because she became conditioned to violence in the same fashion a sideshow freak learns to tolerate the sharp point of a nail or some Holy Rollers become immune, bite by bite, to a rattlesnake's venom. She worked at the plant, tended to Gates, cleaned their shotgun shack of a house and kept her distance from Curt, always on edge, never taking a whole breath. The best she had day to day was a phone call with her mama on the semiprivate line or a trip to buy groceries, where she might run into a friend and chat for a few moments without worrying about what kind of wrath a word or a pause between sentences could incite. Even her dull job became a sanctuary of sorts, the back and forth of the looms and the clacking of machines a monotonous comfort.

Sex was a forced march. Curt would arrive home from his job as a diesel mechanic, carrying his silver thermos and rounded lunch pail, his shirttail neither tucked nor all the way loose, and tap her away from the stove or washing machine with a blunt "let's go," undoing his trousers as he spoke. For a couple years, she actually found a measure of hope in his demands. When he ordered her to take off her clothes, she understood exactly what he wanted, she felt odd relief he was still interested and she believed she could some-how tame him, screw the mercurial cruelty right out of him and fix their troubles. Nothing changed, though, except that Mason was born in 1960, three years after his brother. Sadie Grace told the doctor to make certain Mason would be the last.

Gates and Mason, even as youngsters, did not enjoy the same safety from Curt's physical side that their mother did. As soon as they were upright, smacks, wallops, kicks, spankings and belt lashings came from their blind sides, helter-skelter. Who knew when or why. Six months would pass quietly, calm—Curt would chuckle at Red Skelton's black-and-white skits, repair a broken bicycle chain, cook venison steaks and quiz the boys about their schooling, rewarding them with a slingshot or Silly Putty or a single-blade pocketknife if their marks were satisfactory. Then he'd erupt twice in a week. Out of nowhere, Gates received a hellacious beating for taking a Sun-Drop cola from the fridge, despite getting permission from his mother. Another time, Curt chased him down and flogged him with the butt end of a fishing rod for no discernible reason; Curt just shot him a look and the boy ran and it was innate almost, the tug of feral instinct for the father to catch his son and flail away. Not surprisingly, the boys learned to scatter when Curt would cant his head and curl his lips and demand to know "what you lookin' at?"

It was Gates, growing and gangly, who rebelled first, trying to fight back. Curt would light into him, and Gates would kick and bite and claw and launch impotent punches that his father easily blocked, often catching the boy's wrist and wrenching it until he took a knee. Young Gates became a furious, angry kid whose resistance and wild rushes made Curt that much worse, and Curt would frequently subdue him with a choke hold and taunt him: "You wanna hit me, boy? Hit me now—come on, let's see you do somethin'." During these melees his voice was always battened down, his words deliberate, pointed. Curt Hunt never took a drink of alcohol, never lost his temper in the sense he simply flew hot after reaching his limit and never seemed shamed by his violence.

For a while, Sadie Grace would stand nearby and beg him to leave the children alone, but it didn't take long before she was jumping in and wrapping herself around an arm or a leg, protecting her sons. Finally, she hit the bastard. It was summer of 1964, and Gates was seven, wearing a bathing suit and no shirt, no shoes, in the yard rolling a beach ball to Mason, and their father arrived home from his job, called hello to both his sons, and as best everyone could tell, grew angry because they weren't inside the instant supper was ready forty-five minutes later.

He stalked through the door and gave the top of Gates's head a good whack, and Gates told him he was a shitpot, kicking him in the calf to underscore the elementary-school profanity. Curt went straight to the choke hold, trapping the boy's windpipe in the crook of his arm and heaving him off the ground. Gates began sputtering and his eyes bulged and his face filled with blood and he pedaled the air with his naked feet. Sadie Grace came up from behind and whopped her husband in the rib cage with a cast-iron skillet, the warm grease splattering her hand and staining his blue shirt. He released Gates, ate his meal alone and warned Sadie Grace he'd kill her in her sleep if she ever got between him and his sons again. Then, pretty as you please, he tinkered in his shed, listened to the radio, ate a molasses biscuit and climbed into bed without washing up, his grimy boots and white socks discarded by the toilet. "Night, y'all" was all he had to say as he passed his family, timid on the sofa.

Sadie Grace took to stashing the boys at her mother's more and more, telling Curt they wanted to spend time with their grandma. The brothers slept in a tiny room on pallets made of quilts and cheap fuzzy blankets, in a house that smelled of analgesic rubs and musty clothes, while Sadie Grace stayed with Curt and made excuses and told lies and fell on her sword and watched the mad-man she'd married go from Jekyll to Hyde at the drop of a hat. Sex was rape for her by now. Curt would lead her to bed and roll her over and pound away, and it got so intolerable she'd half-puke, the acid burning her throat and seeping into her nose so that she had to cram it back down with a sick swallow and packed-in air.

Gates and Mason pricked their fingers and made pacts and swore all kinds of oaths, and they shuttled between their home and their grandma's and watched their mother do all she could to defend them when the pitched battles were fought, clinging to Curt's waist or leg, hitting him with a double fist, pushing, shoving, whatever it took to free them or keep the torment to a minimum. Curt would just shuck her off or hold her at arm's length and continue punishing his sons. It was Gates who got the brunt of it, and by the time he was ten, he never failed to take a sacrificial stand in front of Mason and suffer a backhand or an ass whipping in an effort to stick the bull's neck with a few lances or give the younger boy a running start. By rights, many of Gates's welts and bruises were not his own.

There came a day when the two brothers together—Gates at fourteen and sinewy, Mason on the cusp of adolescence—could give Curt a run for his money, and whether it was coincidence or not none of them ever knew, but on a glorious day in 1971, Curt Hunt didn't come home from work, simply up and left. He didn't even stop for his clothes or tools or arrowhead collection, hitting the road with a woman who kept the books at the garage. He never returned, and rumor had it they'd moved to South Carolina. No cards, no let-ters, no child support, no visits, no phone calls, no explanation. Dead gone. Mason's classmates catcalled him and raked him with taunts, and he pummeled the bejesus out of one of the Fain kids after the little snot announced in the school cafeteria that Sadie Grace was now a prostitute, an eleven-year-old's mixed-up dig that was dumb and inaccurate but to-the-marrow hurtful.

Without Curt's check, the family went from making ends meet to free lunches and blocks of gooey government cheese, though Sadie Grace signed up for welfare reluctantly and as a last resort and would drive to Mount Airy when she needed groceries so her friends and people she knew wouldn't see her redeeming food-stamp coupons for canned beets and value packs of hamburger. She took in sewing on the side for extra cash, the boys received used clothes and hand-me-down shoes from the better-off families at the big Baptist church in Stuart, and the county kept a concerned eye on the Hunt boys, watching them with a generosity that was never condescending or meddlesome. When Sadie Grace honestly reported her seamstress earnings to Mrs. Tatum at the welfare office, they weren't recorded for the state, and the family carried a steep tab at the drugstore, toward which Sadie was allowed to pay five dollars a month, an installment schedule that made it possible for her to keep her pride but had a negligible effect on her debt.

She dated on occasion, but a third-shift job and two ragtag boys kept her strung out and frazzled, and she'd seen enough of men for a while anyway, which isn't to say several of her suitors weren't decent and respectful, and one, a retired Army sergeant, actually discussed marriage. She didn't frequent the honky-tonks or doll up and drive to the bars in Greensboro, spurned her married supervisor's advances and promises of a raise and a newer car and, unlike some of her friends, never brought men by the house when the kids were there, "uncles" who would lavish extravagant attention on the children in hopes of bedding their mothers, promises of fishing trips and BB guns forgotten after sex and a free meal.

She stayed wed to Curt for nearly six years after he departed, fig-uring a divorce was an expensive formality, a luxury that would gain her nothing, and when she finally visited a lawyer and made a down payment, it was Mason who asked her why she'd gotten tangled up with such a bum to begin with. "I suppose I mistook quiet for reli-able and solid," she said. "And nice looks for character. Then along comes Gates and I didn't have any choice. You just kinda get your foot caught in a trap, and there's nothin' much you can do."

Gates grew into a community darling, a joker and a football star, his ferocity on the field and violent, freight-train hits almost pitiable at times given that most people recognized the story behind them, and it shouldn't have surprised anyone when it became apparent a huge anger and a sturdy frame were the extent of his talents as a player and a person—by his final year of high school, he couldn't take the slightest bit of coaching or criticism, he couldn't bear not being king of the hill as a freshman at Virginia Tech, and he damn sure couldn't tolerate correction from some sissy English professor, stubbing up and pouting and then skipping class altogether, gone from college by Christmas.

Mason weathered their father differently. He was studious and self-contained, his own redoubt, a reader who appreciated the distraction of science fiction and the promise of *Ragged Dick* and *The Count of Monte Cristo,* a pupil who delighted his teachers, a kid who came from zilch and wore brogans and his brother's ill-fitting winter coat and still was elected student body president, prom king and "most likely to succeed." He occupied himself with every club, field trip, sports camp and school activity available, and he spent many a Saturday cheerfully volunteering at the pound, mopping urine and scooping dog crap, always making it a point to bring the strays and castoffs table scraps, a leftover chunk of biscuit or the burned end of a wiener, whatever he could scrounge, last suppers for most of the animals before Wanda the supervisor pierced them with a lethal needle and they yelped and lost their breathing and she burned them in the incinerator out back. Wanda told her sister you didn't need a Ph.D. to understand why he spoiled the skittish ones—the curs with lumps and cuts and tucked tails—more than the rest.

And while he didn't have his brother's size, swagger or aggressiveness, Mason was a gifted athlete also, a left-handed first baseman who earned a free ride at James Madison University and did well enough on the field to get drafted in the middle rounds by the St. Louis Cardinals. Ever practical, he thanked them for their offer of twenty-five thousand dollars and a minor-league contract, told them he probably didn't possess the skills to make a living as a big leaguer and accepted a substantial scholarship from the University of Richmond's law school. A torts professor gave him a part-time job, his grades were superior, his outlook sanguine, his prospects sound.

No matter how busy he was with classes or work, he never failed to keep his mother in mind, doted on her, surprising her with simple gifts and then the entire first check from his summer job at a Richmond law firm, occasionally returning home to sit with her on the brick steps and eat watermelon slices or plink snap beans into a thick glass bowl, the two of them jawing about local concerns, everything from a neighbor's cancer scare to the big Saturday-night Rook tournament. By his third year of law school, his break from Stuart was looking clean as a whistle, his way clear—clear until he discovered himself on Russell Creek Road, caught in Gates's slipstream, jarred and rattled, shit coming at him he hadn't bargained for.

At Allison Rand's core was a patent invitation to sex, and there was nothing she could do about it, even if she'd wanted to: her eyes were green, honeyed embraces, slightly languid but permanently in on a very private joke, her hair blond, her smiles given more to satisfaction than mirth, her shape, from calves to breasts, overtly appealing. She was an inch under six feet but never seemed large or clumsy or heavyset, moving in fluid, breezy steps, gliding into a room, reaching for a cocktail and encircling it with fingers that suggested caress rather than grip. She was blessed with a voice perfect for her build, neither flighty nor leaden, and a quickness in conversation that was natural and unrehearsed. She had a tender heart and kind disposition, and to her credit she never lorded her appearance over other people. Even so, an occasional acquaintance would keep her at a distance and flay her name with whispers and gossip, tut-tutting about her wardrobe or habits or sports car or trips to Bermuda or boyfriends or the "arrogant" way she reclined against the railing during the Foxfield steeplechase, sipping a mimosa and making nice to everybody's date or husband. To the petty and envious, she was a bitch by beauty, and she'd come to accept the cold shoulders and lukewarm smiles for what they were, deciding the trade-off wasn't so bad, not so bad at all.

Allison met Mason late in the summer of 1985, after he'd graduated from law school. He'd taken the bar examination and been offered a job at McCloud, Flanagan in Richmond, recommended by one of his professors who did freelance consulting for the firm. They were at a bookstore in Shockoe Slip, Allison to hear a popular author read, Mason because he saw the crowd spilling onto the sidewalk and stopped to see what was happening. Allison caught a glimpse of him standing in the overflow near the shop's doorway and made no bones about nudging the woman beside her and turning back for a second, obvious gander, happy to spy the rare man who made her first cut: taller than she, handsome, possibly literate.

The author was reciting from her novel, and Mason hung around for twenty ponderous minutes listening to the story of a maddening husband and wife on a picnic, ants invading their sandwiches, their conversation about a sickly child. When the writer finished, Allison sidestepped to the end of a folding-chair row and turned to leave. Mason was lingering at the threshold of the store, watching her, waiting to find out if they were going to advance any further. He gave her a direct smile as she walked toward him.

"Hello," he said, cocksure. "I'm Mason. Nothing like a stiff shot of prose in the afternoon, huh?"

"Hi," she said, her eyes up and down, not long on his face. "Allison."

"I think we noticed each other during the reading."

"We did, yeah," she answered.

"Did you enjoy the show?"

"Yes. I think she's an excellent writer. How about you?"

"To be honest, I saw the crowd and was curious. I don't read much for pleasure. Wish I did."

"Ah, what a clever opening," she said impishly. "I'll rise to the bait." She moved away briefly to let a pair of chattering ladies pass. "What is it you read—not for pleasure—that you want me to ask about?"

Mason laughed. "I'll try to refine my pitch in the future. I'm a lawyer, a very new one. I took the bar exam in June, and studying for it provided me with all the reading I needed, thank you. I'm starting at McCloud, Flanagan soon."

"Do you think you passed?" she asked, and it hit Mason that everything about her, from the five-word question to her shortish skirt to the way she subtly spread her hands at the end of her sentence, was tinged erotic, the effect like moisture weeping through dam fissures, a puissant promise not quite held in check.

"I studied hard," he said. "Stayed up late, didn't shave, ate bad food, worried myself silly—did all the right things."

"What kind of lawyer are you?"

"I don't know yet, to tell the truth. Are we playing twenty questions?"

"Let's make it ten," she suggested. "Your bar exam for today. We don't really have time for twenty."

"I agree." He put his hands in his pockets, leaned against a bookshelf. "Have at it."

"Okay. Hmmm . . . Favorite lizard?"

"Gila monster." He smiled.

"Me, I'm a chameleon girl myself." She produced a tube of lip balm from her purse and began applying it while she spoke. "Joy buzzers, cigarette loads, rubber snakes or invisible ink?"

"Joy buzzers."

"Good choice, though they all have pizzazz." She dropped the tube into her purse, letting it go near chest level so that it free-fell through the air before landing. "Ever read Gertrude Stein?"

"Lord, no. I guess I don't mind laboring for a payday, but I don't aspire to be in a fistfight for three hundred pages, either." He stood straight, quit resting on the shelf. "She was a lesbian, yes? Of the wool-socks, pomade persuasion?"

"You should give her a whirl. She's amazing."

"We could have a deal breaker there."

"Last one," she said.

"You've got plenty more left."

"I know." She fluffed the side of her hair. "This is important: best painter ever?"

"Huh." He studied her and noticed she really did seem to be

putting him to the test. "Well, I'd say either Vermeer or Salvador Dalí. Those were my favorites from the art class I took at JMU to fulfill my elective requirements, and names like Cézanne will land you in trouble when you're not sure how to pronounce the *a*." He hoisted his hands from his pockets, realized a store employee was watching him and definitely not wishing him well.

"I've heard it both ways." She hunted through the contents of her bag without removing anything. "Either's fine with me," she said, not looking at him.

"Where're you headed? I've got enough cash to buy us a drink or two, maybe a cheap dinner if you play your cards right."

"Let me see your driver's license, please." She'd finished with the purse.

"Why?" he asked.

"Well, I like to get an idea of people at their worst, sort of reverse beer goggles. Plus, I can make sure you're not some ogre who lied to me about his name."

Mason gave her his license, and she held it in her palm and finger-read the information with her free hand. "Yikes! You favor Mr. Bentley, the guy who lives above the Jeffersons." Her eyes were lined and painted like a pharaoh's daughter, her hair an eighties Glamour Shot canopy. She smiled, white teeth, nicely sized and spaced and aligned.

"Really? I thought I looked more like Gary Cooper."

"Gary Cooper after a jailbreak or a bender at Studio 54, maybe." Mason grinned at her.

"You and I were born in the same month," she noted. She finally met him eye to eye, a tiny flirt.

"So how about the drink?"

"I'm with my friend, and I shouldn't leave her," she said, checking her watch.

"Bummer. So am I at least allowed a question or a driver's license inspection?"

"Okay, but the clock's running." Mason noticed she had very little accent, finished off the g's and didn't linger on her vowels.

"Worst song ever?"

She answered immediately. "I'll give you three. This is the kind of important info people need to prepare and have at their finger-tips. One: 'Honey,' by Bobby Goldsboro; two: 'You Light Up My Life,' by Debbie Boone; three: 'Stairway to Heaven,' Led Zeppelin. Honorable mentions go to anything by John Cage, 'Convoy'—"

"Whoa now," Mason interrupted. "Hang on there. I'm filing a protest. It's not fair to use obvious novelty tunes."

"And finally, Neil Diamond and Streisand dueting on 'You Don't Bring Me Flowers'—terrible, painful commercial dreck. Being a boy, you will, I'm sure, object to the 'Stairway' inclusion, but I stand by that choice. It's so overwrought and dramatic, a screeching, loud, pompous, white-bread cliché."

"Pretty compelling list," he conceded. "You won't find me defend-ing Robert Plant." He touched her at the elbow, a small come-on, almost a brush, his hand cupped, palm up, not much to it. "You're sure you're going to kneecap me on the drinks? I'd be glad to treat your friend. Bring her along." He glanced at the crowd inside. "By the way, I know who John Cage is. I took a music appreciation class, too."

"You're nice to ask, but I can't. My last name's Rand. It's in the book. A bunch of us are going to a big party tomorrow night on Monument Circle—you'll see the cars if you want to come."

They met that way, and they never embellished it or rearranged the facts or romanticized the circumstances or colored their motives. Years later, with no qualms and her head held high, Allison would tell close friends Mason simply wanted to fuck her from the first second he glimpsed her—no more, no less—and that was a compliment of the highest rank, a comforting connection, because say what you will, relationships, she was convinced, ignite in the eye. The most unassailable marriage has its roots in the quick math, the sine qua non, the base yes or no, the "bedrock issue," she was fond of saying, often pausing to enjoy the pun when she explained her thoughts. There's much more that has to come, many more integral numbers and symbols in the equation, a slew of other calcu-lations, but by golly who wants to spend a lifetime with a sexless buddy, playing Scrabble or bridge, fussing over seating arrange-ments at a dinner party and sneaking nome early from work every now and again to a bottle of Chardonnay and a mail-order vibrator. "Lay the block, *then* worry with the wallpaper and crown molding, you know?" she always remarked when she was on the subject.

They met up at the bash she'd mentioned, and it ran on until dawn. Mason drank sparingly—doing so, he frequently informed his hungover pals, gave him superpowers around midnight, when everyone else was stoned, sloppy and reckless—and Allison switched from white wine to White Russians to white powder, white being her party motif for the evening, she declared. A cab carried them to her town house, where they kissed and rolled and rubbed and tangled up on the floor, the couch, the huge mahogany dining room table and finally her bed. Her skirt got pushed to her waist, her blouse was mostly undone and her bra loose, and Mason shed his shirt in the hallway near her door, but that's where she stopped it, skin on skin, skin on cloth, exquisitely incomplete, a cocked pistol. She made them a breakfast of fried eggs, toast and cold smoked salmon, and they napped till noon, her head on his chest, her knee against his thigh. He left with her phone number, walked to a bus stop and went home happy as a clam, his recovered shirt all the way open, Eddy Grant's garish "Electric Avenue" looping in his skull, unshakable.

Mason was footloose that summer, at the tail end of a catch-as-catch-can romance with a feisty law student named Brenda who'd already packed her bags for a job in Boston, so with a clear conscience he phoned Allison the following morning and, not finding her, tried again that evening and three times the next day. Unable to afford a ritzy florist, he bought a quality bouquet of flowers from a street vendor, took the bus to her neighborhood, attached a note and had the doorman send up the gift, tipped the guy a dollar and then—when he didn't hear from her—fretted that his lilies and daisies and single sweeping gladiolus had been tossed into the trash or forgotten during a shift change, never making it to her. A week passed, and she didn't call.

He next saw her at the Border Café, a raucous bar in the Fan District, where he'd gone with two law school friends to knock around and make a meal of the free "Thirsty Thursday" promotional hors d'oeuvres, mostly overcooked chicken planks and greasy wings with tepid ranch dressing. When Allison arrived, he and his friend Frank Eggleston were chatting up two college girls from VCU, though Mason had left several times to stand in line and fill his small plastic plate and bring Frank and the women fifty-cent cups of draft Natural Light. Allison blew in with a group of noisy people, and as soon as she spotted him, she waved and smiled and didn't hesitate, cut through the crowd, beelining toward him. She kissed his cheek and introduced herself to Frank and the women, who resented the intrusion and coolly said, "Nice to meet you" without offering their names or any sense that she was welcome. "I loved the sweet gift," she said. "Sorry to interrupt, but I wanted to say hello." She focused on the woman beside Frank. "What a gorgeous top," she remarked, sounding sincere.

"Oh, thanks," came the curt reply.

"I'm glad we ran into each other," Allison said to Mason. "Stop by the bar and visit if you have a chance."

"I will if Master Frank and the ladies allow me time off from my manservant duties, fetching fowl and keeping their chalices full of grog."

She briefly bunched her lips, amused. "I've never thought I'd care for a manservant. Now a stableboy, something sort of D. H. Lawrenceish, that might be the ticket."

Frank dipped his head and pushed his tongue into his cheek. He peered sheepishly at Allison, then caught his friend's eye. The two women hammered her with a stare that said, "You may be prettier than we are, but you're still a big classless bitch, D. H. Lawrence or not."

Mason didn't seem to notice. "I think, technically speaking, Wilbur Post was a stable boy. You're setting your sights on Brylcreem and cardigans, are you?"

Frank performed a quick Mister Ed riff, mimicking the horse's speech. He ended by observing that Mister Ed reminded him of Carol Channing for some reason.

"Nothing wrong with a snazzy dresser, Mason," she said. "Nice to meet you ladies," she added. "You too, Frank."

Mason kept track of her for another fifteen minutes or so, then excused himself under the pretext of using the restroom and threaded his way through the crowd to where she was standing at the bar. She was talking to a man and another woman, and from what Mason had observed, the man was making it apparent he had designs on her, leaning in to listen, handing her glass to the bartender for a refill, offering an aside no one else could hear. He pivoted a shoulder toward Mason as soon as he arrived, blocking him from Allison. Mason didn't like him in the least, and wouldn't have even if they weren't interested in the same romance. Allison introduced him—Clement Watkins, Jr.—and he shook Mason's hand a little too vigorously, smiled too aggressively and spoke with too much volume, as if he were pissing a circle around her with words. He was snarky and impatient and didn't bother to conceal it.

"Clement was just saying how crowded it is here," Allison said blandly.

"Cheap beer and free food will bring out the masses," Clement cracked. Despite the swarm of people and stifling heat, a white cotton sweater was tied around his neck. He was wearing snug shorts that halted before they reached mid-thigh.

"Lured me here," Mason said.

The other woman pressed closer to the bar, her drink held above the crowd, out of harm's way. "I'm switching to tequila," she said to Allison.

"We're just back from St. John," Allison mentioned, turning to face Mason, her expression and intent impossible to decipher.

Clement took this as an invitation to slide his arm around her waist.

"Hey, great. Hope you had blue skies." Mason was deflated, a bit embarrassed. His common rearing had never been a concern for him before, but for whatever reason, he suddenly, for a moment, felt like an interloper, smelling of high-dollar cologne—an extravagant birthday gift from his mom—and dressed in slacks he'd ironed himself while eating leftover KFC from the bucket and watching a *Dallas* rerun, a bare mattress and sleeping bag in his bedroom, a single fan blowing through the apartment to lessen the suffocating tenth-floor humidity.

"Thanks again for your kindness," Allison said cryptically.

"Ah . . . oh," Clement said, raising an index finger to his lips. "Are you the Romeo who sent my sweetheart the bouquet?" He was nearly as tall as Mason, with sharp, alert features and long brown hair that made him attractive in the casual fashion of men who are at ease around sailboats and tennis courts and know how to fox-trot at black-tie galas, who rarely wear socks and favor money clips over wallets.

"Pardon?"

Clement didn't flinch. "I asked if you sent flowers to Allison."

"I did, but what is it to you?" Mason lowered his cup of beer.

"It's a free country, Marlon," he said, unruffled. "Send away. I just like to know where my competition lies." He directed a wolfish smile at Mason. "Though for the short term, not to put too fine a point on it, I can't see any reason for you to hang around here hitting on my girlfriend."

"Mason, not Marlon." He kept his composure. "And I suppose you're right. But things do have a tendency to change. Not many men can get away with wearing a cape over the long haul—you, Underdog, Elvis, French kings. Never know."

"What, pray tell, are you talking about?" Clement asked. "My first beer made me a little incoherent, too."

Mason patted his throat. "Oh damn—my bad. That's a *sweater* tied around your neck. Sorry." He bulled his way forward and kissed Allison's cheek, surprising her, and he peered at Clement, told him he'd enjoyed meeting him, deadpanned it with a wink in every sylla-ble, and what was Clement going to do, quick as it came, in a jammed bar, with a guy as big and audacious as Mason. "Hope you liked the flowers," he said to her. "I delivered them myself."

"Yeah, well, don't forget, Underdog could fly," Clement said. "He was the star of the show."

Later, a friend of Allison's, at her bidding, approached Mason and requested his number, and Allison woke him at three in the morning, inviting him to meet her in twenty minutes for biscuits and gravy at a diner on Cary Street. She poured vodka from a flask into her tomato juice and sprinkled the drink with a lemon squeeze, and they talked for two hours, shared the saturated biscuits, a BLT and a piece of pie with meringue topping, selected from the glass display case near the cash register. At first, Mason was sore about their earlier meeting at the bar, and he sat back against the wooden booth and frowned and tucked his chin and—even though he realized he should've been far more cavalier—wanted to know why she was keeping company with a guy dressed for the local theater troupe's *Chitty Chitty Bang Bang* revival.

"If you didn't think he was impressive, you wouldn't be so curious, now would you?" She took a sip of her doctored juice, looking at him over the glass's rim.

"I'd ask you the same question if you were dating Grendel or Sasquatch—flummoxed doesn't mean I thought he was impressive."

"I don't get the *Chitty Chitty Bang Bang* reference. I don't think it's technically too accurate."

"How about effete and goofy? That's what I was aiming for."

"Clement is neither. If he were, I wouldn't see him. He's an architect, a published poet and a ranked amateur tennis player. He spent a month in El Salvador, not for the politics, mind you, but just trying to help out. He was stabbed in the arm and arrested once while he was there. I would hope, Mason, if you and I were together in a bar and another man showed an interest in me, you'd give him his walking papers, same as Clem did with you."

Mason mentioned he didn't care for poetry, informed her of his Matchbox car analogy, adding he'd need to see the hospital report before he believed Clement Watkins, Jr., had been wounded in the course of tending to the poor and unfortunate in another country. "Maybe he was nicked by a cricket bat or beaned by a snooker ball—I'd come closer to believing one of those."

She sawed off a chunk of biscuit, loaded it onto her fork and offered it in his direction, stopping near his plate so he'd have to leave his small sulk and move forward to get it. "You're blown up like a toad," she teased. "Jealous as a schoolboy."

He relaxed and took hold of the silverware and food, fed himself. "I'm not anything. I was a little—what's the right word?—*surprised* to discover you had a boyfriend after we spent the night together."

She cocked her head playfully. "So, what, you expected me to sit home arranging my figurines and reading the Brontë sisters, waiting for you to call?" She idly bumped a piece of piecrust with a spoon. "Listen, Mason, it's more complicated than you might think." Her voice changed, her face sobered. "Clement and I have been on and off for a while now, and we'd booked this trip months ago. He's about eighty-five percent for me, if you know what I mean, and that's more than a lot of people ever have, so I've been sorta trying to figure out if I've reached the max. It's like a dress that's flattering but not perfect, the kind you'd wear to work or to an important party but not to your five-year high school reunion. And who knows about you, okay? Or even if it matters long-term, since we've known each other for all of a few days. There's no need to be upset about it, not really. I'm sure you've probably been in the same situation."

"I guess," he answered. "Most everyone has. At any rate, it's decent of you to explain. I had a great night when we met, and—see there—not only did I call, but I sent flowers, too. It'll be my stated goal to move the meter to at least ninety percent."

They began dating the next evening and eight months later decided they'd see only each other, though with the exception of two ill-advised reunions with Brenda and a dizzy weekend of shacking up at Virginia Beach with a girl he met at a poolside bar, Mason didn't take advantage of their open-ended arrangement, and all his wandering came during the first month of their courtship. When they finally had sex it was unhinged and passionate, a celebration that began as she was helping him hang curtains in his austere apartment, and despite her bacchanalian zigs and zags and a bearing that rained down frank allure, she confided to Mason she'd been with only four other men, all of them serious beaus except a professional soccer player in Monte Carlo.

Allison was a painter, and a very talented one as best Mason could tell, and she made her living that way. She had no patience with Reagan but thought Tip O'Neill was a blundering, backroom hack, she never failed to acknowledge the donation hats in front of walleyed saxophone players and street-corner beggars, she attended the Episcopal church most Sundays—a Saturday night of merrymaking notwithstanding—and dragged Mason along and, most important, she seemed to have no malice, no scores to settle with anyone, no bruises, no trigger points, a bright woman whose sunny nature was never mistaken for naïveté. Oddly, she'd been to a series of colleges, but held no degree. She'd studied in Rhode Island, Paris, California, North Carolina and at a diesel school in Nashville, explaining to Mason she learned what she needed to know and left before the superfluous hours of calculus and medieval history.

Her rich, daredevil father had perished in a scuba-diving accident, became lost in an underwater cave and exhausted his air, a horrific death counted down by the needle of an oxygen gauge, and she often told people her mom died later of a broken heart, but the truth was cancer had gnawed up Sophia Rand's pancreas when her only child was twenty and nursing her at home, doling out pills and changing giant diapers, honoring a frightened parent's plea not to be hospitalized and given over to the custody of antiseptic strangers.

On a chilly, wet Thursday in the fall of 1986, she admitted to Mason she was afraid the dope and partying were chain-ganging her, and she asked him to miss work and look after her while she dealt with it. He rented a house at Nags Head, where he took care of her for eleven straight days. They walked on the beach, fired late-night bottle rockets toward the dark-gray ocean, prepared mac and cheese from a kit, cooked seafood spaghetti, carted Whoppers and fried-flounder plates from town to their kitchen and played Monopoly for real money and then sex so that "taking a ride on the Reading" became part of their private lexicon. Without any warning or preface, she woke up at dawn in their second week there and started filling her suitcase and said she was ready to go home, done. "Thank you," she told him as they were poking down a sand and grass driveway, aiming toward the hardtop. "I love you."

It was on the return trip she revealed something else, that she'd been "fortunate with money," the beneficiary of a grandfather's trust, not enough to make her rich, but enough to make her comfortable, a windfall of close to two hundred thousand dollars every year.

"Shit," Mason joshed, "let's get married."

Chapter Five

Less than a year later, in April of 1987, that's what they did, got married by a priest at St. Stephen's Episcopal Church, not too far from Allison's town house. Mason was making solid money by now, and Allison had recently sold out a twelve-painting opening, and they set aside three weeks for their honeymoon, first visiting her flighty aunt in Naples, Florida, then stopping to spend time with Sadie Grace, who baked them a lemon chess pie and unpacked photos of Mason, everything from his baby shot naked in the bathroom sink to his blue-tuxedoed prom picture. Without protest, Allison accompanied Mason to a trailer park to meet Gates, and when their visit was finished, the brothers hugged and exchanged sincere good-byes and she covered Gates's hand with her own, told him she was pleased to be his sister-in-law, wrote down his address and sent him a note the next evening, enclosing a quick sketch of the Patrick County mountains, highlighted with a splash of watercolor. From there, they traveled to a rented cottage in Cape Cod, which they scarcely left for two weeks, under each other's spell, slaphappy each morning when they awoke and remembered—oh, wow, damn—they were wed.

Their daughter, Grace Hannah Hunt, was born on September 8, 1988, and she was a delight to her parents, especially her father, who'd occasionally feared during Allison's pregnancy that whatever had haunted Curt might be recessive in him, might somehow bubble in his blood and turn him into a belt-swinging beast where his child was concerned. He grew ever more bumbling and protective as Allison's due date neared, became a sweet, devoted oaf, but at her urging he chose to wait outside the delivery room, elected not to loiter about underfoot mouthing slogans from behind a surgical mask as she ached and strained and tore giving birth. When he held Grace for the first time, he clutched her to his chest and knelt, his knees on the hospital's hard institutional tile, his eyes astonished by a face that jotted down everything superior from her parents. "We did it," he said to Allison, his whole attention on the baby, his voice raspy. True to form, drained and weary after a taxing labor, she blew him a kiss, proud and relieved and over the moon with her infant girl and giddy husband.

For the next several months, Mason took two-hour lunches and frequently worked half days, and despite their lip service about how happy they were for him and how they believed family was paramount, the partners at his firm grew disgruntled with his productivity and office habits. Mason recognized the tension but didn't give a damn, and in the late summer of 1989, he was hauled into a partners' conference and informed by a guy wearing a flamboyant red tie and matching suspenders that the firm respected his commitment to his daughter—and good for him, fine and dandy—but thirty billable hours a week would not be earning him a corner office or a partnership check. "You're a crackerjack lawyer, Mason," the managing partner chimed in, "by far the best associate we have. But it's like we bought a Porsche that we can only drive at thirty miles per hour. We're telling you now so you won't feel ambushed or mistreated when we make promotion decisions."

Mason wasn't insulted. He'd known what was expected when he signed on—fifty billable hours per week, minimum—and he wasn't pulling his share of the load, plain and simple. "I appreciate the heads-up," he replied, surveying the table and making eye contact

with everyone in the room. "Believe me, I'm grateful for the latitude so far, and I understand the economics of this firm. Still, it's
altogether possible—assuming it's satisfactory with you ladies and
gentlemen—that I've found my niche. I'm happy with my pay,
happy with my status and happy with my hours." He stopped and
rolled around a smile, signaling he recognized how his response
would play with many of the lawyers listening. "Most likely, I'll be
content as this firm's first associate-for-life." He paused again. "The
understudy without ambition."

Allison was a darling from the get-go, come what may. "You know
I can manage this by myself," she informed him that same evening,
the family at their kitchen table, Grace shoveling up banana pieces
with tiny soaked fingers. "I hate for you to be kept behind because
of us." She shrugged. "Or, for all I care, you can quit today. Makes
no difference to me."

"I'm okay. Hell, they're paying me close to eighty grand, and I'm
around you guys enough to not miss the important parts. I figure
I've got it made."

"You realize you don't have to do twice as much, pay off a family
debt, prove something . . . because of Curt, because of *your* father."
Her heel was tapping a wooden chair leg. She was twisting her wedding ring. "I just wanted to clear the air. To mention it. Once."

The suggestion irritated him. "Curt-fucking-Hunt," he croaked
after a deliberate silence, "has nothing to do with me and my
daughter."

"Good." She made her voice comically deep, mocking his boss, a
man with wavy silver hair and monogrammed cuff links: "We love
having you home, in all your goldbricking, underachieving glory."

An interesting by-product of his vocational stall was that Mason
appeared in court frequently and tried a number of cases, almost
always the dogs, Hail Marys and quagmires no one else wanted
attached to their résumés or partnership review files. "I'm the
Hamilton Burger of Richmond," he quipped to friends. "Wile E.
Coyote, attorney at law." Because he had nothing to lose in most
instances, he was free to learn on the fly, and he became confident
and adept in the courtroom, discovering how to corral evasive

witnesses with cross-examination questions, mastering the tricks and rhythms of a jury proceeding, and sorting through which technicalities were critical and which didn't amount to a hill of beans. He was never unprepared or indifferent, and his clients were well served. Judges and other lawyers respected him.

And so it went, until the clerk of the Patrick County Circuit Court, a gracious, lanky man named David Hanby, phoned Mason at his office in Richmond, and not finding him there, located him at home, watching Grace while her mother touched up a painting that was almost ready for a gallery in Delaware. It was 1993, May, and Grace was closing in on five years old. When the call came, she was alternating between a coloring book and a battered Etch A Sketch her namesake grandmother had purchased at a Stuart flea market. Mason was surprised to hear from Hanby, alarmed at first. "Everything okay there?" he quickly asked the clerk. "Mom? Is something going on with Gates?"

"Oh, no. I saw Sadie Grace at the church potluck last week, and she was fine, fit as a fiddle." He cleared his throat. "I assume Gates is still at Powhatan. I know that's a burden for you and your mother. I'm real sorry for you both."

"Thank goodness," Mason told him. "I'm relieved. It's not every day you receive a call from home, out of the blue."

Hanby chuckled. "Well, I certainly hope I'm not interruptin' you. I'm glad to see you high-powered, big-city lawyers are able to knock off early." His tone made it apparent he was kidding; if anything, he was impressed to find Mason cooling his heels on a Tuesday afternoon.

"As I understand it, the office runs better if I'm absent," Mason replied in the kind of modest give-and-take that was a mainstay in Patrick County, and also had the advantage of leaving Hanby with an impression that was more favorable than the truth of the matter. "What can I do for you, Mr. Hanby?"

"Ah. I'm calling on behalf of Judge Richardson and our bar." Here he was precise, his diction stilted, the syllables flags and trumpets. "I'm going to connect you with the judge, but I wanted you to know our commonwealth's attorney, Tony Black, is leaving to take a job in Roanoke. I think you recall Tony?"

"Sure. A good guy, good lawyer. He prosecuted my brother. I thought he was fair and professional. He wrote my mom a nice letter after the trial. Sent an overly kind and unsolicited recommendation to Richmond when I applied for law school."

"Well, I doubt it was overly kind," Hanby remarked. "We're all very proud of you."

"Thanks," Mason said, his mind jumping ahead, trying to anticipate why the circuit court judge in Stuart had business with him.

"People know how you've taken care of Sadie Grace and how well you've done for yourself in Richmond. And I remember that home run you hit to win us the regionals."

"I had good coaching and talented teammates," Mason demurred. The Patrick County way, he recalled: unhurried, genteel, sidling up to the point without too much haste or urgency. He smiled, for some reason enjoying Hanby's slow, discursive civility. Mason knew the clerk would get there when he got there.

"We'll miss Tony. Big shoes to fill."

"Yeah, he's been in office a long time."

"It's a very, very important job, servin' as the commonwealth's attorney," Hanby said.

"Yes. You hold people's lives and property in your hands. I agree." Grace showed him a jumble of black Etch A Sketch lines and squiggles before shaking them away. "Brilliant," he mouthed to her.

"Judge Richardson has to appoint someone to fill the vacancy, then we'll have an election."

"Okay . . ." The first hint of wariness arose in Mason's voice. Surely this wasn't why Hanby was calling.

"After thinkin' it through, the judge and the lawyers are prepared to offer you the job."

"Me?" Mason sputtered. "The commonwealth's attorney? There? In Stuart?"

Hanby was forceful. "You're what we're lookin' for, Mason. A smart, honest man who's familiar with Patrick and its people."

"Well, you know, I mean . . . I'm flattered to be asked, but I'm very much invested here, and—"

"I realize you'd be leavin' the catbird's seat," Hanby interrupted. "A high-class firm, a big city, excellent pay—but you give it some thought. There's a lot to recommend this part of the state, and oodles of people are behind this. People who want to see you come home." He hurried ahead before Mason could speak. "I'm goin' to put Judge Richardson on the line. Hope to see you soon. I'll pass along your regards to everyone."

Judge Frank "Tunk" Richardson repeated essentially what Hanby had told Mason, formally extending an invitation to serve as the county's appointed prosecutor until the election in November. Richard Rogers was the president of the bar, and he took the phone next, promising he'd polled all the lawyers in town and no one would oppose Mason when he had to stand for the office. Not wanting to seem rude or conceited, Mason thanked them both and told them he would sleep on the generous offer, fully intending to call them back the next day with feigned anguish and a firm rejection, a tough decision, he'd say, but he'd have to remain in Richmond.

Oddly, when he stepped into Allison's studio and mentioned the offer to her, she seemed intrigued—this despite his tone of voice and ironic brow, which conveyed exactly how he sized up the idea. "So what do you think?" she asked. "Lovely, rugged country there. I've always been partial to Stuart."

"It's behind me. Sealed, padlocked, stored in the archives." He took a breath and exhaled it through his mouth. "Sort of a disconnect now, a greatest-hits recollection of the place and that's about it, very bloodless. We've discussed it before, my sentiments."

"I know. But you've never had any animosity. I've never heard you mention you hated Stuart or Patrick County. People were good to you, you had friends, you were a star athlete, your mom was a saint, you had some fun times."

"Good and bad both. Like anyone else. But that's not the point; that's not why we would or wouldn't go." He was standing at the border of a drop cloth. He stooped and took a brush from a bunch in a quart jar. "No movie theater, no airport, no galleries, no plays, no museums, no colleges, no circle of smart, educated friends, no bookstores, no restaurants with tablecloths." As he ticked off each shortcoming, he tapped his palm with the brush. "One public high school. A nosy, gossipy, inbred culture. Turnip greens and corn bread. Coon hunting. Fundamentalist, intolerant churches that frown on makeup, a glass of wine and women in slacks. Moonshiners. Square dances. Squinty-eyed hunchbacks in bibbed overalls who refuse to let their kids receive a free measles vaccination, swearing it's government poison."

Allison laughed. "Is a squinty-eyed hunchback like a gnome? Same as your basic bridge troll? You forget I've been there—it's hardly that primitive."

"I didn't say it was, entirely." He was slowing down, catching himself. "The county's blessed with a lot of positives. Life there has its own proud pace, and the great majority of people are trustworthy and helpful in a pinch."

"And I'm sure, Rex Reed, you'll really miss those movies and plays." She gave him a mischievous look, her lips curled with amusement, her eyes in a caper. "When's the last time you went to either?" She flickered a grin before turning serious. "The Bible-thumpers and busybodies I can do without, but maybe we should at least think about this. You can nitpick any city—Richmond, for example, is too crowded and clogged with traffic and socially stratified and overpriced. You could say that if you were being harsh. Too much crime here, way too much. Too much third-generation money. Too many snooty, pretentious people."

"Are you serious?"

"I'm not—well, I'm not saying one way or the other. I like change and movement. I always have. The idea of a home with land and a view of the mountains sounds okay. I've been in this same town house for who knows how long now, sort of doing the identical things. Why not break the routine? I mean, at least think about breaking the routine."

"I enjoy the routine," he protested.

"You know, a rut's a routine with a little deeper groove."

"Are you insinuating you're restless or stifled here? Bored?" The notion caught him off guard, and it showed in his expression. "I hadn't picked up on that."

She walked to him and took the brush out of his hand. "I'm happy as can be, Mason. I've loved every day we've spent together. But I think we're coming to a spot where if we stay here, we'll be staying here for good. Permanently. Which may be great. I say let's just take a look around. If not Stuart, then let's keep an open mind. There's a lot here for Grace, but she'll probably never have a yard or pet a horse or splash in a stream. I want us all to be in the best possible place. I adored the three years we lived in the country when I was a little girl, our house in Arkansas. It's not totally abstract for me."

Mason tried to suppress a smile. "You make Patrick County sound like a cross between Walden Pond and some fanciful PBS show. As best as I can recall, having lived there for eighteen years, I never splashed in a stream or touched a horse. We did have a yard, and it was a pain in the ass to keep it mowed." He let the smile form. "Hey, if we do it, if we move, I can teach Grace how to skin a bear and live off the land. How to roll her own cigs. Drive a Trans Am. Find water with a divining rod. Plow with a mule. Whittle in a rocking chair. Tell the weather by reading the stars. The whole shebang, all the earthy, mystical, folklore shit only we rustics know."

Allison laughed, bent at the waist and folded her arms across her belly. "Don't forget she'll need to know how to handle a longneck in a bar brawl."

"There we go." He was still smiling.

"So call them back," she urged him.

The playfulness vanished. He was quiet for a moment. "I guess the whole deal with Gates clouds things, too. Not a situation you want to be reminded of every day—your brother the imprisoned drug dealer." He'd never told his wife about Wayne Thompson's shooting, nor did he ever intend to. "But I suppose we can pay my mom a visit and mosey around. It's a good enough place—hell, it's a fine place in a vacuum if you want that kind of life. I'm just not sure I can change gears from what I'm used to."

Allison walked to the big window that framed their avenue. "I know there are some parts you can't really erase, that'll always be stamped on you. But try to take a fresh look. No regrets if we do it this way, right? And I'm going to try to come at it different, too. I've always seen it as your hometown, a quirky little village we spend a day or two in. It may be strange if I think about it, you know, more long-term." She stared out the window, completely turned away from Mason, her shoulders uncovered except for the two fabric straps of her top. "But, jeez, the city is getting monotonous," she said, her voice flat. "I've thought about the West, too. Some new scenery couldn't hurt my painting. Or this nice town I visited in high school, outside of Boston, called Maynard."

"Who woulda thunk it," Mason said. "Jerry Hall wants to park the jet and raise chickens."

On the first day of June, Hanby, along with Richard Rogers, met Mason, Allison and Grace at the courthouse that dominates the sloped, quarter-mile-long Main Street in Stuart, and they were soon washed over by hospitality and goodwill and the enthusiasm of old friends who'd heard the rumor Mason was planning to assume Tony Black's job. There were free plate lunches at the Coffee Break, welcome-homes and recountings of key hits and baseball championships. As they toured the street surveying the stores and businesses, seeing what was available, Mason's old biology teacher, brought low by a stroke and relying on a cane, told him from a mouth that only half worked he was "tickled to death" for him, especially in light of what Mason had overcome. Grace was scared of the wracked, deformed stranger, but Allison didn't flinch, squeezing Mason's hand as the afflicted man struggled to enunciate his words, her eyes switching back and forth between her husband and his former teacher. Dinner with Sadie Grace was at the swanky winery restaurant in Meadows of Dan, and that night Grace was fascinated by a fat, thieving raccoon who sat on his haunches in the midst of Sadie's overturned garbage, filling himself with black, agile paws.

They stayed for two days, spending the night at Sadie Grace's, Mason serving as a tour guide for his wife and daughter, showing them the county's pig paths and obscure beauty, winding their car up Squirrel Spur at dawn to watch the sun saunter out from the

Blue Ridge Mountains, then dropping by Barnard's Store in Kibler Valley, where cantankerous Bill Barnard presented Grace with a piece of horehound candy and Mason paid a quarter for a cold Pepsi. Sadie Grace played it close to the vest, waiting until they were about to leave for Richmond to tell them how much it would mean to have her granddaughter nearby. They made two more trips to Stuart, studied the elementary schools, the doctors, the homes for sale, the cost of living. They considered Wrightsville Beach, flew to Boston and tooled around Maynard, and contacted the chambers of commerce in Fairhope, Alabama; Bozeman, Montana; and Charleston, South Carolina. Not yet ready to quit on Richmond altogether, they toured several open houses on its fringes, thought about a home close to the city but not so engulfed by it.

But the more time Mason spent in Patrick County, the more he warmed to returning, and he confessed to Allison that part of the attraction was tied to a clichéd sense of accomplishment, the valida- tion he would feel as a poor local boy who'd struck it big and was coming home to parades and fanfare, a success story in spite of everything. They decided to move in late July, finally persuaded by three circumstances. They received a call from their Realtor informing them a forty-acre farm was available in Patrick Springs, a spread with a stream, a barn, a view of Bull Mountain and a jaunty porch surrounding the front and flanks of the house. Additionally, that same day's *Richmond Times-Dispatch* reported there'd been yet another shooting on Hull Street, and a frustrated councilman was quoted as saying the city's schools were a failing mess, not likely to improve.

They visited the property with Grace two days later and tried out the place for a night, rocked on the porch and watched the deer slip into the pasture and take up their twitchy grazing, their ears erect, tense, restless, searching. After they sat with Grace and talked her to sleep at her grandmother's house, they ventured to the barn with a bottle of mediocre Merlot the owners had left for them, and they drank straight from the bottle and had sex that was far more carnal than poetic, finishing with Allison gripping the rough-hewn oak board of a stall front, naked, and Mason behind her, his hands tight on each side of her waist, his bare feet digging in the dirt.

The next morning they signed the paperwork agreeing to purchase the farm. The Realtor presented them with a country ham in a coarse cloth sack, and they held hands as they left his office, a copy of the contract folded in half and sticking out of Mason's hip pocket. They kissed next to their white Volvo, for everyone to see. Strangely, though, during the return ride to Richmond, Allison seemed distressed—she was fidgety, unhappy with any of their music, unable to get comfortable in her seat, squirming, impatient with Mason's chatter. "I hope we're doing the right thing," she said at a stoplight in Danville, but she didn't have any more to add when Mason attempted to draw her out.

"We can always call them and try to cancel," he said when she revisited the subject fifty miles later. "Forfeit the escrow payment and forget about it." He peeked at her, hoping to get a read. "I don't understand the change of heart."

"I'm not saying there *is* a change of heart, okay? This is just such a major step. It's pretty damn overwhelming when you actually do it. Talking about it and looking at brochures is one thing, but . . . now . . . it's happening." She was sitting with both feet pulled up on the seat, her knees encircled and gathered against her chest. "I'm really excited," she insisted. "It's just I can't help thinking, looking back, about how much I've changed. I hope I don't miss, you know, the glamour—well, that's not the right word—the sort of cutting edge or whatever. I mean, I don't miss it now. I love you and I'd die for Grace—but I don't want to wind up faded and drab, a fishwife or something. That's a huge part of what I'm saying."

"I can't believe you'd feel that way." Mason looked across at her, lifted slightly from the gas. "You're as brilliant and sexy and talented as the day I met you, and where we live isn't going to change any of that." He glanced at the highway, then checked her again. "There's not a more irresistible woman on the planet—Picasso crossed with Brigitte Bardot. Margaret Thatcher's brass. Men will always drop what they're doing and fall in line, no doubt about it."

"It's hard to explain."

"What's hard to explain?" he asked.

"I don't know." She sighed. "I'm trying to make sense of stuff. I hope I'm doing this for the right reasons."

"Well, I thought we'd talked about the reasons. You wanted to leave Richmond more than I did."

"We've talked about it," she said, peeved.

"So what's the matter?"

"Nothing," she answered dully.

"There has to be something bothering you."

"It's okay."

"Is there a message I'm supposed to be able to decipher from your clues and heavy hints? Last night we're on cloud nine, we just bought a new house, and now you're weird for reasons you can't explain to me. Your neck's starting to splotch, so it must be pretty serious."

"Can we get Twizzlers at the store?" Grace interrupted from the rear of the car.

"Maybe, honey," Mason said, pegging her in the mirror when he answered.

"The next place," she said.

"Okay," Mason answered, distracted.

"The next place."

"Yes."

"I've tried to tell you as best I can," Allison said. "There's no reason to beat me up about it."

"We're making the right choice," he said. "And I'm hardly beating you up."

"Yes you are."

"No I'm not. I'm simply trying to understand your problem."

"Well, I suppose there is more to it, but I don't want to talk about it with you in this mood."

"What mood?" he demanded, tossing his hands so they slapped against the steering wheel.

"The mood you're in." She was almost to tears.

"This is stupid. What's wrong with you? Why're you so emotional all of a sudden?"

"You wouldn't understand anyway."

"Not unless I'm Mandrake the Magician and can read your mind."

"Stop! My Twizzlers!" Grace wailed.

"I'm sorry, honey. I didn't see the store."

"You promised."

"The next one. You watch and tell me when it's coming."

"You told me a story," Grace said sullenly, feeding on the discontent in the car, sensing her mother's withdrawal.

"It wasn't on purpose," he assured the child. "I'm sorry if I've pissed you off," he said, returning to Allison. "I was only trying to get at what's plaguing you. I suppose I'd have been better off simply ignoring you and the method acting you've been doing for two hours, all the bottled-up angst over there." He barely waited before continuing. "Of course, then I get blasted for *not* asking, for being inconsiderate and self-centered."

She was composing herself. The red splotch on her neck had stopped its attack. "I'll remember this the next time you're in a bad way. I will."

"Whatever," he said, defeated. "You'd think we'd be celebrating." He was almost to another store but couldn't stop in time to make the turn. "Oh damn."

"Stop! You said you would." Grace was instantly bawling, revving up on big gulps of air and loosing them with all the shrieking disappointment she could muster.

Mason pressed the brake more abruptly than was called for and veered to the shoulder of the road. He jammed the Volvo's shifter into Park, turned off the ignition, exited in a huff and trudged back down the side of the highway to a gas station, cars whizzing by, their warm whooshes butting into him as they passed. He bought a pack of Twizzlers, a liter of orange drink, a giant bag of M&M's and a box of cookies. "Go to it," he said to Grace, handing her the cache of goodies as soon as he reached the car. "Knock yourself out."

"Pick one, please," Allison said to her while Mason was jerking on his safety belt and clicking it secure.

The child studied the bag's contents, reached in and removed the M&M's. "These," she said.

"Hand them to me," Allison calmly directed her.

Grace complied, and Allison poured out a handful of colored chocolate and returned it to the girl, then took the rest of the treats, rolled down the window, and tossed them onto the ground, still in the bag.

Grace didn't bat an eye, didn't protest, and she started in on the candy, content and mute. Before accelerating onto the highway, Mason checked his daughter, swiveling so he could see her. She held a single red M&M pinched between her thumb and first finger and bit into it with her front teeth, peering at her father, church-mouse silent, too canny even at age four to utter a word.

"So you're not going to tell me what it is?" he asked again as they drove off, but Allison completely ignored him.

A conscientious wife, she apologized two days later, made him a nice meal and wore her pricey perfume, promising him her bad patch was nothing more than stress from the decision and certainly had nothing to do with him. "I can't wait for us to get there," she said. "I'm ready."

Chapter Six

"We was wonderin' if you could help pay for your daddy's funeral," asked the woman whose voice Mason heard for the first time ever when she said hello. Johnette was her name, and she requested the money before she told him Curt was dead, a cart-before-the-horse rush that left Mason—blinking, jolted—to inquire if his father was in fact deceased.

" 'Course he's dead. Why else would we be wantin' you to help bury him?" The response was a cocktail of bitchiness, impatience and entitlement. She was calling from Marion, South Carolina.

"I haven't seen him in years," Mason said. He was in his Richmond office, the James River viewable if he maneuvered his chair close to the window and strained his neck. "Why're you calling me?" Flabbergasted, he heard his voice change registers. "So he's gone, huh?" he said before Johnette was able to respond.

"You still his son, ain't you?" she answered.

"And who, exactly, are you?" he demanded. "How do you know Curt?"

"I'm his wife."

"His wife?" This wasn't the woman with whom he'd hightailed it out of Stuart. "You were married to Curt?"

"Common law," she said dourly. "We was common-law husband and wife."

"Ah, I see. So you and Curt shacked up for a while."

"We was together for nearly three years, thank you."

"Well, last time I checked, there's no such thing as common-law marriage in this part of the world."

"Call it what you want, he was my husband. So are you goin' to pitch in?"

"Tell you what, Mrs. Common-Law Curt Hunt. Put me down for a thousand, and we'll just knock it off the six-figure unpaid child support tab he ran up with my mother. How's that?"

"It's a damn sorry son who wouldn't want to see his own daddy properly laid to rest."

"It's a damn sorry daddy who'd walk out on his family and abandon them. And that's not the worst of it."

"Well, he left you somethin', but you can bet you ain't goin' to be gettin' it with that kinda bad attitude."

Mason snorted into the receiver. "There's nothing he could leave me I'd be interested in." He snapped back his desk chair so he was looking at the ceiling. "Thank you for calling. Lots of luck finding anyone who'd pay for Curt's funeral. Good-bye." He gave the phone a rude toss onto the carpet, where it lay bleeding long-distance rants and threats and profanity until Johnette ran out of steam and ended the call.

He allowed what he'd heard to steep and spread until it had his whole mind. He remained reclined in his seat waiting to see how it would strike him, sitting there as if he'd chugged some mysterious potion and was tensely awaiting the results, but nothing came, nothing moved or stirred or broke or changed, nothing big or small, not so much as a nibble of melancholy because he'd lost his father for good. Allison was at their town house packing for the move to Stuart, and he called her with the news, and she was soft and comforting on the phone, her words cushioned. She offered to drive to his office; he told her there was no need.

After a few minutes, he stood and gazed through the window at the city's ragged backside—bridges, warehouses and construction cranes—and he became angrier and angrier precisely because he felt so little. His dad had passed away, and instead of a grief born of bottomless love and a blood bond, nothing was registering, and that missing hurt was the final of Curt Hunt's thefts, the capstone of his selfish, ill-tempered life. Mason laid his head on the cold, air-conditioned glass, then let his weight follow and closed his eyes, twenty-one stories high, pitched forward.

Gates phoned collect while Mason was still at the window. Mason never refused his calls, which came at least three times per week on a direct line, and he sent cash to keep his brother's canteen account solvent, listened to his carping and plans and schemes when prison was grinding on him, rounded up a firm secretary to type the wacky jailbird pleadings Gates sent along for comment and correction and did whatever else he could to make Gates's meager confines tolerable.

"You hear the news?" Gates asked after the operator had finished with her questions and Mason had accepted the charges.

"Yeah, just now."

"So the devil is dead," Gates said, the sentence almost singsong.

"So I'm told. How'd you find out?"

"A lady from South Carolina called and left a message with the warden."

"I forgot to ask what killed him." Mason could hear the prison hubbub on his brother's end, jeers and shrill hostility, the occasional echo of metal against metal.

"I'd like to think the Good Lord hunted his ass down and hung him up by his heels and beat the holy shit out of him."

"I doubt the Lord has that much time to devote to individual cases."

"So we're attendin' the funeral, right?" Gates asked. "You're going to spring me for a day?"

"Hell no. I'm not about to go to his funeral. Have you lost your mind?"

"Listen, Mason, no one hates Curt more than me, but it's my one chance to get free of this shithole, okay? If you pay for an off-duty cop, they'll let me out for the service. I consider it a mini-vacation. Hell, it'll be about the only thing our sorry dad has ever done for me. If you don't want to make the drive, hey, cool, that's fine, but please loan me the cash so I can spend a few hours in civilization, maybe eat a Big Mac and some fries and smell air that doesn't stink."

"I'll make the arrangements. Sure."

"Thanks, Mason. I don't know what I'd do without you." A man in the background screamed at another inmate, cursing furiously.

"I suppose I should call Mom," Mason said, dreading the chore. "Let her know."

"Yeah, I guess."

"I'll have my secretary contact the prison." Mason paused. "When's the funeral? I didn't even think to ask."

"Day after tomorrow. Hell, Mason, just come and visit me. You don't have to sit through the service or take part in anything. After everybody's cleared out, maybe you and me will have the pleasure of pissin' on old Curt's loose dirt."

"We'll see."

Almost on impulse, Mason left for South Carolina the morning of the funeral, unable to rest, setting out at four thirty, dark and muggy, a Styrofoam cup of black convenience-store coffee his companion, the radio neglected, a map in the passenger's seat, the headlights forlorn on the interstate, eating into the distance. He'd left Allison a note: "Gone to the funeral. See you tonight." He was grateful when the sun brightened the sky and more cars joined him on the highway, felt better in traffic and color.

He located the funeral home and was greeted by a professionally solemn young man with a gold bracelet and a droopy boutonniere. Mason was early, and the lad sympathized with him about his "loss," then ushered him into a small chapel for some private time with his father, stepping dramatically backward through the double doors and pulling them closed as he withdrew, bowing slightly all through his departure. Mason caught the scent of funeral flowers, and the full-throttle air-conditioning braced him, shocked his skin. Curt's casket was in the front of the room, a gaudy floral heart atop spindly metal legs posted beside the body. A sash with gold glitter words bisected the arrangement, but Mason couldn't make out the letters from a distance.

He walked to the casket, aware of how many steps he took, counting them in his head as he went. He heard the air blowing from vents, tasted a sour current in his spit, noticed the sway in the floor when he stopped a few paces short of his dead father. GONE TO GOD, that's what was written on the sash. He didn't hesitate or reflect or ready himself before looking down at Curt. The mortician's best art couldn't conceal how diminished the body was, wizened and faint, as if a considerable portion of him had left the earth ahead of the remainder. It struck Mason that he was staring at painted-up dregs, sediment in an ugly blue suit, dross prettified by rouge, powder and a belly full of sawdust. He was relieved in a certain sense that the remains were so different from the dreadful man he remembered, so diluted they were unable to summon Curt in any meaningful way.

He stood there for several minutes, taking a long look at his father, finally touching one of his entwined hands—clay cold— before turning away, recalling how powerful they had seemed to him as a boy. He took a seat on the first pew, bowing his head and dabbing at his eyes with his sleeve, emotional because of what he'd never had, crying-mad because of such a fundamental disappointment, gypped and betrayed by his own damn daddy.

Johnette arrived with her three sisters and two grown sons, wearing sunglasses and solicitously attended by this flock of relatives, woozy and weak-kneed until she learned Mason was present. She recovered from her grief and regained her strength long enough to dicker with him about payment for the funeral, smoking a cig and exhaling from one side of her mouth, wagging a finger at Mason and leaning forward in her chair when she spoke. She tapped the ashes on the floor of the business office, where they were meeting by themselves.

"You don't jest get to come here and enjoy all this for free," she informed him. "No more than you'd expect to walk into Dollywood or the demolition derby or whatever without payin' for a ticket. Especially since you're his son and rich as Midas." She was in her fifties, fleshy, with an abundance of dyed-black hair and a round, attractive, gentle face that gave no warning of the harridan underneath.

"So how much is my ticket to the Curt Hunt farewell tour?"

"I don't see why you shouldn't pay it all, especially bein' such a smart-ass. The whole six thousand and change." She expelled a stream of smoke. "And you better believe you ain't gettin' the stuff he left you with your present attitude."

Rank curiosity got the better of him, and they negotiated a payment of five hundred dollars to Johnette Flippin for "reimbursement," and she sent one of her sons to fetch Mason's legacy. The boy returned twenty minutes later with two large toolboxes and a letter, belligerently announcing to Mason he'd taken the socket set for himself, because that's what Curt would've wanted. "I'm sure," Mason said sarcastically. He put the letter in his suit pocket, saving it for a less hectic setting.

There were maybe twenty-five people at the service, and Gates arrived immediately before it got under way. "Hope they hired a Primitive Baptist," he said, laughing, as he and Mason and an off-duty cop sat outside in the swampy South Carolina air, flying, humming pests occasionally lighting on their necks or hovering around their ears, their zzzzzz sounds like tiny drills. "The longer the better." Gates was sausage-wrapped in a suffocating black suit, a wool monstrosity that had him sweating all over himself, even with the coat removed. It was the suit he'd been wearing the day of his conviction in Patrick County. He'd gained fifteen or so pounds, and his skin was eerily white, as if he'd been bleached, colorless except for dark, concave sinkholes beneath his eyes. Yet he seemed fairly chipper, fairly upbeat.

"You not going in?" Gates's keeper asked.

"Hell no." He laughed. "I'm plannin' to sit right here and visit with my brother." He was in leg irons, but his hands were free. "Enjoy bein' outside and the fresh air."

"Nothing to me, one way or the other," the man said, then introduced himself to Mason. He moved to another bench to allow the brothers some privacy, and a funeral home employee brought them all cold sodas.

"You recognize anyone here?" Gates asked. "Who the fuck would come to Curt's funeral?"

"I'm pretty sure I saw a representative from the Joan Crawford Foundation," Mason cracked. "Then there was the ambassador from Dante's innermost circle. The guy with the fur hat was Rasputin, I think." He sipped his drink. "Seriously, I ran into our cousin, the redheaded kid who used to come by with Curt's sister. He works for the railroad. Seems nice enough. Mostly it appears to be the high-white-trash clan of his last squeeze, this Johnette bitch."

Gates lowered his head and aimed for Mason's ear. "So you're headed back to Stuart," he said confidentially. "It's a done deal."

"Yeah. Pretty strange, huh?"

"Strange, maybe, but good for me, I'm hopin'."

"In what way?" Mason tensed, set his drink on the bench but didn't release it.

"Shit, Mason, you'll be the man, the commonwealth's attorney." His face grew animated, his voice quieter. "I didn't want to mention anything on the phone, but for damn sure you can pull some strings for me now. Get me out on probation or find a loophole or have 'em lose my file. We both realize how this shit works. You can help me, get me out from under this. You know I got a raw deal anyway. You'd just be putting things right."

Mason frowned. Shook his head. "I couldn't do anything if I wanted to, okay? Are we clear on that? More important, you need to understand that while I will continue to help you in any legal way possible, there is no frigging chance I'd even think about doing something that would leave me or my family at risk." He locked on to his brother, eye to eye. "Don't ever ask me again. You hear? Forget it."

Gates ducked his head. "Hey, cool. I know what's what. I understand. Just keep me in mind. If the chance ever comes up, I know you'll go to bat for me."

"I'll do my job, pure and simple."

"Man, I'm proud of you," Gates said, changing his tack. "No matter what happens."

"Yeah."

He thought about sharing his father's letter with Gates, but decided against it, unsettled as he was by his brother's desperation and convict's wheedling. They made small talk until the funeral concluded, the deepest notes of an organ's closing hymn vibrating outside to where they sat. Mason had no interest in attending the graveside service, so he wished Gates well and slipped the cop two twenties and told him to make sure they enjoyed a good meal on their return, steaks if possible. Before leaving, he phoned his office in Richmond and instructed his secretary to contact the bank and stop payment on Johnette Flippin's check.

He opened the letter sitting in his car, the engine cranked, the air on high, battling the trapped South Carolina heat in the interior. The letter was in his father's hand, the script unlearned and shaky:

> To Mason,
> So I hope you are find. Me I'm not to good. They tell me I have some Cancer. I am in the hospitel. I wanted you to have all my tool's when I am gone. Johnette will give them you. I'm sorry I haven't been there allways. I don't no why you an your brother and Sadie had it in for me. Why you hated me and done me like you did but I wonted you to have my tools cause there's no bad feelings from me. I for give you. An your mom and Gates to. I hope you for give me. Take care, your dad.
> love, Curt S. Hunt

Mason read the note three times, and when he finished, he was left with a weak, sad grin. "Perfect," he said out loud. "What else did you expect?"

Chapter Seven

"It's not like I have a periodic table of the elements nailed to my wall."

Those were the first words Mason ever heard from Custis Norman in person. Mason had gently rapped on Custis's office door and poked his head—cautiously, politely—through a small crack without violating the threshold. Custis was at his topsy-turvy desk, facing away from the door, his feet plopped on a credenza, a phone receiver jammed between his cheek and formidable shoulder, a newspaper folded down into a fourth of its size held aloft, the crossword puzzle visible from where Mason stood, peeking into the room.

" 'Symbol for tin,' and it's not *t-i* or *t-n*. What kind of feeble-minded vice president are you, anyway? Shouldn't you know this, being's how you guys make metal?" He twisted toward Mason, then slid his wing tips off the furniture one at a time. "Gotta fly," he said, hanging up the phone.

Custis was impossible to miss in small-town Stuart, and during visits home from college and law school, Mason had seen him on occasion, collecting his mail from the post office or inflating his tires at the old Gulf station, but they'd never crossed paths close enough to actually meet. Robust, imposing, hefty, bigger than Mason in every respect, over six and a half feet tall, Custis was a force of nature with quick brown eyes, blunt features and black, black skin. A thicket of dreadlocks, carefully barbered and groomed, corkscrewed out of his leonine head. "My brother in Memphis," he explained, glancing at the phone. "You must be Mason Hunt." He came around the desk, covering the distance in two nimble strides. He wore a wrinkled seersucker coat above khaki pants, and the idiot faces of Larry, Curly and Moe spilled down his tie. "Welcome."

"Tin is *s-n,* if I'm not mistaken," Mason said good-naturedly. "Strange what kind of junk sticks in your mind. Maybe that'll help break the stalemate." They shook hands. It was late in the summer of 1993, Mason's first day at his new job.

Custis was the assistant commonwealth's attorney in Patrick County, a position he'd held for twelve years, and Mason had twice talked to him on the phone, wanting to make sure he wasn't stepping on toes or leapfrogging Tony Black's legitimate successor. "I have no desire to be the man," Custis had assured him. "I catch enough grief as it is. You can handle the complaints, midnight calls and tongue-lashings from the guy who says he controls a hundred votes and is guaranteeing your defeat next term 'cause you won't fix his wife's reckless driving ticket. And yes, they did ask me about movin' up. Judge Richardson checked with me before they began looking elsewhere."

Forty-one the day he met Mason, a graduate of Tulane and William and Mary's law school, Custis had landed in Stuart after an unsatisfying stint in northern Virginia, where he'd loopholed policy-holders out of their insurance proceeds and spent twelve-hour days defending his firm's most important client, a pharmaceutical company, against a class-action suit brought by a gazillion plaintiffs with kidney damage. Wanting to do his bit and actually take some genuine wrongdoers to task, he'd responded to an advertisement Tony Black had posted in *Lawyers Weekly* and decided to give Stuart a whirl. At the very least, he figured the bush-league credentials would serve as a solid stepping-stone to a larger city and better work, his apprentice's dues fully paid. In the meantime, how bad could it be?

THE LEGAL LIMIT • 113

On his second evening in town, he'd sat for twenty minutes at the Kountry Kitchen Diner without so much as a glass of water or a menu, and when he located the owner, Luther Beasley, a spindly, red-nosed man wearing a cook's apron, the skinny hick took a drag from an unfiltered cig and—not fazed by Custis's size—told him, calm as you please, his tone dry and weary, his demeanor creeping up on exasperation, like a parent reminding a child about a winter coat or a hot stove, "We don't serve niggers here. Everybody knows that. Sorry."

But despite all the predictions and speculation that followed Custis's dismal treatment, the new black lawyer didn't file suit against the peckerwood owner of the Kountry Kitchen or invite the NAACP to investigate or raise a ruckus in the media. Custis simply avoided the bigot and his deep-fried business and kept the wrong to himself. As luck would have it, the Kountry Kitchen was robbed eighteen months later, and it fell to Custis to prosecute the case, which he did professionally and successfully, accepting Luther Beasley's mumbled, embarrassed " 'preciate it" and shaking his tentative hand outside the courthouse, thinking to himself how pitiful and dog-dumb the scrawny man was, a creature cast by the tools of a retarded deity, a brute who'd dropped his tail and learned to clothe himself like a human.

Surprisingly, though, Custis gradually discovered that most people in the area—Luther Beasley and his ilk notwithstanding—didn't care one whit about his race so long as he let them alone and told the truth and met his obligations. Seven years after arriving, Custis was elected to the town council (against a leash law, for a stoplight at the intersection of Routes 8 and 58), his 126 votes the second-highest total among eleven candidates, and every year the daffy old matrons from the DAR Society invited him to speak on Dr. King's birthday, where he told them about discrimination and they innocently used the term "colored," as they had since they were children. There were no bruised feelings—any correction seemed pointless to Custis, and the ladies knew they weren't prejudiced, most of them having supported Custis in his campaigns—and the hostesses and their guest sipped Russian tea and enjoyed finger sandwiches and from-scratch cake, good humor the order of the day.

Asked at a black lawyers' conference in Detroit how he could stomach Stuart, Custis chuckled, clasped his hands and gave a practiced reply: "Archie Bunker lived in Queens, Andy and Barney in Mayberry. Take your pick. I prefer the odd hillbilly in a sheet and cornpone slurs to white lip service and worrying whether or not I've strayed past Checkpoint Zulu into a neighborhood where I don't need to be." So instead of leaving, he bought a house on Chestnut Avenue, tilled and planted his own vegetable garden, kept company with a pretty widow by the name of Inez Rucker and took to the place and its people, frequently traveling to Richmond and Washington for long weekends but rarely missing Ted Martin's Wednesday-night poker game and always showing up to stir apple butter at the Woolwine Fall Festival. He even joined the local theater troupe, where the other members agreed he did the best Sky Masterson ever.

He and Mason became fast friends, and their size put a goodly fear in defendants on those days they entered the courtroom together, "a whole lotta justice rollin' at you," as Custis liked to say. "The Yin-Yang Towers" was Judge Greenwalt's admiring tag upon initially seeing them in district court. When their paychecks arrived from the state, Mason, without any fanfare, directed Sheila Shough, their secretary, to put them both in the office account and split them equally, despite his being much larger than his assistant's. "Only fair," he told Custis. "As soon as I get up to speed and can pull my weight, we'll see about changing things." They never did, even though it took Mason only six months to become acclimated; he began racking up convictions and commanding the courtroom, always articulate and prepared, his many hours in the Richmond trenches paying off. Still, he wasn't a tyrant or a prick, and the defense lawyers and the community knew you could count on him and Custis to offer a break or compromise if it was warranted.

Mason first became indebted to Custis during the Brett "Shug" Cassidy drug trial. Fourteen months into Mason's tenure as commonwealth's attorney, he indicted Shug for ten counts of cocaine distribution and a variety of other crimes. Wild, erratic and unpredictable, Shug Cassidy was rumored to have shot and killed a client from West Virginia who was slow to pay his coke debt, and he lived in a compound of trailers surrounded by mongrel dogs, chain-link fence and jackleg surveillance cameras. Lived at the end of a dirt road that led into Whitlow Hollow, scores of store-bought orange-and-black NO TRESPASSING signs tacked to the trees. In case the signs didn't make the point, he'd located a piece of warped, propped-up plywood at the foot of the driveway and covered it with hand-painted threats and "bewares" vowing violence to anyone who came snooping around the Cassidy property.

Soon after the indictment, Mason began receiving notes composed of pasted magazine letters that warned him to steer clear of "Mister Cassidy" and drop the charges or bad things would certainly happen. One afternoon, Allison called Mason and reported a car kept easing down the road to their house, slow and deliberate, halting in front of the porch, then crawling away, the driver and passenger cloaked in hats and sunglasses, the license plate obscured. Of course, the cops couldn't prove anything or locate anyone when they hurried out with Mason to check on her, and it certainly wasn't a crime to meander down to someone's house a time or two. A week later, a quick strike came at three in the morning, a roaring engine and yelling and cursing and spinning tires and a gun discharged into the air, a doll with a severed head and fake blood and another anonymous note tossed onto the doorstep, poor Grace scared to death by the noise and disruption, and Mason—who was, after all, Curt Hunt's son—had seen enough.

The next day at work, still fuming, he informed Custis what had happened and told him he planned a thoroughly personal visit to Shug Cassidy's.

"Let's go drop by the sonofabitch's right now," Custis declared, standing up as he spoke. "No reason I can see to wait."

"I didn't tell you so you'd go with me."

"I know." Custis opened his desk drawer, removed a nickel-plated .38 and dropped it into his coat pocket. "I'll drive."

It was early fall, cool and crisp, the leaves perishing in color, the summer's humidity gone so the air wasn't noticeable unless a wind kicked up or a field of orchard grass shimmered and yielded to weather arriving late in the afternoon. The season and the gun caused Mason a flash of uneasiness and put him in mind of his brother. Still, as they were making plans to confront an armed drug dealer, it seemed wise to anticipate the worst.

Custis's El Dorado bottomed out twice as they approached Shug's fortified home, and they were escorted in by a pack of barking, frothing, snarling dogs of all colors, builds and sizes, fifteen or twenty of them, Mason estimated, the more aggressive ones leaping against the side of the car, their muzzles and teeth and pumping claws right beside his face, slobber and dirt fouling the window glass.

"Shit, Mace, I do hate them damn dogs." Custis looked directly at Mason.

"Can't swim either, can you?" he said, laughing.

"Nope."

"Hand me the gun," Mason said.

"Oh, so you're gonna tell me those Cujo-lookin' hounds don't cause the hair on your neck to raise up, too? Don't act like you're not fazed by this, Mr. Racial Stereotype. Mr. Bull Connor. You know they fired Jimmy the Greek for that kinda attitude. 'Can't swim either,' " he mimicked. "Hey, here's a thought—why don't you just dive in and use your aquatic skills on 'em?" He handed Mason the .38. "Bullet comes out the small end," he said, screwing on a smile. "Maybe I can kill a couple with the car. They've already managed to destroy my paint."

Shug and another man were standing outside a cinder-block garage, staring at the Cadillac, doing nothing about the dogs, sneers on their faces, a holstered pistol strapped to Shug's hip. Mason forced open the door, and a dog that was predominantly German shepherd lunged toward him, grabbing his pants at the thigh, the animal's top and bottom teeth sinking into his flesh. He shot the dog, then another. Then a third one even though they'd all turned tail. He popped a final cur as it was scampering off but didn't kill it; it yelped and squeaked and dragged its wounded, bleeding hindquarters underneath a ratty trailer skirt and started whimpering and manically licking at its injury. Mason trained the gun on Shug. Custis was out of the car, in the mix, beside his friend, step for step.

"Ain't got no right to do what you jest done," Shug announced.

"Nosir. I'll have your job for sure, Mason Hunt. You and your pal Kunta Kinte both. Got it on tape." He pointed at a camera dangling from a power pole. "My Uncle Jacob's rightchere as a witness, too." He appeared only marginally disturbed by the death of his dogs, and he and his uncle seemed smug, pleased to have goaded the commonwealth's attorney into a sticky situation. "Don't know why you got such a hard-on for me, Mason. First them unfair charges, now this. I recken this proves what I been sayin' all along." His mouth was creased into an obnoxious, taunting smile.

Mason stopped in front of Shug, very close to him. "Take the gun out and give it to me."

Shug complied, then took a step away and raised his hands to shoulder height, palms showing. "This is gonna look awful bad on your part," he said, the words spoken slowly and laced with spite. A confident grin revealed yellowish teeth, one chipped. A tatty beard framed his mouth.

Mason gave both Shug's gun and his own to Custis. "You and I know you're guilty, Mr. Cassidy, guilty as can be. You sold a bunch of dope to an undercover cop and, speaking of video, we have a fine little film of you, starring as Shug Cassidy, dumb-ass drug dealer."

Shug lowered his hands. "Maybe you're confusin' me with your brother. Your family's got right smart sperience in the area of sellin' shit on tape, right?"

The uncle cackled at his nephew's reference to Gates, and Custis popped him with a meaningful stare and asked what the hell was so funny. "Nothing, I guess" was the reply.

"Excellent answer," Custis told him.

"Here's the point of my visit, Mr. Cassidy," Mason said, crowding in closer. "Don't you ever even *think* about bothering my family again. Don't send me any more notes, don't have your punk-ass henchmen drive by my house, don't so much as look at our property or come near any of us. Clear?"

Shug didn't give any ground. "Don't know what you're talkin' about." Squinting, he pointed his chin up at Mason. "Sure don't. But I figure a man like you controls that kinda thing hisself, dependin' on who he treats fair and who he treats not fair."

"I will make your life a living hell, Mr. Cassidy. You have my promise."

"Like I say," Shug answered, "I ain't never been involved with none of whatever it is that's eatin' at you. But a man like you, for his own sake, concernin' not me but other peoples, a man with a pretty wife and a fine daughter—Grace, right? Goes to Patrick Springs Elementary?—a man like that oughta be darn careful to always do what's best and fair." He finished with another hateful smile.

Mason jerked him up by the collar, pushed him away to arm's reach, then lit into him, and when Shug's potbellied uncle brought out a section of pipe he'd hidden underneath his shirt, Custis just about wrenched his arm off and rammed his bald head into the cinder-block wall of the garage three times for good measure before hauling him to the ground and planting a foot in his spine. As he was busting up Shug, any number of thoughts tumbled through Mason's mind, his rage unchecked, the sensation of knuckle finding bone and the surge of adrenaline and his choppy breaths all familiar and queerly agreeable, like the wicked taste of nicotine after a long absence. Custis had to yell at Mason to make him stop the beating, but he had to shout only once, and he didn't have to lay hands on Mason or pull him off. At the end of the fight, two buttons were missing from the front of Mason's shirt, and there was blood on the cuffs and sleeves, as well as his coat and pants, all of it from Shug Cassidy, who was drawn up on the ground, a red, battered lump, finally quiet.

Mason looked at the camera above them and traced its black cord into the side of a double-wide. He walked past Custis and entered the trailer. A window-unit air conditioner was lying on the den floor, an expensive TV was wedged into a corner, a matchbook collection was cased and displayed on the wall. Mason located a VCR in a rear bedroom where the line entered from outside, removed a cassette tape and returned to Custis, who still had Shug's uncle subdued, a pistol in each hand.

"Give me the gun again," Mason said.

Custis didn't waver. He offered the .38, butt first. Mason walked toward Shug, who'd sat up from the dirt and was patting his face with both shirtsleeves, his legs splayed in front of him.

"You ain't got the balls," he dared Mason, his voice ruptured, the words full of phlegm and saliva.

"Careful, Hoss," Custis said.

Mason made a show of squaring himself to the man on the ground. Mason's hair was pushed to one side, his navel visible through the gap in his shirt, his suit coat jacked too high on his neck, his trousers dog-bitten, his tie cockeyed. He raised the gun. Extended his arm to its full length. Custis was mutely committed, trusting Mason, crossing the line with him. Mason set the trigger. Closed an eye. Sighted. Shot. Twice. Shug Cassidy fell forward, his fingers digging into the dirt and sparse grass, his mouth rounded, his eyes bugged. Behind him at the edge of the trailer, the wounded dog whined, then collapsed onto its side, dead, shot through the head and neck. "Put the bitch out of her misery for you," Mason said as he was pivoting to leave and Shug lay belly-flat in his yard, scared and manhandled and speechless, at least for the short term.

"Quite a predicament I've gotten us into," Mason remarked as they were bumping over Shug's driveway, several of the dogs baying and barking behind them but keeping their distance, not chasing after the car. "Sorry." His tone was collected, and he was watching the rutted road, staring out the windshield. "There's no way I'm going to mention your involvement in this, Custis. It was completely my problem, completely my doing. As far as I'm concerned, you weren't here." He sighed, looked at the guns beside him on the seat. "Shit."

Custis smiled so broadly that Mason could see an arc of gold dentistry at the rear of his teeth. "Kind of you to offer, Mason, but impossible to pull off. I'm in this up to my ass. And I'm a grown man, you know? I came with you full well aware we weren't making a Welcome Wagon visit." They reached the state road and the tires took traction against the pavement.

"This could cost us our law licenses," Mason said. "Not to mention a criminal charge or two."

"No doubt." Custis hadn't accelerated yet; the Cadillac was

coasting along, barely doing twenty. He looked across at Mason. "Which is why we take the offensive on this shit, Mace. I've already started formulating our plan." He slowed even more and a car raced past them.

"Really?"

"Does Pastor Odell from the Samaritan Apostolic Holy Temple of the Rugged Cross drive a brand-new Lincoln?" A habit of Custis's, answering with rhetorical questions, some of which were child's play, some of which were arcane and puzzling.

"I assume he does, given the context."

"We need to come out swinging."

"I have to admit the thought crossed my mind, but I hate to pull you into my mess."

"I'm already in your mess," Custis replied. "I signed on for your mess. We're past that debate." He drove the car off the highway into the lot of a vacant convenience store. The gas pumps had been removed, leaving a cement island occupied by a few weed sprigs and crimped pipe ends, and the windows were patched with silver duct tape and weathered cardboard. "No need for us to take the fall for a piece of shit like Shug Cassidy. Being noble isn't the same as doing right."

"You're sure?" Mason asked.

"Yep."

"I mean—"

"Damn, Mason—don't wear me out on this. I'm gonna stand with you."

"The only other thing . . . I . . . I hate the hypocrisy of it. We're about to become the same as they are, no damn different."

"Hardly. This guy is a lowlife drug dealer who never so much as earned an honest dime and was harassing your family. You took care of business. He'll still receive his fair trial and all that jazz, still have his day in court beyond a reasonable doubt." His voice rose, almost squeaked. "And if you want to couch it in legal terms, you acted in self-defense. Is there any doubt you had a right to intervene on behalf of your family? Bastard was threatening your little girl." He rested his forearm on the steering wheel, twisted sideways. His tone returned to normal. "I've told you before and I'll tell you again: Justice ought to be a bottom-line proposition. I've been doin' this a lot longer than you, and I've decided it's misguided when we worship musty old words in a text at the expense of innocent people's suffering. Thomas Jefferson and Learned Hand and hearsay rules ought to come into play if we don't know the truth or if it's a close call, not when we have the guy on tape, Technicolor friggin' guilty. We should be concerned with how the soup tastes and not so damn worried about the particulars of the chef's hat."

"I'm not in much of a position to argue with you. I'm only hesitating because I don't want to put you in a jam. If you're okay with rearranging this, then so am I. I can't see much reason to ruin our lives over a little self-help and the niceties of how to deal with a criminal who endangered my wife and kid."

"Exactly. So here's the scenario as I see it." He clicked the car into Drive and gassed it back onto the road. "I catch a call from a guy who claims to be Shug's uncle and says he wants to talk to us about his nephew."

"Has to be the uncle—I've done the same math."

"Says he'll only talk to us, wants to see us. We meet him at the top of Shug's drive, we're—"

"Skeptical and cautious," Mason interjected. "He lets on to us that Shug's still in the trade, still selling drugs, and he's worried his nephew's sinking fast, running with some dangerous people and will wind up dead or in more trouble."

"After some chitchat, he invites us to follow him, claims he wants to show us something." Custis was nodding his head as he spoke.

"The weakest part of our story," Mason added, "but the best we can do."

"We arrive at Shug's, next thing we know, they've let a bunch of dogs loose on us."

"A trap," Mason said. "The scoundrels jumped us."

"Dog bites you, we have to kill a few and defend ourselves." Custis's nods became more involved.

"We get the drop—"

"On Shug and the uncle."

"Even though they attacked us first. And we have—"

"Shug's pistol and the pipe and fingerprints on 'em both to prove what we're saying."

"As well as the bite on my leg." Mason almost spoke over his friend.

"Who knows he's been threatenin' you?" Custis asked.

"You, me, my wife, the sheriff, my daughter."

"I'll speak to the sheriff," Custis volunteered.

"The big picture is that Shug started this," Mason said.

"And we finished it." Custis paused, remembering something. "Make sure you lose the video."

"Really? You think I should?"

They looked at each other and laughed, the giddy, crazy, guilty, fevered laughs of two adolescent boys who'd just vandalized a mean teacher's car and vowed never to tell.

"Done deal," Mason declared at the end of their tear.

"Amen," Custis said.

"It's weird," Mason said after they'd quieted down and Custis was searching for a cassette tape, "how life's full of so many overlays and echoes. Small stones in your shoes you can't get rid of, riddles . . ."

"Ain't any stones in your shoes, and you aren't your brother and you damn sure aren't Aristotle, nope, so don't start wallowing around in any jibber-jabber."

"I'm just saying this was strange for me," Mason replied, perking up. "I'm fine." He cocked an ear, frowned. "What the hell are we listening to?"

"Luther V., my man."

"Ah, yes. The warriors return from battle to the smooth, overproduced sounds of soulful R&B." He grinned. "Wouldn't Wagner or AC/DC be more appropriate?"

"No reason for you to go philistine on me—Luther's always the man."

"Maybe if you're gay or really ancient."

"Never know. Could be my lady Inez is only for show." Custis gave him an over-the-top wink, and they both laughed some more.

They drove directly to the magistrate's office and swore out all manner of warrants, leaving behind the pipe and Shug's pistol as evidence before traveling to the ER for treatment and photographs of Mason's bite. Shug arrived forty minutes later with his uncle, wheeling down Main Street in a slick-as-a-button 1982 Ford pickup, the tailgate dropped, a clump of dead dogs in the bed, a few flies circling after he parked and limped into the courthouse. He was soon joined by his hotshot lawyer from Rocky Mount, but the magistrate, a beefy man with a clubfoot and a stubborn temperament, steadfastly refused to issue warrants for the commonwealth's attorney and his assistant. "No way on God's green earth am I gonna have Mason Hunt arrested on the word of a snake like Shug Cassidy" was how he stated it to Shug's apoplectic lawyer.

Allison knew immediately what had happened, and she nursed Mason's wound and laid her head against his shoulder and took Grace by the hand and sat her on her father's tender lap and told the child Mason had punished the dreadful men who'd scared her in the middle of the night. The state police interviewed Mason and Custis, left them together while they were questioned and barely took notes, a pro forma visit if there ever was one. "I mean, why in the world would we go to this guy's house unless they'd invited us?" Mason asked them. "What—for no reason I wake up and recruit Custis and say let's ride to Shug Cassidy's and shoot his dogs and start a fight and while we're at it take his pistol and a piece of pipe with his uncle's prints on it? How much sense does that make?"

"Exactly," said the state police investigator. "We see it the same way."

Months later, a special prosecutor from Harrisonburg tried Shug, and Judge Richardson sent him to the penitentiary for a long stretch and the state seized the vehicles and land he'd purchased with the dirty profits of a decade in the dope business. Most everyone in the county had a version of the truth concerning the dispute between Mason and Shug, but no matter how it was understood, no matter who went looking for whom, Mason Hunt had kicked an ass that needed kicking, and people were well pleased with their commonwealth's attorney, impressed by his grit.

After Shug's drug trial, Mason and Custis requested the charges they'd lodged against him be dropped—he'd already been stiffly sentenced, they suggested—and they never so much as uttered another syllable about what they'd done in the years that followed, this irregular lawlessness that kept them tethered and bound, and sometimes when the one would finish the other's sentence or there was a mention of the Shug Cassidy case, there'd be an extra blink or a look-away, perhaps even a faint grin, and they'd both know why and take a peculiar satisfaction in the contours of their friendship.

It rained the morning after the melee at Shug's, *plinks* and *splats* sounding off the new aluminum gutters on the Hunt house, the sky a dull gray monochrome when it finally got a dose of light in it, and Mason was up early, drinking black coffee at the kitchen table, content with the somber, shrouded day. Allison came into the kitchen wearing long pajama bottoms and a tank top, barefoot, her hair gathered away from her face. She helped herself to the coffee and flooded it with skim milk, then added a sprinkle of sugar straight from the bowl.

"You know I love you," she said, sitting down opposite him at the table, clutching her mug with both hands. "More than anything in this world."

Mason keened his head and let out a wary breath, realized he was being forewarned. There was no "good morning" or disjointed account of a dream or yawning, stretching transition from sleep to composure—she was bursting to turn loose some unwelcome fact, and this was the balm that preceded the sting. "So what's up?" he asked, sitting straighter in his chair, rubbing his stubble against the grain.

"I need to talk to you."

"I gathered as much," he said, inspecting her face. "I know the drill."

The mug was still in her hands, held above the table. She hadn't tasted the coffee. "I expect you're going to be angry."

"It only makes it worse when you dillydally and give me thousands of disclaimers."

"I was so taken by what you did to that Cassidy man."

Without thinking, Mason glanced at his bandage. A dark red stain had soaked through the gauze, and the white tape had separated from his skin on one side. He was sitting there in a robe and boxer shorts and cheap black flip-flops. "Yeah, well, I hope my conflict with Mr. Cassidy doesn't cause me trouble down the line."

"It won't." She seemed to have forgotten about her mug. "So, well, so . . . do you remember how, uh, pissy, I guess you'd say . . . how pissy I was when we were coming back from buying the house? We were driving to Richmond and you pulled over and got Grace a bagful of candy?"

"Yeah. You've already made amends for that." He noticed the loose knot in the robe's belt, wasn't looking at Allison while he spoke.

She finally lowered her cup. "I was upset because—and please don't take this and lawyer-twist it—I wanted to make sure I wasn't leaving Richmond for the wrong reasons. Wasn't running away."

"I thought we discussed the reasons," he said.

"We did." She folded her arms, then unfolded them. "There was a man there, in Richmond, who was interested in me. Romantically interested."

Mason immediately focused his full attention on her. "What the fuck does that mean?" He gripped the edge of the table and pushed his chair away, started to stand but didn't. "So what did you do about it, Allison? Huh?"

"Nothing. I mean nothing serious."

"We wouldn't be having this conversation if you weren't feeling guilty, now would we?" He was still attached to the table, holding on. "I—"

"Who the hell was it?" he asked.

"It doesn't matter."

"Of course it matters."

"Why?" she asked. "If I didn't act on it, what difference does it make?"

"I'd like to know who's trying to cut my throat and steal my wife so I don't end up at some party shaking his hand and wishing him well and trading stock tips. 'Situational irony' is the term, I think. Plus, since I seem to be in fighting trim this week, I guess I need to know who to beat the shit out of—lots of men in Richmond."

"It doesn't—"

"And why the hell am I just now hearing about this? Tell me that." Mason released the table.

"Listen. It was Norris Deaver, and I didn't do anything, okay?"

"The greasy little cretin with the colored glasses? The art gallery pussy who sniffed his wine at the restaurant and then wouldn't drink it, made such a frigging scene? *Him?*"

"Mason, calm down." She raised her voice, trying to shift the battle. "He came on to me, and I put a stop to it."

"Did you have sex with him?" He stood and glared down at her. The robe was open, his hands were on his hips.

"Absolutely not. No." She looked at him square. "I didn't."

"So what *did* you do?"

"Could you please not wake Grace?" she asked.

"If you answer me."

"Maybe I *should've* kept this to myself." Her voice was firm.

"Yeah, and choke on your own conscience."

"I was at a point where, I guess, I doubted myself. No one wants to be a thick-ankled babushka cooking potatoes and cabbage and suckling babies on floppy tits, okay? My painting was stalled, I'd started questioning—"

"This is going to be a bad cliché, isn't it? 'I needed my worth affirmed, needed to know I'm attractive, so I screwed another man.' Nice. Profound. Very original." He sat in the chair again, scowling.

"I even sort of tried to broach the subject with you."

"Funny, I don't recall your ever asking me if you could have an affair, but it might've slipped my mind."

"I was flattered by the attention and it came at a time when I needed it, but the sum total, Mason, all I ever did was have too much to drink at lunch and let him kiss me once, and I'm sorry and it was wrong and I'm telling you now, and yes, I'd probably kill you if you did the same thing." She dropped her head, and all the defense and resistance drained from her. In an instant she went to pieces, a collapse that started in her lips and undermined her whole face, tears welling and spilling over red rims. "Mason, I swear on our child that was it." She sucked a breath and took a napkin from the wooden holder and wiped her eyes. "You are such a wonderful husband . . ." She stopped, the words hoarse and drowning. "I've always known I love you. It was more . . . I just considered it, thought about it, and I wanted to tell you so our slate would be clean. Nothing bad between us."

"You promise that's it? You thought about having sex with this dickhead and he kissed you?"

"Yes," she said, the word delicate, almost sough.

"Anything else?"

"No. I needed to tell you. I love it here, and there's not an inch of doubt anywhere. Everything is perfect. I wanted this gone, this single, stupid little mistake."

"Okay," he said. "I believe you." He thought for a moment. "I appreciate your being honest."

"But you're mad at me." The squall was leaving, her eyes clearing.

"You bet I'm mad. Who wouldn't be?"

"I'm sorry, but I had to deal with this. For my own sake. In the long run, I think having the temptation and not giving in should tell you tons about how committed I am. This was a tough period for me, and our marriage and our sweet girl had such a pull that I barely even broke faith. It's a good test, a good challenge. It was wrong and I'm apologizing, but there's an upside."

"Yeah—that'd make for a splendid Ricki Lake segment. I think you're being a little too self-congratulatory there, Saint Allison. The image I have is of this greasy, pretentious asshole pawing all over you and you deciding whether or not you plan on sleeping with him, picturing what it would be like."

"You don't need to be so rude about it. I'm sorry, and I love you and I will work to be a great wife because you deserve it and it's what I want to do. I don't know what else I can say."

Two weeks later, when Mason had passed through his mope and forgiven his wife, she invited him to skip work, and they rolled around in bed all morning and got up to speed again, watching TV game shows and snacking on Swiss Cake Rolls and dry chocolate cereal. They sent Grace to a babysitter after school and visited their neighbor's farm pond, where they took out the johnboat and cast plastic worms for the last of the warm-weather bass, cutting up and playing around until the boat tipped and they both tumbled into the water, Mason first, grabbing Allison as he went. Groping, kissing and laughing, they rode home with Allison perched on the car's console, wrapped in a scratchy picnic blanket, goose bumps on her arms and legs, naked except for her underwear, her hair stringy and damp, her hand in her husband's wet jeans all during the trip to their house. They had sex in the driveway, and afterward they went upstairs and she lit a lone, well-used candle and they squeezed into a hot bath together, still careful of the four punctures in Mason's thigh, the hurt.

To his surprise, he did seem more attached to his wife following her admission, and she to him, and they rocked along in the bull's-eye for several years, hit the jackpot, raising their daughter on forty bucolic acres and painting and practicing law and reveling in what was happening to them, time, place and desire aligned and serendipitous, so much so they'd occasionally just sit on their porch—the air chilly or hot, it didn't matter—and not say the first thing, tuned in to every newborn moment, the sensation so sublime and penetrating that Mason, alone one night after Allison had left for bed, actually lifted his hand to see if he could feel the spell and pull it down and make it tangible.

The fulcrum that would rearrange everything arrived in 2001, and like so many other momentous beginnings, it slipped in plain and middling, the kind of commonplace intrusion that goes unnoticed until someone realizes—too late, of course—where the pox was birthed and says, *Oh shit, oh my, why didn't I realize it way back then, when it was nothing, when I could have fixed it, before the briar scratch raged into gangrene?*

Chapter Eight

"What'd he blow?" Mason asked Custis. They were sitting in Mason's office, both of them in chairs on the client side, files stacked indiscriminately near the edge of the desk. It was March 2001, early, before the office opened for business. Custis had brewed them a potent pot of coffee, and they were eating slices of sweet breakfast cake with brittle plastic forks. Although Custis generally had carte blanche to dispose of cases as he pleased, he and Mason met each Monday and shot the breeze and talked about sports and discussed the week's dockets, especially any trials that might prove difficult or unusual.

"Point-oh-eight." The legal limit for blood alcohol content in a driving-under-the-influence case.

"What's the kid's name again? Doesn't ring a bell with me."

"Lonnie. Lonnie Gammons. He's twenty-one."

"Who're his parents?" Mason took a bite of cake.

"His dad's long gone. His mother raised him by herself." Custis checked a file. "Her name is April. April Gammons."

"Good folks?" Mason asked through a mouthful of cake.

"Definitely."

"Connected or rich or high-profile relatives? Too much prominence always makes it harder to cut 'em a break."

"Nope. And not trash nouveau, I'm happy to confirm."

Mason wrinkled his brow. " 'Trash nouveau'? Haven't heard the term before. Did I sleep through a seminar at the convention?"

"Minted it myself, Mace." Custis grinned. "It refers to the newest breed of white-trash royalty, the haughty third-generation simps who inherit the last of a little coin and hang around the family business thinking they're the cocks of the walk. Get the picture?"

"I'm beginning to."

"Their grandfathers wore the narrow ties and dress hats with those tiny curlicue feathers sticking out of the felt band. Lived frugally and made buckets of money sawmilling or manufacturing furniture or truckin' freight. Fine men. Their fathers took over the business and the profit margins sagged—couple wives, aborted plant expansions, expensive condo at Myrtle Beach, too many bourbon nips before quittin' time—and now you've got these saltine kids with an attitude and the damn *Internet*, shoppin' at Banana Republic online and drivin' the roads in a hocked-to-the-gills BMW even though they fucked up freshman year at two different colleges. The first in their clan to write a bad check. Lie on a credit card application. Buy a case of Natty Ice at Wal-Mart because of the buzz it packs for cheap—trash nouveau. I toyed with 'uber-neck,' but it doesn't carry quite the same wallop."

Mason chuckled. "Very apt, Custis. I think you've outdone yourself. Sociologist that you are, why don't you hip-hop on over to the Old Dominion and field-test your new nomenclature on the leather-vest crowd at the counter and see how they take to it. 'Axe' them for their reaction. Run it by a focus group." He ended with a big, broad smile.

"Yeah, there you go—I'll get my clipboards and the number-two pencils."

From the start, Custis and Mason had enjoyed a comfortable, freewheeling give-and-take where race was concerned, clashing only once, when Custis returned from court with a strut and Mason called him George Jefferson and sang the chorus of "Movin' on Up" in front of Sheila and a lady from the clerk's office, injuring Custis's feelings for reasons that seemed thin to Mason. Mason had apologized but was puzzled because the ribbing was far less raw and point-blank than some they'd both delivered in the past.

"So the Gammons kid is okay?" Mason asked, back on topic.

"Yeah. An honor student who was valedictorian of his class here at the high school. Scholarship to Virginia Tech. Works a job at college. Even the sheriff's wife called on his behalf."

Mason swallowed the remainder of his coffee. "Was he cooperative with the cop?"

"Nice as could be. Very apologetic. Didn't do badly with the field-sobriety tests, speech was normal, mild smell of alcohol. They caught him at a road check—luck of the draw."

Mason thought for a moment. "A DUI will break his mother's back paying for insurance. Pretty much ruin his opportunities after college. Probably wouldn't hurt to find him a little breathing room."

"We're usually flexible with point-oh-eight. I mean, it's the lowest rung of the ladder, just barely there, and the simulator came up an eleven instead of a ten, so his lawyer can argue the machine's off a fraction. I know a few months ago we reduced that Arrington guy's case when he had an eight and no record. Gammons told the cops he'd been drinkin' champagne at a weddin'. Claimed he'd never tried alcohol before and didn't realize how much he could or couldn't drink. From all reports, he's probably bein' truthful. His lawyer's Charles Aaron—claims the DUI will cost the kid his scholarship. I've got some sympathy for him."

"So what do you want to do?"

"Reduce it to reckless driving and a fine, send him to liquor school, stick him with a hundred hours of community service, make him walk for thirty days or so."

"Sounds good to me," Mason agreed. "You certainly have my blessing. Make sure you let him know we're doing him a favor. Aaron, too."

The same day, while Mason was eating lunch at his desk and reading the *Roanoke Times*, Gates called from the penitentiary, collect as always, and Sheila announced he was on the line. For the first time since he'd been sentenced, he was surly with Mason, combative and bitter. "I have a question for you, Mason" was how he started the conversation.

"What?" Mason asked. "What's up?" He assumed Gates was calling to unspool yet another harebrained defense theory, the most recent prison wisdom that would provide him the keys to his cell. Mason's tone was terse and prickly, betraying his annoyance.

"What exactly are you doing to help me beat this charge and get outta this place?" He didn't pause for an answer, plowed ahead. "I mean, actual positive steps you've taken. I've been here for ten fuckin' years, Mason. Ten years in this hole, and I don't think you or Mom or anyone else gives a damn."

Mason's hackles rose. "You mean beyond sending you weekly care packages and money twice a month and typing your thirty-page habeas pleadings free of charge and intervening so you could be transferred closer to home and driving Mom to visit you and accepting every collect call you've ever placed? I'm sorry if that's inadequate by your standards. I'll see what I can do about a personal chef and a water bed complete with a hooker."

"Crumbs, Mason. Crumbs and window dressing that don't move me one inch closer to leavin' here."

"What exactly is it you have in mind, Gates? Huh?" Mason was angry, his voice loud. Custis opened the door between their offices and looked in. "You cool?" he asked quietly, and Mason nodded, waving him away.

"Listen, Mason, you and I both know you can pull a string or two for me, okay?"

"We've had this conversation before—there's nothing I can do. I might as well be an astronaut for all the influence I have in your case. I'm not a judge, I'm not the governor and I'm not the parole board. And I'm not going to arrange something unethical, even if I could."

"Exactly. No shit." Gates was shrill, belligerent. "You're king of the hill in your big house, everybody's darling, callin' the shots, and you really don't care what becomes of me. There's no reason in the world you can't take five minutes to walk up and see the judge and put in a word for me. Or call somebody in the system. You're the commonwealth's attorney, for fuck's sake. Why won't you even try?"

"You know, Gates, you are absolutely an unappreciative dick."

"Yeah, well, you just try and remember how many times I saved your ass. Runnin' and cryin' when Curt was on your tail—and this is how you repay me. How you take care of your big brother. Shit, Mason, there're guys in here whose court-appointed lawyers fight harder for them than you do for me."

"This is the last time I'm going to tell you: There is no magic bullet, no escape hatch, no error in your trial. No attorney can help you. You were guilty and your trial was clean and the law was followed. Every court you've appealed to has affirmed your convictions. Why? Because you were selling dope and then elected to lie on the stand. End of story." Mason exhaled a rough, abrupt breath. "While we're on the subject, let me remind you how *you*, Gates Hunt, stubborn asshole, refused to take a plea agreement that would've had you free by now. But—"

"Yeah," Gates interrupted, almost yelling, "which shows what the correct sentence was, the five years they offered, and now I've pulled more than that and I'm still here. How can anyone say I'm being treated fairly?"

Mason laughed sarcastically. "You know, Gates, when some dumb shit falls for Carol Merrill's lovely arm sweep and sparkly evening gown and trades his new washer-dryer combo for a donkey because he picked the wrong curtain, Monte doesn't allow him a do-over. You had your chance."

"Fuck you, Mason."

"Drop dead," Mason snapped and slammed down the phone.

Gates called back immediately, but Mason told Sheila to refuse the charges, left him hanging.

Two months later, in May, Mason and Allison hosted a costume party at their house to mark Allison's birthday, her fortieth, and it was a hoot and a success. The big day fell on a Wednesday, and Allison was determined to celebrate accurately, deciding not to move the party to the weekend. Loads of people came, and Mason dressed like Captain Hook with a plastic sword and buccaneer's striped shirt, and there was only one glitch, only one uncomfortable moment, which occurred early in the evening when Mason greeted a friend's husband—a man he'd never met—and offered him a fake dime-store pirate's hook only to discover the poor fellow had in fact really lost a hand and was extending the genuine article, a stainless-steel pincer attached to a prosthetic forearm. Later on, after a round of drinks, the man joked about the awkwardness and told Mason not to worry. Allison was a knockout vampire, and Grace, who was allowed to stay up late and enjoy the party, was a twelve-year-old hobo, a getup she insisted on no matter what, declining more conventional choices like a princess or genie or rock star or Simba's lioness wife.

After the last of the guests left, at close to one in the morning, Mason brushed his teeth and drank a glass of water and called for Allison to come to bed and she didn't answer. He called again and then walked through the living room and the kitchen, plates stacked in the sink, trash bags filled and cinched. He went all the way to the opposite end of the house, to Allison's studio. The door was pulled shut but not completely closed. He pushed it open and saw her, without the long black wig but still in her ghoulish makeup, wearing loose green army pants instead of her costume bottom, her Gothic, pale vampire blouse above the pants, listening to music, a brush in her hand, painting.

She turned when she sensed him there, stopped her work. The canvas was part of a suite she was preparing for a New York gallery, her best ever as far as Mason was concerned: a rhino peered over a man's shoulder, contemplating a table of cheese, crackers and wine, the hues piercing, the details painstakingly precise. She smiled at him, the both of them happy, rapt. Neither said anything. She returned to her easel, and Mason left her alone, checked on their daughter and went to bed. A whip-poor-will switched on in a front-yard tree, and the bird's three-beat racket kept Mason from falling asleep right away despite how tired he felt.

Allison was beside him, conked out, when he woke at seven; he'd not heard her join him, didn't know how long she'd been there. He had to shake and poke and cajole Grace to get her going and dressed for the school bus, but they did enjoy a nice breakfast together, French toast and scrambled eggs, a bit more than usual since Mason didn't have to be at his office until ten, a precaution he'd taken in light of the party. He tidied the kitchen, filled the dishwasher, hiked the trash to the top of the drive, showered and dressed for work, kissing Allison's cheek as he left the room. She didn't respond, only moved her feet slightly under the covers.

That same afternoon, Sheila Shough was at her desk chatting with her friend Vicki about the Hunts' party when the phone rang. It was one thirty. Mason was in his office talking to a family about a trespass problem, and Custis was upstairs in the office's small law library, doing research. Sheila listened for less than a minute and dropped the receiver, which hit her desk, then the carpet. She abandoned her friend without an explanation, just said "Oh God" and lost her color and headed for the stairs to fetch Custis, the cord catching her shin as she left, nearly pulling the base of the phone onto the floor.

Custis was seated at a rectangular wooden table, surrounded by law books, and Sheila was crying by the time he saw her. Frantic. He stood, and before he could speak or ask why she was upset, she said, "Mason's wife. It's Allison. The police called . . . Terrible." She walked to the closest chair and collapsed there, cried and cried and wasn't much good to anyone for several hours.

Downstairs, Custis found the phone disconnected and bleating, and upon discovering that Sheila's friend Vicki had no answers or information, he hustled out the door and spotted a state trooper, Darrell Bowling, striding toward the office. They met under the office's awning, and Darrell stood close to him, gripped Custis's biceps and spoke in a voice that knew how to modulate dreadful news. "Mason's wife was in an accident in Patrick Springs," he said, his eyes tracking Custis's. "The intersection at Charlie Martin's old store. Vehicle come through the Stop sign and T-boned her. She was dead when the rescue squad got there." Darrell shook his head and removed his hat. "Impact was as bad as I've ever seen." He'd released Custis's arm. "Tough," he said. A tear appeared, but he didn't bother with it. It didn't affect his posture or the clarity in his voice. "Me or you?" he asked. "You want me to give him the news? I was on my way to do it."

Custis had both hands on top of his head, his elbows angled. He kicked the ground and bowed at the waist, stomped a half circle before twisting back to face the trooper. "You're sure? It was her?"

"We're sure. T. J. Meade and Bryant Pruitt were first on the scene."

"How?" Custis asked, his face pained, his hands still raised. "I mean, what happened?"

"From what we can tell, this driver in a Ford, a full-size pickup, didn't see the sign—happens all the time—and tore right into her. How many accidents we had there, Custis? Fifty? Sixty? Lord only knows."

"Who was drivin' the truck? Is he hurt?"

"Boy by the name of Lonnie Gammons, a college kid. Home for a long weekend before exams or some such. He's got a few cuts and scrapes, but that's about it. Always happens like that, huh?" Darrell hesitated and cleared his throat. "Bryant says this Gammons fellow was in court not so long ago with a DUI. We checked, though, and he was okay to drive. Wound up with a reckless driving and a thirty-day suspension, so he was perfectly legal."

Custis lowered his hands and arms. He stared at Darrell. "Oh shit. How about this time? Was he drinkin'?"

"Nosir. Straight as an arrow. Not a drop. Zero on the alka-sensor, nothing in the car. He's all to pieces over it, cryin' and whatnot. He's at the ER. You hate it for him, too. It'll stick to him the rest of his life."

"Well, maybe it should," Custis said, frowning. "Damn."

"Just one of those things," Darrell said. "An accident nobody intended."

"I'm gonna let you break it to Mace." Custis loosened his tie and unbuttoned his collar. "I need to check on somethin'. You stay with him, Darrell, don't leave him alone till I get there, you hear?"

Darrell knocked on Mason's office door and asked the group of elderly men and women inside if they could excuse themselves. He told them in a quiet voice there was an emergency, and it was important that he speak with the commonwealth's attorney. He stood formal and erect, his dark blue hat in hand, his gaze downward, as they filed from the room.

Mason rose as Darrell was closing the door. "What is it, Darrell?"

The trooper made it a point to be near Mason, went to where he was standing, within easy reach. He didn't beat around the bush. "There's been a bad wreck, Mason. Allison was in it." He waited a moment, swallowed. "I wish I wasn't the one tellin' you, but she didn't make it. I'm so sorry."

And that was how Mason heard the news, how he discovered his wife was dead. He was silent for an instant, folding in his arms to his chest, his hands gripped together underneath his chin. Everything seemed to lag and warp, then his legs lost their resolve, tumbling him down into his chair. "Allison's dead?" he asked the trooper. "My Allison?"

"Yes."

"Oh God." Mason left his arms pressed against his chest and cocked his head toward the ceiling and sealed his eyes, clenching his whole face as if he were trying to fend off Darrell's words. "You have to be wrong."

"I'm gonna sit here with you," Darrell said. "For a while, anyway." He took a seat and tugged a folded white handkerchief from his uniform pocket, did his own grieving. They'd known each other since elementary school, two local boys who'd grown up together.

"Where is she?" Mason asked after a few seconds. "What happened?" He paused, balling his hair inside a fist. "What am I going to do?" Tear on top of tear sliced down both cheeks. Several kept going and wet his lap, his sleeves.

"I reckon she's still at the hospital. You'll need to make some arrangements, but there's plenty of time for that. I'll drive you when you're ready. Whatever I can do."

The phones were ringing and not being answered. Sheila wobbled into the office sobbing and Darrell allowed her a brief stay before helping her leave, steering her away with a gentle hand on her shoulder.

"The wreck was at Charlie Martin's intersection," Darrell said when they were alone again. "Pickup come through and didn't slow down."

"Did . . . ? The car . . . How did it happen? I mean . . ." Mason slumped forward. "Did she . . . ?"

"It was over in a second," Darrell promised him. Two decades of dealing with covered gurneys and disemboweled automobiles had taught him what needed to be heard. "She never knew."

Mason just stared at him, shell-shocked, slowly throttling down, his vitality leaking from every pore, like a child's mechanical toy sucking the last juice from weak batteries, wallowing to a harsh, metallic stop. They could hear voices in the waiting room, the phones were still noisy but not being attended to, and through the window, Sadie Grace was visible, hurrying from her car, the door left open behind her.

"There's one other thing about the wreck I, uh, need to tell you," Darrell said.

Custis had jogged to the *Enterprise* office and found Gail Harding, the paper's editor. Because it was Stuart, she'd already heard the miserable report and didn't seem altogether surprised to see him. She told Custis she was heartbroken and asked after Mason and reached out and squeezed Custis's huge hand, got mostly fingers. They walked to a corner and Custis leaned against the wall. "Here's the deal," he said. "It's gonna surface that this Gammons boy was in court for DUI not so long ago. He was a good kid, Gail. College, job, scholarship, raised by a single mom. No record. Everybody and his brother callin' to support him. I reduced the charge. If I'd left it alone, he would've been suspended for a year and not drivin' today. Instead, I gave him his license back after thirty days. Shit."

Gail's face registered the news. She shook her head from side to side. "It's not your fault." She peered up at him. "And I'm not just saying that. You did the right thing for the right reasons. Don't beat yourself up over it. Heck, the way kids are, even if you'd taken his license, he might've still been driving. Suspended or not, people get behind the wheel. Who can say, Custis? And who could've known?"

"Well, people are gonna start gossipin' about it, and I'm sure it's a story with some appeal in certain quarters, so I just wanted to put it on the table, here and now. Mason had nothin' to do with the decision, never even knew about it. It was my case, my call. Now I gotta drag up there and tell him."

"I'm so sorry for all of it," Gail said. "But the kind of man Mason is, he won't hold it against you."

"Doesn't make it any easier." Custis sighed and pushed off from the wall. "At any rate, how 'bout you printin' the whole ball of wax, let the radio know and maybe the *Roanoke Times*. I'll get my ashes and sackcloth and wait for the MADD pickets and the minions from the cable networks." He smiled but didn't mean it.

"So Mason wasn't involved?" Gail asked, though the answer probably wouldn't have made any difference in terms of her story.

"Nope. Completely me. He's always trusted me to manage my cases. You're welcome to check the paperwork."

"No reason to."

There were several people in Mason's office when Custis arrived, and he went directly to his friend and they wrapped each other up, embracing and holding tight. They were emotional and unguarded, but neither was crying or overwrought. Custis's mouth was so close to Mason's ear it almost touched: "This is totally on me, brother. My fault. I hope you'll forgive me." The room was quiet except for sniffles and the gentle, padded sound of a woman's steady weeping, and most of the visitors heard what Custis said.

"It couldn't be helped. Not your fault. No one could ask for a better friend or partner." Mason had recovered somewhat, was operating on adrenaline and numb instinct, his world pared down to the very next noun and verb, the person immediately in front of him, the effort to blink and breathe. The rest was nothing, scrambled— gray, grainy static beyond shrunken margins. He made space between them so he could see Custis. "I was right there with you, and—"

"I wish I could have it to do again," Custis interrupted, talking over Mason. He took a step away. "I can't tell you how . . . how . . ." He gave up, hung his head, wiped a wrist across both eyes. "I can't believe it."

"I know," Mason assured him.

"It's God's will," said a lady from the Baptist church standing beside Sadie Grace. She meant well, had come to see what she could do to comfort the family. "As hard as it is to understand, we know Allison's in a far better place."

"Yeah, and so is our daughter," Mason snapped. "Maybe the Good Lord should have his spectacles checked before he goes down the list again. Or get better information from his agents on the ground. I don't want to hear that shit right now." He was allowed the breach of faith by everyone there, even his churchgoing mother, and the Christian lady who'd made the suggestion understood why he was so distraught and didn't think poorly of him or take umbrage. "How about riding with me and Darrell to the hospital?" he said to Custis after the room fell silent, and the three men started to leave the office, the trooper leading the way. Mason stopped at the threshold and addressed his mother. "I'd appreciate it if you could go by the house. I expect I'll need some help."

"Of course," Sadie Grace told him. She crossed the room and touched him on the arm, sixty-four years old, her knee not completely reliable, the joint sabotaged by arthritis.

The family night was held at the high school auditorium because so many people wanted to pay their respects. The wait stretched into the parking lot, some in the line straight from work and still wearing their blue shirts and steel-toes, others in coats and ties, overalls, sport jackets and Sunday best for many of the ladies. A few visitors barely knew Mason but came because they'd received a fair shake in court or a kind hearing of a past problem, and even reclusive old Hazel Overby, a widow with a dip of snuff rolling around her dentures, stood for hours waiting to see the Hunts. No telling how much food was brought to Mason's house, plate upon plate, chicken, cakes, casseroles, pies, baked beans, cold-cut trays, country hams and Crock-Pots filled with stew. The local arts co-op collected nearly five thousand dollars in memorials. All the Patrick County attorneys wrote checks to fund an Allison Hunt scholarship. There was not enough room in the funeral home's chapel for the flowers.

After a simple, two-hymn service, several hundred people drove from the chapel and encircled Mason and Grace at the Stuart Cemetery, virtually every one of them nicked or saddened by the death. Standing there graveside and wearing a dark suit, Mason was struck by the thought that spring was not the season in which to die. A burial was incongruous and wrong during a time of dogwoods and blithe perennials, stories of empty tombs and rolled-away rocks, and frenetic children combing fields full of poorly concealed, brightly dyed eggs, one always golden. With the world being rebirthed all around him, Mason mourned underneath a tent on a mat of artificial grass, holding his child's hand, occupied by his own concerns, the preacher's words disintegrating into the air, too frail and slight for the huge outdoors, pulverized by the vault of sky and the hard, ancient mountains. He returned to the grave twice that day, knelt and touched the turned dirt, red clay flecked with mica, trying to make sense of what was happening to him.

Grace was devastated. Gutted. Mason had collected her from school and sat her down in her grandma's kitchen and slow-walked her into the tragedy, the worst experience in his forty-plus years, bar none. For five nights, he made a pallet and slept on the floor beside her. He allowed her to miss school for two days, doing what he could to answer her questions, comforting her when she cried and indulging her with movies and rich desserts. The child took a stab at making breakfast for her dad the day following the accident, and once he had to hustle after her when she set out with her pink and yellow backpack and a claw hammer, planning to find Lonnie Gammons and put a beating on him. They did the best they could, the both of them staggered.

Gates, meanwhile, remained in the pen, didn't make the trip to Stuart—he and Mason were still at odds, their communications more and more infrequent and often by letter. "I've got enough to put up with," Mason had told Sadie Grace when she broached the subject of bringing him home for the funeral. "I don't need that monkey on my back, more to vex me." To his credit, Gates did call Mason on his own dime—glibly promising to keep his brother in his "thoughts and prayers"—and he had a peace lily dispatched to the funeral home. "I know it's a bad time to ask," Gates said before his last pay-phone minutes expired, "but did you have a chance to look over the motion I sent you? I mean, I'm not askin' you to do it now or anything, that wouldn't be decent, no it wouldn't, but just when you get past all this. In the next day or two. I've got a deadline." Mason was so enraged that he went barreling to his office, found the envelope full of ponderous longhand on notebook paper and burned it. He shook the ashes into a box and sealed it, leaving instructions for Sheila to return the package to the penitentiary.

Not long after the service, Mason discovered the lie Custis had told for him, and he immediately wanted the truth to be known, thanked Custis but refused to let him be blamed for something not wholly of his making.

"Why you wanna go and do that?" Custis asked him. They were sitting on the porch at Mason's. Sadie Grace was inside molding hamburger into a meat loaf, supper for her son and granddaughter. "What good will it do you or Grace or Allison? The fact of the matter is I'm the one who really pushed the issue with the Gammons kid. My case, my call. It's a wrinkle you shouldn't have to deal with. You know how people can be."

"Our case, our call. I'm not going to be a coward and hide behind your skirts, Custis, much as I appreciate the gesture. I could've stopped it." He sighed and stared at the pasture, the grass greening and uneven. "Can you believe this? What a damn mess. What an unfair, one-in-a-million, Greek tragedy cluster fuck. The day after her birthday. We were set, too. Perfect with each other—I loved her and she loved me." He watched a line of ants curving across the porch boards. "But I'll make sure everyone knows what's what. I'm as much at fault as you. Hell, more at fault—I'm the boss."

"Which assumes both of us did somethin' wrong. In our minds, at least, we have to realize maybe we didn't, Mason. We didn't cause this. You could argue we're no more to blame than Gammons's driver's ed teacher or the guy who sets the exam schedule at Tech. For any number of reasons, you don't have to carry this bag, and you shouldn't. You couldn't see around the corner. You damn sure didn't mean for it to happen."

Mason dipped his head. He wasn't looking at Custis when he spoke. "So why're you scrambling all over the county flogging this lie?" He grinned slightly but didn't lift his eyes.

" 'Cause I knew what you'd think, and I knew it would come up even though it shouldn't. It's a tiny bit of aggravation I wanted to take off you."

Mason looked at his friend but didn't answer. He proceeded to walk inside and tell Sadie Grace about his involvement, and he called Inez Rucker, Custis's lady friend. He wrote a letter to the editor, which Gail Harding returned to him unpublished. The community didn't know precisely what to believe, and ultimately only the most moronic of the jackasses and dolts viewed the collision as anything but a Byzantine fluke, simply horrid bad luck. Still, Custis and Mason both suffered their decision like a millstone, and sometimes when he thought about Lonnie Gammons and the crash at Charlie Martin's intersection, Mason would curse out loud or bang his fist against a wall or a counter, seething.

After nearly a month, at night he took to sitting on the sofa in her studio, the stuffing pressing through tears and slits, a rough blanket from a Mexican vacation partially covering the cushions. He would gaze at the spot where he last saw her awake and wonder if the rhino was finished, if it would suit her. At dusk one warm evening, his doctor buddy Vince Castillo dropped by to check on him, and he told Vince he was out of whack, felt like he'd become saturated and was sinking, a dreamy, suspended free fall, aimless and soupy, breaking up and dropping at the same time, destined for the muck. Vince gave him a prescription for Valium, but Mason didn't fill it, couldn't see where it would change his circumstances.

Chapter Nine

For Mason, loss played to form: he was bewildered, then furious as a wet hen—frustrated and quick-tempered—and finally, depressed, swamped by sadness.

Early on, Sadie Grace spent most of her nights with him and her granddaughter, pitching in with the cooking and the household demands, and friends frequently stopped by to say hello or coax him over for a meal or mention a fishing trip or invite him to a Saturday-evening movie. Midway through June, his old pal Claude arrived unannounced with wild rabbits he'd killed and skinned, and he and Mason visited in the den, telling high school tales and recounting Gates's antics, marveling at how popular he'd been. "Nobody could charm 'em like your crazy brother," Claude said. They'd gotten comfortable, the conversation oiled and rolling. "Ol' Heaven's Gates. Remember that? How he'd say to the girls, 'I'd be delighted to let you enter and take you on a tour you'll never forget.'" Claude laughed and clapped his hands. "What a lady-killer, huh? Always . . ." He caught himself and took a furtive, self-conscious peek at Mason. "Aw, shit, man. Here I am supposed to be cheerin' you up and I go and put my foot in my big mouth. My bad."

Mason shook his head, forced Claude to look at him. "Don't fret about it. Every reference to a woman or wife won't cause me to fall apart. I'm not that hopeless, okay?"

But, in truth, he *was* floundering, and eventually he yielded to his mother's nudges and encouragement and started attending church regularly, eager to find some solace in religion, some tonic that would set him right. He and Allison had occasionally gone to the Presbyterian church on Staples Avenue, hitting the high spots like Christmas, Mother's Day and Easter, and they'd sent Grace to Vacation Bible School there, where she learned snippets of scripture and fashioned crafts from Popsicle sticks and pipe cleaners. Mason shopped around a bit, even tried his mother's True Gospel House of the Risen Lord, an Independent Baptist affair, but the service was too long, too hardscrabble, too strident, too tent-revival, electric-bass theatrical. He finally decided to pin his hopes on the Presbyterians. So, perplexed and sucker punched, seeking a hint as to why his wife had been killed for no discernible reason, he spent the summer in Sunday worship and Wednesday-night Bible studies.

He found the congregation to be generous and sincere, the minister thoughtful, the denomination's doctrines worthwhile, the charity laudable and the entire enterprise a wrenching waste of his time—before hearing the organ and beholding the stained glass, he already knew sin was wicked, tithes were a necessary burden and his neighbors deserved better treatment and more attention. What he couldn't discover was why in blue blazes his wife was no longer with him. The sermons and messages were simply not on topic for him, missing his needs with a defiant regularity, and the frequent suggestion that he and the others occupying the pews were not meant to solve the majesty of a grander scheme—the trite fallback "The Lord works in mysterious ways"—seemed like a sophist's crooked masterpiece, a squishy dodge requiring a much bigger buy-in than he was willing to make. After three months, he felt as if he were an ignored schoolboy, raised high off his seat, his arm shot straight up, straining to catch the teacher's eye, never called on or acknowledged.

One morning late in September, disturbed by a rocky, sleepless night, he appeared at his preacher's study, demanding more than the clergyman could give.

"Why did my wife get killed in a car wreck?" Mason asked, agitated and unshaven, having rushed through their pleasantries. Reverend Hunsicker had offered decaf coffee, which Mason declined. It was morning, the air outside brisk but not bitter.

Using his index finger, the preacher slid his reading glasses farther up his nose. "Pardon me?" The men were separated by a desk, alone in a modest basement room, books spilling from cardboard boxes and red plastic milk crates.

"Why is my sweet, talented Allison dead, when the fools and criminals and drunks, the flotsam and jetsam who fill the courtrooms, can't be killed with a sledgehammer? Why does my daughter not have a mother? How can this be authored—or allowed—by a benevolent God? And if your answer is 'sometimes we can't understand His purpose,' I don't want to hear it. That's not an answer, it's an excuse."

The preacher looked at him with sympathy, an earnest cast to his features. "I wish I had an explanation, Mason. I do. I don't think it's fair either, to use the term generally, as it relates to the here and now. Her death was tragic. Difficult." He ducked his head, emotional. "But you've got to hold fast to your faith. Continue to pray." His voice was low, on the verge of a whisper. "Continue to humbly petition the Lord and ask for peace of mind. The Lord answers prayers."

Mason considered what he was about to say. Ran through it silently. A space heater kicked on, humming and glowing orange. "No offense, Reverend, but the whole prayer routine seems like a parlor trick to me, an elegant variation on the Amazing Randi's act or the Magic Eight Ball game. Let me see if I understand: We're supposed to pray, but the request only comes to fruition if it's God's will, correct? So if we don't get our cancer cure or new job or marriage saved or rent money or spouse to quit drinking, it wasn't His will, and we're okay with the rejection, but we're still positive we're blessed by our Almighty. He simply knew better than we did." Mason hesitated. He gestured with both his hands, tossing them out disgustedly. "And if we win the prayer lotto, well there you go: We sing hymns and give thanks and rejoice, praise be, because the Lord delivered a new car or jammed the coffers of the building fund. Who could doubt the connection? Our prayers were answered. It's a can't-lose gimmick, a damn shell game—I hate to say it, but it is. I mean, how far are we removed from the days when we bowed to Zeus because we burned a goat and chanted his name and the thunder quit?"

"I understand why you're so disappointed—"

Mason interrupted. "The prayer thing is a side issue for me anyway; I've got a bigger bone to pick. No matter how you cut it, either your God allowed my innocent, undeserving wife to get killed— omnipotent neglect, I guess you'd call it—or He intended for it to happen, and that's clearly screwed up given the world's infinitely more deserving choices." Mason sighed and bit his lip. "This isn't . . ." He slouched in his chair. "This isn't working for me, Reverend. I appreciate your decency, I appreciate the good hearts in this church, I appreciate the fine deeds everyone does for the community, but my wife is dead, and it's cruel and random and there's nothing here to change any of those painful facts. No hard feelings, and for what it's worth, I think you're a good man. Very considerate. Problem is, your employer needs to do a better job stocking your store—can't sell what you don't have."

Reverend Hunsicker trailed Mason to his car, and he phoned and visited in the weeks that followed, and he listened to Mason's vehement complaints, absorbed his criticism, struggled to brace Mason's faith, did all he could to transfer a certitude he possessed but Mason didn't. Mason, though, had made up his mind, and the preacher's many efforts and devout entreaties bounced off a man who was too angry to listen and too far gone to care.

For the next several months, into the onset of winter, Mason was a bear in court, brutal to the chronics and petty criminals, the wastrels who stole small items from unlocked sheds or forged a check lifted from their very own mama's purse, the worthless recidivists who whined and whimpered and boohooed, always begging for *one more chance,* another trip to rehab or a suspended sentence, clutching their prison-ministry tracts on the stand, swearing fealty to a new way of life for the sixth or seventh time. But nothing riled him more than shiftlessness, flagrant sorriness, and pity the stupid crook who made the mistake of dragging his aged mom or crippled grandmother in to testify how she knew her boy had learned his lesson this go-round, was sure to shape up if he could come live with her. "Nice," Mason would sneer at these defendants when he questioned them. "How proud you must make your family."

Also, the county's habits, quaint bent, erratic pace and unpredictable characters—its offbeat country charm, if you were in the mood for it—began to prick him, weighing on his patience, like a medicine that had been splendid and effective, then suddenly went toxic. "It's a *wharf* rat, not a *wolf* rat," he declared to Mo Jenkins, the humble hired man who helped with the yard, cleaned the gutters and mowed the pasture. "And while we're at it, the dog is a *Rott*weiler, not a *Rock*weiler." Rustic became irksome—the slow-ass pickups that never gave a turn signal, the farm tractors, hay wagons and old people in muddy Buicks that clogged the main highway, the stores that didn't sell a respectable dress shirt, the endless chatter about nothing, the same-old, same-old all along every route. Then there was the sort who got everyone's goat, the snaggletoothed clods who drew a government check they didn't deserve, slurping their bowls of pinto beans bombarded with chunks of corn bread, green feed-store hats still on their heads while they ate in a restaurant, no manners whatsoever. "It's all I can do," Mason told Custis, "not to knock the piss out of someone. I used to like this shit. Now it drives me crazy."

Unable to stay still for very long, he skipped meals, ran extra miles at the high school track and added reps to his gym routine. Always fit and athletic, he lost eleven pounds he shouldn't have lost, the majority of it through his face, or so it appeared to the people around him. "Mason really looks like he's bad off," Sadie Grace's cousin mentioned at an elementary school fund-raiser. "He ain't hisself, is he?"

There was one mild, interesting deviation. When the special prosecutor consulted Mason about offering Lonnie Gammons a reckless-driving plea, he didn't object, insisting only that Gammons lose his license for a year and be required to volunteer at the hospital ER. "His punishment's really not my main issue," Mason said obscurely. "He's a dumb kid with no daddy." After court concluded, Gammons, scared and remorseful, standing beside his plain, threadbare mother, choked out an apology, and while Mason only frowned and grunted, he didn't curse the kid or lunge at him or threaten retribution, allowed him his say, a tiny forgiveness.

Coal-fed ire takes its toll, of course. The bile and twenty-four-seven, high-end fury couldn't last forever, and gradually Mason wore down into the last phase of his suffering. After the searching and confusion, and after the rants, anger and days of looking to pick a fight for no real reason, he grew weary, blue. Gloomy. He realized what had happened to him, his sad state, standing at a convenience-store counter on the first day of the year 2002, gazing at a Peg-Board on the wall behind the clerk, caught up in the hairbrushes, rubber bands, fingernail clippers, combs, playing cards, off-brand condoms and colorfully wrapped patent medicines, unaware he'd been asked three times, very politely, if he was ready to pay for the gas he'd pumped. He was so distracted he never responded until the clerk touched him on the sleeve and said, "Are you okay, Mr. Hunt?"

Most everything in the world had become a detour or trapdoor for him, sucking him away into chutes and sluices of the past, leaving him distant and dumbstruck. A court reporter's painted fingernails as she adjusted a microphone summoned Allison's hand around the green throat of a wine bottle, pouring herself a glass for breakfast soon after they'd met. A sloppy Hardee's restroom took him to his father's sink in the old shed and the dried, dirty webs of black grease that fanned from a bar of Curt's Lava soap. A glimpse at a DMV transcript in juvenile court and he was drinking sloe gin fizzes with Gates, underage but ready with a fake Wisconsin operator's license when the Myrtle Beach bartender asked. Passing the Stuart hospital carried him to the day the nurse handed Grace to her mother, thirteen years ago. And an ordinary convenience-store hairbrush had ended up in Allison's hand, gliding through her hair while she sat before an antique mahogany vanity, the strokes rhythmic, music without sound. "I'm fine," Mason assured the clerk. "Didn't mean to ignore you."

Worsening his dislocation, he would dwell on change and what had gone missing. Nothing seemed to be nailed down. Nothing could hold. Driving around Stuart one morning, he passed the spot where Smokey's Restaurant and Motor Court used to be, and he coasted to the side of the road, staring at a flat patch of grass and the yellow lines that marked the blacktop. First the motel rooms were razed, then Smokey's became the Lumberyard Grill, next it was Skip's Seafood, and forty years later there wasn't anything left, only a curve in the new four-lane, the Mayo River rechanneled to accommodate the expanded highway, the building bulldozed and the debris hauled away in dump trucks, the kitchen equipment sold to a junk dealer, the old site buried under asphalt and steamrolled earth, Smokey and Ada Fulton and their homey café thoroughly vanished save for a few photos at the county historical society.

Following the holidays, in January of 2002, an unexpected ice storm encased the county, bejeweling branches and power lines and broomstraw fields, and Custis marched into Mason's office for their usual Monday-morning meeting wearing galoshes and a wool scarf, his coat still buttoned to the neck. He tossed a large yellow envelope onto Mason's desk.

"What do we have here?" Mason asked, glancing up from a Code of Virginia volume.

"Important business." Custis sat down. "Inside you will find both your *Allman Brothers at Fillmore East* CD and your Jimmy Cliff CD. I got one from your car, the other from the stereo at your house. I took the liberty of defacin' them with a screwdriver before smashing 'em to pieces. I'm tired of walking into this office or your house and hearin' 'Whipping Post' and 'Many Rivers to Cross.' Enough of that shit, Mace. It's time for the handkerchiefs to go. Time to rejoin the rest of us." He smiled, hoping to get a rise.

"I'm sorry, Custis," Mason said without conviction. "I know I haven't been much good to anyone."

"Listen. You gotta rally. It's awful what happened, but let's draw a line and look at what's left, what comes next. It can't be all bad. Plus, your daughter deserves better."

"I've never, ever neglected my daughter. In fact—"

"Yeah," Custis jumped in, "in fact you've been too damn nice, like a Stepford father or something. Grace thinks she's taking care of *you*. Kids can tell when the train's jumped the tracks, Mace. You ain't foolin' her." He finally loosened his scarf and undid his coat.

Mason put his elbows on the desk, his chin in his hands. "I suppose you're right. Hell, I know you're right. But I can't change how much this punishes me, every moment of every day."

"Well, amigo, Uncle Custis has a plan." He reached inside his suit jacket and produced another envelope, this one white, letter-size and thick. "For you." He stretched the envelope across the desk and Mason took it.

Mason lifted the flap and removed the contents. "Puerto Rico?" he asked, befuddled. "A ticket to San Juan?"

"Me and you, Mason and Custis, sampling the high life come next week. We're gonna forget our troubles and jet to hot weather and drink. We'll sit by the pool, and if the opportunity presents itself, roll up on the fine tourist women. Start the new calendar with a bang. Turn the page in style. Your mom's taking care of Grace, the docket's clear and you'll notice those aren't just any tickets, nope, they're two first-class rides across the ocean. We're gonna fly away from winter for a while and find you a party. Gamble, drink, carouse, burn the midnight oil. The brochures should tell you all you need to know."

Mason laughed. "I'm not a big drinker, Custis. You know that. I've never gambled in my life."

"All the better. It's healthy to explore new vices."

"How much is this costing you? I can't let you buy me a trip."

"Not costin' me a penny, Chief. I had Sheila write the check from your personal account." He grinned at Mason. "I paid for my own, naturally." He leaned back in his chair. "This is a done deal, Mason. Pack your bags."

Mason studied the ticket. He flicked his eyes up at Custis. "Why the hell not? I've got to do something. A break might be what I need."

"Make no mistake—this isn't going to be a break, okay? This isn't a change of venue so you can be unhappy by the pool instead of in the woods. This is about a crushed-velvet, seven-day, groove-on, roof-off, Mayor Marion Barry party. And I'm drivin' the bus."

"I'll be sure to bring my festive clothes." He grinned a little, cheered by his friend. "Thanks."

Two days later, Gates phoned Mason at the farm, around ten at night. It was the first call since November, as their relationship had continued to decline at a steady clip, especially after Mason had burned Gates's legal papers and returned them with a short, hostile note.

"It's me," Gates said. "Callin' to check in." He sounded tense.

"I know it's you. Collect call tipped me off."

"Right, yeah." It seemed unusually quiet at the penitentiary, no shouting or clamor coming through the receiver from Gates's end. "So are you makin' any progress, you or Mom, on getting me some help? Thought of anything?"

Mason resisted the impulse to hang up. "No" was all he said.

"How come? How come you've forgotten about me? I don't understand."

"Anything else I can do for you, Gates? Any new business before the secretary adopts the minutes and we close the meeting?" He actually looked at his watch, even though he was standing in his den, wearing sweatpants, nowhere to go, Grace bumping around upstairs preparing for bed.

"I just wanted to give you one last chance." Every word was coiled and deliberate.

"Or what?" Mason quickly asked.

"Or else. I've been patient long enough."

"Excuse me, Gates? Are you . . . are you threatening me from there in the pen, miles away? Are you? Have you lost your fucking mind? Let me guess: you've met a guy who belongs to a motorcycle gang or some hood with ties in New Jersey and this new buddy owes you a favor. You're a damn joke these days, Gates. A joke. You ought to be grateful for everything we've done, but that wouldn't be your style, would it?"

"Don't say I didn't warn you or give you a million chances."

"Whatever, Gates. You—"

The line went dead.

When Mason woke up at the Wyndham El San Juan, the sun was jitterbugging about on the ocean, his room was bright, the balcony doors were wide open and a set of long, translucent drapes was hanging free and swaying with the breeze. Custis was missing; it was 10:16 according to the red digits of the clock next to the bed. Mason walked out onto the balcony and surveyed the blue-green water, the buildings ringing the beach and the hotel pool, already filling with tourists. He located ESPN on the TV and unzipped his suitcase to start putting away his clothes. Not long after he began, he heard a card slip into the lock and looked up, saw Custis holding the door against his hip, boxes and bottles on the ground, grocery bags cradled in his arms.

"How 'bout givin' me a hand?" he said to Mason. "The bellhop got me this far."

Mason helped him carry in two cases of beer, half gallons of rum and vodka, a bottle of Courvoisier, champagne, mixers, food, napkins and plastic cups. The small fridge was overwhelmed, so they filled a sink with ice, dumped in several beers and the champagne and covered them with a bath towel.

"You were serious about the big vacation," Mason said. He was sitting at the foot of his bed, still wearing his boxers.

"This is just a down payment, my man. No more than the pre-party appetizer." Custis was occupied with a boom box, searching for an electrical outlet.

Mason laughed. "The minibar would have lasted me a month. I don't know who's going to help you slay this dragon."

"Never want to get caught short."

"No worry there." Mason yawned.

"Let's see about improving our situation and headin' to the pool. It's eighty degrees, and I'm already feelin' a very promising, platinum kinda vibe take shape." Custis had the box operating. He was piling chips, nuts and snacks onto a table, next to the liquor.

"Jeez, Custis. What is that? Rap? It's bad music generally, even worse before noon."

"A little old-school to get your blood pumpin'. Wu-Tang Clan. Come on, Mason. Dentists listen to this shit." He was nodding to the beat. "And I don't have any Conway Twitty, so it'll have to do."

"Now I discover this wicked flaw, stuck here with you for a week." Mason stood, took his swim trunks from a drawer, dropped his boxers and changed into the trunks and a button-front cotton shirt. He talked as he was dressing, naked for an instant. "Some tone-deaf turd carves the sweet spot out of a real talent's song— steals it, to be blunt—then litters it with studio tricks and seventh-grade rhymes while his cousins and low-life friends yelp in the background. Awful. The worst of it, Custis, is you have to know the chump with the gold teeth and Fatty Arbuckle pants, the brother with the mike, has about as much talent as a block of wood."

Unfazed, Custis was pouring a beer, taking care not to let the foam get away from him. "By the end of the trip, you'll be sold on Wu-Tang. I'll bet you fifty bucks, confident you'll be such a fan you won't lie just to win the cash."

"Done. Bet."

"I got another little treat for you," Custis announced.

"I hope it's an improvement."

Custis reached into his pocket and came out with a clear bag, dark across the bottom portion. He held it up with his thumb and first finger, letting it dangle. "A little smoke to boost our spirits."

"Well, now." A few fine lines formed at the corners of Mason's eyes. He extended his chin a tick forward. "Where in the world did you get that?" he asked, more amused than surprised.

"People sell it, you know." Custis tossed the bag to Mason, who caught it with cupped hands.

"Damn, I mean, here—you bought it here, I hope?"

"Of course."

"What if you'd gotten caught or—"

"Not to worry—it's all taken care of."

"How'd you find it?"

"I bought it from the concierge. But, hey, I charged it to your credit card, so I'm in the clear when the DEA arrives with the black helicopters and night goggles."

"You what? You—"

"I'm just fuckin' with you," Custis said, laughing so hard he snorted.

Mason relaxed, a grin twisting into his lips. "Smart-ass."

"I paid a kid on the beach fifty bucks; he seemed enterprisin'. Runs a Jet Ski rental right below the hotel." Custis sipped his beer. "So you gonna take advantage of my acquisition?"

"We'll see, I guess. I've told you before I've never tried it. No lie, I never have, not even with Gates. Allison used to dabble a bit. I mean, I don't have a major problem with it. It's not a moral thing or whatever. Just never had the urge, especially when I was playing baseball and trying to stay in shape. Hell, it's no worse than alcohol, right?" He was distracted, concerned with the bag. "Don't see too many potheads beating their wives or holding up the liquor store, all jacked up on grass. Hmmm." He fingered the dope through the plastic. "You do this much, Custis? At home, in Stuart?"

"Never shit where you eat, Mace. And it wouldn't be quite right-eous for me to prosecute people and then burn one during the drive home from work. I might party a bit when I'm visitin' out of town, with friends in D.C. or Atlanta. It's all politics anyway—reefer madness, you know? One toke, you'll become wild-eyed riffraff, playin' the jazz piano and kickin' in doors to support your Mary Jane habit. Comes down to it, the moonshine and apple brandy we laugh off and wink at is probably far more harmful."

"I'm not saying I disagree."

"Since we're on the subject, I appreciate the fact you've never pressured me 'bout my, uh, what should I say, my appearance and libertarian streak. Don't ask, don't tell has been a good policy for us."

"Sure," Mason said solemnly. "But now that I've learned the truth, I'll be firing you. Can't have a druggie on the state payroll, can we?"

"Damn, what a bitch. You'll probably give me bad references, too. 'Course, you the man holdin' the reefer. I don't have the first idea how it got in our room." Custis grinned.

"You know, why not? Let's smoke some. You're absolutely right—I need to loosen up. We're on vacation in a foreign country, miles away from everything and everybody, and I've been through a hellacious year. Who'd begrudge me a simple misdemeanor? Fix us a joint."

"It's not quite a foreign country, Secretary Albright. Last I checked, Puerto Rico is a U.S. commonwealth, but—"

"They speak Spanish—close enough for me."

"Comin' right up," Custis said. "Attaboy. Grab yourself a cold Corona to wash it down." He gestured toward the bathroom. "I knew this was gonna work out. Damn straight." He took the pot from Mason. "There's an opener on the back of the door—say what you will, that's takin' care of your guests, yes indeed. A fine omen, Mace. Your accommodating hotels know to hook you up with some convenient hardware on the door or right under the sink. What would you prefer—French-milled soap or a place to open your malt liquor?"

"So this stuff is going to make me high, correct? Giddy and fun? Carefree?" Mason was on his way to the beer.

"Do electric razors and Chia Pets command the stage at Christmastime?"

"That would be a definite yes." Mason opened a beer. The metal cap hit the floor and rolled toward the tub. He chuckled. "It's not even eleven o'clock, and we've got seven days of this in front of us."

"Wake and bake," Custis said.

"I don't feel anything," Mason declared. They were standing in the hallway, waiting for the elevator to arrive. "What's it supposed to be doing?" He took a drink of beer. "Maybe we need to go back to the room. Or maybe your merchant on the beach took you for a ride without the Jet Ski. Sold you a bag of nothing."

"From the smell of the goods, we're okay on that account. Perhaps if your tight ass would relax and slide into it, we wouldn't have to smoke a bale to get you buzzed." Custis was wearing a shirt and swimsuit that matched, green, red and black, a "gay Jamaican's pajama ensemble" Mason had teased. He'd added some beads and bright bands to his hair. The shirt was mostly unbuttoned, and he'd purchased a new pair of leather sandals for the trip. Mason could smell cologne.

"This is the worst elevator I've ever seen. We've been here for decades."

"It does seem slow," Custis agreed. "Any idea where the stairs are?"

A mother and her small son approached and stood beside them. The woman was holding the boy by the wrist, and he was twisting and squirming, his shoulders and nose red from the sun.

"The elevator's not too swift," Mason informed her. He switched his beer to the hand on the other side, away from the kid. "We've been waiting forever." He smiled at her, then her son. She zipped him a stern look.

A moment later, she took a step forward and pressed the call button. It illuminated, turning white around a black arrow. Her boy peered up at Custis and Mason, and the elevator arrived almost immediately. *Ding.*

"Oh, wow," Mason said. "Good thing you came along, ma'am."

Custis was struggling not to laugh, his huge hands covering his face, looking out through spread fingers. He gestured for the woman and her son to go ahead. "We'll take the next one," he said, avoiding eye contact.

The doors shut, erasing the woman and child, and it was on, oh was it ever, the two men giggling and high-fiving, happy almost to the point of tears. Mason hadn't felt so good in months, and by the time they found chairs at the pool, he was enraptured with the number pi, punching Custis's arm and saying, "I'm serious, think about it, it's this aberrant number, one of a kind, that goes forever, that never terminates or repeats. It can't be stopped or finished, not by anyone. What an amazing fucking phenomenon—infinite, invincible. Damn." He asked the waitress to bring him something "sweet and lethal," and he and Custis enjoyed the sun, the warmth, the new scenery, the separation from home, both of them stoned as cats, their world rendered in concentrated colors and heavy outlines.

They ate plates of French fries for lunch and visited the room to smoke another joint. When they returned to the pool, a DJ was playing music and people were dancing and drinking, the resort afternoon starting to hit its stride. The DJ selected "Electric Slide," and a rush of people, mostly women, popped up and started dancing. More vacationers trickled onto the pool deck as the song progressed, some with drinks still in their hands. Swaying, clapping, spinning, the group moved together, side to side, up and back, one large woman flamboyantly adding extra shakes and gyrations to every turn in the choreography, her giant rear and huge breasts jiggling like nobody's business.

"Shit, Custis, here's our chance," Mason said, high and half-serious. He was propped up in a chaise longue, a fresh piña colada balanced on his stomach. "Though I have to admit I don't know how to do the dance."

"Well, that's a plus. Here's a little secret for you since you've been on the shelf a while: no man who does the electric slide is ever going to get laid. It's a universal truth. Take a look at the pigeons and goofs you got out there. Ain't a woman alive who's gonna be impressed by a bunch of stiff-kneed, upright, counted-out cracker moves—it's barely above a hoedown. Barkin' up your do-si-do and checkered-shirts tree. This shit is for the jesters and the wannabes on the undercard who don't know any better. Don't embarrass me."

Mason set his piña colada on the ground. "I knew that," he said, laughing until he began coughing. "So when do we make our move? We listening for Luther? The Bruce Lee Clan or whatever it was?"

"Wait for your pitch, Mace. Don't need to be swingin' at the slider in the dirt. Your man Custis will give you the assist. Try not to screw it up."

As good as his promise, an hour later Custis had corralled three women at the pool bar, and they were traveling with two affable couples, all of them from a North Carolina doctor's office, sent to Puerto Rico and the Wyndham every year courtesy of their plastic surgeon boss.

Custis beckoned Mason to the bar and introduced him to everyone there. Two golfers from Ohio, still in their long pants and knit shirts, joined the group, and Custis somehow recruited an attractive older lady who had been reading a paperback book by herself the entire day. He ordered a round for everyone, and Mason commandeered a waitress's tray and served the drinks, a mock bow and a request for a tip following each delivery. By four thirty, after shots, ribald jokes and several slapstick dives off the board—predominantly cannonballs and jackknives—the celebration had moved to Custis and Mason's room, more people along for the ride, twenty or so in all, strangers mixing free drinks and chugging beers, music blaring, the women in bathing suits and skimpy cover-ups, sticky with coconut-scented oil.

Custis and two of the North Carolina women found their way to Mason, who was pouring rum into orange juice and eating from a bag of corn chips. One of the women was named Liz; the other's name he couldn't remember, but he'd taken to calling her "the Contessa" because of the way she handled her Cosmopolitan at the pool, sipping it daintily with her pinky pointed away from the plastic cup. The women were tipsy and loud, very flirty, both attractive, and Liz hadn't changed from her two-piece, was flitting around the room in flip-flops, a tattoo decorating her ankle, smoking cigarettes.

"Reggie says you guys know tons of celebrities," the Contessa said to Mason. Custis had introduced himself as Reggie, and Mason was Holden, though Mason kept forgetting to use the aliases and caused everyone confusion. Having misunderstood him at one point, the golfers were addressing Custis as Festus, and naturally Mason became Marshal Dillon.

"You could say so. Yep." Mason raised his drink. "Cheers. Everybody okay alcohol-wise?" His speech had started to slip, s's and d's affected the most.

"I told your skeptical self twice," Custis retorted with feigned offense. "Now you gotta come and ask my partner. Being sports agents, you tend to encounter a few folks with a profile."

"I thought you were lawyers," Liz said. She was a blonde with short hair and slender legs and arms.

"We are," Custis told her.

"You want a milkman doing your important sports-agent business?" Mason added. "Of course we're lawyers. Ask me a legal question." He took a swig of his drink and shuddered. "Whoa—little too strong there, bartender." He scrunched his face. "Oh shit, I *am* the bartender."

"So who do you know famous?" the Contessa demanded. She was blond also, taller than Liz, with longer hair. It might've been the dope, but it appeared to Mason that she'd had her lips and breasts altered. Probably a job perk.

"What we do is confidential," Custis told her. "I can't be chattin' 'bout our clients to strangers at a cocktail party."

"So we have to take your word, huh?" Liz pressed him. She was smiling, impaired, bullshitting and enjoying it.

"Reggie says you played baseball." The Contessa was addressing Mason.

"I did."

"College All-American, three years with the Mets," Custis said, clueing his friend.

"True, true. Swing for the fences. That's my motto."

"I think you two are makin' this up." The Contessa pouted her exaggerated lips.

Custis shook his head. "My, my, my. Ye of so little faith. Wait right here." He left, rummaged through his suitcase and located his cell phone. "You've heard of Deion Sanders, haven't you?" he asked when he'd rejoined them, phone in hand.

"Sure," said the Contessa.

"The football player," Liz noted. She shook out a cigarette and touched Mason on the arm to ask if he had a light. He didn't, apologized. One of the golfers tossed them a plastic Bic. She lit her cig and touched him again, seemed very close. "Do you guys have any tequila?"

"Afraid not," Mason replied. "It's one of those tastes you acquire as you get older. Like onions. Or black coffee. Or rare meat. We're not that mature yet." He laughed at what he'd said, his own rambling. Slightly dizzy and too warm, he set down his rum and orange juice, aware he needed to take a break. He opened a Coke and drank it from the can.

"So just to satisfy you ladies, I'm gonna put Deion on the line and let you say hello," Custis announced. Try not to say somethin' stupid, and don't mention Tim McCarver. Not a word about Tim."

One of the golfers overheard the conversation and sidled up beside the Contessa. "Sweet," he said. "You know Neon Deion?"

Custis made a show of holding the phone in front of him and pushing two buttons. "Motherfucker's on speed-dial—you could say I know him." He placed the phone against his ear, waited. "Where Deion?" he said, his voice high, the tone purposefully aggressive. "Tell him his man Reggie's callin' from San Juan." A knot of people had now gathered around Custis; the music had been switched off. "Deion, man, this is Reggie," he said, evidently to someone on the other end. They bantered for several minutes, the exchange about a Porsche and a barbecue restaurant in Memphis. "Listen, 'PT,' I got a lady here wants to shout at you—it might raise Reggie's stock if you say a word or two, if you take my meanin'. And don't forget to call me about the variety show with CBS—it's gonna happen." He transferred the phone to the Contessa, and she talked awhile, laughing and sipping a beer, before telling the man on the line he could be anyone—how did she know he was really Deion? The golfers suggested a football question, which he correctly answered, and finally Mason heard her say, "Okay, I will," and she disconnected the call and handed the phone to Custis.

"What? What'd he say?" Liz asked her. "Why'd you hang up?"

Mason was as ensnared as everyone else, buzzed and tripping, wondering about the conversation. He caught Custis's eye but couldn't read him.

The phone rang, and Custis turned it so the Contessa and Liz could view the screen. Mason craned to see as well. "Saunders, Deion" appeared on the caller ID. He answered the call after one ring, thanked Deion for the effort and said good-bye. "Deion says to tell you hey," he told Mason. "You can check the area code, too, ladies—Atlanta."

"Holy shit," said the Contessa. "It really was him. Did you see that?"

"Impressive," said one of the golfers. He slapped a high five with Custis, then Mason.

"I suppose now you'll want me to call Columbine and prove to you we were *there* for two weeks, tryin' to lift spirits and contributing free legal services to the families. Some sad, tragic shit," Custis said somberly.

"You've convinced me," Liz told him.

"Me, too," Mason agreed, and everybody laughed.

As soon as he could, Mason pulled Custis aside and asked about the call. "So you know Deion? Really? How come you've never brought it up before now?" He dropped a chip on the floor and stooped to retrieve it. "How'd you do that?" he asked, tossing the chip toward an ashtray and missing.

Custis's eyes were red. "I know my cousin in Atlanta, Deion *Saunders*," he chuckled. " 'Course drunk white folks at a party usually don't catch the *u*, now do they? People go straight for the 'Deion' and hell, if they did pay attention, how many people know the difference? Sanders or Saunders. Deion and me, we've had that play for years, bread-and-butter, my man." He bumped his Corona against Mason's soft-drink can, a toast. "Custis has traveled all the routes before. Consider me your personal cartographer."

"Shit," Mason said. "Damn." He toasted again. "Slick, slick, slick." He laughed. "The maestro." He swallowed some Coke. "Reggie."

Before too long, Custis, Mason, Liz and the Contessa were in the bathroom with the pot, the women hell-yeah good to go when the dope was offered. Mason took only a small toke this time, not wanting to tumble off the revelry cliff and end up passed out before sunset. They made plans to eat dinner together, and Mason and Custis, with handshakes and promises to do it again tomorrow, shooed the party away, switching the CD to jazz, declining the golfers' invitation to catch a cab into the city and hunt for a strip club. They showered and dressed and met the women at a hotel restaurant, ordering wine and Bailey's with dessert. Together, they were the kind of voluble, high-flying foursome—large men, one black, with short-skirted blond women—that caused people to look twice or cheat their eyes over a menu and follow them to their table.

The hotel lobby was bygone elegant, in the vein of Batista's Cuba: marble, chandeliers, polished wood, three energetic bars, live music, well-dressed people dancing with dramatic dips and cha-cha-cha feet and a dark-skinned man with a full mustache rolling cigars beside the casino entrance. Liz wrapped her arm inside Mason's, and he escorted her to the center bar, the busiest of the three, where she ordered a martini that was impeccably made and served with a flourish. They tried the casino, roulette and blackjack, Custis doing his best to explain the smart strategies and Mason, sloshed and reckless, betting whatever felt good in his gut, somehow not losing his shirt.

Another trip to the room for pot and the night became spotty for Mason. He and Liz made it to the beach, a bedspread on the sand along a seawall, and he kissed a woman other than Allison, remembered it had been years and years, and it felt oddly good, the breeze and her mouth, the lights around them dots, low-hung bogus stars. They had sex, in the shadows, tucked into a hitch in the wall, close and restrained, the bedspread pulled over parts of them, people walking next to the ocean below where they were, the tame waves repeating the same sound over and over.

Mason passed out and woke up to several people quarreling by the pool, and he was lost, spinning, didn't know where he was, stoned and drunk, and he guessed maybe he was in his front yard, near the barn. Allison was there with him, he could feel her, and he closed his eyes. "Oh shit," he said, realizing it wasn't his wife, his stomach stinging, his thoughts haywire. The woman with him was different, and it wasn't the right neck or shoulder. The way she lay against him was foreign, too low on his chest. He dozed off again, sick and not sure of much.

The next time he came to life, a hotel security guard was crouching beside him, amused and kindly. "Hola, amigo. Good morning." The guard had a flashlight but was merciful with the beam, keeping it away from Mason's eyes. Liz was gone.

He revived enough to tell the man he was a guest at the hotel. He didn't seem to have a key or all his clothes, and he wasn't certain of his room number but knew how to get there. He recalled his own name and his wallet was still in his pants pocket, enough information to have him returned to their room after a walkie-talkie contact with the front desk. He slept until noon on gritty, sticky sheets, finally shaken awake by Custis.

"Rise and shine, Party King." The Wu-Tang Clan was on the box, harsh as ever. "Nice to have you conscious." Custis grinned.

"I feel awful. Uhhhh. Damn." He dragged a pillow across his face. "How're you so chipper?" he asked, the question muffled.

"Plenty of water, no hard liquor after midnight, food before bed. I'd suggest you consider dialing your party back to a steady six or seven instead of red-lining it at ten."

"Try zero. I'm done." He removed the pillow. "You're the fucker who kept at me. Kept pouring the poison down my throat and egging me on. Big of you to worry now."

"I apologize." Custis took a seat and began strapping on his sandals. "So'd you do okay with the lovely Liz?"

"As best as I remember, yeah." Mason sat up against the headboard. "You?"

"Not as fortunate, I'm afraid. It's one thing if you're a white woman to dance and kiss and talk shit, bump and grind; it's a different story to close the deal with Mr. Johnson. Black man's got two battles to fight with a white girl—it's tough enough to get any woman to sign up for a one-night stand, much less jump races."

"Really? Huh. Seemed to me, Mr. Mandela, the only fight you had was keeping the Contessa from screwing you in public. Hell, Custis, she was grabbing your crotch in the lobby."

"Trust me, it's not as easy as you might think. 'Course, I've still got six days to make my case." He finished with the sandals and stood. "But I'm happy for my buddy. Glad to see you catchin' fire again. Not standin' against the wall moping."

"Yeah." Mason swung his feet out of bed, sat on the edge with his head thumping. "It goes without saying it was bittersweet. And now I wish I hadn't fucked her." He put the heels of his hands against his temples and rubbed small circles. "I shouldn't have done it." He flopped back onto the mattress.

"You've been in the monastery for eight months," Custis said. "It's okay."

"To top it off, I didn't even think about birth control or AIDS or whatever."

Custis folded his arms. "I swear, it's like lookin' after a child. A handicapped child."

Mason didn't leave the room until almost five o'clock. Custis, Liz and the Contessa checked on him twice during the afternoon, Liz explaining she'd hated to leave him alone on the beach and had tried to wake him several times before she stumbled off, afraid of what might happen to her. Worried, she'd sent a man from the hotel to check on him. He ate some pasta and a bowl of soup for dinner and went to sleep early. He told the maid she could skip their room. He never showered.

A day's rest helped. Mason recovered, and they finished out the week with the remainder of the marijuana and more moderate amounts of alcohol. They took the women to watch the cocks fight but stayed for only one raw, to-the-death battle, all of them put off by the loser's missing eye and limp neck. Relying on Custis's recommendation—"trust me on this," he promised them—everyone agreed to stay in for an evening and watch *Cannonball Run*. Custis had discovered the movie at a video store in town, and he rented a VCR from the hotel. They closed the drapes, started the movie, smoked dope and ate a box of Whitman's candy, the sampler, high as Georgia pines, selecting a piece of chocolate on the lid diagram and then tracking it down in the maze of brown wrappers and yellow cardboard. "Hell, that's Sammy and Dean Martin," Mason exclaimed, walleyed and chewing the solid square with the messenger boy's image. "I hope they win. This is great, Custis. Excellent choice as always."

Mason had sex he could remember with Liz the night before she was due to fly home to North Carolina, and they walked on the beach afterward. His conscience hurt him as they were having an early breakfast the next morning, seated outside on a restaurant's veranda, and he told her his real name and what he did for a living. Solid black birds with yellow eyes and black legs and feet were flying around, hopping from table to table, diving into abandoned plates, skittering and flapping, extracting scraps and the crumbs of pastry sweets whenever they had the chance. The waiters would shout at the birds in Spanish and wave at them with white cloth napkins. There was only one other couple at the restaurant, older, sharing a newspaper.

"I hope you aren't cross with me," he said. "It was fun meeting you. I didn't think we'd be seeing each other as often as we did, or I would've been honest when we met. Or at least corrected Custis and told you my name."

"Not at all—it means a lot to me you wanted to tell me the truth and so forth." She tossed a toast corner to a bird and seven or eight others swooped in, screeching, fighting for a bite. Two waiters gave her an unhappy look. "So how much better or worse is the rest of the story? You know, are you married or engaged or like, I don't know, serious with someone?" She'd told him she was twice divorced—but amicable with both her former husbands. She had an eight-year-old son.

"My wife was killed in a car wreck last May. This is the first . . . you're the first woman I've given any thought since then. I have a daughter named Grace. She's the center of my universe. I probably ran up a two-hundred-dollar phone bill calling her."

"Oh my, I'm so sorry," she said. "Bless your heart." She was absently twisting an empty Sweet'N Low packet around her finger. "How terrible for you."

"Yeah." He watched the birds, kept his eyes off Liz. "Yeah, it is. But being here was nice. Thanks for taking such fine care of me. I've been really struggling."

He carried her heavy blue pleather suitcase to a cab at the hotel's entrance, and they exchanged numbers, kissed and hugged and talked about seeing each other down the road, although Mason wasn't sure he'd be up for it. Custis hit him with an empty beer can when he confessed he'd ratted them out to Liz, laughing and shaking his head and screaming "Judas" while Mason tried to justify breaking ranks.

"So you feelin' better?" Custis asked after he'd finished the needling. "You off the skids?"

"Not really. I'm improved, I guess. The problem is, I mean, well, spending time with these women, who were okay in their own way, pleasant and entertaining for sure, makes me realize how I'll never replace Allison. But I'm going to quit feeling sorry for myself—that's the important thing. Getting some perspective, stepping away from Stuart and a place so . . . so . . . saturated with Allison and me, yeah, that's been helpful. I'd like to think I can miss her and not have it ruin me." He blinked and looked away, gazed at the carpet. "I appreciate your going to all this trouble," he said. "It's great to know you can count on someone, a friend. I'm grateful, Cus. Thanks."

"My pleasure," Custis said quietly. He emptied potato chip crumbs from a bag straight into his mouth. "Let's hope our new girl-friends don't go broadcastin' everything they know, huh, Mason? I still can't believe you gave her the real goods."

"You owe me fifty bucks—I still hate the Wu-Tang Clan." He didn't look up.

Chapter Ten

When he returned to the farm, Mason set about anchoring his life again. He apologized to Sheila, the other lawyers in Stuart, his mom and his friends, telling them he was sorry he'd been so moody and unbearable. They all claimed to understand, assured him that grieving came with the territory, charitably lied and said they really hadn't noticed anything out of the way. He talked to Grace at the kitchen table and promised her they were over the worst of it and suggested they'd now just take care of each other double and enjoy what they were fortunate enough to still have. She took in his words, listening with her head slanted up at him, her mother blooded into her looks and mannerisms, her gangly legs. "Triple," she answered him, and seemed relieved, smiling and wiggly, happy to have her father reformed, done with his hangdog stares and late-night pacing.

A week later, he cashed a sick day and stayed home to pack Allison's clothes in cardboard boxes and haul them to the Martinsville Goodwill, keeping only her wedding gown, his favorite cocktail dress and several blouses Grace fancied. He gave her perfume and cosmetics to Grace, who wrapped the bottles, tubes and compacts elaborately and tucked them away in her dresser.

Following a cordial negotiation with the owner of the New York gallery that had dibs on her last piece, he drove the rhino to a Winston-Salem shop and had it framed, holding on to it for himself. He sorted through Allison's studio, carefully storing her books, sketches, paints, brushes, easel and canvases in the attic. He cried on and off while he did it, but he didn't flag or let himself become sidetracked. He and Grace invited about thirty neighbors and friends to stop by for a get-together, where they unveiled the framed painting along with the room's new pool table and a big-screen TV. They decided to leave the ratty sofa as it was and didn't disturb the hodgepodge of drops and smears on the floor where the easel had stood. Custis christened the table, taking the first shot.

Mason placed a photograph of Allison on his bureau, secured her jewelry in a box at the bank so it would be safe for their daughter, filed the estate paperwork at the clerk's office, and finally returned the calls of the lawyer who managed her trust. She'd left the stipend to him, now close to $275,000 a year, the change of beneficiary instruction dated three days before they'd wed. He took steps to transfer it to their daughter at his death, signing the forms and faxing the documents from his office the same morning he received them.

He dutifully sent Liz several photos from Puerto Rico and phoned her a time or two so he wouldn't feel like a cad, and they met for a meal in Greensboro, but removed from the perfect hothouse of a weeklong island romp—all pool drinks and pot and blank slates—their romance withered. He was relieved when she allowed in an e-mail as to how she'd begun seeing someone from Durham and it would be difficult for her to keep in contact. "Dumped your timid ass, didn't she?" Custis razzed him.

He visited Reverend Hunsicker and mended fences, told him he was still miffed and couldn't make sense of his predicament, but at least had come around to a general notion of deism, was back to Jefferson's armchair creator, a god who fashioned the universe and occasionally ventured from his lair long enough to add another ring to Saturn or adjust the thermostat a few degrees in the Amazon.

"That's a beginning," the preacher beamed. "Something's better than nothing."

"Yeah—I think I'm pointed in the right direction," Mason replied.

In the months ahead, he gradually became a man who learned to crutch his loss, compensating until the dreadful became routine, *his* normal, shit he just incorporated and dealt with, same as diabetics with their insulin or a car you always have to park on an incline so it can be push-started, making do.

Chapter Eleven

"Remember, we're probably only gonna have one crack at this," Jay Lane said before he walked through the door to the Patrick County Commonwealth's Attorney's Office. "Our first pitch needs to be a winner, Gerald. It'd be nice to snag this guy."

"Yep," Gerald Hooper said. It was the spring of 2003, the countryside starting to bloom in Stuart, the sun finally sticking around past suppertime.

The two men introduced themselves to Sheila, mentioned their appointment and were ushered in to see Mason without having to wait. Mason met them and shook hands and welcomed them. Custis was there too, perusing the *Enterprise,* and he made it a point to cross the room and greet both men, calling them "Mr. Lane" and "Mr. Hooper" even though they were younger than he. Everyone took a seat.

"Mr. Hunt, I'm here in my capacity as the governor's assistant chief of staff," Lane said without any arrogance or pretension. "Gerald works with me in Richmond."

"That's what Sheila told me when you phoned last week. You

didn't need to drive four hours to speak to me. Can't imagine what's so important."

Lane shifted in his chair. "Glad to do it; we felt our business was serious enough we should visit you personally."

"Okay," Mason said.

"As you know, this region is really hurting, your county in particular. You have the second-highest unemployment in the state, the textile and furniture industries are absolutely kaput, jobs are scarce, the economy's dead as a horseshoe nail. You've lost Tultex, DuPont, Spencer's, J.P. Stevens, Fieldcrest Mills—the list goes on forever."

"I hear they're plannin' layoffs at United Elastic," Custis added.

"It's bad, yeah," Mason said. "Truth be told, I don't know how people are going to make it. Ten years ago, I'd never have believed it. The shame is most people here will give you a good day's effort for their paycheck."

"Well, I'd like to cut to the chase," Lane said. "Are you familiar with the Tobacco Commission?"

"Generally. What I've read in the papers."

Hooper spoke up. "The Tobacco Commission, Mr. Hunt, is the entity tasked with disbursing the commonwealth's share of proceeds from the federal litigation with various cigarette manufacturers." His recitation was crisply delivered, no doubt polished before scores of newspaper reporters and subcommittee muckety-mucks. He sat erect in his chair. "The stated goal of the commission is to promote growth and development in communities such as yours. Over the next two decades, the commission will distribute four-point-one billion dollars to localities." He lingered on the "billion" part.

"I'm all for it," Mason said. "We can use it."

Lane looked at Hooper, then back at Mason. "We're here on behalf of the governor to ask you to serve as a board member. We feel you would be an excellent representative."

"Really?" Mason picked up a yellow pencil from his desk. "I wondered why you gentlemen were driving down here; we assumed it was about an extradition or something sensitive with the attorney general's office." He started tapping the pencil's eraser end against his thigh. "Huh. Why me? It's no secret I hate politics and politicians."

Lane laughed politely. "Your senator, Roscoe Reynolds, recommended you. You're extremely well thought of in this area, and the people here need a voice, an advocate, someone to honestly take care of them where this money is concerned. You have a fine record as a prosecutor, plus you've had a taste of Richmond. And it's precisely because this isn't a political job that we think you'd be a great asset."

"Listen—if there's big money, there'll be politics." Mason laid the pencil on his desk blotter. "In fact, in my opinion, they're one and the same."

"Sad but true to some extent," Lane agreed.

"What would I have to do?" Mason asked.

"Obviously, this isn't the local library board or the Lion's Club parade committee. It's a serious, heavy-duty commitment. It would involve twelve to fifteen meetings a year, the thorough review of hundreds of grant requests and frequent consultations with other members and staff. It's no picnic, and we can't pay you, but it would be a huge service to Patrick County and all of Southside."

"Essentially, you would be on the board of a multibillion-dollar corporation," Hooper explained. "A board that would make critical decisions affecting you and your community."

"Pretty cool gig," Custis remarked.

"You think?" Mason glanced at him.

"Maybe you could score us money for the office revitalization project we been discussin'—the Jacuzzi and wet bar for the law library and matching sharkskin suits for key jury trials." Custis grinned at the two bureaucrats.

Lane didn't seem upset by the joke. "If you'd like, Mr. Hunt, the governor would be willing to speak to you directly about this. Your participation is a priority for him."

"Why not, Mace?" Custis had turned serious. "You might do some good. Might help pull us out of the ditch."

Mason was quiet. He pursed his lips. "I'll sleep on it, if that's okay with everyone. I'll speak to my daughter, too. How about I give you an answer tomorrow?"

"I'll leave my card and my cell number," Lane said. "We appreciate your time and your allowing us to interrupt you."

"Jeez—they make it sound like you're Lee Iacocca or Commodore Vanderbilt or somethin'," Custis kidded him after the Richmonders were gone. "Evidently, the whole enterprise will collapse unless you sign on."

"It's their job to make people feel important. They're professional sycophants, a level above your common jester with bells on his shoes. Apparatchiks minus the vodka and tiny dacha."

"At least they seemed like good sports."

"Yes, they did," Mason answered.

The following afternoon, Mason phoned and accepted the governor's offer, became a board member of the Tobacco Indemnification and Community Revitalization Commission. He agreed to the appointment because his community was broke and suffering and on the brink of ruin, and he figured he could do as well as the next fellow when it came to showing up at a meeting to wrestle for pork-barrel dollars. He also took the job because he needed something to keep him sharp, a challenge. The business of a rural commonwealth's attorney's office tended to turn routine after a while, stale, and Mason was determined he would never fade into the ways of a sad-sack country lawyer, like the ham-and-eggers doing basic wills for seventy-five bucks a pop or poor old Wally Walters, Jr., harrumphing and hooking his suspenders, a blowhard with a fat tie and brown shoes who last opened a proper legal text during law school, waving his hands and spouting moldy truisms in court, his arguments so obvious an imbecile could see them coming. Mason didn't want to stagnate and peter out at the county line, and this would allow him to stay in circulation.

"Seems like it'll help me and could help the area," he informed Custis. "I'm making the right call, don't you think?"

"Does the ambitious local weatherman, angling for a network

promotion, don his slicker and broadcast live from the eye of the hurricane?"

Twelve days later, on a Tuesday, Ray Bass was standing beneath the metal awning at the Patrick County Commonwealth's Attorney's Office. "As much as I hate doin' this, we take it seriously," he cautioned his companion. "We've got one chance. We're gonna get one read, and that'll be it. Quick and sudden—that's the plan."

"Absolutely," replied Rick Minter. Out of habit, he pushed back his blazer and checked his holstered gun. Spring was sailing along by now, the yellow forsythia bushes past their peak, the hardwoods awakening, the bugs hatching from the dirt and beginning to grow active in the evenings. The crickets and cicadas were the most noticeable, shrill and steady, their sounds everywhere and always at a distance, encircling the outdoors like sheets of noise tacked to hill-tops and high, sturdy limbs.

Bass and Minter introduced themselves to Sheila, and because they weren't expected, didn't have an appointment, they had to wait in the lobby for nearly an hour before Mason returned from district court. Mason buzzed Sheila at her desk, and she walked with them to his office and showed them in. Mason stood and the men reached across his desk to shake hands. He'd met Minter before, but didn't know Ray Bass. Mason sat down first, then the two visitors, almost in unison. Bass didn't waste time addressing what was on his mind. "We appreciate your seein' us on such short notice. Agent Minter and I realize you have a busy schedule."

"Always happy to help when I can," Mason said. Minter and Bass were state police investigators; Mason had worked with Minter on a 1998 homicide, the stabbing of a man by his live-in girlfriend.

"We have some good news. A break on a case, an old one."

"Great, let's hear it." Mason noticed both men seemed uneasy and stiff, their shoulders squared off toward him.

"Remember a shooting years ago, back in the eighties, a boy by the name Wayne Thompson was murdered?"

Mason felt his skin tingle, juiced with adrenaline. "Yeah. Uh, yeah, I do." He crossed his legs.

"Well, we've turned up a witness—a Frederick Wright—who says the killer confessed to him. He says a man named Allen Roberts is the shooter. We checked, and this Roberts was a suspect originally, but nothing came of it. Roberts and the deceased were in an argument earlier in the evening, a dispute about a pool game as best we can tell."

Without meaning to, Mason gripped the edge of his desk. His collar and cuffs suddenly felt scratchy, binding him. "So this witness, this Wright fellow, so, uh, you believe he's reliable?"

"Passed a polygraph," Minter assured him. "I can send you a copy if you want it."

"Yeah. Please." Mason stopped pinching his desk. He put his hands in his pockets. "Is that it? A witness? And why, pray tell, does Mr. Roberts confess after all these years? What's his relationship with Wright?"

"They used to work together. Drinkin' buddies. Wright tells us they were sharin' a bottle and Roberts says he needs to get it off his chest. Admits he shot Wayne Thompson. Wright didn't know what he should do, so he told his brother-in-law, who's a deputy in Floyd. The brother-in-law contacted us."

"I'm not sure how strong a case we can build from a drunk's ramblings. Hell, maybe he did say it, just flapping his gums. Or maybe your witness misunderstood or has some grudge. Polygraph or not, I'd need more. Over and above all that, I know Allen Roberts pretty well—it's going to be a tough sell for you to convince me he's a killer."

"I agree," Minter said. "A good lawyer'd clean our clocks." He barely paused, but changed the set of his head. "'Course, we got the gun. We have the murder weapon. A thirty-eight. Lab is positive on the match. Found it at Roberts's house." Minter was short and skinny. His hands were interlocked at his belt buckle, his black shoes were planted on the floor. He seemed stock-still.

Mason eased his chair backward, rolling on brass casters and speaking at the same time. "That's impossible . . . impossible to, uh, imagine, but lucky, I guess. A real break, it being so many years ago. The shooting. Incredible you'd find the gun after so long."

Reaching inside his coat, Bass produced a report from the Division of Forensic Science, placed it on the desk and gave it a small push. "No doubt we have the pistol," he said. The paper hung on the wood and didn't slide very far.

Mason left the report alone. "So you want me to indict Allen Roberts?"

"Well, we think we're pretty close—a confession to a disinterested witness and the gun."

"What's Allen say about this?" Mason asked. "Have you interviewed him?"

"Denies it. We talked to him yesterday. Won't give an inch." The way Bass was sitting, Mason could see his silver badge. It was attached to his belt, above the hip. "Says what he said in 1984—claims he ain't involved."

"I see," Mason mumbled. He was thinking of the Burger King Dumpster, the muted, unremarkable sound the cylinder and bag made when they landed, the kid taking a smoke break.

"Not to step on toes," Minter said, "but your brother was a suspect, too, wasn't he? I saw where Danny Owen had questioned him."

A flatbed truck passed by the window and took Mason's attention. After it cleared, he saw Roy Lee McAlexander hobbling from the grocery store to his house, a translucent plastic sack in each hand. Probably toting beer home to get snockered. "He was. But he was with me and lots of other people. For what it's worth, I was there for his interview. He—" Mason was seized by a thought that caused him to break off and bring a finger to his temple and fisheye both cops. "He didn't have anything to do with it." Every word stuck on the roof of his mouth as if it were coated in flour. He hoped his face and neck weren't mottled.

Bass and Minter didn't reply right away. They reminded Mason of the summer toads at the farm, always biding their time beneath a floodlight or brightened transom, vigilant brown lumps watching . . . watching . . . watching . . . watching, waiting for a gnat or moth to dip too deep and become food for a sticky, darting tongue. The three men sat there in a fierce silence—at least a full minute—until Minter spoke. "You okay takin' on the case—any conflicts or doubts?" His voice was carefully formal. Stilted.

"I'll do just fine. Thanks for asking. I might talk to Allen myself. Have the sheriff bring him in."

"I don't think he'll give you anything new."

Mason shrugged. "Just the same, it wouldn't hurt to see if he'll talk to us. Never know what might come of it." He glanced out his window again. Roy Lee was gone. "So what did Allen say after you told him you'd located the gun there? Was he present when you found it?"

"Claimed he'd never seen it," Bass answered. "He wasn't at home when we arrived and executed the warrant, so we served it on his wife." Bass was tracing the bright outline of his badge with his index finger as he spoke.

"Where exactly was this gun?" Mason asked.

"Buried beside an oak tree."

"Allen lives on ten, fifteen acres, right? And you knew to dig at exactly this spot because . . . ?"

"Because that's what Roberts told our witness," Minter said. "Roberts told Frederick Wright where the gun was located and, lo and behold, that's where we found it. Pretty powerful stuff, huh?"

"Why would anyone bury a murder weapon in their own back-yard and then tell a drinking buddy where it was?" Mason asked. "There's something screwy here."

"Well, like I said, we have ourselves a believable witness, a lie-detector test, the weapon which done the shootin' and a confession. You're the lawyer, but I like our odds." Minter rocked forward. "Why *wouldn't* you hide the gun on your own place, where nobody but you has access and you can keep watch?"

"Why wouldn't you throw it in Smith Mountain Lake or bury it on someone else's property?" Mason asked.

"Who's to say, huh?" Bass stuck Mason with a tight, prickly smile.

Mason picked up a legal pad and wrote Roberts's name across the top along with the words "gun" and "confession." He stared at the pad and pretended to consider the facts he'd been given. He faked concentration and made a whistling sound, almost a hiss, air pushed through his teeth and dry lips. "Definitely worth taking a look at," he said, still focusing on the pad. "Definitely." He mustered enough grit and composure to raise his eyes and face the cops. "I didn't mean to harangue you guys—just playing the devil's advocate. Better to find the problem here than at trial. I need to have all the bases covered before I charge someone with murder, but it seems like you've done your homework."

"I understand," Minter said.

"Send me everything you've got. I'll have the sheriff take another pass, and we'll go from there."

"Affirmative," Bass said, already rising. "Thanks for seein' us."

"Fuck," Mason muttered after he heard the men speak to Sheila and knew they'd departed. "Damn." He ran his hands through his hair, stopping at his crown, and sank into his seat with his palms pressing against his skull. "Damn." He was utterly rattled, feverish, sick all over, poisoned by the ambush, dizzy, his lungs choked with pitch, snakes squirming in his guts. He took his hands down, noticed they were trembling. "Thank you, Gates," he said aloud. "You piece of shit."

Outside, as they were striding toward their gray Ford, Bass caught Rick Minter with a sidelong glance. "Gee," he said, his mouth pointed at the ground, acting nonchalant for the benefit of anyone watching. "Maybe there's somethin' to this. He looked like we'd slapped him upside the head, and then it took dynamite to get him to move on a slam-dunk case." Bass kept walking, his partner close by. "Let's have the tape transcribed soon as we can." He patted his blazer's breast pocket. "Man, I hope we got everything, especially the 'impossible' part."

The following morning, Sheriff David Hubbard and Investigator Roger Wilson met with Mason in the sheriff's private office. Across the hall, Allen Roberts was by himself in a sparsely furnished room, the door shut, a half-empty soft drink beside him. At Mason's request, Wilson had telephoned Agent Bass and received several faxed pages and an overview of the murder case against Roberts.

"He ain't admitting to it," the sheriff informed Mason. "We've been at it for an hour. He claims he doesn't know anything about the gun and didn't shoot nobody. Roger's given him a pretty thorough talkin'-to."

"He's not gonna change his story," Wilson said, frowning. "I mean, you know, it is what it is." He was gray-headed, wearing a maroon windbreaker. Above him, on the wall, was a framed picture of the entire police force and staff from the year 1999, taken on the courthouse portico. "I gotta say, Mason, I'm a little surprised, what with the kinda person Allen is. We were in school together; I've known him all my life. He just don't seem like the type."

"You and the state police been on this for a while?" the sheriff inquired. He was a tall, strong man with a black mustache, a cattle farmer from off the Meadows of Dan mountain. Shrewd and unflappable, he rarely raised his voice and was popular with his employees.

"I heard about it yesterday for the first time," Mason said.

"Kinda strange they didn't include us or give us a courtesy call," the sheriff mused.

"Yeah," Mason agreed. "You guys mind if I talk to him?"

"Be my guest," Wilson said. "You want us to be with you?"

"No need."

"Tape recorder's in there—on the table—and we Mirandized him soon as he got here."

"Can't say I ever recall you questionin' a suspect," the sheriff remarked. "Isn't that a little tricky—what if he admits somethin' to you? You'd be in a fix, wouldn't you? You couldn't prosecute him if you were a witness, right?"

"We'll cross that bridge if we come to it," Mason told him. "Roger's probably correct—he's not going to change his story. I just want to get a feel for this, see how he's reacting."

When Mason opened the door, Allen Roberts was smoking a cigarette and his knee was firing up and down like a sewing-machine needle, rapid and kinetic. He was dressed in bibbed overalls and a blue shirt, weathered boots splattered with specks of white. He'd worked at the same job for over twenty years, hanging Sheetrock for Clark Brothers Construction. Seeing Mason, he stubbed out his cigarette in a thick glass ashtray already filled with butts. "Hey, Mason," he said.

"Allen," Mason said quietly. He checked to make sure the recorder wasn't running. "Sorry to see you under these circumstances." As a precaution, he removed the cassette from the machine and laid it on the table.

"Mason, I swear to you on my mama's grave I didn't do this," he blurted. He took a fresh Camel from a pack in the chest pocket of his bibs. He couldn't get the first paper match to strike and had to use a second one to light his cigarette. He inhaled and blew out shaky smoke. "I know it looks bad, but damn, Mason, you know me. This is some kinda crazy nightmare."

"It would have to be," Mason said. He bent forward so both his palms were flat on the table, his arms rigid and bearing his weight. "Look at me." He said it gently, without any suggestion of malice or command.

Roberts tried, but his eyes were waterbugging all over the place.

"I know you didn't do this, okay? Don't worry. Go home and kiss your wife and drive to the store and punch the clock. As long as I'm the commonwealth's attorney, you will never be charged. Do all you can not to worry. You're innocent. You have my word nothing will happen to you. My firm oath." Mason pinned the man with a stare, honed, intense, sincere. "You hear me, Allen?"

"I don't . . . This ain't some kinda confusion, is it, you tryin' to get over on me?"

"Nope. You need to walk out of here and keep your mouth shut." Mason straightened up.

"I don't understand, Mason. This don't make sense. That ain't my gun, and I damn sure didn't bury it under no tree and I didn't kill Wayne. I never seen him after he left the Old Dominion. As for this Fred Wright, he showed up for a few days on a job we was doin' over in Ararat, and I had one beer with him in Mount Airy. He was gone the next week, and I sure as hell didn't tell him I killed a man."

Roberts was flying through the words, the cig wasting in the ashtray, forgotten. "Back when this first happened, my ex–old lady done told the cops I was with her, but now I'm afraid she'll switch her story 'cause she's pissed at me over the divorce. There goes my alibi. Have y'all found her yet? Last I heard, she was stayin' with her mom in Yanceyville. Did they keep a copy of her statement—maybe you can find it. Danny Owen was the police who talked to us."

"There's no need. I believe you. This is a terrible mistake." Mason smiled. "Come on—I'll walk you to your car."

"You sure? I . . . I . . . I don't know how the pistol—"

Mason shoved out an upturned hand—final, suffocating, brooking nothing—to cut him off. "Judge Richardson used to tell people you don't need to run to catch a streetcar you're already riding. You're on the streetcar, Allen. This is finished for you. I'm sorry we've scared you to death, sorry the system has failed you. Forget about this and put it behind you."

"Honest? You're positive?"

"Positive." Mason kept his hand in the air. "One other point: don't speak to the police anymore. If they come to see you again, you simply say, 'I don't want to talk to you. I want a lawyer.' That's the rule, no matter what they promise or what they threaten." He took down his hand. "Don't even get started with them. Slam the door. Hang up the phone. You'll only get burned by answering their questions. That includes the cops here in Stuart as well."

"Believe me, I've learned my lesson. I ain't makin' a peep next time they come around."

"You understand you don't have to talk with them about anything. Not the crime, not the gun, not even our conversation right now. Just refuse and request a lawyer. We clear?"

"Yeah. Keep my mouth shut and right off the bat say I want me a lawyer."

"Exactly."

"So I can go?" Roberts asked tentatively. "Me and you's okay with each other?"

"You're free to leave. We're done."

Roberts came around the table, a burly man with a full beard and hands damaged by decades of hammers and drywall compound, and he hugged Mason, crying and sobbing and wiping his eyes and nose with a balled red bandanna he pulled from his back pocket. "Thank you, Mason. Thank you. Lord in heaven, thank you. I got me two kids to feed. Two boys. I thought I was a goner. You're a good man."

"Not really," Mason said. "But I appreciate your saying so."

That night, Mason made a mess of dinner, scorching the mashed potatoes so they tasted like he'd mixed in the bottom of the metal pot, and he and Grace had a round about her school dance and her sixteen-year-old "boyfriend." She called her dad Hitler and barricaded herself in her room and was still sullen the next morning, mulling through breakfast, barely deigning to speak. After she'd stalked off to the bus, Mason called his mother for advice, and she promised to drop by and lend a hand. "It's only a phase," she assured him.

Before leaving home, he sat on the porch and gazed out over the pasture, watching the newborn sun scale the sky, listening to the seasonal birds celebrate their return, but he missed his wife and was pained by his loneliness, the magic spooked from his sanctuary. Forty acres and not another soul to be found. He fretted about how much he'd given away, how much truth the cops had assayed from his surprise and stumbling and clumsy playacting. Somehow, without tipping his intentions, he needed to communicate with Gates, and he had to do it quickly. Feeling claustrophobic and cramped, he drove to Stuart with the car windows rolled down, already fatigued, running on four hours of fitful, sketchy sleep and three cups of coffee, the last one black with grounds in almost every swallow.

When he arrived at work, Mason discovered Custis was busy in juvenile court, already gone. Around noon, after three impatient, wasted hours, Mason finally heard him next door and went into his office. John Coltrane was on the wall, along with framed degrees

and a picture of Custis wielding a gavel at a town council meeting. He was still carrying his files under an arm, standing beside his desk, reading pink phone slips.

"Mace, hey. Check this out: Judge gave our boy Benny Watson twelve months for assaultin' his wife. If a man ever had it comin', it was Benny. You shoulda seen the fucker when they dropped the twelve on him. Priceless. It's why I love my job."

"I'm glad it—"

"I was thinkin' maybe we could implement some kind of recognition system for kick-ass victories, something along the lines of the Ohio State football team, you know, where you get a sticker for your helmet, a buckeye for every exceptional game. We'd give each other rewards to wear on our lapels—gold stars or justice scales or a set of miniature cell bars or perhaps exclamation points. Might help morale. I know I'd go the extra mile." Custis did his best to appear sincere.

"As successful as we are, I'm sure we'd use up our lapels in no time at all and have to go with auxiliary sashes or chevrons."

"Killjoy," Custis said with mock disappointment.

"I need to talk to you about grand jury," Mason stated with a new, different voice, pared down and serious. He folded his arms into his chest. "How come there's a first-degree murder indictment for Allen Roberts on my desk?"

" 'Cause I put it there," Custis answered.

"Since when did you start preparing indictments in my cases?" Mason was testy.

"Since always. I was only tryin' to help. The state police called while you were gone yesterday, about four thirty, and asked me to draft it for you so we could have it done for June term. Agent Bass was the dude's name. Said to check with you, but you were up to speed. Sounds like it's a pretty righteous case from what he told—"

Mason interrupted. "So now we're taking our marching orders from the state police?"

Custis clenched his face. "Damn, Mace, what's in your craw? Huh? The cops called and asked, and seein' as how we're the good guys and they're the good guys and we work together I attempted to be accommodating. It's not like I tried to hide it or sneak it in—the

cop said you were ready to go, and I did it so you wouldn't have to. Assistin', like my job title suggests. I don't give a damn if you submit it or toss it in the trash." He glared at Mason.

"Exactly what did Bass tell you?"

Custis set down his files. "Said we have a confession and the gun and a motive. From what I gathered it was Law School 101, ripe fruit ready for the pickin'. He led me to believe you were on board."

"Well, I'm not. There's more to it." Mason dropped his arms.

"Hey, cool, whatever. I just work here." Custis was still perturbed.

"So we won't be taking it to the grand jury. Not in June. Not ever. We on the same page?"

"Same page, same chapter, same book, same library, same universe," Custis answered.

"Good."

"No need to be so damn hateful about it," Custis said, more hurt than angry.

"Sorry." Mason pivoted and left the room, returned to his own office and shut the door. A few minutes later he went back and apologized to Custis again. "I shouldn't have snapped at you," he told his friend.

"No problem." Custis's suit jacket was draped over the highest peg of a wooden hat rack. His cuffs were unbuttoned, his sleeves rolled up. "What's goin' on? Why're you so torn outta the frame 'bout this?"

"No reason in particular—bad couple days, that's all. It's not really connected to the murder case. Things in general could be better, I guess. I'm fine."

"You sure? You seem awfully tense."

Mason flicked his hands, grimaced. "You know, trying to deal with an eighth-grade girl, not sleeping worth a darn, worrying about work."

"Can't be easy rearin' a chap by yourself. Especially when they start thinkin' they know more than you."

"True."

"Hey, here's an idea." Custis maneuvered a foot onto the corner of his desk. "I've got ten pounds of top-notch ribs—I'm talkin' primo eatin', first-class—I brought home from Memphis last weekend. I was savin' them for me and Inez, planning a big event, but I'm sure she wouldn't mind if we sampled a few early. I'll chop some slaw, cook my special baked beans, have you come by and fill you up. Nothing like a good meal and cold beer to float your spirits."

Mason smiled. "I appreciate it, but—"

"Before you blow me off, let me also mention I have a little Puerto Rican panacea I imported from Tennessee as well. Follow what I'm sayin'? Seemed to cure your woes last time you were in the dumps."

"Ah. Well, that was a singular experience for me." Mason checked behind him to make certain no one was listening. "I'm afraid Rasta Mason has retired his dreads."

Custis chuckled. His other foot joined the one already on his desk. "Your choice to make. It'd be strictly a medicinal use, my man. A remedy for what ails you. I got the major entertainment goods ready, too. My own mix CD, with War's "Spill the Wine" and Renaissance man William Shatner lettin' it loose on "Lucy in the Sky with Diamonds." A gem of a Cypress Hill cut. Plus I found *Bride of Frankenstein* for a dollar at the video store. I'll bet the ranch ninety or so minutes of under-the-influence, black-and-white mad science will put you in a far different mood—can't beat sparks flying in the lab and all those crazy sets."

"Nope. Not for me, although I will have to admit San Juan was big fun. Still, I'd just as soon you don't ever mention the topic again." Mason was firm but there was no scold in his words. "I'm grateful for the food offer. Thanks."

"You don't need to be backsliding on me. You're done with the blues, okay? I can't afford another trip to resurrect you."

"I'm fine," Mason promised him. "I shouldn't have jumped down your throat about the case."

"Yeah." Custis smiled. "Don't do it again."

Mason made it to Sheila's desk before he stopped and headed back to Custis's office for the third time in ten minutes. He tapped on the door and invited him to lunch, offering to pay. They ate at the

Coffee Break, underneath the antique posters for Flatt and Scruggs and Chet Atkins and the autographed fender of Michael Waltrip's race car, suspended from the ceiling. Custis ordered three hot dogs, double potatoes and a diet soda. Mason had a chicken salad sand-wich he didn't finish. When the booth behind them emptied and the customers were at the cash register, Mason removed a blank check from his wallet and wrote it to the order of Custis Norman in the amount of fifty dollars. On the memo line, he printed "Retainer." He placed the check beside Custis's napkin.

"What are you doin'?" Custis stopped chewing and tucked his chin. "Why did you write me a check for fifty bucks? We bein' charged off the tourist menu or something?"

"Pick it up, please."

Custis took the check. "Okay."

"That's a retainer. I'm hiring you to be my lawyer—"

"You don't have to pay me to do legal work for you," Custis inter-rupted. He was offended. "What's wrong with you? *Hiring* me? What could you possibly want me to do?"

Mason hunched over the Formica table and squeezed Custis's wrist. "Listen to me. For once, be quiet and listen. I'm hiring you as my lawyer. I'm in the middle of a nasty legal situation, and I think you might've just inadvertently become a witness against me."

Custis pulled his wrist free. He pushed his plate to the side and cocked his ear. "Sorry. I'm lost."

"Here's everything you need to know and everything I can tell you: This Allen Roberts case isn't about Allen. It's a smoke screen. I know for a fact Allen didn't shoot Wayne. There are people, most notably these pricks Bass and Minter, who have it in for me. I'm ninety-nine percent sure this whole Roberts investigation is a sham, a test. A trap of sorts." Mason was whispering, hoarse. "So now you're my lawyer, okay? You and I are going to walk up the street and cash your check at the bank and from here on out we'll have attorney-client privilege."

"I don't need no check to go to the mat for you, Mace. You oughta know that by now. We've been in too many foxholes too many times. Been through too much."

188 • MARTIN CLARK

"I understand. And I believe you. Just the same, this will make it easier for us both if push comes to shove down the road."

"Your call. If you think we need to, then off we go to the bank." Custis cupped his hand over his mouth. A gold ring cut into his dark skin. "But I'm not up to speed here. I'm still fuzzy. Why would the state police be fuckin' with you? Have you done somethin'?" He removed his hand and located his water glass. He thumped free an ice cube and began crunching it, the bulge switching from cheek to cheek.

"I didn't shoot Wayne Thompson, if that's what you're asking. Obviously that's not the problem." Lois the waitress breezed by with a coffeepot and Mason hesitated. "Neither did Allen Roberts. He's totally innocent."

"Okay."

"You know my worthless brother was a suspect in the Thompson shooting," Mason said cryptically. He stopped talking and mashed his sandwich with the flat side of a butter knife. "My brother is now very angry with me." He fussed with the knife and sandwich some more. "I was his alibi for certain parts of the evening." Another emphatic, pointed pause, the dull tip of the knife piercing the bread and all the way to the plate by now. "I'm not able to say much more, but I hope the fog's lifting a bit."

"Shit." Custis was rubbing and squeezing his chin between his thumb and forefinger. He appeared distressed. "Yeah, I'm gettin' closer, but I'm not sure I'm there yet."

"I've given this a lot of thought, and here's the plan if you're agreeable. You need to call Agent Bass, tell him you've drafted the indictment, conferred with me and we're ready to charge Allen. Also inform him he'll have to be here for June grand jury to present the bill and testify. We'll run our own little experiment. You watch and see—there's not a chance he'll go in front of that jury and recite his bullshit under oath. You watch. We'll call his bluff."

"You told me no less than an hour ago we weren't gonna go after Roberts. Not ever."

"I said we wouldn't indict him," Mason replied. "I still don't think we will. I'll give you the script for the call while we're walking to the bank."

As soon as Mason and Custis returned to work, they went into Mason's office, closed the door and had Sheila ring Agent Bass. They were squeezed side by side between a desk and a credenza, the receiver not flush against Custis's ear so Mason could eavesdrop on the conversation.

"Agent Bass," Custis said when he picked up, "Custis Norman here, from Stuart. Afternoon to you. We spoke the other day about an indictment in the Roberts case. First-degree murder of Wayne Thompson."

"Yessir," Bass said, his voice bland, professional.

"I spoke to Mason and he's good to go, very much invested in your case. We both agree we should move on it next grand jury, in June."

"Okay. So you talked to Mr. Hunt and he definitely wants to proceed?" He labored on the last word, unable to hide his astonishment.

"Absolutely. Mason and I went over it together and we had the sheriff bring Roberts by for tea and crumpets and a little visit. Mason's convinced you guys have the right man."

"Okay, well, I'm glad he's come around. He seemed a little iffy when we saw him earlier in the week. So he personally approved this?"

"Yeah. Mason can be cautious. That's his style. He'll prod and poke and put you on the spot, but once he's sold on the facts and has analyzed every speck of evidence, he's like a junkyard dog."

"So, what, you guys are going to indict? June?"

"Yeah, just like you wanted—that's why I'm calling. We need you or your partner to present this to the grand jury. How about you be here around nine thirty on the fifth, and we'll send you in first and have you back to Salem before they even miss you." Custis widened the gap between the receiver and his ear.

"Well, uh, I guess, yeah, I think we can be there. Let me check and call you right back. I'm thinking we might already be scheduled to be somewhere else . . . already subpoenaed."

"Can you let me know kinda quick?" Custis asked. "I realize it's just April, but we don't need anyone fumblin' the ball in a murder case."

"Sure. We'll do our best."

Custis hung up the phone. "No way he's coming, Mason. Fucker was crawfishin' on me to beat the band."

"He certainly doesn't seem so enthusiastic all of a sudden." Mason leaned against the credenza.

"So where does this leave you? I'm not likin' the vibe I'm gettin', and the way I'm thinking this thing is traveling."

Mason was preoccupied, gazing down at the bottom of a rickety file cabinet, the last drawer of which was pitted and dinged, marred by the first hints of rust. "Still in a jam," he said distantly, "but at least I know who my enemies are and how this was supposed to operate."

Two hours later, Bass's supervisor called and requested that Custis delay the indictment and not submit it, told him neither of the agents would be available and, more important, there had been a "reevaluation" of several critical factors in the investigation. "So let us know," Custis told him. "Far as we can tell on this end, we're on solid ground and eager to take this one to trial."

Chapter Twelve

The Saturday morning after the cops came to Stuart, Mason cornered Grace and attempted to make her answer him with more than a grunt or sarcastic frown or sullen, dismissive snort. Having wandered out of bed around ten thirty, she was watching the big-screen in the room where her mother used to paint and was still wearing pajama bottoms and a man's plaid flannel shirt that evidently had some connection to her be-all-and-end-all sweetheart.

"What?" she said irritably when Mason straight-armed the control at the TV and the sound fell off incrementally. "There's a mute button, you know," she remarked. "So you don't have to readjust it to where you want it."

"I appreciate the tip—been feeling the first twinges of carpal tunnel lately." He managed to sound jovial. "I've come to brighten your life," he said, silly and clownish, keeping several days of temper under rein.

"Wow."

"I thought, given the gorgeous weather, you might like to spend the morning with me. We could go to Dobyns and try a little trout fishing, then visit your grandmother's for a late lunch. I could use the break, too. Work's been merciless." He made a cast with an imaginary rod and cranked an invisible reel handle. "I haven't so much as wet a line since we moved here, and your uncle and I used to love the streams in the spring of the year. Any interest?"

"Ick. No. Why would I want to be stuck in the middle of nowhere and catch slimy fish?"

"Next plan: Let's drive to Stuart and buy a cool kite and take it to DeHart Park. Pack a picnic."

She didn't even answer. She watched silent TV.

"Okay, last option: I'll take you and a girlfriend of your choosing, anyone but the obnoxious Wray kid whose parents I can't stand, to Hanes Mall in Winston and you can buy overpriced, faddish clothes and act like you're older and hipper than you actually are. Maybe a movie, maybe Chili's for dinner."

"Really?"

"Yep. A reward for your good nature and delightful attitude as of late." He smiled crookedly, ironically. "I prefer the fishing or kite flying, of course, since at the end of the day we'd have this huge PAX channel moment, a touching father-daughter understanding where everything would be heartwarming and shot through a colored filter. We'd be beside a fantastic yellow stream or a shimmering red lake and soothing classical music would be playing as the camera panned in. I'd tell you how much I love you, and you'd puckishly punch me on the shoulder. Drop some cuddly line while we're frying the fish over a campfire."

"If we go, will you not hover and not be totally nosy and *promise* not to embarrass me?" She was growing excited.

"I'll do my absolute best."

She wound up inviting two of her friends, and Mason drove the three chattering teenagers to the mall. The girls all rode together in the backseat and huddled and giggled and tried on clothes at the Gap and Abercrombie & Fitch and did all they could to keep Mason at a leper's distance. Outside the discount cinema, they begged, wheedled and whined and repeated "pleeeez, Mr. Hunt" and "pleeeez, Dad" like it was some powerful, sacred chant when he considered whether he ought to allow them to see *Queen of the*

Damned. He didn't yield, however, and they bought tickets to *Ice Age*. Mason sat in the last row and the girls in a far right corner close to the screen.

He was pleased to have the respite and the dark, and he sipped a fountain cola and picked at a tub of oily popcorn, concentrating on his complications with the police. Midway through the movie, he looked over the rows of rounded seat tops toward the front of the theater and found his child's silhouette, and it made him mad as hell, livid, thinking about what was happening to him and what a weak, craven brother he was tethered to. The dim theater put him in mind of Richmond and tending to Grace during the early-morning hours, when her nursery was illuminated only by a gentle night-light and the streets and city were peaceful, particles of the baby's sweet powder glinting in the gray glow after he changed her. "I will kill Gates Hunt before I let my daughter lose another parent," he vowed, mouthing the words as Sid the Sloth hammed it up on the screen.

When Mason called Sadie Grace early Sunday and pitched a trip to visit Gates, she protested that she didn't want to miss church and drive four hours to Powhatan. "Preacher Logan from Greensboro is coming, and he always has a good message. I just hate to miss it, and I saw Gates a week ago."

"Well, I haven't been in a while. Grace is spending the day with the Anderson kids, and I'd certainly appreciate the company."

"Oh, Mason," she sighed.

"I'll buy you lunch and you can smoke in the car," he offered.

"Honey, you know I'd love to spend time with you, and you know I love your brother as much as a mother can, but to tell the truth, I'm not up for listenin' to him fuss and say ugly things about us. It's the same old song, same old accusations, same old crazy junk. I go see him faithfully, but it's kinda like the way I go to the doctor for my flu shot. He sits there all puffed up, and he's got more gripes than Carter's got liver pills. I'm right tired of it."

"I'm not disagreeing with you, but maybe if we both go it would be better."

"I know y'all are feudin', so why now? Can't we wait till next Sunday? Give me a little more warnin'?"

"Next week is tough for me, and I've got Grace situated today. I want you to go *because* Gates and I haven't been on the best of terms lately. Your being there will help, I think."

Sadie Grace relented, of course, her mother's conscience captured twice, first by Mason's hopeful entreaty and then by the guilt of avoiding a trip to see her imprisoned son, no matter how rude and undeserving he was. "I can't say no" was how she phrased it, none too thrilled about the prospect.

During the trip to the penitentiary, they listened to an oldies station and a full hour of a preacher on the FM band, a man whose purified, dulcet voice was tinged with accessibility and soft-pedaled seduction. Mason's relationship with his mother was unassailable and deeply rooted but starting to blur. They'd cycled through the stark divisions between parent and child and begun the pivot at which Mason would watch over *her* and remind her she shouldn't do this or that and telephone to make sure she'd remembered the dead bolt at night and slip her cash she was far too proud to request regardless of her needs. Driving together, they didn't have very much conversation, but that was okay with Mason, a point of pride actually, how well he and his mother could abide silence, their comfort during the lags and frequent quiet spells. They felt at ease when nothing was being said, trusted each other's nature, and didn't prattle on for the sake of talking or chigger from topic to topic because they thought it necessary to always keep balls in the air. They'd ridden without a word for fifty miles when Mason pulled into the prison lot and said, "Thanks so much for doing this."

Not surprisingly, it took longer than usual for the guards to produce Gates in the visiting area, the delay, Mason surmised, the result of a scramble to get him wired, cue his handlers and reiterate his instructions. He was fraudulently upbeat when he appeared, smiling and pumping Mason's hand, acting delighted to see his brother. Mason noticed he twisted his torso before he embraced their mother, gave her mostly shoulder and ribs, not risking a complete hug.

"What a super surprise," he gushed. "My two favorite people. You didn't have to drive down here on such a pretty Sunday."

Sadie Grace was immediately suspicious, and it showed in her posture and how she arranged herself in her chair, quickly on guard, her purse deep in her lap, her hands defensively clutching its strap. "I'm glad you're so chipper, Gates," she said. "It's nice to see you happy."

"Oh yeah. Hey, why not, huh? I can't believe you brought Mason, too. How long's it been, brother?"

"Several months," Mason replied. "I'm relieved you're not still angry with me. I was a little afraid to come after you were so mad at me and threatened to . . . to . . . you know, do whatever it took to cause me problems because I couldn't get your sentence reduced or help you with court."

"I'm not sure I remember exactly what you're talkin' about but, heck, whatever it was, it's behind us. We'll always be brothers, me and you. Sometimes I probably say crap I shouldn't to you and Mom both. It's bad here, difficult to keep your head screwed on." Gates was prison-pallid, underbelly white, and he was near enough for Mason to smell him; Mason well knew the scent, a dank, vinegary, rotting odor that infested the convicts' skin and came from inside them, couldn't be washed off by the occasional communal shower and two-bit soap.

"How're your classes?" Sadie Grace asked. Gates was a credit or two shy of a community college degree.

"Almost there, almost done," he told her. He'd taken a seat. An institutional metal table that ran the length of the room separated him from Sadie Grace and Mason. Other families visited nearby.

"Good for you," she said, still wary, still awaiting the inevitable ambush.

Prison cooks down time for its inhabitants, boils it away to concentrate, so the long-termers always seem hyper and rushed, their speech and habits accelerated, jumbled, telltale. They can't wait. Can't wait. Hurry. Press. Squirm. Even out of the joint, they eat and talk and live like a clock's about to expire, the curtain drop. Jumpy, scrambled, hasty, anxious. Gates couldn't curb his convict's instincts, couldn't stick with the drill, had to make his pitch *now* no matter what, no matter how forced or clumsy. "Mom, uh, you mind if I speak to Mason in private for a sec? It's good to see you, sure is, but man, it's been so long since I saw my favorite little brother. I'm just so tickled he's here, and, well, maybe, uh, we could talk about some personal stuff if we were alone. Not that I don't appreciate you and your sacrifices. You are one more wonderful mom."

Sadie Grace didn't bother to quiz him or attempt to unravel his motives. She patted his hand, stood, smoothed the front of her blouse and said—without inflection—"Bye, son." She showed Mason a chilly look and tersely informed him she'd be in the car.

Before she'd even reached the officer at the steel door to the visiting area, Gates ducked in toward his brother. "Damn, Mason, I'm glad you came." He dropped his voice confidentially. "Listen, the, uh, the cops were here like last week and they were askin' about that thing back in the eighties, you know, the deal on Russell Creek Road." He bored in closer, almost touching Mason's face.

"Huh? Say what? What're you talking about?" Mason gestured broadly with his hands for the benefit of any video surveillance. "Russell Creek?" He leaned away from his brother's smell.

Gates remained hunched over the table, his voice almost a hiss. "Russell Creek, in Stuart. 1984, Mason. You and me."

"I'm lost," Mason said calmly. "Slow down and just tell me what it is you want me to know."

"The initials 'W.T.' mean anything to you?"

"Uh, Wu-Tang Clan?" It was the first usable match that popped into his mind. He was taking a devilish pleasure in watching Gates grope and scheme, becoming more frenetic as each obvious snare failed to do the trick. Soon they would exchange a hard, mean glare and Gates would realize the jig was up, but he wasn't there yet, was still trying to dupe Mason and give the police a taped admission to improve their case. "Why are you speaking in code? I have no idea who or what you're referring to."

Gates had grown itchy and flustered. "Wayne Thompson. 1984.

You and me. Him bein' shot." He wiped the back of his hand across his mouth. "That clear enough for you?"

"I guess. Why would the police be interviewing you about Wayne? You didn't have anything to do with his death. I know that better than anyone. You're innocent. You were with me or our friends the whole day. We never saw him after he left Denise's place. I wouldn't worry if I were you."

"Well, I am worried," Gates screeched. "Somehow they know, Mason. They know it was me and you." He grasped Mason's wrist, squeezed.

"What're you talking about, Gates?" Mason asked. "Have you lost your mind? Are you all right?"

"I didn't admit anything, but they're on to us."

Mason pried away his brother's grip. "I'm going to call the prison first thing tomorrow and have the doc take a look at you. I have no earthly idea why you're freaking out, and you sound paranoid. Are you taking medicine? Some kind of prescription they have you on?"

"Hell no."

"I'm sorry I can't help you, Gates. I have no clue why you're so upset. Wayne Thompson died years ago, and you and I had nothing to do with it. You sure you're not on something? You okay?"

"Damn it, yes, I'm fine. Me and you—" His mouth opened but the next words stalled and he was momentarily lockjawed and pop-eyed, dumb as a post, and then he began a slow, deflated retreat into his chair, part slink, part crumple, like the stopper had been yanked from a blow-up valve in his middle and air was wheezing out. "Me and you need to decide what we're gonna say about Wayne's shooting. Unless you're plannin' on sittin' there and pretendin' you don't have any idea what happened and leave me holdin' the bag." He kept at it, but he was losing his fire, knew he'd been discovered and had no chance. His last few words trailed off and blended into the other conversations around them.

"Gates, as best I can tell, you and I are on different planets. No one's going to cause you or me any grief over Wayne Thompson. How could they? We didn't do anything. You need to take a breath. Who's been to see you? The cops, you said? Maybe you're overreacting to something routine. I'm worried about you—this isn't normal."

"Right. Yeah." The hate and stench were so strong they almost translated visibly. He was a corpse in a baggy orange jumpsuit, seething, haunted, beaten. "I can't believe you, Mason. You're gonna fuck me again."

Mason feigned hurt. He worked his hands some more. "I'm not aware of ever having done anything to you. I've always tried to go the extra mile, no matter how much dope you sold or how many times you came to me needing a loan or a favor. No matter how many times you lied to me or our friends or our mom. No matter how many jobs you pissed away. We've always stood by you." Any court or jury that listened to the recording of this conversation was going to receive Gates's entire despicable résumé, from soup to nuts.

"Thanks so much." Gates was buried in his seat.

"I'm sorry I've upset you. I don't know what else to do. This is why it's so damn difficult to visit. I really am going to have them send a doctor by." Mason stood and peered down at Gates. For a second or two, he burned his brother with an incensed, blistering stare that belied his charity and pleasant demeanor and spoke what he'd come to speak, and there was no doubt Gates took his meaning, understood they were now enemies rather than kin, understood Mason was aware he'd gone Judas.

"I'll leave a twenty for your canteen account," Mason promised, his voice honeyed and sympathetic. He offered his hand, an effort requiring considerable discipline, but Gates childishly refused it. "Good-bye, brother," Mason said, the syllables so loaded and somber that Gates dipped his head and knew he'd been cut loose forever, cleaved and kissed on each cheek and dismissed into the desert.

As they exited the parking area, Sadie Grace kept her focus on the highway and said in a stern voice, "Trouble has a way of rubbin' off to the people around it."

The sun had warmed the car's interior, and Mason switched on the air-conditioning, the first use since last year. "I know. Better than most people, I know."

"I don't have any idea what you two have goin' or why we came today, and I don't care to find out. But Gates is trouble. It pains me to say it, but he is. You need to steer clear. You've made a life for yourself. You've got a daughter to raise. Gates has too much of his daddy in him." She touched her eye, though there was no tear apparent. "I take my share of the blame, too. I could've made different choices."

Mason looked at her, but she kept to herself. "We were lucky to have had you," he said to comfort her. "You did everything anyone could have. More, in fact. No telling what would have happened if you weren't around. You are a saint and a godsend." He patted her knee. "I can handle Gates."

"You remember the story of Joseph?" she asked.

"I seem to recall he had a fine coat. And a good run on Broadway." Mason smiled.

She finally faced him and recited from memory: " 'So when the Midianite merchants came by, his brothers pulled Joseph up out of the cistern and sold him for twenty shekels of silver.' I've read that verse a thousand times. Brothers who would sell a brother 'cause they're jealous and petty. Selfish. Tradin' their own flesh and blood. It can happen, Mason. It happened in the Bible."

"I doubt we could get the full twenty shekels for Gates," he joked.

"Oh, no. It'd be the other way around, believe me."

"I understand—I was only kidding."

"Watch yourself," she said. "You've been good to Gates. You should have a clear conscience. You don't owe him. Don't risk your good name on him."

"I wish it were that simple." He decreased the car's fan. "Along those lines, let me say I was glad to drive you to see him after you asked."

"Huh? I asked? You called me. I'd rather been at Sunday service."

"Maybe I'm mistaken, but I think you wanted to go, and I volunteered to take you."

Their roles briefly reverted, and his mother eyed him as if he were sixteen and seeking a white lie about his homework or where he'd been when a girl called the house asking for him. "You're a good son," she said. "Always there if I need something. It was nice of you to take me. As best as I can remember, I asked you to." It came out almost primly, and she seemed curiously gratified, eager to be maternal and help her boy, even if she didn't know the specifics and even if it required her to discount the truth, her church teachings and the Ten Commandments crowded to the rear where her son was concerned.

The world seemed to swap ends the next morning. Early rather than late, the sky looked like a sketch pad full up with doodles, scribbles, crosshatches and blots of bold lavender and flaming orange, as if evening had arrived hours and hours prematurely. Clouds imprinted the hills and swales with slow-moving shadows. The light lacked power. The day seemed to have ripened at birth. Mason drank from a cup of coffee on the porch and figured the strange doings augured poorly for him, assumed he was receiving some sort of supernatural tip-off that his woes would only increase as time went by. He scanned the farm, half expecting to catch a glimpse of a mad owl beating its wings or an apocalyptic horse rearing in the pasture.

Grace trudged down the drive to await the "crappy old bus" her father made her ride. She continued to dwell in a province that excluded Mason, but at least after the peace-offering mall trip, the malice seemed to have vanished from the gulf between them—now he was simply out of her loop, irrelevant rather than loathed. Soon the bus lumbered to a stop with a swinging red sign and blinking lights, the doors folded in on themselves, and Grace mounted two big steps and was swallowed up, the doors' black rubber strips reuniting and sealing shut. Betty Smith, the driver, waved at Mason and pulled away, taking the bus through its gears. Mason's coffee had gone cold, and he left the cup sitting on a railing, walked through the dew-damp grass to his car.

Sure enough, Custis was in a tizzy, pacing around his office when Mason located him at work. He had neglected to brew their coffee, and there were no donuts or bakery sweets or honey buns to eat while they talked about the coming week's cases. His attention snapped to Mason the instant he entered the room. "I can't fuckin' believe this," Custis brayed.

"I had a feeling," Mason said, resigned, ready for the bad news.

Custis shook his head. His dreads flipped and flopped. "Seventeen pounds. I've gained seventeen pounds since San Juan, Mace. I'm the damn affirmative-action Michelin Man." He parted his suit coat and turned sideways. "Why didn't you tell me how fat I've become?"

"I didn't notice."

"Well, part of the problem is this damn confab we have every Monday. We sit here and eat trash—no telling how many calories I'm crammin' in because of this little ritual. But no more." He faced Mason and jerked open his belt with a frustrated tug to the right. "Look. Can you believe this? I can't even hook my damn britches." With the belt loosened, a gap was apparent at the top of the zipper where the pants should have fastened. "Man, I gotta take steps."

"So that's why you're so wound up? You think you've put on weight?"

"Ain't no *think* to it," Custis replied, refitting his belt.

"Sorry. I honestly hadn't seen a difference. You carry it well, big as you are."

"Damn. No more bread, I can promise you that. No more desserts."

Despite his own difficulties, Mason laughed out loud. "Well, why don't you try the LA Weight Loss program?" he said sincerely, after the amusement passed. "I've heard several people say it's effective. They opened, what, a month ago? In the building next to Hudson's Drug. We walk past there five times a day. Art Anthony claims he's already dropped nine or ten pounds."

"It's like every other small-town business. It isn't anything but

Frieda Compton in a flashy smock surrounded by a bunch of dumpy posters and silk plants, just tryin' to scrounge a buck. She bought the starter kit and went to three training sessions in Greensboro and that's the high-water mark of her expertise. I'll bet you she's smokin' cigarettes in the back and feasting on Little Debbie, and we both know her husband's fat as hell and basically a slob. She doesn't know nutrition from a hole in the ground."

"My, my. No need to be so cynical."

"Yeah, well, it's true." He adjusted his pants. Centered his belt buckle.

"You're welcome to go with me to the gym. I exercise three or four times a week, and it's the best cure there is. I'll show you the ropes. You'd enjoy it, and it'd be a treat to have someone to talk with. Break the monotony."

"I might. Thanks. Maybe I'll sign up. I know I really should."

"Heck, I'll buy you a three-month membership."

"I'll give it serious thought. Kind of you to offer." Custis turned and walked behind his desk. His chair was of the standard office variety, four legs with rollers and a lever on the side that adjusted the height. He settled in and reached for a file. Mason stayed where he was. "I'll at least make the coffee," he told Custis.

"Okay," Custis said. And then, boom, a pin gave way and his seat collapsed and slid down its metal support and lost all its altitude and hit bottom so that Custis's chin was about level with his desk drawer, his startled eyes alligatoring over a *Michie's Jurisprudence* volume.

Mason couldn't help himself and tore out of the room laughing. "I'll find the workers' comp forms," he shouted over his shoulder. "It's slapstick hour at the commonwealth's attorney's office," he quipped to Sheila as he approached her desk, still in stitches over his friend's misfortune.

Chapter Thirteen

"A Mr. Carson from Richmond is on your line," Sheila announced to Mason. It was Tuesday, two days after Mason's visit to the penitentiary.

"What's he want?" Mason asked, not recognizing the name.

"Said it was personal." Sheila was coming through over the phone's speaker, but she was close enough to his wall that Mason could also hear her in the room next to his. Each of her words sounded doubled, the muted voice on the other side of the wall piggybacking the clear version on the phone.

Mason felt a hitch in his stomach. He wet his lips and picked up the receiver. "Mason Hunt," he said.

"Mr. Hunt, good morning to you and thanks for taking my call. My name is Carter Carson."

The man was too courteous and too affable to be a cop. Mason swelled his cheeks and quickly sighed out a breath, relieved. "No problem. What can I do for you?"

"I'm the executive director of the Tobacco Commission, and for starters let me welcome you aboard and thank you for your service."

"Oh. Right. I'm looking forward to it."

"Great," Carson said. "Your first meeting is June thirtieth, and I'll be sending you a packet of information in the next day or so. More to the point, there's one grant proposal that impacts your area, a request for a public-private partnership with a company called Chip-Tech. They're basically a computer component manufacturer wholly owned by Caldwell-Dylan."

"Ah—there's a name I've heard. Caldwell-Dylan is none other than Herman Dylan, correct?"

"Exactly, Mr. Hunt."

"The Iceman. I've read about him. Got rich in frozen foods."

"It would be fair to say he's somewhat controversial, but there are people in business and government who swear by him."

Mason found a paper clip and began bending it straight, trapping the phone between his chin and shoulder. "From everything I've seen, he's definitely a mixed bag. What concerns does he have in our neck of the woods?"

"According to his application, he's interested in bringing Chip-Tech to Patrick."

"Huh. Well, more power to him."

Carson's tone dampened. "Of course, he wants us to kick in a healthy six mil, he wants your county to waive taxes for five years and lease him a shell building for cheap, and he wants discounted water and sewer."

"How many jobs do we get for our largesse?"

"Seventy. But bear in mind that number is 'an aspiration' as per his application. If you read the fine print, the commitment is for fifty-five positions with an average wage of nine dollars an hour."

"I guess that's fifty-five more than we have now."

"True."

"I appreciate the call and information. Thanks for the warning."

"My pleasure. It's what I do." Carson chuckled. "And if I were you, I'd brace myself for a little cold weather. Keep the down jacket handy."

The police, meanwhile, had decided they were best served by making a formal appointment with Mason, trading away surprise for the grind of dread and worry. Late Wednesday, Ray Bass called Sheila to schedule a meeting, and she assumed he and his partner were coming to see the commonwealth's attorney just like every other cop who requested an hour to review a case or ask advice or prepare for trial. She booked Bass and Rick Minter for Friday morning, and Mason learned of the visit Thursday afternoon when Sheila handed him his schedule for the next day.

"Shit," he said, staring at the photocopy of her calendar page.

"I'm sorry. Is something wrong?"

"No. No. I didn't mean to curse. Seems . . . seems like a lot to do, that's all."

"I can switch stuff if you want me to," she offered.

"Nah. It's actually not so bad." He almost asked her about the appointment with Bass and Minter but immediately swallowed the impulse, realizing there was nothing she could add and that the inquiry would only draw attention to a subject he preferred to keep off everyone's radar.

Convinced that the cops would sooner or later be on his tail, Mason had devoted a fair amount of thought to what he should tell Custis when the pincers began closing and the state police arrived in their unmarked Crown Vic for an interview, ready with Gates's accusations. Custis had left earlier in the day, and Mason drove directly from their office to his friend's home on Chestnut Avenue. He parked behind Custis's new Caddy, left his suit coat in the car and knocked on the front door. There was no answer, but Mason was able to hear loud music and dull thumps, and he could sense a vibration in the wooden porch, movement that began inside and traced out along joists and planks and registered in his feet. He knocked again, and when Custis didn't respond, Mason eased the door open and shouted hello. The music dropped. "Who is it?" Custis yelled from another part of the house.

"It's me. Mason."

"Damn. Maybe you should knock."

"I did." He spoke louder than normal.

Custis stuck his head around a doorframe on the opposite side of the room. "Who's with you?"

206 • MARTIN CLARK

"Nobody. Why? You smoking crack back there?"

Custis came through the door. He was wearing tennis shoes, white tube socks, gray athletic shorts and a red T-shirt that didn't make it all the way to the elastic band at the top of the shorts. A strip of brown belly skin wallowed in the space between the shorts and shirt. "I'm workin' out, smart-ass." He was sweating and breathing hard.

"To what? The sound track for *American Graffiti*?"

"It's a Richard Simmons tape. It was all they had at the library, okay?"

Mason smiled and put his hands on his hips. "Richard Simmons is a category-one flame, and the routine is for fossils and ancient women with canes and artificial joints."

"Actually, Mace, it's pretty damn rigorous, and even if it wasn't, what exactly would you suggest for me?" He glanced at his stomach. "I mean, you know, right now, old fat women would be about my speed."

"I told you I'd buy you a gym membership and we'd go together."

"You think I'm gonna stroll my lardass into a public gym lookin' like this?"

Mason sat on a sofa arm. "That's why you go, Custis. To get in shape."

"When I can go and people aren't thinkin' I'm 'Rerun' Berry, I'll go."

"Your choice," Mason said. "It's good you're exercising. Wherever you do it, it's a positive."

"Yeah. I can't believe how this shit creeps up on you."

Mason faked a wince. "Friend to friend, seeing your baby-doll shirt and kneesocks, I've got to say lifestyle changes are definitely in order."

Custis balled a fist in Mason's direction and raised his middle finger. "Fat or not, I can still beat you down. You'd be smart to not forget it."

"Amen."

As Mason balanced there on the leather arm of Custis's couch, about to confess his involvement in a murder, it occurred to him how frequently settings fail to match important moments, how critical, wrenching events that deserve the dignity of a hearth or respectable office or church altar wind up poorly staged, jammed into the first empty space available, willy-nilly, revelations loosed and souls bared at gas pumps, bowling alleys, carnivals, bus stops, department-store toilets, the surroundings be damned. Mason took stock of the revved-up oldies and Richard Simmons's exhortations and the comical red shirt, but he decided they probably didn't mean anything or make much difference. Perhaps the absurdities might even make his burden more tolerable, draw off some of the poison. "Have a seat," he said to Custis. "We need to talk."

"Uh-oh. That doesn't sound cool." He pointed at Mason with his index finger. "Hang tight." He left and returned wearing a bulky sweatshirt that kept his middle concealed. "Problems with the situation we discussed at lunch?" he asked, twisting the top off a bottled water.

Mason heard the plastic seal break. "Afraid so."

Custis perched himself on the edge of a recliner. "I hope you know I haven't forgotten you or ignored anything we discussed. I took it to heart, but I figured you'd get back to me when you needed to. It's been weighing on me, though. Sure has."

"Thanks. Well, the time is here, I'm sorry to say."

"I got a fair idea of your troubles, but I'm hopin' I'm wrong." Custis lifted the hem of his shirt and patted his face.

"We're in confidence here, right? Attorney-client?"

"Yeah, Mace." The question obviously annoyed him. "We cashed the check. If my word and my friendship won't hold, we can always count on the technicalities."

"I wouldn't be telling you this unless I trusted you. I've never had a better friend. The check may end up keeping *you* off the griddle—it's more for you than me."

"Whatever," Custis groused.

Mason moved from the arm onto the sofa proper. "I apologize for dragging us both into such a mess. I'm particularly sorry that over the long haul this affects you, too." He stared at the oak floor, noticed a dark, swirling knot in the wood. He thought of his wife, how he never told her he'd protected his brother and allowed a killing to remain unsolved, for years aiding and abetting a criminal. He stopped studying the floor, jacked up his posture and met Custis eye to eye.

Mason told him the story. He omitted nothing and included every detail, from the number of Budweiser beers he'd drunk before the shooting to Gates's clumsy embrace of their mother at the prison.

Custis listened without interrupting.

"It's been a shackle for nearly twenty years," Mason said at the end. "To this day, I don't know what the answer is, what I should've done. I mean, there I was, sucked into it, surprised as hell. Of course, if I'd had a crystal ball and could've seen what a prick Gates would prove to be, I'd have reported him to the cops. But in 1984, Custis, we were both young and he was my *brother*. You've probably heard what a beast our dad was, and I owed Gates for taking care of me. We were really a pair in those days, close. We wouldn't have made it otherwise." Mason sank into the cushions. "Still, I broke the law. There's the plain old moral issue, too. Law or not, I probably had an obligation to tell the truth." He turned silent, pensive. The upbeat music continued in the background. "I've often wondered," he said after the pause, "and I've never said this to anyone before . . . I've wondered about Allison. Maybe in the big scheme of things her wreck was my payback. My punishment. Sort of to teach me a lesson about loss. Karma. You could find a certain divine symmetry if you wanted to."

"Nah. No. I doubt it's anything punitive. You're readin' passages that don't exist. Anyway, your theory wouldn't be tit for tat. It'd have to be Gates's wife for the score to be even."

"Maybe there's a penalty and interest. The toll goes up. Who knows?"

"It was bad luck," Custis said. "No more, no less."

"So you won't think I'm a moron, this isn't a staggering turn of events for me, what Gates is doing. Hell, it's almost predictable. It's nagged me for years and years, like a damn open sore, and I guess I've always understood it was a possibility. A cutthroat brother with leverage will definitely make you lose sleep. A year and a half ago he actually called and threatened me, and even though neither of us mentioned it, I couldn't help but wonder if he was finally desperate enough or pissed enough to sell us both down the river. It was like he was ready to launch the missiles. But I thought I was okay, or at least reasonably safe, because I didn't see how he could use this to his advantage or hurt me without screwing himself worse."

"Well, I had this close to puzzled through. From your big ol' hints at lunch, I figured you knew Gates was guilty or involved in the Thompson guy's death. I didn't realize you were there while it went down. Dumped the gun. Bald-face lied for him." Custis took a slug of water. " 'Course I damn sure didn't guess he was tryin' to lay his crime at your doorstep." He screwed the cap onto the bottle. "Some dilemmas can't be solved. Yours is murky. Tough. I can't say what I'd have done in your shoes. Me, I'd pimp the truth for either one of my brothers or my parents. No doubt. Family trumps the Code of Virginia. Plus, it wasn't clear-cut murder—this dumb-ass evidently was lying in wait, and then decides to chase you two down, curse Gates, call him out and threaten him with a stick. A good lawyer could generate a lot of smoke with those facts."

"A club. It's accurate and it makes our case a bit more presentable."

"Yeah. Exactly." Custis concentrated for a second. "Hell, it's probably the low end of voluntary manslaughter. In hindsight, it might've been wise for you to have leaned on Gates, maybe persuaded him to fess up. This is Patrick County, after all. You go huntin' for trouble and find it, even if you find it in spades, people usually are pretty understandin' of the person who dished it out. He'd have had a strong case with a lot of mitigation. Seven or eight years, that's what I'd do with it if it were mine. Can't imagine a jury callin' it much different."

"Fat fucking chance Gates would've pled to anything. And who can say what Tony Black would've offered or a jury would've done. Let's not forget Wayne Thompson was drunk and there were two of us and my star-athlete brother had a good hundred pounds on him and a car to drive away in—it's not as if Gates was cornered and had no option except to shoot the guy."

Custis stood. "Yeah, well, be that as it may, the big concern is your situation now." He folded his arms. "Let's game this thing out."

Mason recovered his posture and sat more erect. "Okay. Thanks."

"How 'bout you drop it truthful? Tell the gospel." Custis walked across the room and settled into a different chair. "Come clean. By my math, you're guilty of, at most, accessory after the fact. Misdemeanor. The statute of limitations is a year, so you're good to go. Can't be prosecuted. With this scenario, there's the added advantage of your punk-ass brother receivin' his due."

"Far too risky," Mason replied. "Huge downside. Believe me, it's the first permutation I went through, too. But here's the problem: I really think all it would do is guarantee me a murder trial. See, if I tell the truth, Gates's story suddenly has credibility. I was in fact there, I did dispose of the gun, I did lie, I did help construct the alibi. Any prosecutor or cop worth his salt is bound to ask why I did those things if I'm not the shooter or at least a willing participant from the get-go. Moreover, the second I choose the honesty option, the best I can hope for is a damn swearing contest with Gates in front of a jury, and even if they kind of believe I'm being straight, you and I both know it's human nature for them to be angry and find some way to nail me. Why should a guy who helped hide a murder walk away scot-free? Or they pop me with a nice stiff sentence for being a hypocrite and sending people to jail for all these years despite my own dirty laundry." Mason bowed his head. "God, it sounds awful, doesn't it? When you put voice to it—when I hear it out loud—I can't help but feel I *have* done wrong."

"Well, you did break the law. But you didn't shoot anybody, and you tried to honor your brother as best you could. Let's not forget who's the polecat in this piece."

Mason looked up. "Yeah—I guess that makes me like a flunky or henchman. So I'm Renfield. The captain of the Wicked Witch's winged monkeys. Great."

Custis hinted at a grin. "So the only other option is balls to the wall. We play it like you've been playin' it, and when the cops come tomorrow, we find the props and costumes and act our asses off. Big surprise. We're stunned. We're the Prefect of Police in Casablanca. We pound away at Gates. Who the hell would believe Gates Hunt, a drug-dealin' felon? You're gonna go to trial against a well-respected commonwealth's attorney based on the word of his felonious, vindictive, piece-of-shit brother? We do all we can to convince them they got a loser."

"I agree." Mason shifted his weight. "But like I told you, my worry is I can't exactly recall what I said to Bass and Minter in our discussions about the gun. They knew I was flustered, and now I'm betting my slip is on tape. I was so rattled I said something close to 'that's impossible' or 'that can't be,' and they really flagged it."

"But you covered yourself, right? Muddied the water? If there is a tape, it's bound to be ambiguous. It's not like you confessed. We pass it off as professional skepticism."

"Yeah, but it's one more little brick for their house."

"No way a judge or jury would convict you if that's the whole case, everything in their satchel. No chance, Mace." Custis stood again. "I can't imagine they'd be dumb enough to even indict you if that's all they have."

"Well, you know what we say about close cases: too good to ignore, probably not good enough to win. Some you simply have to take to trial, no matter the probabilities. It's tricky for them, too, just like it is for us from time to time. If the press discovers the state police have credible evidence that a commonwealth's attorney committed a crime and they refuse to file charges, they'll get skinned alive in the newspapers—along with the attorney general, and I don't need to remind you they're political animals in that particular office."

Custis scowled. "The more I'm in this business, the more I dislike it. Hell, about half the crap we do is either boondoggle or placating people who don't deserve it. All these rituals and fictions that absolutely shit on common sense. The worst of it is, the rest of the world's come down with the same disease: The chumps at airport security harass wheelchair granny so we can justify askin' the guy with the sword and prayer rug to let us search his suitcase. Clerks have to see an ID from the BMW lady in the pink sweater and three-carat diamond so they can press Lawanda when she breaks off the first starter check from her new account to buy her strawberry blunts. Fewer and fewer folks have the guts to do what's obviously right if it means catching a little abuse in the process. Everything's a damn referendum or a jury trial or left to the rabble in the name of egalitarianism." Custis was agitated when he finished, his mouth strict. He returned to the recliner but kept standing.

"We can't do much about all that except deal with it," Mason replied. "Besides, I've got my own dragon to slay. You and town council can fix the country's shortcomings, okay? The bottom line is it'd be a difficult decision for any prosecutor to make, especially if I sound like a crook on the tape, assuming there is a tape." Mason smiled. He crossed his legs. "Better not let the officers in the Urban League hear you spouting such heresy. If they discover you've signed on with the fascists and plantation owners, you'll be banned for life. Lose your Stokely Carmichael card."

"It's just wrong to indict someone because you want to pass the buck and don't have the courage to tell the papers and whoever else to kiss your ass. That's all I'm sayin'." He was still disturbed. "As for my bona fides, when brothers run the planet and we fuck it up, you can take me to task on it. Till then, this is your show and you guys are the ones who've allowed it to fall apart. Most of the time, democracy ain't really been the black man's friend, now has it?" He strafed Mason with a look. "So you'll know and not embarrass your bumpkin self, it's Kwame Toure. He changed his name."

"I was only kidding," Mason said. "Ranting and tilting at windmills and soapboxing isn't really doing much for the problem at hand. My problem."

"It pisses me off. Sorry."

Mason cleared his throat. "For me, the big issue is not jamming you up. I'm here for advice, but this is my mess and I don't want to take advantage of our friendship or pull you over the cliff with me. I guess we've sort of been down this road before, years ago when my family was threatened. I appreciate your help, but you need to take care of Custis first."

"If my situation changes, I'll tell you," he said, the passion ebbing in his voice.

"I mean, you know, tomorrow I'm basically going to mislead the cops."

Custis nodded. "You're not under oath, and I'm not plannin' on sayin' too awful much. I'll be there listenin' and learnin'. In the end, no matter which way you come at this, it seems pointless and wrong for you to be charged and have your life ruined. Who benefits from that? You're a good man, a good father and a good son. Not to mention a good friend." Custis sat again. He rubbed his hands over his face. "Whatever punishment is fair, I'd say you've served your sentence, carryin' this cross around as long as you have."

Mason walked toward him and Custis stood and they met chest to chest and slapped each other on the back, and Mason left without either of them saying anything else, Richard Simmons still counting to the beat and chanting encouragement.

That night, from his table at the seafood restaurant, Mason saw Jasper Griffith's pickup circle the parking lot and take a space near the end of a row. He had a dog cage in the truck bed, stuffed full of rowdy bluetick coonhounds. Mason and Grace were eating dinner, two popcorn shrimp and whitefish specials, and for reasons that were impossible to pin down or articulate, she was in a good humor, her fickle sulk suspended for the moment, lightning caught in a jar. She was talkative and agreeable, chatting with her dad about school, cheerleading, friends, boys and whatever else struck her fancy, eating one tiny shrimp at a time after spearing it on a fork and twirling it in cocktail sauce. Already dreading his morning appointment with the cops, Mason had no appetite, but he was enjoying his daughter's generous mood, and he sipped his tea and ate a hush puppy and a few bites of broiled fish. Jasper came through the door, by himself, dressed in Carhartt coveralls and new brown boots, and while the hostess was collecting a menu and scouting out an empty booth for him, he noticed Mason and tramped across the restaurant to where he and Grace were eating.

Jasper was a bossy, opinionated man with a big yap who thought highly of himself and his place in the community. He'd inherited land and a few dollars from his crotchety dad, and he sold used cars and did excavation work and swapped and traded odds and ends, especially antique furniture and Depression glass. He approached Mason's table, said hello and, remarkably, slid into the empty chair beside Grace without being invited, announcing in a determined voice he wanted to take care of a legal matter that wouldn't keep.

A large part of Mason's job was listening to the oafs and dolts who tugged on his sleeve at the high school play or cornered him at the grocery store to tell him their bullshit, convoluted legal woes and ask him to do the impossible, to snap his fingers and settle a decades-old boundary-line dispute, force a landlord to repair a mobile home's grievous plumbing or persuade a deadbeat dad to ante up his child support. It was the bane of every small-town lawyer, the thoughtless boors who swooped in with no respect for place or privacy and invariably began the intrusion by declaring, "I need to ask you a legal question," as if they were entitled to put any attorney to work on the spot, wherever and whenever, for free, for as long as they wished. Now here was Jasper Griffith, a grating, self-important man, sitting beside Mason's daughter, interrupting their meal and the first decent conversation they'd had in weeks.

Mason raised his eyebrows and cocked his head. He'd said a curt hi, but that was the extent of it.

Both elbows on the table, Jasper remarked he'd "thought about visitin' during business hours but hadn't had a chance," then launched into a diatribe about a hundred eighty dollars he was owed by Oneal Pack for a used transmission and set of rims.

Mason interrupted him while he was indignantly rambling on. "Jasper, my daughter and I are in the middle of our food, and I was enjoying our time together."

"This ain't gonna take long," Jasper remarked, oblivious.

"No, it's not. If you have a problem, call Sheila, set up an appointment and we'll discuss it."

"No need to get snotty about it, Mason."

"I'm not. I'm simply telling you I don't appreciate you busting in on us."

"Really?" Jasper was a short, wiry man with ruddy skin, always clean-shaven and fussily neat. He usually smelled of sweet hair tonic.

"I'm simply asking for a little common courtesy."

"Unlike all you hotshots up there in Stuart with bankers' hours, I have to actually work, so it ain't always real convenient for me to call your secretary and sacrifice my entire day so I can suit your schedule."

"Then your problem must not be too urgent. Certainly not urgent enough to warrant discussing now. My daughter and I are going to finish our supper. By ourselves."

Jasper smirked. He jerked his chair away from the table and shot to his feet in a huff. "You need an attitude adjustment, Mason. I've known you and your family all your life, and you're gettin' too big for your britches. You're Curt Hunt's boy, not some king. On top of that, you're a public servant, son. You work for us, not the other way around. It's a shame when a taxpayer, the man payin' your salary, can't have two minutes of your precious time. You better hope nobody runs against you next election, I can promise you that much. I can swing a bunch of votes."

Mason set his fork on the table, took hold of the napkin in his lap. Already frazzled and close to the margins because of his police stress, he considered whether he ought to stand and put his finger in Jasper's stupid face and light into him. Very quickly, he was thinking "why the hell not," even though he ordinarily would've dismissed the likes of Jasper Griffith with silence and a stern stare and returned to his seafood and tea, aware that a public spat with an imbecile was the worst kind of quicksand.

Before he could speak or act, Grace twisted forty-five degrees and said to the man who'd challenged her father, "It wouldn't make any difference who ran against my dad. My dad would win." She sounded mad, defensive and slightly scared. She glared at Griffith. "I think you are a rude idiot. You suck."

Mason glanced at Griffith, then switched to his daughter. "Grace, I don't . . ." He hesitated, felt his shoulders go soft, his breathing decline. "You know, come to think of it, you're right, Grace. I agree." He reached into his hip pocket, took out his bill-fold, removed a five-dollar bill and held it in Griffith's direction. "Here's fair reimbursement for your part of my salary, your share of all the whopping taxes I'm sure you pay." He waved the five in the air. "Go on, take it, Jasper. Take it so I can be rid of you and won't have to listen to your nonsense from now on."

Several other diners were watching, and a waitress with a tray of refill pitchers and extra hush puppies had halted her path to the Hunts' table.

"This little display is gonna cost you more than any five dollars, you mark my words." Jasper didn't lower his voice. "And if I was you, I'd think about teachin' my youngun a lesson on respect." He looked sideways at Grace.

"Good-bye, Jasper," Mason said coolly. "Tell Mr. Griffith good-bye, you uncouth heathen girl," he said to his daughter. "And please don't tell him he's an idiot or that he sucks."

"Good-bye, Mr. Griffith," she singsonged through a huge, insincere smile.

"Comb your hair next time you leave home so you'll look like somebody," Griffith said to Mason before he turned to walk away, one of his four or five stock lines and his attempt at a parting shot. He stomped toward the metal and glass double doors at the front of the restaurant, waving off the teenage hostess and her single menu as he passed her on his way to his truck.

When the waitress arrived with more water and tea, she congratulated Mason and Grace for laying into Jasper. "He talks and talks and talks and just worries you to death. The same old dumb sayings again and again about 'comb your hair so you'll look like somebody' and how he's always 'fine as frog hair split three ways.' Ugggghhh. He was achin' for a comeuppance, Mr. Hunt—good for you. And you too, sweetie," she said as she was tending to Grace's glass. "He runs us to death and tips you two quarters or some pocket change, which ain't even worth the effort. I'm glad he's gone."

After the waitress moved to the next table, Mason addressed Grace in his paternal voice. He leaned closer to her as he spoke. "I appreciate your pluck, and I'm tickled you wanted to defend me, yes I am, but let's not make that kind of language a habit."

"Okay," she said, intuitively understanding he couldn't let on how pleased he was with her, how gratified. "But he did suck," she said.

"Enough. Hush." He raised a finger across his mouth. Her hair was as light as her mother's and she was already tall and blessed with Allison's slender, elegant hands, but she favored him, too, most noticeably through the mouth and chin, and he loved her fully, adored how he and her spectacular mom were etched into her in so many ways. "Finish your plate," he said gently, gesturing with his fork. He prayed he wouldn't soon shame her, leave her with scars and clipped wings, and for the first time since his travails began, he considered the possibility of jail and the prospect of his unlucky mother raising another kid.

Chapter Fourteen

The next morning, Mason made Ray Bass wait in the lobby for thirty minutes, and when Sheila knocked on the door and showed him into Mason's office, not only was Minter with him, but to Mason's surprise his friend Ed Hoffman was there as well, the last of the three to enter the room. Hoffman had been employed by the state police for over two decades, and he was a perfect cop—honest, fair, deliberate, smart and reliable. He and Mason had worked together on several cases in the past, and Hoffman had invited Mason to his car on the last occasion he'd been in Stuart for a trial and they'd sipped top-shelf bourbon from paper cups to celebrate a favorable verdict. Hoffman was paunchy and bald but utterly average in every other physical regard, an ordinary guy given to plain dress and brief, direct sentences.

Mason was sad to see him there, hated to disappoint a man he respected. He spoke to Hoffman first, striding out from behind his desk to greet him. "Well, well, what a fine surprise," he said. "A visit from Kojak himself." He was nervous, juiced, struggling not to muff his lines. He shook Hoffman's hand. "Hope you're okay."

"I'm good," Hoffman said unenthusiastically.

Mason welcomed the other policemen and returned to his desk. "Sorry to keep you waiting. I apologize. We're swamped today."

"No problem," Minter told him. They were all silent while he and the other officers took their seats. Something metal—a ring or watchband—dinged a chair arm. Coins jangled in a pocket.

"What's on the agenda, gentlemen? I assume you're here about Allen Roberts. The old murder from eighty-four?"

"You could say that," Bass replied.

Mason pretended not to pick up on the pointed answer. "I think Custis told you we were prepared to go. Last I heard, you guys wanted us to hold off, so we did. It seemed like a solid case to me— what happened? I was planning to track you down and go over things again, and Sheila told me you gents were coming today. Thanks for making the trip."

Minter was fingering a gold button on his blazer. "Mr. Hunt, we, uh, we're here because we have information we need to discuss with you. You personally. Believe me, we don't take any pleasure in this. No sir."

"I'm not following you," Mason said. "You've already told me the facts and given me the evidence we have for trial. I'm satisfied and ready to indict, but obviously there's some sudden reluctance on your end. How about you guys just tell me what's on your minds? I'm lost."

Minter buttoned his jacket. "Mr. Hunt, we have a report— credible—that you was heavily involved in this shooting."

"Huh?" All at once, the lines and creases in Mason's face deepened. "Pardon me? Involved? Involved how?"

"The truth is you're a suspect," Bass said somberly. "We're here to question you based on everything we've learned. I'm sorry."

"Question *me*? Question me about what? You're telling me you think I know something about Wayne Thompson's shooting?" Mason glowered at Bass. "You can't be serious."

"Serious as a heart attack," Bass answered, holding his ground.

"So you're a part of this?" Mason asked Hoffman. "You're here with these two because you believe I'm involved in a murder? Am I understanding this right?"

"You're my friend, Mason," Hoffman said sincerely. "I go where my job takes me."

"That's helpful," Mason snorted. "So what is it—this is fucking insane—what is it I'm accused of doing? And who the hell is accusing me?"

"Your brother," Bass said.

"Beautiful. There you go." Mason rocked back in his chair. "You're here in my office, all full-tilt *Dragnet,* because my dumbass, drug-dealing brother said I somehow had a hand in a twenty-year-old unsolved murder? Come on." He sat forward and brought his heels down hard. "That's rich, guys. You should be embarrassed. Credible? Gates Hunt?"

"Well, we think he—"

"Hold on a minute—I'm going to bring Custis in here. I want him to hear this, so when everybody has to account for themselves down the road, there'll be no mistaking who said what."

"We'd prefer you—"

"I don't give a damn what you'd prefer, Mr. Bass," Mason snapped. "If you don't like it, you can pack up and leave for all I care."

None of the three police officers responded. Mason used the phone to summon Custis, who rolled into the room a few seconds later and playfully punched Hoffman on the shoulder as soon as he recognized him. "It's my boy Ed Hoffman, fashion-plate and slickster extraordinaire—the hip quotient in Stuart just went off the charts." The razzing was harmless; Custis also admired Hoffman. "Nice to see you." He approached Bass and Minter and shook hands, calling them both by their first names. "What's cookin'?" he asked. "Everyone seems a little grim." He was standing beside Minter, facing Mason.

"You know, Custis, I think I'll let Officer Minter tell you. Or his partner. I'm not sure I can actually spit the words out of my mouth."

Minter peered up at Custis, who was big enough and near enough that the cop had difficulty fitting all of him into his vision. "Well, to be blunt, to, uh, not sugarcoat nothin', and I don't take any joy in doing this, well, we have information Mr. Hunt, Mason, was involved in the death of Wayne Thompson. The 1984 shootin'." He quit straining to see Custis and refocused on Mason.

"You're shittin' me," Custis whooped. "Say what?"

"Nosir," Bass said gravely. "This is for real."

"You tryin' to tell me you think Mace is mixed up in a crime, this deal you two were so hot to trot on a week ago? Wanted me to indict Allen Roberts?" Custis smiled. "You're pullin' my chain, aren't you? Let me guess—it's practical joke week down at the station house and you get bonus points for dupin' a lawyer."

"They're serious, Custis," Mason said. "They think I'm complicit in this murder because none other than the oracle of truth himself, my righteous, holy brother, has evidently told them something or other."

"Ya'll ever spent any time with Gates?" Custis asked. "Huh? Everybody in this town can tell you he ain't to be believed. Good Lord. Hell, I was workin' with Tony Black when we prosecuted him—you shoulda heard his version of events on the stand. This is crazy." Custis was very convincing. Several of the words were squeaky high; he expanded the *a* in "crazy."

"It's not just Gates," Minter said.

Custis walked behind Mason's desk and sat on the corner of the credenza, close to Mason, opposite the three policemen across the room. "So what else could it possibly be?" he demanded.

"This makes perfect sense," Mason interjected before anyone could answer. "Now I see. Sunday, when I visited Gates, he was raving about how people were trying to blame us for the Thompson murder. He was loony. Berserk. Hell, I called the prison doc the next day to have him examined. I thought he was losing his mind. But you geniuses put him up to that, didn't you? You wired him and had him try to snake his own damn brother."

"Gates was wired," Ed Hoffman said. "Sounded like maybe you were speechifying right smart when you were talkin' to him. Making your argument."

"What the hell is that supposed to mean, Ed?" Mason asked.

"Funny you'd all a sudden decide to drive to the pen for a visit," Bass said. "How long was it between trips? Months?" There was no deference left in his tone. "You two been on the outs for who knows how long and then—snap, crackle, pop—there you are about the time you get wind of this investigation."

"My mother asked me to drive her. Why don't you check with her? While you're at it, ask her if she has even a jot of faith in her older son's word."

Bass theatrically scratched his head. "Strange how the logs show she went regular as you please every other week till you and her made your trip last Sunday. She hadn't been back-to-back since the Pilgrims landed. Maybe things had started to click and you needed a chance to eyeball your brother."

"This is some powerful evidence you guys have. I drove my mom to see my brother. Shit, Ray, you got me. Wow. I surrender." He extended his arms. "I'm done. Cuff me now."

"Returnin' to my question," Custis said, "tell us why you think Mason's wound up in this shooting? I'm hearin' you represent that his brother's makin' claims."

Bass reached inside a file and produced several typewritten pages joined by a single staple. He didn't read from them or offer them to Custis. He rolled the papers into a tube and clutched them with both hands. "Gates Hunt has give us a statement which says Mason and him were stopped by Wayne Thompson after they left the home of Denise Puckett, who was Gates's girlfriend. Mason had been drinkin'." He caught Mason's eye and spoke in his direction, holding the gaze. "Accordin' to your brother, you and him and Mr. Thompson had a disagreement on the side of Russell Creek Road. Gates says he and Thompson were arguing over Denise; she'd been datin' both of 'em. Gates and Thompson have a scuffle, a fight, but Gates whips him pretty easy, just kind of pushes him away. Then Thompson sets in on you, Mason, sayin' unpleasant things about your father and how you guys—you and Gates—have ganged up on him. He starts at you with a club." Bass slapped the papers against his thigh. "Gates says you were mad and scared and shot him when he was cursin' you and comin' at you. Favorable to you, he says you claimed you only meant to nick the deceased, not kill him." He hit his thigh again. "What's the old saying? You're the guy who brought a gun to a knife fight. Except with you and Mr. Thompson, it was a little blackjack, not even a knife."

"That is a fucking complete and absolute stone-solid lie. Totally untrue and made up by a damn worthless coward." Mason was so livid, so indignant, so rabid, so furiously unrehearsed that Minter ducked his head and Bass shrank back against his chair as if they'd been flogged by fierce weather, wind and thunder. Mason pushed out of his seat, stood and slammed his fist into his desk. *Whump.* While the noise from the first blow was still lingering, he hit it a second time. *Whump.* "And you motherfuckers treat it like it's from the pope." His face pinched and red, Mason yanked at the knot in his tie, loosening it. "And what did my brother want in exchange for this valuable information? Wait—let me guess. He wants to get out of jail." Mason was yelling.

Ed Hoffman watched impassively, his hands idle on his bump of a belly. "Nada. Nothing. He knows we can't help him." Hoffman shrugged. "Don't want a thing. Made me think there was less chance of him lyin'. Why would he? He did ask about a pardon. I told him we'd be happy to write the governor on his behalf. Also informed him the governor will say no."

Custis put his hand on Mason's shoulder, but Mason kept standing.

"He'll want more," Mason sputtered. "You mark my words. Gates never does anything unless it's calculated to help him." He wasn't as fiery, had quit shouting. "Even if he realizes there's no benefit, I wouldn't put it past him to do this because he's a jealous, petty, mean, common punk who blames everybody but himself for his problems. He's mad at me because I won't bend the rules to help him. Envious because I've worked hard and have a life and he's squandered his."

"Actually, he ain't got that long left to pull," Minter said. "He tells us he only wants to clear his conscience. Wants to start with a clean slate."

"You guys are loadin' up on Mason because of a convict's uncorroborated song and dance?" Custis was calmly fishing, attempting to extract as much as he could from Minter, Bass and Hoffman.

"The boy pretty well passed a polygraph," Hoffman said casually. "Two of 'em. Two different examiners."

"Pretty much?" Custis asked. "Pretty much doesn't cut the mustard, does it, Ed?"

"We know Gates was there when it happened. He knows who done it. Mason was with him. Mason hid the gun. Mason did the alibi. He's twice truthful on those points, Custis. Passed with flyin' colors. I don't like it either."

"He's a sociopath," Mason said. "He probably believes his own cock-and-bull fantasies."

Custis removed his hand from Mason. "He flunked the only one that counts, didn't he, Ed? You asked the sorry turd if Mason shot Wayne Thompson, and your boy Gates went south, didn't he? Even a practiced liar like Gates Hunt couldn't trick the box on the grand-prize question."

"We don't have to tell you our case, Mr. Norman," Bass chimed in. "But let's just say we wouldn't be here unless we were fairly confident of his version of events and had verified it."

"He failed on one and the other was inconclusive," Hoffman said. "I don't mind tellin' you. You're entitled to know. Get the results for trial anyway."

"What a huge surprise," Mason said sarcastically.

"But damn, the men with the voodoo say he's Abe Lincoln on everything else." Hoffman wasn't combative, wasn't gloating.

"They can say he's Malcom X," Custis replied, "and they can confirm it till the cows come home, and we all understand it's not admissible in court. It's worthless to you at trial."

"True," Hoffman agreed. "You asked. I told you. You know me well enough to know I'm not goin' off half-baked. There's a reason I'm investigating. Another small nugget: Gates knows details. Information which wasn't made public. Knows about the club. How the car was positioned. Location of the body. Lights were on high. Details."

"Hell, Ed," Custis scoffed, "everybody knows everything in Stuart—people are all up in their neighbors' business. Rescue squad guy tells his wife what he saw at the scene, she tells her mom, the cat's outta the bag. Can't say I'm impressed."

"I'm just addin' the numbers, Custis," Hoffman said. "Same as you'd do."

"So it's still only my brother's wild accusations," Mason said. "As I'm understanding you, you've confirmed by a polygraph I didn't shoot the victim, and my brother was there and knows who did. Seems to me you're talking to the wrong guy."

"Nice lawyer trick, but that ain't exactly what the results was." Bass was firm, dogged. "If his version is true, then you've been lying 'bout every kind of thing, whether you shot the boy or not."

"So it's his brother's word and a lie-detector test you can't use?" Custis wanted to see how much more Hoffman was willing to give.

"Nope. Bass and Minter recorded Mason. Their first trip to talk to him." Hoffman's hands hadn't moved, and his head hung slightly too far forward, as if it were oddly weighted and straining his neck. "Mason spooks bad when they tell him they got the gun. The gun from the shootin'." He was trained on Custis, speaking as if Mason weren't present. "Sounds guilty. Says it ain't possible we could have the weapon. They jumped him with a little setup. You listen to it, Custis. See what you think. You can tell."

Mason flew hot. "Wait. Hold on. Wait a minute. So you sons of bitches faked a whole damn criminal investigation attempting to get a rise out of me?" He decided to glare at Minter. He jabbed a finger at him. "You tried to . . . to . . . test me by making up an entire fucking case?" He was surprised at how angry he actually was.

"Man, that's some bad shit there," Custis remarked. "Crooked shit. Is that true? You fellows were scammin' Mason and me?"

Minter and Bass seemed momentarily cowed. Hoffman didn't hesitate: "Yep. The Roberts case wasn't real. We ran it by the AG's office. We were extremely careful what we told Roberts. We never accused him of anything. Never arrested him. Asked him a few questions. Played around in his yard and came up with a gun. Let him know we had it. We've explained to him since we were at his house that he's not a suspect. 'Course, we had to tell his wife and write him a letter since he lawyered up on us. Slammed the door. Wanted nothing to do with us. Mad."

"That's the type of police manipulation that should land you fuckers in a world of hurt," Custis said, frowning as he spoke. "I hope Allen Roberts sticks a stake through somebody's heart. You're out of line, Ed. I'm surprised."

"It's frigging illegal to lie to obtain a search warrant last time I checked," Mason said disgustedly. "And serve it on Allen's wife."

"Never happened," Hoffman replied. "They walked onto his land, made a show for everybody to watch and flashed the fake gun. No more. Asked Mr. Roberts about the shooting and about the gun. Two or three questions. No accusations. They gave his wife their business cards and a paper with our addresses and phone numbers. There was never no warrant. We told you it was served on his wife so you wouldn't be askin' Mr. Roberts about it. We created the rest. The witness Frederick Wright was a Salem cop we sent to Roberts's job site. Posed as a carpenter, a subcontractor. Him passin' the lie-detector test was baloney. We had to be sly. Do it different. You're a smart man and a lawyer. If Mr. Roberts has a gripe with us, we'll deal with it. His situation don't help you none, though, Mason. Whether we was right or wrong with how we treated him. Not as I can see."

Mason wasn't finished. "Cat got your tongue, Officer Minter? Don't have the guts to admit how you tried to have me indict an innocent man, scared the shit out of him and abused the system? Broke every rule in the book and fabricated evidence to deceive me? You can go to sleep tonight knowing—*knowing*—that your ass will be investigated the second you walk out of here. You and your dipshit partner both. Hope you weren't counting on a pension. You guys are totally off the rez."

"Do what you have to do," Minter replied. "See if I care. If I was you, I'd be more worried about my statements on the tape than how we got 'em. Remember, you're the fool who pulled Roberts in and grilled him, not us."

"I didn't say shit on your tape. You three are acting like I confessed or something."

"Help me here, but didn't your sting prove Mason's innocence?" Custis surveyed all three cops. "Huh?" He bunched his lips and pretended to be piecing the facts together for the first time. "Man, I gotta tell you, as the assistant commonwealth's attorney for this county and the brother with over twenty years' experience in this office, Mason reviewed the file with me and green-lighted it. I mean, come on, he told me to call you and agree to indict."

"Never would've happened," Bass said. "Misdirection."

"Hell, it did happen," Custis insisted. "I'll show you the damn paperwork. We were ready." He stood. "In fact, seein' how you guys are playin' this, I'm gonna have Sheila go fetch the actual document and give you a copy for your file, so you'll know we were on the up-and-up and ready to take it to the grand jury."

"Appreciate it," Hoffman said.

"I'm not impressed," Custis remarked. "This isn't like you, Ed."

"I'm trying to be as fair as I can," the officer replied.

"Anything else we should know?" Custis probed.

Hoffman smiled, a grin without any happiness. "Sorry. Have to turn off the spigot. You'd be entitled to this stuff anyway before trial. But it ain't our ace. I'm not at liberty to divulge any more. I would if it was possible."

"Your ace?" Mason asked, trying to sound sure of himself. "Sounds like you'll need it, because so far you've shown us a two and three of clubs."

"I wouldn't be so cocky if I was you," Bass said smugly.

"I will tell you," Hoffman added, "that Judge Williams down in Henry County has already appointed a special prosecutor. He's calling the shots now. The attorney general's office is basically through."

"So who's the turncoat prosecuting a fellow commonwealth's attorney?" Custis asked. "Based on this bullshit evidence."

"Went through nineteen people to find somebody," Hoffman replied. "Least that's what I'm informed. You should take that as a compliment, Mason. Recognition of your good reputation. The guy they finally got is a reckless little shrimp from Waynesboro, name of Leonard Stallings. Ink addict this one, with big plans for himself. This would be a hide for his trophy wall. I wish for everybody's sake we'd done better in that area."

"You want to talk about the shooting?" Bass asked. "Tell us your side? We've somehow managed to jump off track, but we're here to interview you. It'd probably be helpful to us all if you cooperate. Help you and us."

"Yeah. Take out your pad and pen. Listen carefully to my cooperation. Write this down. My brother is a liar. I didn't shoot Wayne Thompson. I have an absolute alibi which you can confirm from the old files. End of story, end of our interview."

"It only makes it worse if you—"

"Mr. Bass, I'm afraid I'm not going to be swayed by the Dick Tracy strategies they taught you in the three-hour interrogation class at the academy. What—next you're supposed to offer me a cigarette or a free soda? I'm not a junkie or a dim-witted thief. We're done. I'm innocent, so there's nothing to discuss."

"I was only trying to give you a chance—"

"You heard Mr. Hunt," Hoffman interrupted forcefully, respectfully. "He said we're done, and so we're done." He shot Mason a frank look. "This is bad for the both of us. Ugly business. I'm not happy with none of it. But the truth is, as much as it hurts, unless things change, come this fall, Stallings is gonna insist on an indictment. He'll skip June grand jury. Too rushed. Case still needs our report from today and a little more prep. But it's comin'. Let me know if anything occurs to you between now and then." He finally disturbed his hands, lifting them to chest level. He matched fingertip to fingertip but kept his palms spread apart. Head bowed, speaking almost inaudibly, he said, "It would be awful to try and help a man and have it switched around on you. A brother. Your favor used against you."

Mason could feel Custis beside him. He smelled the chemicals in Custis's dry-cleaned suit and a pungent edge on his breath. He waited for Hoffman to set the hook with his eyes, to invite him into an easy, compromised door, but Hoffman cut it off there, never showed anything more than the top of his shiny head. Mason avoided the temptation to answer, and the police filed out, gone.

Cautious and rattled, Mason and Custis remained tight-lipped after the cops exited the room, their positions unchanged, Custis propped against the credenza, Mason listless in front of his high-backed leather chair, the seams outlined by decorative brass nailheads. Eventually, Custis shuffled to the door and closed it, first checking outside the office to make certain no one was within earshot. He flopped into the seat Minter had just left, his huge, thick legs stretched and splayed.

"Damn," Mason said.

"No shit," Custis replied.

"*Damn.*"

"Man-oh-man, this saga all of a sudden got ill. Severe."

"What else do you think they have?" Mason asked. "I mean, hell, what else *could* they have? Huh?" He picked up the phone and had Sheila confirm that the cops were no longer in the building. "They're bluffing, aren't they?" he said when he'd finished speaking to her.

"I don't know, Chief. It wouldn't be Ed Hoffman's style to threaten cards he's not actually holdin'. I'm worried sick. He's shrewd, too—you hear him talking about how awful it'd be for your own brother to take advantage of you? Ed's no chump. 'Course, I figure he's doin' all he can to benefit us, revealing as much as possible."

"Damn."

"I know. I'm hard-pressed to see how we're gonna beat the odds on this, Mace. Sounds as if they're waiting for the grand jury, and ain't much we're able to do. I swear I think this Stallings mother-fucker's going to drop papers on you." Custis shook his head, stopped, then shook it even more vigorously. "You talk about this and think about it and it's all abstract and just like that they show up with the badges and bullets and pepper spray and it grabs you by the collar and completely mugs you, whales on you, real as can be. I gotta admit it kinda caught me off guard."

"Maybe they're bluffing," Mason repeated without much conviction. "They ran an elaborate sting to start this, right? Gates simply can't give them a shred of hard evidence. He can't. It's impossible." Mason's color had seeped away—his skin was blanched, mushy, the hue of lima beans left simmering too long on the stove. For the moment, there was no fight in him, no resistance. He was limp, squashed, passive, bobbing in the undertow. "Mystery to me," he mumbled. "A few months from now, though, unless there's a hellacious change, I'm going to be arrested."

"We'll figure something out," Custis promised. "And if we don't, we'll coldcock the bastards at trial."

"This is unbelievable, Cus."

"Damn."

Mason recovered some, firmed up. "If you need to, feel free to hop off the bus right now. I mean it. I appreciate your being here today and everything you've done, but—"

"Hey," Custis butted in, "fuck that. I'm your lawyer, right? I'm not about to take a dive on you, nosir, not a chance. I'm not goin' anywhere."

"Thanks. So I guess we just wait for the other shoe to fall, huh? Unless we can magically turn my shitbird brother around, and I don't think we've got too many options where he's concerned."

"Well, let's concentrate on that for a minute," Custis said. "Perhaps we can—"

Sheila knocked and opened the door without waiting for a response. "Sorry, guys, but we're already way behind, and Mr. Gunter has to be at the dentist's and Mr. Stovall has a load of cows to take to the stockyard and everybody's getting impatient. Can I send them in?"

"Yep. Go ahead," Mason told her. He glanced at Custis. "We'll keep thinking and see if we can come up with a solution."

"Definitely," Custis said. He thumped Sheila on the top of her head as they were leaving Mason's office, a silly, playful pop with his forefinger that caused her to laugh and freeze where she stood and ask him if he thought other professionals acted like second graders, childishly harassing staff members. "I don't know why they wouldn't," he kidded her. "Especially if their staff's all grumpy and wound tight and it's not even noon yet."

Walter Gunter, Hubert Stovall, Avery Wood, Marvin Stanley, Lucas Barnette and James Staples were all businessmen of one sort or another, and they were almost the entire membership of Patrick County's economic development commission. They were ebullient when they paraded into Mason's office, beside themselves with grand news, almost squirming, reminiscent of schoolboys waiting in line for their first ride on the Tilt-A-Whirl at the county fair. "Have you heard Caldwell-Dylan is probably comin' to Stuart?" Gunter asked Mason when everyone had crowded into the room.

"Bits and pieces," Mason answered. He was distracted, irritable, his mind elsewhere. He wasn't in the mood for the men's panting enthusiasm, nor did he give a damn—right then—who was planning to locate in Stuart. Still, he attempted to be polite, aware that he might need to call his current visitors as witnesses at his trial to testify how composed he was, hardly acting like a criminal who'd been caught and exposed only minutes before. "I understand Herman Dylan is interested."

"Aw, no, Mason, he's more than interested," Stovall drawled. "So you don't know the latest?" he asked, pleased to be an insider, giddy with his secrets.

"I guess not, Hubert. Why don't you enlighten me?" Despite his best efforts, Mason sounded nettled, and the men noticed and dialed back their smiles and high-octane exuberance.

"Yeah, well, Mr. Dylan isn't just interested. He's as good as here. We got it from the horse's mouth."

"Oh?" Mason raised his eyebrows.

"Yeah. We was guests of Mr. Dylan's at the Homestead last weekend. He put us up and bought us dinner, the royal treatment."

"My wife got a massage," Lucas Barnette volunteered. He was wearing a short-sleeve shirt and striped tie, khaki Dockers. He owned several Laundromats and car washes. "I played golf."

"The point of it all," Stovall continued, "was for us to meet with his top man, this gentleman by the name of Ian Hudgens. Mr. Hudgens showed us a presentation, and he's given us his promise that their company Chip-Tech will come to Stuart if you can lock 'em into a grant from the tobacco people."

"There're a few other strings as well," James Staples noted. "But we can make it happen. Water, sewer, tax exemptions. A shell building."

"The thing is, Mason," Stovall said, "we need you to get on your hind legs and make them give us the grant. It's the key. You need to hang tough and really fight for us in Richmond at the next meetin'."

"I understand," Mason told him. "But I'm still not as sold on this as you guys are. Maybe missing out on the canapés and lush fairways has left me poorly educated, but from my research so far, Herman Dylan has a spotty record, most notably in terms of staying put after the free money expires. This grant is going to be critical for us—let's make certain we don't trade our birthright for a cup of porridge."

"These are new-paradigm jobs, Mason," Barnette announced. "We're comin' in on the ground floor with an industry that will have a long life. Textiles and furniture are gone to places overseas. Dead and dying. Here's a new beginning for us. Seventy jobs, great jobs, and a chance for many more. Expansion's almost a given. I don't see the downside."

Mason cracked a smile. " 'New-paradigm jobs,' Lucas? That term must have appeared early in the dog-and-pony show. Listen, all I'm saying is let's not rush into an arrangement and waste our money. Four or five years from now, we don't want to see the moving trucks and padlocks on the factory gates. Mr. Dylan has hit the high-way far too frequently for me to be completely comfortable. For starters, it might be wise to extract some tighter guarantees from our prosperous suitor and not just hand him the combination to the vault. I agree it's a business with significant potential for us all, but we have an obligation to negotiate the best deal possible for the county."

Marvin Stanley spoke for the first time. "I'm with you, Mason. No need to burn our resources and wind up screwed. It may be to our advantage, it may not. You ride herd on it and find out."

"Well," Gunter snipped, "I hope we don't dicker and dither and lose the best chance this area's had in years. There are other locali-ties champing at the bit for this factory. I think I speak for the rest of us, and we're convinced it's a sound project. We've seen the num-bers and met the head honcho personally. Let's hope you can arrange the tobacco money. We're ready to take care of the other incentives we can control, the local issues."

"I'll consider your opinions," Mason said tersely. "Then I'll do what I think is right. No more and no less. Thanks for stopping by."

At lunchtime, Mason informed Sheila he needed "to see a man about a dog" and wouldn't be returning, and she'd have to cancel his afternoon appointments or transfer them to Custis. Sorry, but she'd just have to do it. He drove to his house, changed clothes and collected his fishing gear, stopping by the Panda #2 to buy a tub of live night crawlers on his route home. Like most county stores, they kept the big worms in their cooler during the warm months, on the bottom rack beside the eggs, bologna and Jesse Jones sausage, next-door neighbors to the beer and wine. Mason removed a container, took off a lid that was pricked with tiny pinholes and shook the dark dirt to get a peek at the bait, made sure the crawlers were fresh before taking them to be rung up.

He went to Kibler Valley and planted a lawn chair on a skinny sandbar that connected with the bank and fingered into the Dan River. He cut a branch from a maple tree and pared it down to a "Y" shape, sharpened the end and twisted it into the ground, cast and set his rod in the stick's fork. Above him the river was fast and truculent, a series of choppy falls and swift rushes, but it gradually relaxed into a deep, calm pool that joined the sandbar, no bottom in sight, the water good for fishing. The river was noisy where it shot quick and white, the sound penned in by trees and steep hills on both sides. An occasional car or truck would pass on the dirt road ribboning through the valley, none of the vehicles making much speed.

Mason sat there in his chair and let the May sun coat his skin. He studied the eddies and swirls, finding leaves, twigs, foam bubbles or an unfortunate bug, then watched them ride and bounce and dip along, carried off downstream. He felt better, braced, unencumbered. Finally let alone. He'd purchased a six-pack of Budweiser at the Panda, but he left the beer cooling in the shallows next to his chair, untouched. Despite his laziness with the rod, he caught a trout, a decent-size rainbow, hooked through the lip. Pulled to land, the fish's gills fanned open and shut—red and silver, red and silver—and it had a stunted fin in the front, a translucent nub, probably worn to nothing on the hatchery concrete before it was stocked. Mason removed the hook and lowered the trout back into the water. He watched its silhouette dart for the heart of the hole, and he hoped, somehow, he would receive the same courtesy when—and if—his day came.

Chapter Fifteen

The following Monday, Route 58 to Stuart was blocked by a paving crew, ten or twelve dump trucks lined up in one lane, waiting to spread their asphalt, a steamroller idling behind them, flagmen with two-way radios posted at both ends of the project, slouching against their traffic signs, flipping STOP or SLOW depending on which side was needed. "Brown-out season," Curt Hunt had always called it. "You know it's hot weather for damn sure when the Mexicans and coloreds finally start their five months of yearly road work." He'd say it snidely every spring, usually at supper, perturbed for whatever reason, chewing while he spoke, then licking his fingers, dirty grease-monkey nails and all.

Stalled on the highway with the radio mute and the windows partially lowered, Mason listened to the diesel engines clatter and rehashed what he'd decided on the riverbank: There was nothing—*nothing*—to be gained by wringing his hands, fretting, anticipating Armageddon or collapsing into fear and spoiling the days and weeks to come. A trial was the absolute worst possibility, and as wretched and embarrassing as it would be, he was at home in a courtroom and he'd win and be free to raise his magnificent daughter. Afterward, people might whisper or gawk or think less of him, but he'd manage, just as he always had. He'd grown up with a violent madman on his heels, every moment a tightrope walk across an infernal pit, and he was fiercely resilient because of it, impervious, whet-leather tough and able to wall himself off and stand his ground. Custis would help him prepare for a trial if it came to that, and he'd hire a crackerjack lawyer and they'd all go to battle. Fuck it—he'd lived with bigger problems and not knuckled under.

He received the SLOW command and touched the gas. Homer Amos was operating the steamroller, perched in its tiny round se wearing a hard hat and a fluorescent safety vest, and he waved at Mason, shouted hello and called him by name. "Lock 'em all up, Mr. Commonwealth," he said as Mason pulled away, "and keep that ol' assistant of yours straight."

Mason and Custis arrived at the parking lot within seconds of each other, and Custis beckoned him over to the Cadillac and invited him inside. Tucked into the passenger seat, Mason noticed the car smelled of drive-through breakfast biscuits and a splash of top-drawer cologne. He twisted toward the rear, pretending to search the interior.

"What?" Custis asked. "What're you lookin' for?"

"The source of the nice smell. Since there's nothing dangling from the mirror, I thought maybe you were riding high with one of those classy air-freshener crowns in the back window."

"Yeah, well, they were sold slam-out at the dealership when I checked. It's aftershave balm, a skin-care product. It's why I look like I'm thirty and you remind people of Granny Clampett."

Mason laughed.

"So I've been at the grindstone all weekend, Mace, tryin' to crack this. I couldn't sleep."

Mason focused on his friend, barely blinking. "Listen—I'm not going to cave, not going to cower, not going to let it dominate my life. I've made it through rougher times. Hell, this is only a blip on the Curt Hunt scale of discomfort."

"Somehow, we need to yank the switch on your brother and shut him down. He's the key."

"No doubt," Mason agreed.

"It's gonna be impossible for you or me to get a clean shot at him; cops are bound to be watchin' him like a hawk. In fact, he probably wouldn't even speak to us."

"True," Mason said. Leon, the dog warden, walked past the car and wagged two fingers, grinned. Two of a kind, it meant in Stuart. Quite a pair.

"I hate to even bring it up, but you think Sadie Grace could—"

"Nope. No, no, no, no. No. It'll ruin her when this breaks. It'll be bad enough then. More to the point, I'm not about to rely on my mama's apron strings."

"I guessed as much," Custis said somberly. "Don't blame you."

"I can't phone him, and I damn sure can't write. I'm guessing he doesn't have access to the Internet, huh?"

"A whore like Gates, if we can offer him a more attractive prize, he'll change his tune. Feeble as it is, that's gotta be our strategy until we can shake something else loose."

"I've done the same calculations," Mason said. "Gates is their whole case."

"I'll keep at it," Custis vowed.

"Thanks."

"You're positive there's no way they have the gun? Or a witness? Or evidence you've forgotten about? Surprises are cool at birthdays and Christmas, a bitch at trial."

"Like I said, I hid the gun myself and we scraped the barrel. Can't be any other witnesses, or they'd have surfaced years ago. I've been through it with a fine-tooth comb, Custis, and it's a mystery to me."

"Another thing: You know I'm with you—every step I'm right there—but if this goes to trial, you're goin' to need a lawyer besides me. I appreciate what the retainer does, the protection and so forth, and you understand I'd be glad to do the time behind bars for you if it came to that, but number one, you'll need me to testify, and number two, we both realize I can't represent you while I'm an active commonwealth's attorney. The state and the bar would probably take a dim view."

"I know. I've been thinking about who to hire."

"I'll work like the Godfather of Soul for as long as I can, and I'll raise my right hand and be the sweetest witness you've ever seen— you can take that to the savings and loan."

"I appreciate it. I owe you. Someday, somehow, I'll return the favor."

"But if this doesn't disappear soon, you'd better be linin' up a lawyer."

"No need to retain somebody now and have the world gossiping about my problems and telling tales. You and I can do whatever needs to be done until an indictment. Let's keep the situation under our hats for the time being. Maybe we'll get lucky and the lawyer question will be moot."

"I'm committed to beatin' it for you," Custis said. "I won't quit."

"Do I also smell biscuits in here? The bacon, egg and cheese from Hardee's part of your new diet? You sign up for the long-haul-trucker weight-management plan?"

"I've lost seven pounds, thank you. Ain't a man alive who can go total cold turkey."

At his desk there was a pink message slip in Sheila's flowery script informing him a Mr. Ian Hudgens had phoned and wanted Mason to return his call. Mason had her ring him while he checked through her other notes and reminders. Hudgens was in Manhattan, and he spoke with a cosmopolitan's studied lack of accent—his diction to the tee, his vowels neutral and sterile—as if he'd grown up in Saginaw or Butte or Gainesville and taken a postgraduate class somewhere along the line to master the details of hip ennui and whitewashed intonation. He juggled sounding cordial and blandly superior, no small task. "I had hopes we could meet and discuss our Chip-Tech endeavor," he explained after they'd run through their formalities and chitchat about Patrick County's splendid weather. Mason imagined the word "endeavor" leaving Hudgens's lips with its affected British spelling: *Endeavour* was the way he heard Hudgens fashioning it.

"I'm not sure we need to meet," Mason said politely. "You can just tell me over the phone what's on your mind."

"Ah. Yes. Exactly. I'd thought perhaps I could be even more informative face-to-face, but I understand you are a busy man with a full schedule."

"I don't know how busy I am, but I'll be glad to hear you out. We could use a solid employer."

"I'm grateful," Hudgens said. "Though we would be pleased to invite you to New York as our guest and let you have a closer, more intimate look at who we are and how we operate. Mr. Dylan will see to it you are well received—a Yankees game, Broadway, a restaurant of your choosing, whatever engages you."

"Very kind of you and Mr. Dylan, but I'm not sure I'd be entirely comfortable accepting hospitality from folks I'm considering for a multimillion-dollar contract. Might be a little sticky ethically."

"I respect your sensitivity," Hudgens replied. "Of course, the trip would be purely educational."

"So what exactly is it you want me to know?" Mason asked, impatiently enough that Hudgens knew to move on.

"To be candid, some of your fellow citizens there in Stuart tell me you have questions about us and our intentions. Our viability and good faith. I'd like to dispel any reluctance you have along those lines. Cure any misgivings. As your region's Tobacco Commission representative, you will have great influence on our plans to locate in Patrick County. We want to convince you we're an asset for your area."

Mason tried to put a face to the voice—he envisioned slicked-back dark hair, clear skin, slippery eyes, trendy spectacles, a slightly beaked nose. "Feel free to tell me anything or send me information or come to Stuart and make your pitch. To be honest, I've spent a fair amount of time investigating your company's track record, and the big problem for me is your staying power. You gentlemen have a tendency to spend the free money and hit the door."

"I applaud you for safeguarding your community and its investment. Sincerely, I do. But I trust you'll also note our long presence in many, many locales after the grants and incentives have disappeared, often to our detriment. Given your research, you must know our plants have long tenures in Columbia, South Carolina, in Bangor, Maine, and in the modest city of Fremont, Ohio. We understand our obligation to the communities who have welcomed us and dedicated their resources to our arrival."

"True enough. But since 1998, you've shut down five plants in four different states, every one in a smaller locale like ours, and the closings always come, as best I can tell, soon after the freebies expire."

"In many instances, we find ourselves at the mercy of marketplace conditions we can't manage. Taking a manufacturing unit offline is also very costly for us. It's certainly not part of our business model or a systematic component in our integrated strategy. I would invite you to contact Mr. Clay Austin, the city manager for Hopkinsville, Kentucky; he will tell you we struggled mightily to remain intact in his small town, but we simply could not fill the job slots with competent, qualified people. In fact, he will tell you that, if anything, we—Caldwell-Dylan—were sold a bill of goods in terms of the quality of their available workforce. I can only trust you will look at the big picture and not a few isolated realignments."

"I haven't come to a decision yet," Mason said. "And hearing your perspective is helpful. I don't have any agenda except to do the best I can for Patrick County. Once we receive our grant, we're not going to be able to return to the well for a second dip. I'm taking this seriously. I want to ensure we don't wind up in the hands of confidence men and highfliers, our only stake down the tubes."

"And we want to partner with you to make this a worthwhile, profitable relationship for all involved. We are proud of this company's commitment to our workers and their communities. In fact, I'll overnight you a copy of our charitable giving."

"Really? Huh. Excellent," Mason said, his tone suddenly positive, accommodating. "I think charity's critical. I'm pleased to hear you feel it's important to lend a hand."

"We do everything from Little League to fire departments."

"Our fire departments and rescue squads are all volunteer, so any contribution means a lot. They work hard for free and squeak by on fund-raisers and donations. A real shoestring budget."

"A crying shame," Hudgens remarked.

"Recognizing their dedication carries quite a bit of weight wi, me," Mason added.

"I'm sure we will be eager to make a generous commitment if we set up shop in Patrick. I'm delighted we have this as a common denominator. Whether we're awarded our grant or not, I would certainly be honored to cut a check immediately as a token of our goodwill. As an employer, we also value fire and rescue personnel— they are vital to what we do. How does two thousand dollars sound?"

"Great. But five sounds better."

"Five it is," Hudgens agreed.

"Thanks. Make it payable to the Patrick Springs Volunteer Fire Department. They cover the district where I live, and they can use the cash."

"Consider it done. I'll have it forwarded to your office."

"So I take it you're the man to contact about any changes in the terms of your deal?" Mason's voice remained upbeat.

"Changes?"

"Yes. I'm happy to have established this channel," Mason said, smiling to himself, "so we can streamline our negotiations."

"Uh, yes, I'm always available to discuss any issues," Hudgens answered after a moment's hesitation, caught off guard because he hadn't sweet-talked Mason into submission and bribed him with shiny beads and a pittance for the natives.

"Excellent. We can start by adding some assurances in your contract with the county, guaranteed by Mr. Dylan personally or a corporate surety, that you will remain here for a minimum of ten years and provide seventy jobs with a pay scale forty percent above minimum wage. If you fail to do so, depending on when you breach, you refund a pro-rata share of the local tax forgiveness and the tobacco grant. Gives us security, gives you your free money, and we both have every incentive to make your stay in Patrick profitable and lengthy." By the end of his proposal, it was evident the earlier aw-shucks acquiescence in Mason's voice had been feint and flypaper, a snare.

"I see. Of course, we believe the document as written is extremely fair. We find it difficult to be economically bound to situations we have little or no control over. Speaking for Mr. Dylan, I can honestly say we'd thought our reputation, integrity and global success would be sufficient to warrant your county's acceptance of our terms without change." Hudgens sharpened his words: "While it is theoretically possible we could encounter events which require your facility to become superfluous, it is equally possible we could expand threefold wherein you receive more than you bargained for. As we see it, this is classic risk allocation."

"So's a dice game in an alley," Mason said. "Doesn't mean I want to play."

"I mention this as background and for no other reason: As you might guess, there's quite a queue for this plant. While Patrick County is near the top of our wish list, we have other attractive alternatives."

"So you won't give us any guarantees or structure a repayment if you fold your tents?"

"I will bring it to Mr. Dylan's attention, but I'm not optimistic. I doubt he'll want to purchase a sea of monetary uncertainty, and any underwriting via insurance would not be cost-effective for us. There may be a degree of tweaking or a very limited guarantee we can provide, but, much as I despair in saying it, your demands could be a barrier to consummating the deal."

"Hmmm," Mason grunted. "Consummating and getting screwed are close kin in this part of the world."

"Pardon?"

"The commission is meeting soon. I'll let you know what I decide."

"Thank you," Hudgens said. "I appreciate the consideration. I truly believe if you reflect on the offer, you'll conclude it's beneficial to you, your county and Caldwell-Dylan. As best I can discern, you are the only fence-sitter, the only obstacle holding up this transaction. Your various boards and any number of prominent citizens have embraced us and are eager to make this happen. As is. Without change. Perhaps I might send them in your direction?"

"Jeez, no. Thanks. I've already had an earful." Mason chuckled to let Hudgens know there were no hard feelings. "Believe it or not, I have an open mind. See what Mr. Dylan will do. Please at least ask him about my suggestion. I want this to come together, too."

"I will. I look forward to wrapping this up to everyone's satisfaction."

The following afternoon the fire department check arrived, FedExed overnight, and included in the envelope were four third-row-center seats to see *The Lion King* and a number to call for "courtesy round-trip air to New York, plus hotel and transportation." Mason had Sheila return the tickets the very same day, but when he foolishly mentioned the lost opportunity to Grace, she pitched a hissy fit and howled and pouted because she wouldn't get to go and had to live her life in the sticks, set on a dead-end trek to the white-trash backwoods. "Don't blame me," she griped, "if I wind up stuck in Branscomb's Trailer Court with tube tops and purple Maybelline eye shadow."

Mason allowed a parent's amused, wiser-than-thou expression to form, drawing and rolling his mouth, pretending he was trying to derail a smile but—this was the infuriating part—letting on he really wasn't taking her seriously, and she became madder and madder and madder, to the point of tears. Twenty minutes later he knocked on her bedroom door and conveyed through the wood he'd called his cousin Sean in New York, and they now had two *Lion King* tickets for July, as well as a fancy hotel room to boot, a suite at the Waldorf. Within seconds she was in the hall, bouncing, excited, squealing and proclaiming him the best dad in the world. "I'm sorry I was such a baby. Wait till I tell Evette and Monica—they'll die," she said, and off she went to call her girlfriends, her door once again closed to him.

On the anniversary of Allison's death, her daughter and husband rode together to the Stuart Cemetery in the late afternoon and visited her gravesite. Mason knelt and plucked away a few grass sprigs that had trespassed over the boundary of her foot-marker, and he stared down at the dates cut in granite, but, for Grace's sake, he strangled his emotions, refusing to tear up or cry. When she wasn't watching, he shut his eyes and recalled the blind, splendid times before he'd been force-fed forbidden fruit and schooled in what could indeed *happen*, the dandy years before he feared that every tractor-trailer might veer across the center line and worried that every muscle cramp was multiple sclerosis, every belch a stomach cancer's calling card. There'd been a day when he and Allison set their clocks by cocktail parties and the future was simply the next weekend, the next thirty ticks of a second hand, the lazy minutes it took him, sprawled naked on a sagging couch, to recover and have another go at sex. Now, like it or not, his horizon line had evaporated and there was a long view, and it was full of chicanes, perils, hazards and pit traps, enough inevitable bad news to make anyone jittery. He opened his eyes. He caught sight of a man unloading a push mower from a pickup bed, a red and yellow gas can already on the ground beside him.

After they'd been there a while, silent and keeping to themselves, Grace asked Mason if he was planning to stay forever.

"Huh?" he mumbled, distracted. "Stay, uh, where?"

"Here," she answered, childishly put out with him. "Looming. Invading my privacy."

"Oh. Okay. I see. Yeah. Sorry." He was standing by then, and he pawed at the ground with the toe of his black dress shoe. He jingled the coins in his pocket. He blew a kiss toward the dirt and said "Bye, Love," to his wife, said it aloud. Finally, he bent over and moved the flowers he'd brought—red roses, a frivolous gift that would soon wilt in the sun—to a spot a few inches away from where they already were and rotated the vase half a turn, leaving everything just so for Allison, doing all he could for her, even if it was only bustle and fuss and not a soul would notice the difference in the big grave-yard, monotonous with its headstones and chiseled names. "No hurry," he told Grace. "I'll be in the car."

She stayed for fifteen minutes more, and checking on her in the mirror, Mason could see she was speaking occasionally, and as she was leaving she removed a rose from his arrangement and dropped it onto the grass. Her cheeks were damp and her breathing knotty when she returned to the car. Mason met her, and she allowed him to drape her shoulder and walk her to the passenger side, help her with the door. He cooked them a better meal than normal, and after supper they unboxed snapshots and photo albums, but neither of them mourned or strayed into sadness, and Grace smiled at one picture of her mother, beheld it as if she were viewing a movie-poster stranger, and she remarked on how gorgeous Allison was, how perfectly she wore her dress.

On a stale, humdrum morning in the middle of June, Mason was crossing the town's public parking lot, returning to his office after a short docket in general district court, and he thought he heard someone say his name. He checked behind him but didn't break stride until he heard the voice again. He followed it to his left where he spotted a man rising out of a green Honda. It was Ed Hoffman, and seeing him startled Mason so much he quit walking and, like a dope, allowed one of his files to get loose and fall to the ground. Papers went everywhere, but thank God there was no wind.

"Sorry," Hoffman said, approaching Mason. He gestured at the spilled file. "Need me to help you?"

"Hey, Ed." Mason was gathering his papers, trying not to rush or appear discombobulated. "Well, I suppose if you're here to arrest me, you can hold off on the cuffs long enough for me to pick up everything. I need both hands free."

"Nah. Personal visit."

Mason finished collecting the file's contents. Page corners were sticking from the top, bottom and side, slapdash. "Personal in what sense?" he asked.

"Buy you coffee or a cold drink?"

"Do I need my lawyer?" Mason wanted to know.

"Personal, Mason. Off the record." As usual, Hoffman spoke in abbreviated bursts, stinting with his words.

"There's a new coffee shop on Main Street—Stuart's climbing the ladder. You willing to spring for a two-buck cup of decaf?"

"Good coffee's worth two dollars. My opinion it is. I drink it by the bucket." He was gripping a rolled-up magazine, popping it against his palm.

"I'm surprised, tight as you are," Mason needled him.

"I also spend extra for sheets. Third of your life, you're in bed. No place to skimp. Me, I'm a thread-count man. I'll pay top dollar for quality linens."

"Are you serious?"

"I am. Why wouldn't I be?" He continued a beat with the magazine that had no relation to their conversation.

"Any other extravagances?" Mason asked.

"Nope. Not on what the state pays me."

At Firebaugh's Coffee they took a corner table away from the counter and its traffic. Mason asked for lemonade, fresh-made by the owner, and Hoffman ordered a specialty blend that had to be started from scratch, the beans scooped from a canister and ground.

"So what's the 'personal' concern that brings you to my neck of the woods?" Mason asked soon after they'd been served.

"We're friends, Mason. I hate where we're at right now. With your brother. Me and you know you didn't shoot nobody. Least I don't think you did." He stopped stirring his coffee and peered up at Mason, then returned to his spoon and sugar packets. "But it's hinky. Gates is too close to the bull's-eye. Me, I got my idea of what happened. You already know that." He bounced another glance off Mason, who remained impassive.

"I'm listening, Ed."

"Gates Hunt is a dung beetle. Truth be told, I'd bet he done it. Hell, the dead boy wasn't screwing your gal, now was he?"

Mason hadn't touched his drink. Water beads were forming on the plastic glass, on the cusp of trickling. "I'm happy to hear whatever you have to say, Ed, but, uh, help me here, this hardly seems like a personal visit. Sounds to me like this is part two of my interrogation."

"I ain't on duty. I promised you we're off the record. Gave you my word."

"No notes, no wires? You're not recording me?"

"No," Hoffman snarled. "Hell no. We know each other better

than that. You want, we'll step in the toilet and you can shine a light up my ass. I'm not in Stuart, never was."

"I didn't know cops were ever off duty. Exactly how does that operate? I suppose if I were to confess right now, you'd act like it never happened, huh?" Mason took a swallow of lemonade. He kept the glass in the air so it came between him and Hoffman. "So, anyhow, you were saying?" He lowered the drink.

"If I'm readin' this right, you're between a rock and a hard place. For another man's crime. Brass tacks, my friend, I'm assuming you covered for him. Not legal by the book, but understandable between brothers. Don't have to be a genius to solve the puzzle. Unless you're Minter. Minter's fuckin' Sherlock Holmes. He's after you, believes what he wants to believe. You're in Minter's sights."

"I'm still listening, Ed. Let me just say again, I had no involvement in Wayne's death, before, during or after, but I'm happy to listen."

"Gotcha. I understand. My proposal: a polygraph. I'll bind the commonwealth, put it in writing. You pass, you walk. You fail, we throw it away. Can't use it at trial."

"Can't use it anyway, Ed. We've already traveled this road. I'm not about to take a polygraph." Mason put his elbows on the table and laced his fingers.

"Difference being, you pass it and everything ends. That's new. It's a bonus not many receive. Satisfy the examiner, you're done. You fail, we can't hurt you with it. Stallings'll never catch wind of it. He'll never know if you bomb. Also, I'll see to it you only have to answer two questions. One: Did you shoot Wayne Thompson? Two—"

"I didn't," Mason interjected.

"Two: Do you know who did?"

"Lee Harvey Oswald, maybe? Woody Harrelson's dad? Raoul, this international guy with sunglasses I met in a bar?" Mason unlocked his hands. "I don't have any idea who shot Wayne Thompson, and as much as I trust you, I don't trust the lie-box, and more important, I have to question whether you can legally bind our pal Mr. Stallings, even if you wanted to."

"Already thought of that. I'll sign off on it, and Mike Madison in the attorney general's office will, too. We'll write it down. I'll play dumb. Pretend I didn't know we were operating through Stallings. Mike has high regard for you. You were in law school together?"

"Yeah. We were friends in school, then we kept in touch while Allison and I were living in Richmond."

"You can't lose. I'm offering a free spin at the big wheel."

Mason jabbed at the ice in his glass with the wrong end of a butter knife. He spoke while he was stabbing the ice, his head down, Hoffman completely missing from his vision. "I appreciate it, Ed. I realize you don't have too many days off, and it's kind of you to burn your gas and waste one on me. I understand you're trying to help me and respect your job at the same time." He adjusted his gaze to take in the detective. "Sitting here, right this moment, the answer is maybe. I'll give it some more thought, and if I decide to do it, I'll contact you. If I decline, it doesn't mean I'm not grateful. Why don't you see if you and Madison can have something typed up and finalized for me to review?"

"Already done." Hoffman opened the magazine and withdrew two sheets of paper held together with a single corner staple. "Mr. Madison signed. I signed. Place for you to sign."

"Huh." Mason could see the heading of the document: FULL IMMUNITY AGREEMENT. "You're way ahead of me." He laid the knife on a paper napkin, and the lemonade began to spread and dissolve the area around the handle. "Of course, a court might rule the AG's office has no standing and I receive zilch. I'd wind up screwed, jumping through hoops for nothing. Let me sleep on it. I'll probably discuss it with Custis, too." The papers were bowed from their stay in the rolled-up magazine, didn't rest flat on the table. Mason took them and turned them facedown. He pressed them with both hands, trying to mash away the hump. "If I don't accept your offer, Ed, it has nothing to do with my guilt or innocence," Mason dissembled, already building an excuse for his friend. "From here to trial, it's just about strategy, whatever works best."

"No problem. Unless it's cheatin' or illegal, I'll do everything I can for you."

They spent a few more minutes talking about Grace and the professional baseball standings, and as they were heading for the door, Mason noticed Hoffman had left his magazine on the table. Mason reminded him he'd forgotten it, and Hoffman immediately said, "Yeah. Meant to leave it. It's not an accident."

"Oh."

"Good merchandise in there," Hoffman said with odd vigor and enthusiasm.

"Okay," Mason replied uncertainly.

"I'm done with it. Don't need it."

"Maybe I should go retrieve it," Mason said.

"Free country, Mason. You're welcome to. Might learn a lot." Hoffman extended his hand. "I'm goin' home. Treatin' my granddaughter to the zoo. She loves the tigers. Enjoyed the coffee with you. It was worth the price."

Mason accepted his hand. "Take care," he said, and he watched Hoffman leave and never turn around to see what was happening behind him. He had a quick, upright walk, almost ceremonial, like a palace guard or a drum major.

The magazine, Mason discovered, was actually a trade catalog for a company called Tactical Technologies, and one color page was conspicuously dog-eared. It displayed an "audio listening device," model CST 702V, and described its transmitting distance, power requirements, number of channels, size, cost and warranty period. It was endorsed by a police chief from Delaware. The remainder of the catalog was more of the same.

Mason sat back down, took the knife by the proper end and began poking at his lemonade again. He ran through the possibilities, picking apart his clue: It could be no more than Hoffman warning him generally to watch his step and keep his yap shut, simply a friend reiterating the basics, a reminder that the state is omnipresent, the walls have ears. More likely, though, it meant Mason was being monitored, his office bugged, perhaps his home or car. Because he had a lawyer's perpetual fear of eavesdroppers and intercepts, he would never discuss his predicament over the phone, but maybe that was it, a warning not to forget how easily the authorities could obtain a wiretap. He knew they'd miked Gates at the prison, but this was too much song and dance for old news, so he discarded that theory. It was a listening *device,* not a hidden wire or small camera, so it seemed most likely Hoffman was tipping him about a problem in his house or office. And, of course, it was possible that he—nervous, apprehensive, paranoid—was misreading the policeman's intent, seeing haunts and shadows where there were none, and the forgotten catalog was merely a forgotten catalog. No question, he'd run it past Custis.

"What the fuck you think it means, Gilligan?" Custis railed when Mason showed him the picture and informed him of Hoffman's courtesy trip to Stuart. "Mr. Orwell's probably at your house and listenin' to your daughter on the phone tellin' her friends about crushes and math grades. It's no piece of cake to invade a lawyer's business, but who knows, maybe they talked some nimrod judge into a warrant for our office as well." Mason had left the coffee shop, buttonholed Custis at the end of an arson trial and dragged him into a vacant jury room in the old Main Street courthouse. "From now on," Custis continued, "no conversations unless we're positive they can't bug us."

"Well, so far we've not discussed anything harmful in the office— it's been the Coffee Break, your house, your car."

"Unfortunately," Custis said, "come to think of it, maybe we have. We were pretty damn loose with our talk after Hoffman and the Righteous Brothers lit the fuse in your office and left. Can't say I recall the specifics, but we might've been a little too careless."

"Oh shit. Yeah. I'd forgotten. Jeez. Like I need something else to worry about."

Custis concentrated. "Best I remember, it was more along the lines of how inevitable the indictment was. How they were bluffing. Gates's lying. We're probably okay."

"I'm pretty hazy on it. The promise of a murder indictment will do that."

Custis closed his eyes. "Yeah, goin' over it again in my mind, I'm not hittin' on anything they could use to snag you." He opened his eyes, focusing on Mason.

"Believe it or not, I actually think Ed's sort of trying to help."

"It's the best of both worlds for him, Mace, the best of both worlds. He can offer you a sweetheart escape as a friend, and if you pass the test, he did right by you and the system. If you turn him down, he's got himself a little better feel for the case, another reason as a straight-arrow cop to think you're guilty."

"His charity does put me in a jam, doesn't it?" Mason smiled. "The instant he made the offer, it occurred to me what a porcupine he'd handed me. But you have to give the devil his due—Ed's smooth as they come."

"Can't help but like him."

"I'd never say squat on the phone about anything, but this is a wrinkle I didn't anticipate. So I guess it's fair to assume I'm under surveillance—you see it the same way?"

"Is it a rookie error to buy an entire CD after you hear the one good song on the radio?" Custis broke with habit and answered his own rhetoric: "Yes. A big yes. Hell yes."

Chapter Sixteen

Asshole Bingo was the game, and the students had played it in the larger lecture classes when Mason was enrolled at James Madison University. Without fail, the same suck-ups and brown-nosers would—*every single class*—raise their hands and ask some rehearsed question designed to get them noticed and show the professor how much they cared about the subject, how deeply they'd delved into the assignment. How smart they were. The trick for these grandstanders was to humbly pose what they perceived to be a profound question while seeming simultaneously confused and consumed by learning's narcotic majesty. First would come the brilliant soliloquy, next the squinched face, then a calculated pause and, finally, the Socratic payoff. You could always count on a tortured inquiry from Gertrude London, José Perez, Steve Ackerman, Joe Fowles, Eddie Nicholson, Walter Post III, Julie Warriner and the king of the assholes, Roger Patel, whom the students called "Hadji" after the character in the Jonny Quest cartoon.

It was Emmett Montgomery who invented the game, selling bingo cards with the assholes' names arranged in squares for two bucks and a chance to win a pot that occasionally went as high as a hundred dollars. Any student could buy a card, and Emmett held the cash and collected a ten percent skim as compensation for serving as czar and commissioner. When an asshole spoke, the corresponding block was marked on the card. Once a player scored an asshole line, he or she had to finish off the win by joining the class discussion and using the word "bingo" in a sentence. As in: "So, like, they find Gatsby dead in a pool and, bingo, all his wealth means nothing," or "MacArthur fights to the Yalu River and, bingo, he's done." The games usually required two or three classes to complete, and the professors had to have known the deal, but they detested Hadji and his gang as much as anybody and never interfered or sought to shut down Emmett's entertainment.

He and Mason roomed together their last year at college, and they remained close after graduation, visiting and phoning and showing up for each other's weddings. Using thirty thousand dollars he'd inherited from his grandmother, Emmett was one of the first people to discover that, hey, wow, there really might be something to this Internet thing and one of the first to also discover that there wasn't quite as much to this Internet thing as everybody thought. "Pigs get fat, hogs get slaughtered" was his investment mantra, so he dumped his go-go start-up stocks and cyber tulip bulbs well before they crashed, becoming rich enough that he didn't have a regular job and was able to play tons of golf at pricey courses.

Not long after Hoffman's visit, Emmett made the trip from his home in Charlotte to Mason's farm, bringing with him a month's worth of research on Caldwell-Dylan. He hugged Grace and made her blush by announcing how gorgeous she was, this despite the "foul, medieval genes" she'd suffered from her father. Emmett was around five eight or nine, and it registered with Mason that his child was almost as tall as his college roommate, a realization that caused him to feel displaced, the victim of a velocity he couldn't arrest or curtail. The three of them ate together, and after Grace—on her best behavior—cleared the table and loaded the dishwasher, Mason and Emmett moved to the den and went directly to business.

"Looks like a bunch of research," Mason said, eyeing the thick sheaf of papers on his friend's lap.

"Yeah. But I can cut to the chase for you. It's far more likely than not Mr. Dylan will put on his walking shoes once the grants are exhausted."

"Not the news I wanted to hear," Mason said, truly disappointed. "Damn it."

"See, here's the story. To begin with, even the *name* of this outfit is candy-coated. Chip-Tech has such a current-sounding ring, suggesting technology and computers and all the bells and whistles designed to make small towns wag their tongues. Truth be told, they will be sort of involved with high-tech operations and basic component assembly. But here's the rub: Guess what they make?"

"I give up," Mason said. "I've read everything I can lay my hands on, and it seems they make chips and other parts for larger distributors. They claim to have contracts with GE, Whirlpool, two British companies. KitchenAid, I think. I remember sales to twenty or so different countries."

"True. Correct. But what they'll really be doing in Stuart is manufacturing freezer and cooling components, some circuitry, some simple technical guts to run and regulate various industrial merchandise. Hardly Microsoft."

"No surprise there, Emmett. Even I knew the basics from perusing the Internet. This is how you got so rich? Mastering the obvious?" Mason grinned.

"Here's what's not obvious to rookies like you, Slugger. Caldwell-Dylan routinely sets up shop in smaller, distressed towns. Places aching for business, with giant aspirations and whopping grants to spend. The secret is, Caldwell-Dylan's most noteworthy client is a corporation called Aegis Integrated Systems."

"I hope your reservations aren't political, Emmett. The county needs the jobs, and I'm not interested in taking a quixotic ethical stand. Sorry."

Emmett chuckled. "Why am I not shocked? Nope, no worries there. The problem for you guys is simple. Aegis is wholly owned by Caldwell-Dylan. He sells to himself."

"So?"

"So, he sells to himself cheap. Extremely cheap. He'll design your plant to manufacture what he needs for his major-market products at the parent company, use your grant money to subsidize the loss at Chip-Tech and run as fast as he can once you're bled dry. As a result, Caldwell-Dylan can undersell its rivals. For window dressing, he'll engage in small-potatoes contracts with other firms—probably break even on those deals. Five years from now, one of his minions will appear before your town fathers, invite them to audit the books and whine about losing money. Tough business environment, he'll say. The numbers will confirm the loss. Then you're in a bind, Slugger. He's hooked you. Give him more money, more incentives, or he leaves and the bubble bursts. The employees, now accustomed to decent wages and maybe even basic health insurance, will raise hell with the politicians and the local panjandrums. Can't blame people for wanting to keep a good job."

"So he doesn't care if we fold?"

"Not really. Think of it like this: You may as well hand him half the grant in cash and let him pocket it."

"Pretty damn clever," Mason said.

"Clever, legal, aggressive. After spending a little time with your friend Mr. Dylan, I bought his stock. Thanks for the tip." Emmett smiled and tossed his papers onto the floor. "By the way, I'll wager he's expecting cash from other sources, too. I doubt he's stopped his panhandling with just the Tobacco Commission request. There's so much of this money floating around these days. It's a racket, especially if your training costs and start-up expenses are minimal. Watch the news, Mason. The minute the ink dries on this deal, he'll padlock an identical plant either in Florida or in South Carolina, truck it here and bring his managers along with it. They're like a traveling carnival troupe."

"So we're a temporary stop?"

"Definitely," Emmett declared. "His plants with long histories in the same place are the terminal producers, much farther down the line. You're not. The Stuart location will be expendable."

"But we'd at least have the jobs for several years?"

"Oh yeah. He'll hire your people and pay them okay until the government's not underwriting him any longer. He wants a competent labor force, which he'll find here, especially since people are so anxious to have a job. They'll bust their asses for him. Another reason he selects locales with tons of unemployment. He likes the Loretta Lynn, Pentecostal poor because of their eagerness." Emmett leaned over and tidied the pack of papers. "Hope I've been helpful," he said when he finished. "Sorry I can't be any more optimistic."

"Thanks. I appreciate all the insight. I doubt I would've seen behind the wide-angle shots on the glossy brochure."

"The upside, though, is this visit with my home-run-hitting roommate and his daughter. How're you doing? You seem a little, I don't know, faded."

"Hunky-dory, Emmett. Top of the world."

Chapter Seventeen

It was near midnight, June, in the middle of the week, and Custis had driven the Caddy to Mason's farm and knocked-knocked-knocked-knocked on the front door until the porch lit and Mason appeared, disheveled and shoeless, his shirt's buttons out of sequence and the collar folded inside itself. Custis was wearing a Panama hat, a Grambling football jersey, loose jeans and sneakers. "Sorry to disturb you, Mace," he announced the instant the door opened. "But I found a major snag in our case tomorrow. Needs your immediate attention, so I brought the file with me. You mind takin' a look and see if you can offer some advice? It's in the car, or I can lug it to your kitchen—it's a gigantic file." He puckered his mouth and pointed toward the vehicle with a subtle finger laid against his chest.

"I'll walk with you to the car. No need to wake Grace. School tomorrow, you know." Mason rubbed his eyes.

"Who's there?" Grace yelled from upstairs. "Everything okay?"

"It's Custis," he told her, gaining on his senses. "A work question. Go back to sleep." He leaned close to his friend. "Excellent timing, huh?" he whispered, a hand partitioning off his mouth. "We should be in espionage, quick as I am on my feet."

258 •   MARTIN CLARK

They settled into the car, shut the doors and sealed the windows. Custis cranked the engine and tuned the radio to an AM talk show. He was excited. "I wanna hear you say it," he instructed Mason, the volume in his voice held underneath the gabbing from the radio program. "Say, 'Custis Norman is Superfly.' "

"Custis Norman is Superfly," Mason repeated dully.

"A little call-and-response before I dazzle you with my wisdom. Shout it righteous. Let me hear you proclaim it. Say, 'Custis Norman *is* Superfly.' "

"Custis Norman *is* Superfly," Mason intoned.

"Say, 'He's a genius, smarter than Dr. Carver, slicker than Clinton, more mojoed than Miles.' "

"Could we do that one in segments, Reverend?" Mason asked, playing along. "You're asking me to remember a whole lot of new material."

"I've conquered the Gates issue," Custis informed him, his tone enthusiastic, straining at the seams but still contained within the sound of the radio conversation.

"No shit? Really? How?" Mason wiggled himself higher in the leather seat.

"Okay. Here we go. This would be me earnin' that heavy-duty fifty-buck fee you paid me. Remember Otis Jernigan, the dumb cracker we sent to the joint for all those burglaries?"

"Yeah. Mean, worthless, lazy. Been in jail most of his life. Always claims to be cheated by the system and never accepts responsibility no matter how guilty he is."

"Exactly," Custis said. "And remember what he promised you last he was in court? How he'd never rest till he got even with you for prosecutin' him?"

Mason grinned. "He says that every time. Does the same diatribe as they drag him away kicking and screaming."

"This afternoon I received a call from an assistant in the Powhatan Commonwealth's Attorney's Office. Seems our boy Otis decided to make good on his threat. About a month ago he discovered your brother was servin' time with him, and he—dumb shit that he is—sticks Gates with a plastic fork and bashes him with a lunch tray."

"Shame we didn't know in advance. We could've upgraded his arsenal."

"Obviously, Otis isn't aware you and your brother despise each other. This was his big payback."

"I thought they took steps to keep Gates away from our convicts."

"Generally they do, Mason. I asked the very same question. But let's not forget we're dealin' with the Department of Corrections, and he's been there for years. Shit happens. I mean, hell's bells, Corrections ain't much more than DMV with Tasers and riot batons. How huge a surprise is it they make a mistake?"

"So why's this helping me?"

"Patience, my man. They're tryin' Otis soon for the assault. Gates will be a witness. They called here to confirm the threat. Naturally, they want to show Otis's motive, why he selected your brother. They've agreed you and I can do an affidavit so we won't have to trudge to Powhatan."

"Even if we volunteered to go in person," Mason said, anticipating Custis's plan, "I doubt we'd have a chance at Gates without setting off every alarm and trip wire known to man. I suppose there's a slim possibility they might sequester the witnesses and we'd all end up together, but most likely they'll keep him in a holding cell, have him testify and return him to the pen. Not to mention there'll be other people around—cops, inmates, lawyers."

"Here's the Norman stroke: My cousin's husband is a deputy in Henrico County. They're next door with business in Powhatan several times a month, no big thing. Regularly in and out of both the courtroom and the jail. He slips Gates a cell phone. Maybe in the holding area, maybe as he's visitin' the john, maybe as he's standin' around waitin' for the prison van. Gates hits redial and you're on the other end. You probably won't have too long, but at least you can take his temperature."

"Phone records?" Mason asked.

"We use Inez's phone and my brother's. I'll arrange it."

"Can we trust your in-law?"

"Yes, we can. And supposin' we can't, the worst he can do is say he handed your brother a phone at my request."

"Hmmm." Mason extended his arms toward the roof, stretching as much as he could in the interior. "Maybe."

"It's not all the way uptown, but it's not Baltic Avenue either. He won't be wired, I doubt he'll have a minder and we'll catch him by surprise. Even if Minter or Hoffman should somehow learn where he's goin' to be, they won't be hangin' around in the holding cells."

"Why're you so confident of a distant in-law's loyalty? A cousin's husband?"

"Perry's his name. First off, he's a reliable dude. Solid. I've known him for years. Second, he borrowed a grand from me after a bad trip to Atlantic City. His wife has no idea, and he's still on the hook for part of it to the Bank of Custis."

"Excellent," Mason scoffed. "A gambler with secrets from his wife: the optimum ally."

"I'll vouch for Perry. Like I say, if it blows up on us, so what? We admit it: 'Yeah, damn right we wanted to talk to him to see why he was hawkin' wicked reports to the police.' There's a risk, but it's not like we're buyin' Louis Vuitton from the trunk of Street-Corner Harold's Maxima. You *could* argue this seems heaven-sent. Providence's gift. I'm afraid we won't do any better."

"It's your girlfriend's phone—"

"And my brother's," Custis interjected.

"So the records would be difficult to locate," Mason mused. "Gates won't be miked, and he won't be expecting me. The only weak link is your cop buddy, and we can't get burned too badly if he fucks us over."

"So we're clear, Mace, your name won't ever be mentioned. Perry doesn't know the who's or why's or anything else."

"Good enough," Mason said. "Yeah, let's give it a shot."

"I'll take care of it."

"Custis Norman is Superfly. Thanks."

. . .

Rich—real-McCoy rich—when Mason was a lad growing up in Stuart, consisted of a genuine winter suntan and perfectly adequate teeth that had nonetheless been topped off by a few caps and washed bright by bleaches, or even better, a cat's-pajama luxury along the lines of a Piper Cub at the Spencer airport or a T-Bird convertible straight from the showroom floor at Blue Ridge Ford. In college, he'd been wowed by Southern boys whose families owned third homes on Yankee beaches and hired illegals to plant their flowers, dust their shelves and bathe their infants, the help always dressed in uniforms of one sort or another and careful about direct eye contact. Then there was Mason's high school friend Darrell Haney, who'd moved to Orlando and shot the moon in the landscape business before he turned thirty—he'd built a movie theater smack-dab in his own house, started a bank and purchased more heavy equipment than he could possibly use, some of it just so he could rumble around on a dozer devouring whatever he pleased when he returned home to Patrick County for a summer vacation. But upon meeting Herman Dylan for the first time, Mason soon realized that the updated incarnation of the filthy, Rockefeller rich possessed far bigger ambitions than silk stockings, fancy automobiles or even big-ass bulldozers. Dylan, it seemed, had somehow managed to buy off decay and age and the laws of nature, in effect striking a priceless bargain.

After informing a flustered Ian Hudgens that he'd decided Patrick County's grant would be more wisely invested elsewhere, Mason received a call from Dylan himself, an event that prompted Sheila to appear in his office, practically on her tiptoes, and whisper—even though they were alone—the remarkable news: "Mr. Herman Dylan's on the phone. For you. I recognize his voice from an interview I saw on TV." Mr. Herman Dylan noted he had a real estate closing in Winston-Salem, fifty minutes away from Stuart, and he invited Mason to join him for dinner so he could take a final stab at selling the Chip-Tech project. Mason agreed to the meeting but cautioned him not to be too optimistic; they'd arrived at an impasse, and there wasn't much left to discuss. In fact, he'd already told his fellow commissioners he had serious reservations and didn't support the application.

Curiously, Dylan arranged their meal at a Japanese steak house, not a country club or private home or hoity-toity restaurant. Arigato, it was called, and a black limo was already parked by the entrance when Mason arrived. The interior was crowded with people seated eight to a table, and the sounds of knives, spatulas and metal seasoning canisters clanging on hot grills were all around. As Mason was being led to Dylan's table, one of the chefs squirted oil onto the center of a grill and a blaze jumped and then quickly died in a sizzle, and the diners laughed and clapped, entertained. Dylan was seated alone, in a recessed section of the main room that was empty except for him but wasn't blocked or cordoned off. From his private area, he could see most of the other patrons and they could see him. It was apparent that several people recognized Dylan and were attempting to study him without being altogether obvious, especially a group of younger, raucous men who were enjoying beers and mixed drinks with their food, probably a year or two into their first jobs.

When Mason reached the table, a stocky man in a dark suit and sedate blue tie appeared from nowhere and greeted him, and, after the hostess had departed, the man casually asked him if he minded a search and quick "wanding." "Don't take it personally," he told Mason, "but with an individual like Mr. Dylan, we can't be too careful." Mason didn't want to seem overly meek or submissive, so he didn't answer, instead unbuttoned his blazer and slightly raised his arms away from his trunk. Mr. Blue Tie rapidly did his job, so efficiently and discreetly it was likely no one noticed.

Dylan rose and came to where Mason was standing, and they shook hands. "Pleasure, Mr. Hunt. Thanks for coming." He gestured toward Blue Tie, acknowledging him. "This is Matt Strong. Aptly named, I'm fond of saying."

It was then Mason noticed Dylan's appearance: Pushing seventy, he had the hair, skin, countenance and manner of a man two decades younger, and if Mason hadn't known his age from magazine articles and a lightweight, ghostwritten autobiography, he would have been utterly fooled. The scalpel and conjurer's arts had been spectacularly generous to Dylan, so much so that Mason caught himself searching the man's neck and forehead for missteps, scanning his hands to see if the work matched all over. Everyone in Stuart knew Loni Akers had flown to Atlanta so she could have her breasts improved, and the occasional second wife or industrialist's pampered daughter would have her wrinkles and sags banished by a physician, but *plastic* surgery summed it up quite nicely—the results in the provinces were invariably jarring and fraudulent, an incomplete and checkered grab at reclamation akin to a chunk of flashy chrome slapped on a gray, washed-out jalopy. But with enough money to buy and sell Dr. Faustus himself, Herman Dylan was sublimely altered to the point of seeming remade, wealth incarnate, and Mason had never in his life seen anything so beautifully unnatural. Courtesy of Dylan's warlock doctor, Mason now had a new take on what it meant to be well and truly loaded.

He sat beside Dylan and they ordered and the chef began his full routine, flipping a shrimp tail into his hat and juggling the salt and pepper shakers, even coming at Mason with a joke squirt-bottle that shot red string, not sauce.

"I love the whole shtick," Dylan told Mason. "And if you take it easy on the rice, this is some of the healthiest food around."

"It's certainly tasty."

Matt Strong kept his distance, and while Dylan was civil and courteous, there were stretches of silence when he simply ate and had nothing to say. At the end of several quiet minutes, he turned to Chip-Tech without a warning or preface, wiping his lips with a crimson cloth napkin before he spoke. "So you're against Caldwell-Dylan setting up shop in your county?" he said, and returned to his dinner, collecting a piece of chicken with chopsticks.

"I'm not against you or your company, Mr. Dylan," Mason replied. "I want the absolute best for Patrick County. I'm trying to do due diligence as a board member, and part of that was to ask you for a guarantee you weren't comfortable giving. I truly wish matters were different."

"Me, too. Promising to return money already in my pocket isn't going to happen, though, especially since the business world can turn on a dime. One day you're king of the hill, the next day you're obsolete. Gotta be nimble, Mr. Hunt. Flexible and fast."

"I'm not arguing with you."

"So," Dylan asked, pausing to sip his hot tea, "tell me again why it is you aren't in favor of us receiving the grant? Why you're not interested in our jobs?"

"Sure. It's simple—I think you'll take the money and run. I'd rather invest in something a little less likely to be transient. No offense."

"None taken. Where exactly is it you intend on spending your money, if I might ask?" Dylan had stopped eating.

"Well, there are some local businesses which could really become more competitive with a small boost. Nothing on your scale, of course, but half a million might allow Kreager Woodworking to expand and upgrade their heath-care choices, maybe grow by ten or twelve jobs. Same with Mechanical Design and Hutchens Petroleum. They're not going anywhere, and I've never understood why we ignore our own—the local people who've busted their butts and we see every day—in order to fawn all over strangers. I'd also thought of offering financial aid to kids if they'd come back to Stuart as a teacher or lawyer. Believe it or not, we don't have enough lawyers. We definitely don't have enough teachers. The county would have to submit a grant proposal, but I think there are more productive options for us."

"Nothing wrong with that, I guess, if you believe it's as simple as handing these businesses cash and watching them all magically prosper and create jobs. Money, even well-intentioned money, dropped into the wrong sector or spent at the wrong time is money wasted. Like throwing seeds on concrete."

"So's money spent at the carnival." Mason twisted his chair so he could have a full view of Dylan. "They come to your town, everybody's thrilled for a week, and they leave you with empty pockets, Taiwanese teddy bears and a feeling the rides weren't as fun as the year before."

Dylan chuckled. "Besides your guarantee idea, what will it take to earn your support?"

"I don't know," Mason said. "I suppose I'm open to suggestion." He cocked his head. "We've been waltzing around it, but how about you tell me you're not planning to hit and run, that you'll make a good-faith effort to ensure we stay viable?"

"I could tell you most anything I wanted to, but I doubt it'd mean much. I'm not a fan of fools' errands." Dylan smiled, but there was a strain of malevolence in his expression, like the silver edge of a razor blade visible in tainted Halloween chocolate. "Truth is," he said casually, "we'll probably leave in five or six years. I'm not going to sit here and blow smoke up your ass. You've got a handle on the situation. Bully for you—you saw past the fairy dust and slide shows."

"So why am I here?"

Dylan smiled again, allowing more menace to slice through. There were barely any creases at the corners of his mouth. He slid his plate away and rested his hands on the table, one stacked on top of the other. "To see if we can do business."

"How come this one plant in a tiny Virginia town is so important to you?" Mason asked.

"Six million in grants from the Tobacco Commission, a million from the Governor's Opportunity Fund, no local taxes, free water and sewer, a shell building there in your industrial park and about another million and a half from the federal government. Of course, you're the first domino—no local support and no tobacco money screws me everywhere else. Those kind of dollars certainly warrant taking you to dinner and asking for your confidence a second or third time."

"I'm sorry I can't be more helpful." Mason shrugged and flipped up his palms. "I don't know what to say."

"You're convinced, are you, that six years of excellent jobs is something you want to sneeze at? The grant money'll go some-where, so why not to your citizens? Hell, if I was to tell you, 'Mr. Hunt, I'm a philanthropist and hope to give forty or fifty people health-care insurance and thirty-five thousand dollars a year for five or six years,' explain to me again the reason you'd say no? And that's all this is, subsidies and socialism packaged so people can feel good about taking it and politicians can thump their pimply chests and claim they've delivered the bacon. It's all a shell game, and I'm telling you which shell's got the pea under it."

Mason looked out into the restaurant. "If you wanted to write us a check, a donation from *your* account, we'd be tickled pink." He kept his focus on the people in the adjacent room. "Probably even present you with a key to the city and name you grand marshal of the Christmas parade. The bottom line is I think we can do better. I realize there are people who would grab the short-term benefit and be happy, but I'm not one of them. Maybe I'm wrong—maybe we'll lose your plant, my ideas won't hold water, the tobacco money will go elsewhere and we'll wind up left behind. Still, I've decided. For what it's worth, I appreciate you being candid with me." Only when he finished did he face Dylan.

"Lying's difficult when the other side knows they're being lied to. You need a level playing field if you're going to get anywhere with dishonesty." He removed his hands from the table. The chef was gone and the waitress appeared and poured his tea from a small ceramic pot. "I'll offer this also," Dylan said once they were by themselves again. "I can always use smart, tough people in my business. I'd be pleased to hire you on as a consultant. Of course, we'd have to be cautious about how the arrangements were made."

Mason stiffened. He noticed a piece of rice on the table, and he mashed it—soft, tiny, cold—with his thumb, pressing it into paste. "I'm not interested in a bribe," he said icily.

"I didn't offer you one," Dylan replied, not flinching. "I mentioned a business possibility. I'm disappointed you read something corrupt into it. I understand you have no money needs, or at least you shouldn't in light of your late wife's assets."

"I think we're done here," Mason declared. "I appreciate the invitation and the dinner."

"Yes, we are. I'm sorry we didn't make any progress." Dylan finished the last of his tea and clinked his cup into its indentation on the saucer. "I'd hoped we would. Now we leave set against each other. At odds. I regret it, Mason. Damn, I do. You're a likeable fellow."

"Is this your stick since I didn't go for the carrot?"

"I'm not sure I take your meaning," Dylan said with an inflection that made clear he understood exactly what Mason was suggesting.

They left together, Matt Strong at Dylan's elbow, and a bold young man from the drinking group approached Dylan and asked him to autograph a dollar bill. Strong produced a pen and Dylan wrote his name on the currency and wished his admirer well. Dylan paid with a credit card and the three of them walked through the door into the summer air, Mason in the lead, Strong tending to the door for his boss.

Outside, it was more night than day. Cars on the highway had their headlights burning, and the afternoon's weighted heat had lifted. Dylan and Strong didn't hold up at the limo, instead stayed with Mason, following him across the parking lot, not speaking. Mason wondered about Dylan's intent—their tailing him seemed ominous, and neither of them gave any hint as to why they were tagging along. Mason took stock of Strong, and the brute saw him doing it, didn't seem to care. Strong would thrash him, Mason immediately concluded. He looked like the sort who knew about pressure points and vulnerable bones—but certainly Herman Dylan had better instincts than to have a commonwealth's attorney attacked in a public place lousy with witnesses. This was probably just Dylan's method of intimidating him, a silent, unexplained smothering that would end with some elliptical reference and a sinister good-bye.

Mason stopped suddenly. "You don't have to escort me to my car," he said to Dylan. "I appreciate the thought, but I'll be fine." He was firm, bordering on confrontational.

"Oh. Well, okay," Dylan answered, and from his tone, Mason gathered he'd misconstrued the man's purpose. "I didn't know we were going to anyway, but it's . . . it's . . . good to be relieved of the duty."

Mason hadn't moved. "Then why are you following me? You and Mr. Strong? Quiet as mice?"

Having swiftly sized up the source of Mason's anxiousness, Dylan was amused. Glib. "Uh, because we just ate together, finished at the same time and we need to get our car so Matt and I can drive to the airport? As for the 'quiet' part, you'll find I don't talk unless I have something to say."

"You're a long way from your limo," Mason said, but the alarm and accusation had almost left his voice.

"Ha. Now I see," Dylan chortled, although he'd guessed what was coming, wasn't surprised in the least. "Now I see," he repeated, relishing his advantage. He glanced at Strong, who took it as a cue to crack merry as well. "Sorry to disappoint you, Mr. Hunt, but the limo's not mine. I'd bet it's being rented by kids headed to a club or girlfriends painting the town or maybe our buddies who sent their leader for an autograph—the young hotshots could split the cost into very reasonable shares."

"Oh, um," Mason grunted.

"Sorry to disappoint you."

"My mistake. Bad assumption. I thought it was yours and didn't want you to feel, to feel, you know . . . obligated to keep me company." He hoped he wasn't red-faced. "So it belongs to somebody else?" he rambled.

"Yes, it does. Matt and I are Town Car men."

"I'll be damned," Mason said. "I mean this in a complimentary sense, but you seem like a man who'd travel large."

Dylan turned to Strong. "Tell Mr. Hunt our story, Matt."

"So," Matt Strong began as if he'd been waiting in the wings, expecting the request, "one day in the jungle this mouse discovers an elephant up to his neck in quicksand, sinking fast. 'Please, please help me, Mr. Mouse,' cries the elephant. The mouse leaves and comes back with his Porsche and hooks a cable to the elephant and drags him to dry land. The elephant is eternally grateful, and lo and behold, months later the elephant is strolling through the jungle and finds the mouse stuck in the same quicksand, about to go under. 'Remember me, Mr. Elephant?' squeaks the mouse. 'I saved your life. Please help me.' The big ol' elephant steps close as he can to the danger, unrolls his huge penis and tosses it out to the mouse, who grabs it and is pulled to safety."

"And do you know the moral of the story?" Dylan chimed in.

"Be kind to animals?" Mason offered, still off balance.

"If you have a big dick, you don't need a Porsche." Dylan delivered the punch line stylishly, with a raconteur's polish.

"Or a limo," added Strong.

"Or," Dylan said more plainly, "to muscle your fellow man in a parking lot because he won't help you get your important deal done. That would be tiny. Coarse." He held his index finger millimeters away from his thumb. "Not my style."

The phone played a grating, electronic, tinny, accelerated version of the "William Tell Overture," *datta-dut, datta-dut, datta-dot-dot-dah*, and Mason snatched it from the table and pushed the green talk button. He was in the jury room at the courthouse and Custis was with him, the door shut and locked, a handwritten DO NOT DISTURB sign taped to the outside, although it was unlikely anyone would happen by, as circuit court was not in session and there was no reason for people to be in the building. Mason and Custis had been waiting for over an hour, trading sections of the *Roanoke Times*, and when they'd finished with the paper, they began speculating about what Gates and Perry might be up to, the possibilities and pitfalls in Powhatan, two hundred miles distant.

"I'll wager this is my famous brother, the commonwealth's attorney," Gates said as soon as Mason clicked on, before he'd so much as said hello.

"It is."

"Amazin' what you can accomplish when you're motivated, huh, Mason? When you have a vested interest." He laughed sarcastically. "I was about to take a dump, a real pleasure for me, you see, the luxury of a private stall and a bit of dignity, and not only do I get to relieve myself without an audience, but holy cow, a big black deputy gives me a cell phone and free minutes. He's probably not supposed to do that. Kinda like it would be bending the rules to help me have my sentence reduced. Depends on whose ox is bein' gored as to how hard you work on things, doesn't it?"

"What is it you want, Gates?" Mason asked. "Plain and simple, name your price. Why in the world are you doing this? You damn well know I didn't shoot Wayne Thompson."

"Yesterday was July Fourth. I'd like for you to describe your holiday."

"Why? We don't have much time."

"Oh, I doubt your lackey's gonna rush in here and pull me off the crapper. So humor me, make me happy, tell me about your Fourth."

Mason spoke mechanically: "Mom came over and two friends of Grace's, and I grilled hamburgers for them. The kids had some sparklers. Mom made a pound cake."

"And me, Mason, I sat here, like I have year after miserable year, eatin' shitty food and listening to crazy motherfuckers rant and rave. No pound cake, no fresh air, no fireworks, only the same horrible day repeated." Gates paused to let his complaints sink in. "There's your answer, Mason, the key to your legal woes. Nothing new. Same as it's always been. I think if you spent as much effort on gettin' me free as you did settin' up this call, I'd be munching pound cake and lighting sparklers, too. You need to put your shoulder to the task, boy."

"You have less than two years left. We both know you were sentenced before the state abolished parole. You're virtually through anyway."

"Less than two fuckin' years, huh? If it's so minor, how about you come down here and serve it for me?"

"It must make you feel great, whoring yourself for a handful of months and slitting your brother's throat. Selling your conscience for next to nothing. Maybe I can scrounge up thirty pieces of silver for you."

"Hell," Gates spat, "what really bothers me is you shootin' a boy and walkin' free while I'm locked up for half my life. I'm only tryin' to see justice done."

"I'm not taping this. You don't have to recite your bullshit for the record."

"The truth's the truth, Mason."

"But if I somehow get you released," Mason probed, "the truth might change?"

"I'm just lookin' for some brotherly love, you understand? I'm sorry I had to come forward on this Thompson deal, but I've acquired a profound respect for our legal system. I'm into truth and honor now. The flag and our great American country. You do what's right, and it'll all pan out. Even if you did pull the trigger."

"I understand," Mason said.

"Excellent," Gates replied. "You think your cop buddy will mind if I call my lady pen pal? I'm in high cotton here for a little long-distance sex."

"I have no idea why a policeman would offer you a phone, and I certainly didn't put him up to it. I was surprised as heck to hear from you."

"Better go heavy on those law books, Mason. Find that special case."

"Good-bye," Mason said dryly. He folded the phone shut and handed it to Custis. "Major surprise. He wants out of the slammer. He's such a piece of trash, he'll destroy me and my daughter and our mother to save himself the last year and few months of his sentence. Naturally, he'll forget the murder accusation if I spring him. Or so he says—you can never be too certain with a jackal like Gates."

"Well, we got two months till September term," Custis remarked. "Maybe the fucker'll drop dead."

"Superb legal strategy, my friend. Congratulations. Why didn't I think of that?"

A week later, Mason caught sight of Gail Harding, the *Enterprise* editor, as she was leaving her basement office under Stuart Drug and locking up, finished for the day. Mason was swinging by the pharmacy to fill a prescription for Grace, medicine for a mild sinus infection, and Gail waved him over and said she was glad to see him and had been meaning to pay him a visit at the farm. "I have a question for you," she announced mischievously. She withdrew her key and checked the door, grabbing the knob and simultaneously pulling and twisting.

"I have one for you first," Mason replied. "What's with that crazy story about the raccoon? The 'Man Bitten by Raccoon on Main Street' piece? Was it satire or something?"

"If it were satire, Mason, you'd know. It's true. Hard news, as we say in the biz." She was spirited, ironic, her glasses dangling from her neck on a beaded chain.

"You want me to believe a man or woman, whose name you won't print, is strolling down Main Street—right here—and a rabid coon materializes from the vapors and bites him? Or her? The story wasn't a lark or goof? Heaven forbid—you didn't get snookered, did you?"

"I doubt anyone would go through those excruciating rabies shots as a joke. It's just a quirky, weird story, accurate to the last period."

"So why not print the name? Preachers with dope charges, politicians with ugly secrets, information you know will decimate people—you've never sanitized a story before."

"Yeah, a watershed edition for us. It was such dreadfully poor luck, I felt sorry for the guy. I figured everybody and his brother would make fun of him. He'd be a laughingstock for the rest of his life, don't you think? The story works without revealing his identity."

"Only in Stuart." Mason smiled, a smile that expanded into a laugh. "Pulitzer-grade stuff on your end. Invite me to the ceremony."

"I will. Now, on to more important topics." She opened her purse and deposited the office key, which was attached to a plastic Wonder Woman figure. "If this isn't appropriate, you stop me, but, well, I have a friend who's interested in meeting you, a lady. I don't have any idea about your personal life, and she doesn't want to seem brash or intrude or stick her nose where it doesn't belong."

"So who is it?" Mason asked. "This friend?"

Gail giggled, suddenly flighty and girlish. "I'm not supposed to tell."

"Then how would I know if I'm interested?"

"So you might be okay with it?"

Mason shifted his weight. An elderly man in bib overalls walked between them, leaving the store with his pills. The old man said "hey" but didn't linger, and Mason waited for him to shuffle out of range before he continued. "Who knows? Maybe. I'd have to think about it. I've been pretty much a hermit since Allison's accident."

"Yeah, jeez. And everybody's different. We want to absolutely respect your situation."

"So who is it?"

"Well, a teacher at the high school. A teacher you see at the gym."

"Huh. A teacher . . . I see at the gym. I'm thinking . . . I'm stumped, Gail. Sorry."

"Shoni. Shoni McClean."

Mason did a double take so pronounced it was almost slapstick. "She's married, Gail. Damn fine-looking, but damn well married."

"She and her husband are separated. They have been for several months."

"Last time I checked, she was wearing a wedding ring."

"So you noticed," Gail teased him. "Yeah, she still does occasionally, mainly to keep men from hounding her, but she and Mark are history. He moved to Detroit, and they've signed all the legal papers. You'd know more about those matters than I, what has to be done for it to be official. Their split is old hat. You haven't heard?"

"Nope."

"So?" Gail dragged out the *o*.

"I'll mull it over. She seems nice enough from our conversations in the gym. How old is she?"

"Thirty-eight."

"Yikes." Mason widened his eyes, then shrank them back to normal. "Kinda young for me."

"Not really."

"Well, I'll give it some thought." He flicked a piece of lint off his lapel. "Yeah, thanks. I'll probably run it by my daughter, too, if I get that far."

"She's a sweetie," Gail said warmly. "It'd be good for you."

"Since you're not available, I'll have to settle for second best, huh?"

"Another little thing I need to check with you about, Mason." Gail's stance changed, and her voice became less vibrant, the upper register disappearing. "What's this I hear about the old Wayne Thompson murder? I was going through the court orders last month, and there's been a special prosecutor appointed, some guy I've never heard of. The sheriff's no help, claims it's being managed elsewhere and swears he's as much in the dark as I am. I contacted this Stallings, the new prosecutor, and he's like talking to a rock, but he did say you might be involved—that's the word he used, 'involved'—so you weren't able to handle the case. He also sent me a photo of himself for the article, by the way. A lot of smoke, wouldn't you agree?"

She'd taken long enough building the question that Mason was able to keep his poise and answer her coherently. "Beats me. I've had a visit or two from the state police, but you're as informed as I am. Years ago when it happened, they interviewed Gates, and I was part of his alibi for the night, so I obviously have to be careful if there's a charge. Could be a conflict."

"They wouldn't be gearing up like this unless there was something to it, would they?"

Mason brushed his suit jacket again. "The cops who talked to me seemed kind of desperate and scattershot, if you want to know the truth. Left-field, snipe-hunt stuff."

"I heard a rumor Allen Roberts might have some worries."

"Allen's a hundred percent safe. That much I can tell you."

"I'm getting the impression you're not as uninformed as you let on," Gail challenged him.

"Let's leave it like this: I'm giving you all I can, and if the case takes off, I'll be more than happy to fill in whatever blanks need attention."

"They're after Gates, aren't they? Aren't they? He's tangled up in this, isn't he?"

"Come on," Mason said jocularly. "Put away the bamboo shoots and I'll walk you to your car—wouldn't want you left alone with the rabid street animals."

Chapter Eighteen

The following Monday morning there was an onslaught of rain, the kind that came companioned by thunder and capricious gusts, the downpour so strong windshield wipers couldn't clear a view, even on the highest setting, and umbrellas snapped inverted toward the sky, breaking their metal ribs. Arriving in Mason's office, Custis was grumpy and incommunicative, and there was no coffee, nothing to eat.

"I take it the diet's kicking into a new gear," Mason tweaked him. "Tap water and conversation the whole menu for us?"

"If you're hungry, I'd suggest you hoof it across the street and place an order," Custis responded. "Or visit the vendin' machine at the sheriff's department." He was humorless, the comments tart, defensive. "I'm not your toady."

"Ah, but today you are. I was *your* toady last Monday, and I went so far as to bow and scrape to your low-cal demands and had my mom fix that fruit concoction; plus I paid a pretty penny for the fat-free muffins at Food Lion. It's your turn."

"It's raining like hell, Mason, and I didn't stop for anything. Sorry. We got any business to discuss?"

"Not really," Mason said cautiously. "No." He began swiveling his desk chair from side to side, pointless motion. "The diet seems to be going great, huh? What is it now, fifteen pounds?"

"Thereabouts."

"You do anything entertaining over the weekend?" Mason inquired. "Travel anywhere?"

"No. Why're you askin'?"

"Just making conversation."

"I hung around here," Custis said.

"What's up your ass?" Mason demanded. "You think you could possibly be any more surly?"

"I'm not surly. Fact bein', I'm the duke of good cheer. But we don't have any cases to discuss, I didn't bring breakfast and I'm not in the mood to rehash the details of our weekends like we're a couple teenage girls at our lockers. That okay with you?"

Mason dramatically raised his hands and wheeled away from the desk, as if he were at the point of a weapon. "Sorry I asked. Jeez."

"I've got a case in circuit court," Custis declared. "I'll see you later." The wind shifted, and rain sheeted the office window. Thunder boomed and the lights dimmed, struggling and flickering before they healed. "Shit," Custis groused. "Why is it I always catch court on the friggin' nastiest days—I'll be soaked and have to sit there dog-wet for three hours, listenin' to losers and crackheads."

"Oh—you don't know by now? I signed up for the weather hotline, this deal with Zeus and Willard Scott. I buy the forecast a year in advance and use it to make your life miserable."

"Hysterical," Custis said.

"You sure you're okay?" Mason asked. "I mean, obviously something's on your mind. Anything I can do or help you with? I'd be glad to."

"I'm fine. Besides, you have your own cross to bear." He stood and turned to leave, his full back to Mason.

"Hey," Mason said awkwardly, Custis's mood beyond his reach, "you want me to cover for you? It's not a problem, not in the least. I'll be happy to take your docket. Sheila can postpone my appointments, and I'll fight the storm and crackheads for you. It'd be my pleasure."

"No, thanks." He was walking as he said it.

Mason didn't see him for the remainder of the day, and he called in sick on Tuesday, instructing Sheila to continue his cases and reschedule a meeting. "He seem all right to you yesterday?" Mason asked her after she gave him the news of Custis's illness. "Normal?"

"Well, he was kinda quiet. I really didn't have much to do with him. He went to court and went directly home. He wasn't actin' himself, though, now that I think about it."

"Yeah. Guess it was already bothering him. There's a nasty bug making the rounds."

Mason was lonely; there was no avoiding it, no putting it aside. He was lonely partly because he lacked a marriage, the joy of his wife and the salts, spices and flavors of living with a woman, needs as fundamental as water or winter heat and as damnable and visceral in their absence as a punch to the stomach. He *felt* the empty breakfast table and solitary cup of coffee every single morning, *felt* the dead rocking chair beside his own on the porch, *felt* the hours that were simply stock replications, chapters and verses without promise or spontaneity: the clock radio, work, bench presses, a rental video, Grace's school assignments, TV sports, the king bed suspending him in the dark, the twenty-watt hall night-light, the silhouettes of furniture as he dozed off. Still, the bigger portion of his loneliness was self-imposed, a barefoot pilgrimage to a shrine that wasn't yet visible and likely never would be, the monotonous march the best he could do to honor Allison, his way of keeping her with him, a slog of his own creation. He chose to mourn, to assume the habits of a widower, to withdraw into sackcloth and the sanctuary of his forty acres.

Complicating matters, he grew concerned he was doing wrong by his daughter, turning her into his sidekick and best friend by default, steadily dragging her into his own predilections, the two of them Ralph Kramden and Ed Norton, or Sinatra and Dino tearing up the Strip. "Pretty soon," his mother had recently scolded him, "I'm goin' to find you and Grace drinking beer on the sofa together and watchin' the monster trucks. Peanut hulls on the ground. Or you'll have her dealin' cards at a poker game. She's too pretty and too smart to waste. You have to be her daddy, not her barstool buddy. You need your life, she needs hers."

"I know" was all he could muster. "I'm trying. I enjoy spending time with her, though . . . in those rare moments when she'll actually have something to do with me."

Tuesday night, after supper and an unanswered call to check on Custis, he tracked down Grace in her room where she was busy on the computer, sending e-mail. He knocked and entered and sat on the corner of her bed. "Hey," he said.

"Hi." She didn't stop typing or look in his direction. Typical.

"Question for you." His hands were flat on her comforter, at right angles to his hips, pressing craters into the billowy fabric.

She continued with the keyboard.

"Are you listening?"

"Um-hmm," she said.

"I've been thinking . . . been considering the possibility of having lunch with a lady." He'd taken the sentence through several permutations, shaping it, careful to omit the words "date," "dinner" and "another woman." "I'll never do better than your mother, and I'll never stop loving her, but I wanted to ask how you'd feel if I went to eat with someone. A meal. Nothing serious."

She whipped around toward him, and her face reacted as if a bee had found her bare foot in clover: First came a half breath of startled, steel-trap surprise that erased everything and reset her features to zero, then the spasm from the sting hit—damn, ouch—and ran roughshod over her. The cursor was abandoned on the screen, blinking in mid-word: *tho.* "A date? You mean you have a date?"

"No, no, no. I don't *have* anything, and if I did, it wouldn't be a date. I'd thought about getting out of the den for a change and spending time with people my own age."

"Custis is your age."

"True."

"So it has to be a date," she said. She was practically bug-eyed.

"Not really."

"It's just weird. Icky. Gross." She folded her legs into the chair, knees against her chest, flip-flops on the seat. "Sorta awful, you and somebody different."

"Listen, I realize none of this is simple. That's why I'm talking to you. I'm not even sure I want to do it, but it's been over two years, and . . . well . . . here I sit, probably depending on you too much, teaching you how to do a box score and pitch a softball and inviting you to kung fu movies, repeating the identical day again and again like I'm knitting Laertes's shroud or channeling Ben Cartwright, and I assume I need to try to balance myself, inhale some fresh air, not become a hermit and pull you along with me. Plus, the truth is I'm lonely. Not every day or anything," he added immediately, "and I love you and it has nothing to do with you." He looked at the hard-wood floor, the throw rug, the yellow walls, the truncated word on the computer screen. "You're a blessing as a daughter. Yes, you are. I wish things were different and we didn't even have to discuss this, but . . ."

"So who is it?" she asked. "And how come you're trying to men-tion stuff you think I won't understand?"

"Shoni McClean."

"Ohmygod. Are you serious? I'll be humiliated."

"Why? I see her at the gym and she seems pleasant enough."

Grace buried her head into her knees and grabbed hold of her hair with both hands. "She's a slut. Everybody knows it. All the guys in my class call her 'Sexy Shoni.' " She was speaking into her pants legs, but she was loud enough that Mason had no difficulty hearing her. "Why don't you just date Pamela Anderson and get it over with?"

"From what I've heard, she has an excellent reputation. The fact she's attractive doesn't make her a slut."

"You don't know; I do."

"I see."

"Why are you even askin' me if you've already decided?" She popped up and stared at him.

"I haven't decided. I wouldn't do anything unless I checked with you."

"If you think you have to check, it must be somethin' huge, so that means it's a date, like you and her are . . . are . . . a couple." Her chin crumbled and the first mad, wounded tears wet her cheeks. The tears dropped fast, straight. "I can't believe you're doing this to me. I'm not even fifteen. Don't you think I've been punished enough without you making it worse?"

"I'm not trying to hurt you or make it worse. I'm only trying to recover and have a tolerable life. Normal. Happy. The both of us." He slid off the bed. Still crouching, he attempted to take her hands, but she wasn't about to let him, jerked away, slapping and pawing at the air before hunkering down behind her shins. "I love you," he told her, supplicant there as she bawled and thrashed and retreated into her chair, and he understood how she felt, what it was like to be screwed out of a parent, rooked and shortchanged. "Don't worry," he assured her. "We'll be fine."

Don Wiggington wore his soul on display—hooded eyes, fleshy oblong cheeks, a dash of gargoyle running through his wide nose and rubbery lips. His were the sluggishly corrupt features you'd expect to mark a Renaissance cardinal on the take, one robe pocket full of dispensations, the other stuffed with bribes and Medici kickbacks. Unfortunately, what you saw with Wiggington was exactly what you got, and Stuart people kept their distance where he was concerned. He was a big talker, a glad-hander, a regular at the café counters and lunch tables, but everybody knew he couldn't be trusted, knew the story of how, in the eighties, he'd pled guilty to misdemeanor disorderly conduct, a charitable legal arrangement that blurred the true nature of his crime, a sexual overture to a first-grade girl fresh off the bus from Red Bank Elementary School.

Wednesday at lunch, Mason passed Wiggington on the chipped concrete steps of the Coffee Break. Mason was heading in for the cheeseburger and orangeade special, and Wiggington was leaving, three white to-go bags clamped together in his chubby hand, grease outlines already penetrating the paper, turning it slick and translucent.

"Mr. Commonwealth," Wiggington said cheerfully. "Everything goin' to suit you?"

"No complaints," Mason said, slowing between the top step and the landing but not intending to visit.

"I tell you who has no complaints: your assistant, Custis. I seen him in the tall timber this weekend, down at Richmond. How's he gettin' along?"

Mason stopped, straddling the riser from the last step. He ducked his head, not certain he'd understood. "Custis Norman?"

"Yeah." The sun was bright, and Wiggington shaded his eyes with his free hand. "Me and my wife was in Richmond to see our grand-daughter at a dance recital, and Saturday a bunch of us went to the Tobacco Company, the nice restaurant, and there was ol' Custis with a steak in front of him as huge as a mountain." Wiggington laughed.

"Last weekend? Four days ago?"

"Yeah." Wiggington situated himself so the sun wasn't as fierce, dropped his hand.

"Huh," Mason murmured. "You positive it was Custis and it was last Saturday?"

"I'm downright positive. Robbie Unger, a big wheel with Farm Bureau Insurance, took several of us out for dinner. Robbie's close with my boy Louis. Custis was talking to a police officer and a sorta average-lookin' bald guy. Not that I should say anything about another fellow's hair." Wiggington chuckled—false modesty—and raked a clump of comb-over strands off his forehead.

"A cop? How would you know?"

"He was a state man, Mason. Had on a blue uniform and a badge—pretty easy to identify. They was at a corner table, the three of them." Wiggington shielded his eyes again. "How come you're so surprised?"

"Oh, well, Custis, you know how he is. Tight as a tick. I'm stunned to hear he was in a fancy restaurant. Burger King, yeah. Wendy's. Subway. But not an expensive place, not Custis Norman. It's a cinch the other guys were paying." Mason counterfeited a grin. "You should've walked over and handed him your check or something."

He was trolling, sussing out as much as he could. "Given him a hard time, cheap as he is."

"Nah, we didn't have a chance to speak. They was totally on the other side of the dining room." Wiggington glanced at the sidewalk, then back at Mason. "And Custis, he's never really warmed up to me. He's polite, speaks and whatnot, but we've never completely gee-hawed." He gestured with the sacks, lifting and dropping them. "I'm not saying anything against him, you understand. Me and him just aren't as friendly as you and me are. I like Custis a lot. Appreciate all he does."

"I'm sure he thinks highly of you, too, Don. I wouldn't take it personally."

"I don't," Wiggington replied. "See you later." He arranged his hair again and waddled off.

"Later," Mason muttered. He made it no farther than the edge of the landing before veering away, straggling down the steps and crossing Main Street, retreating to his office, his appetite squashed, his skin so hopped up with distress and adrenaline it ached. "Sonofabitch," he said aloud, cloistered by himself and pacing the floor, doing his best to decipher why Custis would lie to him, why his attitude had grown so foul, why he was meeting in Richmond with a state cop and a man who sure might be Ed Hoffman.

Maybe Wiggington was mistaken on the date.

Maybe it was simply a man who looked like Custis, and the cop being there reinforced Wiggington's perception—it would make sense for Custis to be breaking bread with a policeman.

Maybe Custis was in such a vile humor he gave a pat answer about the weekend to escape having a longer conversation, an innocent fib.

Maybe it wasn't Hoffman.

Mason couldn't quit pacing, thinking, stewing.

Maybe Wiggington was lying. Who knew with a guy who'd offer up his pecker to a little girl?

Maybe it *was* a cop and Hoffman and the meeting had nothing to do with the Wayne Thompson murder.

Maybe Custis was trying to help, had a plan cooking.

Maybe—

Sheila opened the door so violently it bounced off the stiff-spring stop and nearly ricocheted back into her. The *thwack* from the door surprised Mason, and Sheila was right on top of him, busting in just as he was circling past the threshold, staring at the plaster walls but not actually noticing them, his arms pinned behind him like bony wings and his hands clasped. She was all to pieces, sobbing and snubbing and mad, her nostrils yo-yoing snot when she breathed through her nose, spit threads running from lip to lip when she fish-gulped air with her mouth. Her neck was red. Her blouse wasn't right. She was an angry house afire.

"Damn," he exclaimed. "What? What's wrong?" He instinctively stepped away from her.

"Custis," she fumed. "He—"

"Is he okay?"

"Yes," she shrieked, "he's okay, but I don't have to put up with his treating me like dirt."

"Here," Mason said, offering her a cotton handkerchief. "Take it easy."

"He called me a moron." She wiped at her nose with her blouse sleeve. "And stupid. He said I was stupid."

"Okay, okay, okay. Okay. Sit down." Mason positioned a chair for her. "I'm sure it's a misunderstanding."

"I don't want to sit down." She stomped her foot and became even more emotional. "I work as hard as I can, Mason. I stay late, I miss opportunities with my kids, I—"

"No one doubts that, Sheila. You're the best in the business, and this place would collapse without you. What exactly has happened? Tell me what's wrong. Try to relax."

"He had no right," she said.

"No right to what? You need to tell me."

"Custis came in last week after circuit court and gave me a discovery motion in that Jack Morris case, the guy with the nineteen larceny charges." She dabbed at her eyes with the handkerchief, and the crying and sniffling lessened. "He said, and I quote, 'Send them all the statements in the file.' I said, '*Every* statement?' and he told me a second time to send everything. So today he claims I've ruined the case because I sent a *witness* statement we didn't have to reveal and he was intending to use as an ambush." She picked up steam again, growing louder: "I'm not a lawyer, Mason. Send 'em all, he told me, and I did what he wanted."

"Wow. Huh. You sure he's not picking on you, just kidding around? You know how he is, especially with you. The rubber mouse, the stuffed skunk in your drawer, the exploding pen, the props and gags. The guy's practically Gallagher. He's always teasing you or thumping your head. Nailing you with paper wads. Acting silly."

She sucked a breath through the flow of mucus in her nose. "He was mean as a rattlesnake and he meant it. He said I was stupid. He said I was a moron."

"Well, I'll talk to him. I'm sure you guys just have your wires crossed. He thinks the world of you. So do I."

"I'm entitled to an apology," she said. "Especially since the whole thing is his fault for not being more definite. He's blamin' me for his mistake."

"I'll check with Custis. You go in the restroom and calm down. Take a few hours off, go home, eat a long lunch, whatever. I'll get this resolved. I promise."

"I'm not goin' anywhere," she said determinedly. "I'm not gonna let him run me out of this office or think he can bully me. No, thank you, nosirree. I have as much right to be here as he does. I'll fix my makeup and be at my desk expectin' him to be a man and say he's sorry."

"Fair enough," Mason said. He slid around her and eased the door completely open and solicitously waited, lightly, briefly, gently touching her shoulder as she went past, making her way to the ladies' room.

As soon as she disappeared, Mason paid Custis a visit. He was speaking to someone on the telephone, and he spied Mason in the doorway, smiled, and motioned for him to come in. A Tupperware tub loaded with carrots, broccoli and cauliflower was on his desk along with a napkin and dressing packet. "Not good," he was saying into the receiver. "It's never promisin' when you order a kitchen table and it comes in a flat box. Mail order's a bitch like that. I'm predictin' obscure directions, pre-drilled holes we can't quite line up and a need for Allen wrenches and pliers. I'll take a stab at it, though. See what I can do. I'll be by tonight 'round seven. Hey, Mason's here—I gotta roll." He said good-bye, hung up the phone. "Inez," he explained. "She ordered this damn table from Williams-Sonoma and—greetings from the factory—it's not assembled, despite the fact it cost a king's ransom. Sweet, huh?" He seemed serene, normal, very much his affable self.

"Never buy grills, bikes, dollhouses or furniture unless they're already put together," Mason said. He shut the door and took a seat across from Custis. "What kind of skirmish did you and Sheila have?"

"Nothing, really. She screwed up a case and I called her on it." He shrugged. "We had a discovery motion, and instead of sendin' the other side only the defendant's statements, she, for reasons known only to her, decided to provide them witness statements as well, a gift you and I both realize they aren't entitled to, and an error that took away my chance to do serious impeachment damage at trial. Why's it an issue?"

"She's crying and bent out of the frame," Mason said softly. "She claims you insulted her, called her a moron and stupid."

"I told her it was a stupid mistake. I didn't say she was stupid. There's a considerable difference. She's the one who then got all up on me and wanted to argue about how I'd authorized it, which is nonsense. I don't need that kind of static, not from her, not from my secretary, not from anyone, so, yeah, I cut her down to size a little bit and called her a moron. She deserved to hear it."

Mason grimaced. "Damn, Custis. Man . . . um, um, um, um. She says you told her to send every statement in the file, not just the defendant's stuff."

"I did no such thing," Custis said, his tone formal. "And supposin' I did, how long's she been doin' this gig, Mace, huh? We're too damn lax around here. This was basic and she was careless and now she's runnin' to you and actin' like a child. I don't have time for this. It's petty."

"Petty or not, do you think you might help me make her happy again?"

"Meaning what?" Custis growled. He glared at Mason, tugging and twisting a dreadlock. Gray had begun to stain his hair and sideburns.

"How about we write it off as a misunderstanding, a bad moment, pressure, whatever, and you jolly her up and assure her you didn't intend to insult her?"

"So she's at fault, and you want me to apologize to her? She's insubordinate, and your reaction is for Custis to dive into his Stepin Fetchit routine, hat in hand, and shuck and jive and grovel? She crosses the line with me first, and I'm the villain?"

"Christ, Custis, give me a break. What's with you the last few days? I only suggested we try to mend fences with the best secretary in the state—who also happens to be our friend—and yeah, for what it's worth, you were wrong to say she was a moron. You should address that with her."

"Right," Custis snarled, his voice larded with disdain. "Here we go. Custis gonna crawl up to the manor house and ask the missus for forgiveness. Well, maybe I'm tired of bein' the house nigger. Maybe I'm tired of bein' Sammy Davis, Jr., and keepin' everybody happy, the song-and-dance man. How 'bout we have her come in here and apologize to *me*?"

Mason wouldn't allow Custis any purchase. "This isn't about race," Mason said, not flinching, making it a point to stand from his chair. "And you know it. It's chickenshit to hide there. This is about you treating another person the way you'd expect to be treated. End of story."

"Everything's about race," Custis said. "You try bein' a black man in Patrick County. You try always bein' the oddity. See how chicken-shit you think it is." He rose, too.

"Sort of like the drawing of me in court last month—the 'Super-cracker' caricature you sketched because I didn't recognize some ridiculous hip-hop term. The flying redneck with the Saltine shield and banjo death ray." Mason hoped mentioning the scene, funny as it was, would diffuse their quarrel and nudge Custis toward civility.

"If the shoe fits, brother."

"You're making a mistake, Custis."

"You're entitled to your opinion."

"So you're going to hide behind your skin color and play the victim and refuse to even speak to your employee? The lady sitting out there at her desk, your friend of over twenty years? Let's assume you're right and she's wrong. You think the correct thing to do is blow her off and declare a race foul? She's doing this because you're black—that's your position?"

"Tell you what. Since you're the philosopher king and have a corner on the morality market and know everything there is to know, I'm gonna glide on through the front door and let you and Sheila take this ship over and sail it however you wanna. I'm gone. You can kiss her ass for me if you'd like. Tell her how sorry I am. I don't care." Custis snatched his suit coat from the rack and hurried past Mason, brushing against him as he went by because Mason wouldn't grant him a wider path, wasn't about to yield or show him the courtesy of a step to the side.

Custis was missing the next morning, nowhere to be found, forcing Mason to hustle between two courts and beg indulgences from the judges while Sheila did her best to placate miffed victims and impatient cops, a disaster of a day that had Mason tired and cranky by three o'clock. He twice sent a deputy to Custis's home and he called Inez Rucker, but it didn't do any good; Custis had disappeared. To make matters worse, Ed Hoffman phoned while Mason was huddled in his office with a pair of investigators, attempting to learn—from scratch—one of Custis's cases during a fifteen-minute recess he'd cajoled from Judge Greenwalt despite a docket that was over an hour behind. Already harried, Mason had to excuse himself and bound up the stairs and answer the call in the library.

"Afternoon, Mason," Hoffman said.

"Ed." Mason was slightly winded. He held the receiver away from his mouth while he recovered, didn't want Hoffman to hear him panting.

"Sheila says you're busy. I won't dillydally. You decided on the polygraph? My offer still stands."

"I'm considering it, Ed."

"This bugger's comin', Mason. Stallings has made up his mind. Sent me to re-interview your brother. Don't care for him, your brother. Sorry sack of shit, if I can say so."

"I'll let you know, and I'm grateful to you, Ed." Mason's breathing was quickly regular. "We'll see, huh?"

"This ain't fair," Hoffman said, and he struck Mason as concerned and earnest. "It's upside down."

"The fair left town in September, right?" An old courtroom saw they'd both used before.

"So I've heard."

"I'm aware this is difficult for you, and I appreciate how generous you've been with me." Mason checked his watch. "I think I told you as much at the coffee shop."

"Keep in touch."

"So Ed . . . so when're you going to tell me more about your secret evidence? The nail for my coffin." The question was clumsy, more desperate than Mason would've preferred.

"Can't. Wouldn't be ethical. Can't tell you jack that I'm not supposed to."

"I know."

"Can't tell you. You might guess it. On your own. Readin' magazines, studying, you might piece it together."

"Yeah, thanks," Mason said. They were both silent. Mason noticed the rows of tan Virginia Reporters on the shelves, numbered law books containing decades of disputes and rulings. "Is it reasonable to assume, if I were speculating, that I need to watch people close to me?" He shut his eyes. Clenched his teeth. Swallowed. The window-unit air conditioner was humming, its control cover sprung open and three knobs visible.

"Always wise in any situation," the cop replied. "Especially them who *was* close to you in the past."

"You're a prince, Ed." But Mason was sick when he said it, numb, and the injury, the wound, was obvious in his voice, a weight so pronounced he slurred the words.

"Don't know why you'd think so. The box is the only route you got, seems to me. Bus is leavin' the station. Call anytime, twenty-four-seven."

Mason used the handrail as he descended the stairs from the library, kicked-in-the-groin pained, his pace a single step and a pause, both feet together on each worn oak board, and he made it halfway to the bottom before he surrendered and sat down and bent at the belly, his hands catching his face, the hell with the cops and their shoplifting file, they could wait forever. He remained in the stairway until he'd squandered most of his fifteen minutes, accomplishing nothing, stymied, wondering, half-ass contemplating disguises and fake passports. He finally collected the waiting policemen and went to court and muddled through the rest of his docket, distracted and indifferent, losing most of the cases or giving away the store in lenient plea agreements.

No Custis on Friday, either. As soon as he had a break, Mason hustled to the clerk's office, scanned the index and found a lawsuit filed by Art Anthony, a boundary-line fight between bullheaded neighbors quarreling over fifty feet of worthless dirt. At the end of the complaint was Art's address, phone number and Bar ID number. Mason copied the ID number onto a scrap of paper. He walked across the street to Art's law office and asked the secretary if he could use their library, a request that was fairly routine, given that Art had more legal volumes than anyone else in town, an inheritance from his former partner, Howard Pilson. Mason had been there three weeks ago to find a criminal precedent from 1903, and today the secretary smiled and inquired about Grace, then told him to make himself at home. "Where's Art?" Mason asked, and discovered he was in Martinsville, involved in a deposition.

Mason shut the door to the library, removed two books at random and placed them on a table. There was a phone in the room's corner, near the edge of a small, junky desk, and he picked up the receiver and depressed the clear, square button for line two. The button lit red. He checked the room, considered locking the door but didn't. He dialed the number for the state bar, got a receptionist and was put through to a lady named Marie Reilly, who was assistant bar counsel. He told her he was Art Anthony, and she confirmed his ID number.

"So how can I help you, Mr. Anthony?" she asked after they'd finished the preliminaries.

"I have a question about attorney-client privilege," he informed her. "I think I know the answer, but I wanted to discuss it with the experts."

"I'm not sure if I'm an expert, but I'll try to help."

"Here's my scenario: Let's say I'm standing on the street and I see my best friend running from the bank. As he passes me, he says something like, 'Can't talk, I robbed the bank and the cops are hot on my trail.'"

Marie Reilly chuckled. "Now, there's an original one."

"Right. So the next day, my friend is arrested, and he retains me to represent him. The trick is, he claims the commonwealth can't call me to testify about his earlier statement, wants to assert the privilege to prevent me from revealing what I saw and heard before I was hired. How do we stand under those facts?"

"First off," Reilly noted, "I'd have serious reservations about taking the case when I was a potential—"

"I understand," Mason interrupted. "Sure. You're correct, no doubt. That's really not my issue, though. I need to know if the attorney-client privilege reaches back to insulate information gained before representation, info or facts that were obtained completely independent of the client's communications and prior to any formal, legally recognizable relationship."

"The answer would be no. Pretty easy one there, Mr. Anthony. As a policy matter, it only makes sense—you're not betraying any client secret or improperly revealing any unique or special insight gained via the representation. For example, a murderer couldn't hire you months after the crime and then bar you from testifying how you observed him shoot his victim. Pretty straightforward, but again, I'd

be extremely hesitant to accept such a case if I had critical knowledge I'd discovered earlier, totally apart from the representation."

"Yeah, thanks," Mason said, attempting to sound chipper. "I'd
pretty much come to the same conclusion." *There's more to it*, he
remembered shouting at Custis. *We won't be taking Allen Roberts
to the grand jury. Not in June. Not ever.* Lord only knew what else
he'd said before he wrote the check. Great.

Brooding on his porch that night, still wearing his suit and tie,
waiting for Grace to arrive home from a friend's pool party, the outside light swarmed by gnats, moths and hardshell bugs, the toads
lying in wait beneath the azalea shadows, Mason recalled watching,
years ago, a deer leap the pasture fence, chased by dogs. Not long
relocated from Richmond, he and Allison had been planting perennials when they heard baying and barking and saw a fawn, still spotted, no larger than its pursuers, jump the top rail, and it was
momentarily a gorgeous sight, graceful and elegant, but the baby
was tired, evidently drained by the run, and its rear legs clipped the
fence, causing it to go crooked in the air and stagger its landing. The
dogs, a pack of them, feral, ugly and wolfish, came into view, wild
brutes breakneck charging, but Mason was certain they'd never
catch their prey, never have the stamina or speed regardless of how
weary the deer was. Its head start seemed enough.

Then another group of mongrels emerged from the woods
below, coming at an angle, and together with the first pack they had
the deer cut off, trapped. It stopped and tried to flee to the right but
was boxed in, and it leapt straight to the sky and squealed and shuddered as the first cur chewed into his thin hind leg. It was mangled
and as good as dead by the time Allison reached it, shouting and waving a garden hoe and not thinking about the danger, Mason beside
her clapping his hands and yelling curses. The dogs trotted to the
edge of the pasture, all together now. They wouldn't leave, just
stayed at a distance, some moiling, some on their haunches, ears up.
Determined not to let them reap benefit from their bloodletting,
Mason and Allison wrapped the dying animal in a sheet and paid the
vet a hundred dollars to put it down. Whispering comfort, Allison

stood witness to its pitiful fading and vowed to kill every one of the motherfucking strays on her property.

Surrounded and abjectly isolated, barricaded against his own particular hounds, Mason rocked in his chair, the night humid and the pasture under patches of fog. It made no sense for Custis to betray him, no sense whatsoever, and that plain inconsistency, along with his belief in Custis's ironclad decency, gave him a dribble of optimism, kept him thinking. There was nothing to be gained, no advantage, no reason for Custis to help the cops and decimate a friend, no grounds for retribution or punishment. Perhaps Custis felt he couldn't lie, felt he was beholden to some rule of paramount integrity that required him to honor the law and hew to the truth no matter the consequences, especially with a murder involved. But why does the guy who invents rough justice with Shug Cassidy suddenly change his stripes and decide to worship at the altar of abstract notions? And why be so suddenly, transparently hostile? Custis would've had to have been in cahoots with Bass and Minter from the beginning, part of their ploy with the prop gun and fake lab reports, the law office wired so he could spin webs and tease out information. But Custis Norman wasn't a tattle or a stool pigeon, hell no, far from it, and they were as close as kin, each other's favorite.

Mason heard the Gregorys' minivan bringing Grace home, and the headlights spoked through the driveway poplars and then into the pasture, animating the fog and coloring three sets of eyes redorange. A buck and two mature does, briefly revealed from the dark, evaluated the vehicle and returned to their grazing, not alarmed or frightened, unaware of any history there in those fields.

Chapter Nineteen

Violet, yellow, orange, white, crimson and many of their shades and variants stacked at least five feet tall—an arrangement of flowers the likes of which Mason had never seen before was waiting on Sheila's desk when he arrived early Monday morning, a magnificent mea culpa from Custis. There was a Mylar balloon fastened to her chair, floating the words I'M SORRY, the apology issuing from the jowls of a contrite cartoon basset hound. A box of Godiva chocolates was beside her computer, a present wrapped in metallic paper was in her chair, but there was no sign of either her or Custis. Driving to work, Mason hadn't known what to expect, but since it was his turn to supply food and snacks, he'd optimistically brought along a bag of fruit, reduced-fat cereal bars, pecan twirls, and two pint-size containers of orange juice, hoping for the best.

He flipped on the light behind Sheila's desk, took another gander at the flowers and the gift and noticed, topping a neat pile of messages for Custis, a slip marked "Urgent: Call Ed Hoffman ASAP." Hoffman had phoned on Friday, right after nine. Mason picked up the small piece of paper, held it between his thumb and index finger, read it aloud to the empty room in his normal voice, then laid it down; he felt no more or less disturbed than he had before finding it. He snooped through the rest of the messages and didn't discover anything else of interest.

Custis had also left a gift on Mason's desk, along with a note instructing him not to open it until they were together. Settling in to wait for his partner's arrival, Mason pried apart the juice's waxy spout, drank from the carton and bit into a pear. He separated the sports section from the *Roanoke Times* and checked the baseball scores. Several bites into the fruit, nearing the stringy core, he saw a sleek black limo pass by his window—an odd sight in Stuart—and make the turn onto Main Street. Almost immediately he heard a horn honk and keep honking. He walked into the lobby, carrying his juice with him, and found the limo parked in front of the office. The driver went briskly to the rear door and out stepped Custis and Sheila, laughing and goofy, their argument apparently behind them, both in fine fettle.

They strolled into the building and greeted Mason, and Sheila gasped at the flowers and teared up because of the balloon. "Custis came and got me in a limousine," she said. "You coulda knocked me over with a feather. Roger saw it and ran screamin' from the bathroom to the kitchen 'cause he thought we'd won the Ed McMahon sweepstakes or somethin'." Her hands were excited while she spoke, embellishing her words. "And I don't think I've ever seen such gorgeous flowers." She smiled at Custis. "Thank you."

"The production's not done, Mrs. Shough. Act two moves to your desk." Custis was beaming, and as Mason saw him there, so sincere, generous and humble, making amends in high style, it was difficult to imagine him as a serpent with a hidden agenda, lying to his friend and sleeping with the cops, Ed Hoffman's recent message notwithstanding.

Sheila oohed and ahhed over the candy, and when she opened the present—bam!—a spring snake uncoiled and rocketed from the box, startling her and causing her to shriek and then wag her finger and promise revenge. They hugged and the rift was repaired, the first good sign for Mason in many a month.

Later, seated in his office, Custis devouring a cereal bar and leaning against the wall, Mason asked if he could unwrap his gift as well.

"Soon, my man. Soon." Custis crossed his legs at the ankles, set a toe against the floor. He was wearing a tan poplin suit and novelty socks with vibrant Dr. Seuss rings. "Listen, Mace, I'm to-the-bone sorry 'bout my conduct last week, okay? Embarrassed. It wasn't professional, it wasn't justified and it wasn't the way a friend should respect a friend. So you got my apology, straight up and no strings. I shouldn't have broken on you like I did, and I hope you can wipe the slate and me and you go back where we were."

"Absolutely, Custis. And if I did or said something or offended you, whatever, you know I'm sorry, too. Basically, you're the best friend I have, and I'd wrestle the devil for you. Last week never happened. I'm relieved you're okay now. It worried me to death, you being so unhappy."

"Thanks. I was goin' through things, and I should've never carried it to work or let it get between us. My fault."

"It's nobody's fault, Custis. I was a pain in your ass after Allison's wreck, completely useless and glum, and I probably still would be if you hadn't helped cure me. I figure you have plenty left in the bank where I'm concerned."

"Kind of you to say."

"I don't want to be a nuisance, but is there anything I can do for you? All you have to do is ask."

"Nah, I'm clear of it." He dabbed at his mouth with a paper napkin, wiped his hands and tossed the wadded napkin into the trash. "I need to give you a heads-up on a situation, though. I hate to do it, hate to have to tell you, but it is what it is."

"Okay." Mason tensed. "Sure." He chain-blinked. He made fists and jammed them partway into his pockets.

"Man, this is a bitch. Man . . ." Custis tilted his head and spoke toward the ceiling. "It has nothin' to do with you or our friendship, but I'm guessin' you'll probably see it differently. Some events, Mace, some events just kinda shake out naturally." He leveled his gaze and studied Mason. "They're what comes next."

"Okay."

"This ain't about you."

"Okay," Mason mumbled again, stuck on the response.

"So, well, uh . . . damn . . . I'm probably gonna be leavin', Mason. Movin' on. New job, new town, new Custis." He shut his eyes and pinched the bridge of his nose. "Not immediately, mind you, and you know I won't put you in a hole. But it's most likely gonna happen, and you should be gettin' ready, lining up my replacement. Takin' measures."

"Why would you leave?" Mason was incredulous. "You've been here forever. I can't . . . I mean . . . shit, Custis. Why? Is there a problem—you certainly don't seem to be too thrilled about your decision. Is it money? I realize we aren't getting rich, but we split what there is to split."

"Nah, it ain't about the cash. Money's cool. But no doubt in my mind I'm takin' the route I need to take. A bigger city, more black folks to hang with, more for me to do. These days, I'm travelin' to D.C. or Atlanta twice a month, and that program gets tedious. I came here planning to stay a year, and I made it with plenty to spare. Truth is, if it weren't for you and Inez, I'd have flown this coop long ago."

"There's nothing else behind this? No undercurrent? You're simply moving to another place because you want to?"

"Amen. Precisely. You and everyone else have treated me like family for the most part. It's time to vacate, though. A man can leave and not be pissed or angry or disappointed. School superintendents and college coaches do it every day and nobody wonders why. Better gig at the next stop."

"So, Councilman Norman, the king of small-town life, is suddenly eager for traffic, crime, pollution, four-figure rent and five-dollar specialty coffee? How do the sly white editorial writers put it? What's the code? You're leaving us for the 'urban' side of the street? Why am I skeptical?"

"You shouldn't be."

"I damn sure can't speak to being a minority—I've only been poor, and you can fix that—but forgive me if I'm not sold when you tell me you're moving so you can be around people in dashikis and go to the jazz club. Better ribs and the Maya Angelou Festival. Nope, not your style, and I should know. Especially when your announcement follows on the heels of your week as Captain Queeg. Hell, you're more content in Stuart than *I* am. Why do I think you're not giving me the whole story?"

" 'Hip-hop culture' is big, too, when George Will opines about us. And the ribs around here are tasty, no complaints." Custis grinned. He took his weight off the wall, stood on his own. "Listen, Mace, no one harangued you when you decided to stay in Richmond after law school. Made sense for a bright lad to want the city. People switch and relocate, okay? You and Allison did. Skipped Richmond for Stuart. It doesn't necessarily mean you've got a secret motive." The last touch of lightheartedness vanished from his expression. "No matter how good of friends we are, you can't be another person. You *don't* know what it's like to be me or to be black in the sticks. You don't. Plain truth. You have no idea how narrow and convoluted the path between Uncle Remus and uppity Negro is. I'm always calculatin'. Always ridin' shotgun. Always wary of the booby traps."

"You've never let on it was a concern. Seems to me maybe you're reading in sentiments that don't exist. Or making false excuses. You've said yourself how much better it is living here with the random Klansman and impotent, obvious bigot than having to cope with a more sophisticated breed of redneck."

"I'm not sayin' there aren't good people here, and lots of 'em. It's just time for me to move on down the highway. Take in new scenery elsewhere."

"Inez?"

"Probably not a long-term proposition once I leave. But we'll see. We'll just play it by ear."

"Wow. Does she know this?"

"Yeah," Custis said. "She does. She's okay with it so far."

"Where're you going, by the way?"

"Atlanta. I already have three job offers. One's with the district attorney's office."

"Seriously?" Mason asked.

"I used Judge Greenwalt as a reference, if you're wonderin' why you haven't been contacted."

"I'll be damned."

"But I'm gonna stay as long as you need me to. Wouldn't think of leavin' you in a jam, though it would suit nicely if I could be relocated by October."

"Thanks," Mason said.

"It's been a pure pleasure practicin' law with you. You're like a brother. Custis and Mason. The Yin-Yang Towers, as Judge Greenwalt tagged us all those years ago. That's what makes this situation so friggin' tough, not where I'm headed. I hate it 'cause of me and you." He was suddenly emotional, and he paused to stare at the ceiling again. "Me and you, we've had a helluva run."

"I don't know what I would do without you," Mason said pensively, almost as if Custis weren't there. "I can't believe it."

"Me either."

"I never saw this coming. Never. I wish I could change your mind. I'll miss you."

"On this end, too."

Mason peered up at his friend. "If you tell me there's no concealed motive hiding in the bushes and give me your word you're not being pushed or forced, if you can shake on those terms, then you and I are square and I'll be satisfied. I'll help you pack and throw you a party. More power to you if this is truly what you want."

"My word, Mace." Custis stepped closer and they shook hands across the desk.

"Done," Mason said hoarsely, but he held the connection a few seconds after Custis relaxed his grip, continuing to focus on his friend, still not altogether convinced, mining for a telltale flinch or twitch.

"So open your gift," Custis said.

Mason tore off the paper and removed the lid from a rectangular box. "A shoehorn?" He grinned. "I mean, it's a superb shoehorn. Don't think I'm not grateful. On cloud nine, even."

"The handle's ivory, carved in Africa, the horn's stainless steel, so smooth sandpaper would slide down it like silk. Top of the line. An inexpensive luxury in your life, and trust me, you'll become addicted. Keep it in your closet and every morning, instead of

fightin' with your shoes and squeezin' and stompin', you can be a
gentleman on the cheap. Find a comfortable chair, take a little extra
time and slip your feet into your wing tips easy as you please—it's a
sweet feelin', Mace. Butler and castle kinda shit." Custis was sincerely enthusiastic. "If you really wanna go uptown, locate yourself
one of those old-fashioned electric buffers with the red and black
whirling brushes and hit that baby before you leave. A few seconds
on each shoe, *zzzzzzt, zzzzzzt,* and you've set a tone for the day,
highbrow right outta the gate. On top of everything else, your shoes
will be stylin' and last forever."

"This, Custis, is why I'll miss you so much. Thanks. I'll give it a
try tomorrow."

"You won't regret it. You'll be surprised what a major difference
it makes." Custis backed away from Mason's desk and nodded at his
feet. "Check out these puppies, smart and fly as you'll ever see. Says
somethin' about the man wearin' 'em, too."

"Why've you been keeping this a secret, Cus? All these years I
could've used a boost to my day, and only now are you inviting me to
the club."

"My bad, I admit it. But better late than never."

Mason put the top on the box. "You didn't have to buy me a gift,
but thanks."

"You're welcome."

"You want the other cereal bar?"

"I'm good," Custis said.

"You can have it," Mason offered.

"Not worth the calories."

"Fruit?" Mason was stalling, fretting, deciding. He'd forgotten
about his own pear, and its white meat was starting to brown.

"Appreciate it, but no."

"Okay."

"I'm gatherin' from the long faces at the council meeting Chip-
Tech's DOA in Patrick County," Custis remarked. "You for certain
against it?"

"Yep," Mason said distractedly.

"You see it as a rip-off? Hit and run?"

"It's not end-of-the-world bad, but we can do better."

"Stick to your guns," Custis encouraged him. "People enjoy the hell out of crack over the short term, too. I'm with you. Don't let a mean-spirited prick like Herman Dylan boss you around, you hear?"

"Uh-huh." Mason drummed his desk with all ten fingers. "Listen, since we're clearing the air, I need to ask you a question." It seemed to Mason his blood was too heavy for his veins, taxing everything inside him. He was on the brink of dizziness.

"Yeah?"

"Yeah. Were you in Richmond last weekend—not this weekend, but last weekend—with a cop and Ed Hoffman? At the Tobacco Company?"

Custis emphatically shook his head before answering. "No, I wasn't. Haven't you already asked me? The Monday it was pourin' rain? Sittin' here in this very same office?"

"I didn't really ask you directly, and it wasn't much of a conversation."

Custis finally sat, his knees splayed in opposite directions. "I didn't lie to you then, and I'm not lying now. Why're you so curious? Whoa. Wait. Hold on. You think me and Ed got something percolatin' to your disadvantage? *Do* you? That's a pretty rude accusation from the guy who claims we're so damn tight, such major pals." Custis stretched his neck forward, leading with his chin, defiant. "Especially shitty seein' as how I've busted my ass to protect you, and I'm still willin' to do my bit—by any means necessary, as brother Malcolm would put it."

"I didn't accuse you of anything. For all I know, you could've met with him trying to help me." The surge of nerves was waning, the threat of dizziness passing.

"No, you're suggesting I'm lying about bein' in Richmond with Ed. Don't try to sugarcoat it."

"So you weren't?"

"Fuck no, Mason, I didn't meet with Ed. Not in Richmond, not in Area 51, not in Timbuktu, not any-freakin'-where. Suddenly, I'm not regretting my decision to leave quite as bad. Who's spreadin' this nonsense, huh? Where you hearin' this rumor?"

"Don Wiggington said he saw you and a man who could've been Hoffman and a uniformed cop at the Tobacco Company restaurant. He was positive."

"And I'm positive he's a pervert, a liar and a troublemaker. I wouldn't believe that seedy SOB if he told me the sun rises in the east. You're in my business because of Don Wiggington? The child molester? I need to slap myself, cause I know this has to be a dream."

"Why's Hoffman calling you? He called last Friday—you didn't mention it."

"I oughta leap over there and knock the shit outta you." Custis was furious. Strident. "I should. You think—you have the balls to challenge my . . ." He was tongue-tied mad, spluttering, so angry he couldn't continue.

"I had to ask, Custis. Wouldn't you?"

"You're not asking," he snapped. "You're accusing me of lying and plottin' against you. That's what's at the bottom of your question, and I resent it."

"If you tell me I'm off base, we won't mention it again. You say you weren't in Richmond, you weren't in Richmond. You tell me you didn't have dinner with Ed Hoffman, you didn't have dinner with Ed Hoffman."

"I shouldn't have to say it three times, but I'm gonna, just so I won't undo the dab of goodwill I've tried to spread this morning." His voice was still heated, but he wasn't as confrontational. "I've never talked to Ed in Richmond or anywhere else on this planet about your case unless you were there. I don't have some secret plan, good or bad, goin' with Ed or the cops. Despite your lack of faith and appreciation, I've stuck with you and will continue to do so come what may, even though reasonable people might say I shouldn't. Understand?" He glared at Mason. "Ed, who is a policeman with cases other than yours, phoned Friday to tell me the forensics weren't ready for the trial we have tomorrow, the Arlen Spencer credit card forgeries. He needed a continuance. I saw the message when I brought the flowers and called him Sunday night at his home." Custis rose from his chair. "Here's the gospel, Mason

Hunt: Like the song says, paranoia will destroy you. You better chill and quit actin' the fool. Remember who's your friend, who's your enemy."

Mason believed him. "Far as I'm concerned, the book's closed, then."

"Far as I'm concerned," Custis huffed, "there never shoulda been a damn book."

Mason managed a weak smile. "You want your shoehorn returned?"

"I'm not playin', Mason. I admit I shouldn't have jumped on you last week, and I came in here today and apologized like a man. But I've never questioned your character, never sunk so low as you did just now. Never would. Like I'm gonna pretend to be your friend and . . . shit, we probably shouldn't be discussin' your personal affairs in here, anyhow. Too many potential ears."

"You're right."

"Shame on you," Custis rebuked him.

"I regret it, Custis. I'm sorry. I don't blame you for being pissed at me. Seems to be the day for apologies around here, huh?"

"Well, you're not finished with yours yet. This insult's got some legs. Your restitution's just beginning."

They didn't have any desire to be Ling-Ling and Hsing-Hsing, eating their meal while a hoard of gawkers scrambled for a peek at the town's newest curiosity, so Mason and Shoni McClean drove to Mount Airy on an August Saturday to have their first lunch together. School had begun, and even though it was still plenty hot, the air was crisper at night and the grass dew-soaked when the sun rose. Yellow leaves were starting in the poplars, maybe five bright inserts in a tree a hundred feet high, the changes still lost among all the green, insignificant.

Mason hadn't told his daughter where he was going or what he was doing. She and a group of friends were rehearsing a play at a teacher's house, and Mason had instructed her to call his cell if she needed him. He was pleasantly excited as he showered and shaved and dressed, and he debated which shirt he should wear and looked at himself in the mirror, gauging his appearance. He decided against cologne and settled on flip-flops with his chinos. It felt good to have a trickle of juice flowing, to finally register something besides dread at the same gray, stifling loop he toured every day, but as he was leaving, he saw Allison's picture, prominent on his dresser, and the lovely reminder caused him to sit on the bed in his silent house and ponder how out of whack this was, how flukish and screwy.

Before calling Shoni and asking her to lunch, he'd parked himself in the room with the rhino painting and scoured his conscience, trying to get a handle on what Allison would have expected of him. He concluded he'd be the jealous, childish ghost rattling his chains and shouting boo at his wife's new suitors, rearranging furniture and shorting light fixtures, a selfish spirit who'd rather see Allison in brown, droopy sweaters and drowning in cats than content with another man. Conversely, she probably loved him more than that, would ultimately wish him whole and attached to life, and he imagined her elegant hand raising a wineglass in a toast, subtle and sorrowful, of course, but still offering her blessing. She'd say something like, "So long as she's not as pretty as I am . . ." because she had always been confident and complete in herself, more assured and more generous than he could ever be.

Mason and Shoni had lunch at a Main Street restaurant called Pandowdy's, and despite his looming legal problems and the undeniable weirdness of a first date, the phenomenon of being both buyer and seller, performer and audience, Mason enjoyed the meal and he was impressed by Shoni, who had the grace and good sense not to discuss her estranged husband and was interested in all manner of things from kayaking to Ingmar Bergman. They discussed law and teaching and mutual friends and the new treadmill at the gym. They chattered past dessert and coffee, staying until two o'clock, even finishing the hard peppermints that came with the bill.

Returning to Stuart on Route 103, they commented on the cement dinosaur, polka-dot elephant and giant pink amphora at the entrance to Slick's Pottery, and they passed an old coot in a metal folding chair, a flyswatter resting across his lap, peddling his wares from a roadside shack, mostly hubcaps and lawn mower motors and dusty glass bottles. They turned around at a white clapboard church and went back to the man's junky stand, where they bought a pair of hubcaps, one shiny prize for Mason, one for Shoni, matching first-date mementos, the kind of calculated craziness that's funny and loosey-goosey and vaguely romantic but would have a veteran husband fussing at his wife and braying, "Why the hell would I want to drop twenty bucks on hubcaps we can't ever use?" Mason kissed Shoni on the cheek at her door, told her he'd see her again soon, he hoped.

At the end of August, now firmly convinced he would be indicted by Leonard Stallings in the September term of Patrick County Circuit Court, Mason traveled to Martinsville and hired a pair of lawyers, Pat Sharpe and Jim Haskins, to represent him. Sharpe was the younger of the two, around six feet, thin, fair-skinned and impossible to rattle in the courtroom, deft at developing his case with thoughtful, compact questions that left witnesses no space to hedge or lie. Haskins was in his sixties, a warrior from the first pleading to the last post-trial motion, savvy and persistent, and he was famous for his impeccable manners, natty suits and cheap black-plastic comb, which he would unabashedly produce, anywhere, anytime, and carefully groom his hair, whether in the middle of a trial or while talking to a friend on a street corner, it didn't matter to Gentleman Jim, and the idiosyncrasy had become a trademark of sorts for him, to the extent that other attorneys and court personnel often cued on it, figuring the comb's appearance likely signaled a turn in a case, big doings, a sign the hammer was about to fall.

After mulling it over, Mason decided to include Custis in their initial meeting, and the four of them gathered in Haskins's conference room, late in the afternoon. Mason explained he was soon going to be charged with the 1984 murder of Wayne Thompson. Saying it, sitting there in Haskins's conference room amid the black leather chairs and fox-hunt prints, saying it caused Mason to come to a dead halt, his own voice repeating in his brain, the awful gravity binding him for several seconds. Finally continuing, he also informed them the common-wealth's case was based on three items: his brother's testimony, an incriminating statement he'd allegedly made during a police sting and some mysterious evidence he and Custis hadn't unearthed but believed to exist, since Ed Hoffman was an honest cop and wouldn't bluff if he didn't have the goods. Mason declared his innocence, repeat-ing the false account of where he and Gates had been on the night of the killing. "He's doing this because he's angry with me," Mason said in a steady voice, "and because he wants me to help him get out of jail. Since I won't do his bidding, I'm sure he'll try to trade his testimony for some sentence reduction or an advantage in the system."

True to his temperament, Haskins was enraged. "What a bas-tard!" he exclaimed, bellicose and combative, immediately spinning out no-holds-barred legal strategies. Sharpe listened intently with his index fingers steepled in front of his face and said, "I'm sorry this is happening to you, Mason."

They discussed options and speculated and debated strategy for over an hour, and at the conclusion of the meeting they were in agreement on all issues save one: the question of the polygraph. Sharpe and Custis thought there was nothing to lose and everything to gain, but Haskins was against the idea, arguing the tests were unreliable, he wasn't sure the agreement was enforceable and it was beneath Mason to participate in a "damn witch hunt." "Those tests are wrong too often for my taste," Haskins said. "You catch an erro-neous reading or an inconclusive, and you better believe this Stallings or the cops will leak it to the court, slip it in, and while the jury might not hear it as evidence, you'll wind up with a judge who thinks you're guilty and that'll color every ruling he makes. Besides, your sympathetic chum Ed Hoffman, who's helping and feeding you under the table right now, might switch teams if he thinks you're lying."

"I'll sleep on it," Mason said. "Grand jury meets on the eighth—I'd need to do it before then. How about you guys helping me with the research, see if Ed and the AG's office can tie Stallings's hands once he's appointed as special prosecutor? I've spent several hours on the computer reading every case I could find, and I think we can rely on the agreement, but I'd rather have a more objective opinion."

"I'll have your answer by tomorrow," Sharpe promised.

"Every case I found references commitments made by the *commonwealth*," Sharpe explained in a call Mason took at his mother's house the next day. "The rulings don't necessarily focus on individual prosecutors except in the sense that they're agents for the state and can therefore make agreements on its behalf. Who better than the heaviest hitter of them all, the attorney general and his authorized staff, to conduct the commonwealth's affairs? Do we really think a judge is going to ignore an immunity offer made by the cop in charge of the case *and* the office of the commonwealth's chief prosecutor? You could very legitimately argue that the attorney general is Stallings's boss and can trump him. Legally, my opinion is the same as yours—we've got the horses on immunity if you want to have a go at the polygraph. Tactically, of course, it's up to you. Jim has raised a number of very valid points contrary to mine."

Ultimately, Mason sided with Custis and Sharpe, concluding that there was a strong possibility of enforcing the deal and defeating any prosecution *if* he could beat the test. Mason himself phoned Ed Hoffman, and they rearranged several schedules so Mason could drive to state police headquarters in Salem and undergo the examination before the grand jury convened. "Who you want on the box?" Hoffman asked.

"I get to pick?" Mason replied.

"So long as it's one of our guys. Or one of the feds."

"Huh." Mason thought about the possibilities. "I'll take Morgan Witmer."

"I would, too. Good luck, my friend. I'm rootin' for you."

Mason spent hours preparing for the test. He would ask himself the money questions out loud and practice saying no, attempting to repeat the deception again and again and again and again until he was immune to it, desensitized. He concentrated on his breathing, the pace of his heart, the adrenaline bumps in his stomach. He rehearsed with a thumbtack positioned in his shoe, pressing it into his middle toe before he began each series of questions to himself, hoping to elevate his breathing and heartbeat so there would be less room for deviation from the recorded baseline, no peaks and valleys. To dull his responses, he washed down a Valium with his breakfast orange juice before leaving for the exam.

Aware the cops might search him or require him to remove his shoes and discover the tack, he parked at a Hardee's in Salem, slit the underside of his middle toe with a razor blade, placed a slender, flesh-colored Band-Aid on the cut and experimented with the pain level. He was satisfied—the fresh slash hurt more than the tack he'd used as an approximation. Pat Sharpe met him at the entrance to the state police building, wished him the best and accompanied him down a long hall with fluorescent lights and dingy white ceiling tiles, several discolored by water stains.

Morgan Witmer was careful not to grant any advantages or favorable treatment. He spent forty minutes asking questions and explaining the test and ground rules before he hooked Mason to the machine with wires, a chest strap and a blood pressure cuff and asked the first question: "Is your name Mason Hunt?"

Mason mashed his cut toe into the floor and monitored his breathing. "Yes." He was still wearing his shoes, perhaps a concession from Hoffman, or maybe the experts weren't concerned with countermeasures gleaned from the Internet, confident they could see through a layperson's most disciplined subterfuge, barefoot or not. The control question was "Have you ever lied about anything to keep from getting in trouble?" and Mason answered yes, aware this wasn't the key inquiry, nor was it really directed at his case. "Did you kill Wayne Thompson?" and "Do you know who killed Wayne Thompson?" were sandwiched between innocuous softballs about the color of his shirt and Mason's home mailing address.

Witmer then repeated the questions word for word, this time in a different order. "You can relax," he said at the end of the second round, and the device's skittering, darting needles went calm over their paper.

Hoffman and Witmer left the room after the exam was concluded, and Mason made an effort to appear relaxed and assured, given that he was most likely being recorded by a concealed camera. Having ambled in to join his client, Pat Sharpe was calm also, a pro, and he projected confidence, chatting about deer season and his son's roster of teachers at elementary school. Ten minutes later, Hoffman returned alone. Dispensing with the customary song and dance and post-interrogation razzmatazz, he stood in front of Mason, his arms against his rib cage, a soldier's posture almost. "So, you want Mr. Sharpe to stay here?"

"Absolutely," Mason said, his mouth dry, his stomach suddenly hollow, realizing from Hoffman's question that the results were not going to be favorable. He saw Sharpe quickly remedy a dejected mouth, masking his own disappointment.

"Well, you got fifty percent. Passed on whether you killed the boy. No surprise there. Showed deception on knowledge of who killed him." He glanced at Sharpe, not Mason. "For me, no surprise there either."

"The test is wrong," Mason protested. He struck the right tone, too: firm, astonished, aggrieved.

"This isn't a police trap is it, Ed?" Sharpe inquired. "The Hail Mary where your polygraph guy actually has no idea, but you claim Mason failed so you can pressure him into admitting something? Hope he'll collapse because you tell him he failed a test we both know is on a par with tarot cards and Ouija boards?"

"Witmer says he's lying. I don't like it either. At least give me credit for not underestimatin' you gents. I'm not interested in screwin' Mason."

"Thanks," Mason said. "You've been completely fair. It's not your fault. I was probably too nervous or overanalyzed the questions."

"I told Witmer to make you a copy," Hoffman said. "You're welcome to have an independent take a look at it. But you and me know Morgan Witmer's a straight arrow." He peered at Sharpe. "Hell, I wanted Mason to pass. This investigation's off track. Wrong."

"So this stays between us?" Mason asked.

"Me, you, Mr. Sharpe, Witmer, your classmate at the AG's office." He reached inside his coat pocket and handed Mason a sheet of paper. "You have the only other copy of the agreement. Morgan can't destroy the test, but you have my word we won't mention it. He's filin' it under my name, not yours. This is deep-sixed."

"So what if an independent examiner will certify he passed?" Sharpe asked.

"If he's credible, we'll talk." Hoffman pulled one side of his mouth taut. "See, Mr. Sharpe, I'm not a man who wants to convict the wrong guy. For the sake of lookin' good. The big bust. Make my bones in the papers. Another pretty letter in my permanent file." His arms were still slack, against his sides. "Here's what I know. What I've known for a while. Gates Hunt killed this guy Thompson. Gates is a dogshit criminal. He has reasons to lie—thinks it'll help him with us. Or maybe he's only bein' spiteful. Years ago, Gates's brother helped him with the cover-up. Brother takin' care of a brother. Young boys, immature. Tough upbringing. I don't know how deep Mason's in, but I figure it's enough to make it bad legally."

"If that's your theory of the case," Sharpe said, "then why are you planning to indict Mason?"

" 'Cause we have the evidence to do it. Sad to say. Mason's gettin' hosed because he lied and continues to lie. Now he's so tangled up, if he tells the truth, it potentially makes matters worse. Gives his jailbird brother credibility." He caught Mason's eye. "Right, Mason?"

"I didn't kill Wayne Thompson," Mason said, the reply rote. "I'm not lying."

"Minter and Bass, good men. They see it different. They believe you did. Truly believe it. There's another thorn for you."

"Any suggestions?" Sharpe asked.

"Me, I'd try to cut a deal for Mason. I'd come clean, toss this grenade back to Gates. Where it belongs. Maybe lock in a misdemeanor, plead guilty, no jail, community service, go after the man who actually pulled the trigger. Probably over the girl. There's your motive. I personally will do everything I can to sell it to Stallings.

People would understand. Brother and brother. I'd recommend an obstruction or the like for Mason. If he quits lyin', damn it. He'd have to testify."

"You can recommend it," Sharpe said, "but Stallings has to go along."

"True. Truth is, he might not. Sense I have, he won't."

"How strong is your case?" Sharpe asked. "How do you evaluate it?"

"As it stands now, I'd lay my bet on us."

Mason smiled. "Are you giving odds, Ed?"

"Nah." For the first time, he appeared perturbed. "By the way, Mason. Morgan said to inform you bitin' your tongue wouldn't skew the test. They can tell."

"Huh? Bite my tongue? I didn't bite my tongue. What a bizarre thing to say."

"I'm just repeatin' what he told me." Hoffman gestured slightly with his hands.

"I've read that you can use thumbtacks or pins or, yeah, bite your tongue, but you and Morgan can look at mine if it makes any difference."

"Doesn't matter to me," Hoffman replied, still irked. "Sorry this went south on you. Wish we coulda done better."

Chapter Twenty

The night before he was due to be charged with first-degree murder, Mason brought Grace to their kitchen table and told her about his likely grand jury indictment and what she could expect because of it: the arrest, the media attention, the gossipy stares and smirks, the uncertainty, the pressure, the whole ball of wax that accompanied a high-profile homicide case, especially one in which the defendant is the county's commonwealth's attorney and a local boy who'd overcome a hardscrabble past. The tale would be terrific fodder for the newspaper writers and ravenous local TV reporters, rags to riches to ruin, the tragic cycle, capped off with neon irony, a prosecutor in danger of a trip to the hoosegow.

Grace went from bored to alarmed to hysterical, her eyes paralyzed in horror, her mouth drawbridged open, mutely pleading with her father: *Oh God this can't be real, can't be happening.* She seemed stricken, spastic, as if her windpipe were clamped shut and no air was reaching her lungs. Her neck filled with pink, sawtoothed splotches, and before Mason could say more or attempt to comfort her, she dumped herself forward, collapsing onto the floor, her knees hitting first with full force. She clutched her stomach and lowered her forehead, rested it against the Spanish tile her mother had bought and set and grouted, every beautiful square aligned, every joint quarter-of-an-inch perfection. Blond hair spilled across the tan hues like pick-up sticks.

Mason joined his daughter on the floor, sitting beside her with his legs folded, his tentative hand rubbing patterns between her shoulder blades. He didn't force the issue, speaking only occasionally to reassure her, and she stayed hunkered down and withdrawn for what must have been half an hour. When she finally was ready to talk, she rocked onto her butt and rested her jaw on the bony point of her knee; she was facing the cabinets beneath the sink, her view slanted sideways, still not directed at her father. Sobbing, she wanted to know if Mason could be "sent to the electric chair."

"It's not possible. No chance. None. I'll be charged with first-degree murder, not capital murder. There's a difference. You don't have to be concerned."

"You swear? You're not just saying it to baby me?"

"I swear," Mason said. "Plus, there's no way I'll be found guilty. This will be terrible, but in the end, I didn't shoot anyone or break the law and I'll be acquitted and we'll be normal around here again. I can't honestly tell you it'll be easy, but we'll be okay."

"Would I automatically go live with Grandma Sadie? At her house?"

"Yes. But I'm not going to prison. If we have a trial, I'll win."

"It's possible, though, isn't it?" She turned and met his eyes, switching cheeks on her knee. The crying wasn't as bad.

"Anything's possible. True. It's possible the oceans will disappear in the next five seconds, but it's not something to worry yourself with, is it? You're becoming too much of a lawyer."

"Why is Uncle Gates doing this? Why?" She dropped her head again, fitting it between her knees. "Why?"

"Because he's petty and selfish and he thinks this will help get him out of prison early. He's trying to trade this lie for a break in the judicial system. Sometimes people who help the authorities, even if they are rotten to the core, are given special consideration."

"I hope he dies."

"Can't argue with you."

"Why is this happening to me?" she asked, and it was the moment that weakened Mason the most, bludgeoned his resolve and pierced his heart.

"It's a big burden. You've had lots to carry, sweetie, too much for a girl your age, none of it your fault." His voice clotted in his throat. "I can't tell you why, much as I wish I could. I'll always do my best for you, though. Always protect you, always love you." He bucked up, determined not to cry and dilute the snake-oil palliative he was trying to sell her. He hugged her with both arms and tipped her toward him, and they remained stuck together on Allison's tile floor, the kitchen quiet except for the soft, soft hum of the refrigerator and the surprising clunk of the ice-maker birthing cubes into its plastic bin. Mason ended the silence when Grace separated from him. "I don't want you to think this is another I-walked-ten-miles-to-school-in-the-snow story from the prehistoric days, another tiresome reminder of how difficult it was for me, but my daddy, your grandfather Curt, was the nastiest, craziest, most worthless parent who ever lived. A complete sonofabitch who gave me nothing but grief. It was hard, but I got through it. Unfortunately, Gates didn't. No matter what, Grace, you have a father who adores you and will never, ever abandon you. Right now, maybe that doesn't seem like so much, but trust me, it'll mean a lot in the future. You always have a safe place with me. I'm an absolute for you. You understand?"

She nodded that she did.

"He ain't my son anymore," Sadie Grace announced, spitting mad, when Mason stopped by her house early the next morning and gave her the news. "After all we've done for him, this is the thanks we get." She was in a housecoat and bedroom slippers, and she appeared older without her makeup, the cigarette wrinkles around her mouth more obvious, her lips pale.

"I'm sorry I have to tell you. I'd like to think you've earned the right to enjoy retirement and take bus trips with your friends and spoil your granddaughter."

"Shut up, Mason," she barked. "You brought some of this on yourself, now didn't you? I've told you a million times to keep your distance with Gates. But you wouldn't listen. Nope. Ignored my warnin'." She was standing, and she jammed her hands against her hips. "I knew when it happened, like a mother always knows, somethin' was fishy. The day Danny Owen come by here askin' questions about that dead boy, I knew Gates was in the wrong. I shoulda grabbed you up right then and gotten to the bottom of this so we wouldn't be having this discussion now."

"Well, I'm sorry you'll have to suffer all the scrutiny and embarrassment." He paused, chose his next words. "I'm to blame to some extent, you're right. But Gates would've done this no matter what, whether I'd been in contact with him or not. It's his last straw. I realize it's awful for you."

"How can he say all this and not drag himself into deeper trouble?" Sadie Grace asked.

"He claims I shot the Thompson boy. A damn lie. Claims he was just there, a bystander. Didn't see it coming, didn't participate. Who exactly can contradict him? It's just me versus him. Pretty cunning on his part—I have to give him credit."

"He's his daddy's son, no doubt. It's in his genes, Mason. Has to be. Curt was a man—if you can call him that—who hit his own baby boys and turned my every hour into hell on earth, and it never caused him so much as a second thought. It's a kind of ugliness you can't understand or explain or remedy."

"I'm optimistic we'll win this, but I wanted you to hear it from me. I hate it more for you and Grace than I do for myself. We both know I've survived worse. I'm more worried about you two than anything else."

Sadie Grace momentarily avoided Mason, seemed occupied by a framed scene on the wall, a reproduction of *The Last Supper.*

"I'll let you know this evening how the grand jury went," Mason promised, "though it's pretty much a done deal."

"Okay."

"I'm sorry to have upset you."

"Well, I shouldn't have gotten ill with you. It's . . . it's just you're all I have, Mason. You and my granddaughter. Sixty-six years on this earth, and my only joy is you and Gracie. Now the single good thing in my life is bein' threatened." She shifted her eyes, stood taller. The crinkles in her face intensified. "I'll tell you this, and me and you will never speak on it again: Whatever I need to say or do to keep you out of trouble, I will. We're goin' to fight fire with fire. We've made it this far, me and you, through thick and thin, and we ain't backing down now, not to a coward like your brother. If this jury decides the way you think it's gonna, I'll be there by your side. With my chin up. You fight as strong as you can, and you don't worry about me."

"Thanks," Mason said humbly. "I love you. Lucky for me, I got your genes and grit, huh?"

Sadie Grace was too wily to alert Mason, but she left soon after their conversation, before lunch, and she showed up at the prison wearing tennis shoes and old-lady dungarees, her thick hair pulled tight into a ponytail, a dab of lipstick her only preparation, and since she'd been coming for years and years and knew the guards, they allowed her to see her son, bent the rules when she told them she had an emergency. Gates sauntered into the visitation area—empty and cavernous on a Monday—and he spread his arms and smiled and said how happy he was to see his mother, but underneath the goodwill Sadie Grace could sense, almost immediately, that he realized why she was there and his great welcome was a sham, fake as fake could be.

She never took a chair. She marched directly to Gates and asked him if he'd told the police Mason had killed the Thompson boy in 1984. For whatever reason, she recited the year. He began his answer, hedging and dissembling, Cheshire cat grinning the whole time, like he was talking to some damn fool instead of his mother, but she soon cut him off—"You are disowned by me," she snapped— and busted him in the face with a fistful of rings she'd added before leaving Stuart. The blow wasn't a slap, wasn't symbolic or a maternal correction, but was thrown with bad intentions, calculated to do as much damage as possible, most of it meant for Gates, maybe a little left over for Curt. Gates yelped and ducked and jumped to the side, and when he looked up his mother was walking toward the exit. He shouted, "Wait, Mama!" and even though it pained her to no end, she kept right on going, holding her tears until she reached her car, where she sat weeping with the engine running for so long that a kindly guard came to check on her and offered his handkerchief.

Realizing his mother was done with him, Gates touched the jagged cuts on his mouth and jaw, then aimed his middle finger at the room's locked door and laughed through the ache, a lunatic's cackle, pronounced and malicious, like Vincent Price or Idi Amin, and the noise tangled up in itself, echoing off the cement and metal.

Chapter Twenty-one

Mason glanced at the photograph he'd been handed. "Uhggg . . . nasty. Why the hell are you showing me this trash? Huh? What's the matter with you?" Disgusted, he quickly tossed the picture onto a polished, rectangular table and went through a pantomime with his fingers, vigorously wiping them on his suit coat to remove an imaginary taint. "Today of all days, why're you plaguing me with this? You know I don't have any stomach for homo porn." He and Custis were tucked away in Art Anthony's law library, under the radar and safe from possible police eavesdropping, killing several hours, waiting for the grand jury to return and Mason's life to be recast. Custis had delivered 116 indictments for the jury, stayed until the four men and three women were sequestered and then left, on standby across the street if he was needed. Special prosecutor Leonard Stallings was there with a single count to present, dressed to the hilt, his secretary along for the momentous event.

"Look closer," Custis said solemnly. He was crammed into a wobbly metal chair, diagonal to Mason, at an angle that allowed him to see only Mason's profile.

"No, thanks," Mason replied. "Gay sex isn't my bag. I'm not a fan of costumed queers caught in the act. Butt pirates, my neighbor calls them."

Custis took the photo and held it toward Mason. "You should look closer."

"Is this about a case? Or some stupid Internet gag? I'm not in the mood, Cus, okay? I have bigger fish to fry. Maybe it slipped your mind, but I'm being indicted for murder as we sit here twiddling our thumbs and passing around your faggot nonsense."

"Humor me," Custis said, his tone constrained, purposeful.

Mason was frazzled, pins-and-needles restless. He snatched the photo and gave it a longer inspection. "Oh damn." Squinting and befuddled, he drew the picture so near that his nose almost touched the glossy paper. "This shit is libelous, Custis." He positioned his chair so they were able to see each other full on. "You realize that, don't you? What—is someone circulating this? I'd be pissed off, too. Bastards used a computer to superimpose your head on a porn guy's body. Pretty respectable job, but you can tell it's a gimmick. Who did this? Where'd you find it?"

"I found it in my mail."

"Say what?"

"It ain't no mistake or trick, no Photoshop, no cut-and-paste." Custis hurried, speaking rapidly. "That would be me in the picture, boss. Sorry to be the one droppin' the bomb on you."

"Huh?" Mason shook his head like he'd been roused from a nap, trying to compose himself. "You?"

"Me. Custis Norman. 'The faggot nonsense,' as you so diplomatically labeled it, occurred at a private residence in D.C., couple years ago."

"So that's you in the picture having sex with another guy? You wearing a cowboy hat and vest and a hard-on?"

"Head 'em up, move 'em out, rawhide," Custis said dryly. "I'm not necessarily proud of it. It's not representative of how I conduct my personal life."

"Damn . . . I'll be damned. So . . . ?"

"Yeah," Custis answered.

"Really?"

"Really."

"Gay?" Mason still wasn't convinced. "No shit?"

"Yes," Custis replied, and he was deliberately formal, no retreat in the word, no shame, no quibble. "You got it."

"Like, *gay* gay? How long . . . I mean, how long have you known? How long has it been?"

Custis chuckled, but there was a bitterness to it. "Quite a while, Mace. I didn't simply sample the buffet, study my options and decide before the deadline came and went. You don't read the brochures, list the pros and cons and select the gold lamé package."

"I mean, hey, whatever. Your business, not mine. Live and let live, right?"

"Even faggots and butt pirates?" Custis pressed.

"I'm not going to lie, okay? This is a shock, not really a revelation I was expecting, especially today, of all days. And yeah, the thought of two men kissing and having sex, well, it's not my cup of tea. Viscerally, it's awfully tough for me to accept. I can't help it." Mason couldn't keep his eyes trained on Custis. "And Inez," he blurted. "You've been dating her for years."

"For years. There you go, Mr. Wizard, a big whoppin' signpost for you. Make no mistake, Inez Rucker is one of the finest, most remarkable women to ever leave the Good Lord's mansion, and I love her dearly. But she's devoted to her dead husband and is waiting for the day they'll be together in heaven—you can laugh and joke and make fun of her, but she believes she's still married. When her Harrison died, she was finished. She has no interest in sex; hell, she sees it as adultery. To her credit, I don't think she's ever tempted, either. It's not like she's fightin' the urge to get laid and have a man in her bed. There are folks who're like whoopin' cranes—one and done."

"So she knows?"

"Duh, Mason. Yeah, she does. It's been a blessin' for us both, a perfect relationship for her and for me. Our interests match like gin and juice, we keep each other from bein' lonely, and our friendship prevents people such as you from pesterin' us about our personal affairs."

"All these years, she's protected your secret?"

"Yeah. She has, despite hatin' the gay lifestyle on principle. Her religion, you know. Your churchgoin' sisters take a dim view of sodomites. She's forever prayin' up a storm for me, but unlike a lot of your hypocrites recitin' scripture, her heart's pure. She truly does love the sinner, just doesn't care for the sin."

"Why're you telling me this now? No offense—I'm happy to listen—but I'd say we already have a full plate. Sort of odd timing." Mason rubbed his temples. "Wow."

"Two reasons," Custis said, sounding rehearsed and prepared, like he was presenting a closing argument. "First, misery loves company, and though that proverb doesn't exactly hit the nail, I thought you might be more understandin', more sympathetic in light of your present circumstances and troubles. Struck me you'd have a good idea how it feels to be up against it. There's—"

"I'm sorry," Mason interrupted, smirking, "but virtually everything you say seems Broadway funny now, like gay double entendre."

"If you're fifteen in the locker room, it probably does."

Mason flickered a smile. He felt slightly less uncomfortable.

"Anyway, here's reason number two. The payoff. I wanted to come completely clean with you. See, I gotta figure maybe you're still questionin' my bona fides, what with this Richmond sighting, me leavin' so soon after you're popped by the grand jury, me cutting a shine with you and Sheila, this whole streak of weirdness we've had lately. You need a clear mind to take care of your predicament, and you deserve to have the entire picture—so to speak—and I'm gonna do my damnedest to be an ally you can count on one hundred percent. Truth is, I *was* in Richmond like the pervert Wiggington claims, and I was with a cop."

"You lied to me?" Mason exclaimed.

"Not really. As we say in court, check the transcript, my man, recall exactly what I represented. I've never had any sneaky dealings with Ed Hoffman, and I didn't meet with him in Richmond. I gave you the bare-bones facts on the subject. 'Course, you never asked me if I was visitin' with our mutual friend Ian Hudgens."

"Hudgens? You mean Herman Dylan's minion?"

"Yep."

"Huh. He's a nondescript bald guy? I imagined him very differently."

"He's a bald weasel," Custis said. "An average Joe with a serious facial tic. Probably the stress and long hours."

"Okay. I assume he was chewing your ear about Chip-Tech, but you'll have to help me with the particulars. Why are you and Hudgens eating steak in Richmond?"

"Simple. They're aware you and I are ultra-tight. He and his taskmaster Dylan wanted me to lean on you."

"To vote for their grant?"

"Aren't you clever," Custis said, stretching every syllable. "We're *Perry* Mason today, aren't we?" He grinned. The sarcasm was genial. "And guess what he used as a stick, once I didn't do the carrot dance?"

"It's starting to make sense," Mason said. He was finally able to settle his eyes on his friend. "The faggot nonsense. They're blackmailing you. You didn't want me to find out." There was a peculiar enthusiasm in Mason's voice, a skip in his cadence. "So you really don't want to leave, do you? Your whole big-city-Black-Panther speech was bullshit."

"They prefer the term *quid pro quo*. A bit slicker, don't you think? I can't stand for my personal details to be broadcast all over our fine Victorian county. I can't. Hell, you're supposed to be my friend, and you're actin' like I'm a leper. Can you imagine everybody else's reaction? The shitstorm I'd suffer?" Custis shot Mason a frank look. "It's a comprehensive slash and burn, too. See, Hudgens had gotten wind of your jam as well and threatened to release the photos right before your trial, thinking—at worst—maybe some of the gay will rub off on you and influence the jury and—at best—we'll have another distraction, two fronts to defend. A bit of lagniappe, as the Cajuns say, a bonus to make me more inclined to persuade you."

"I'm not treating you like a leper. This is sudden—sky-falling sudden—and I grew up fishing, hunting, playing baseball and listening to my mom's Old Testament piety in rural Patrick County, Virginia, the unreconstructed South, and I'm sorry, it's just ingrained, the . . . the distaste I have. I can separate our friendship, and I will, I swear I will, but seeing the photo gives me the heebie-jeebies. It's no different than getting the heaves from rancid meat or retching at the dead-mouse-in-a-heat-duct smell. It's hardwired. Instinct. You know I'm as libertarian as they come, and it's fine with me, do whatever the hell you want, and intellectually I can accept it, but if I saw you cuddling with some man I'd probably puke. I value our friendship, I'm not making moral judgments, but I can't change how I am."

"The term *faggot* is as offensive as the term *nigger.*"

"I suppose it is."

"It's great to know you're so tolerant and broad-minded," Custis said. "Magnanimous of you to overlook the rat stench, or at least hold your nose for me."

"Actually it is, if you think about it. My friendship with you, my respect and affection, trump everything else. I don't care who you sleep with; I'm just giving you fair warning how it affects me."

"Ah. I'm grateful, too."

"I'll try to do better with my language," Mason said. "But how about a grace period if I forget? Maybe for the first three months you don't take away rainbow points or report me to Queer Nation?"

"It's wonderful you can be so glib," Custis remarked. "I'm delighted you're friggin' Richard Pryor when I have to leave my home and my world's toiletized because I refuse to trade on our friendship and compromise my values by dragging you into Herman Dylan's mud. You have any clue how difficult this has been for me? Do you? I didn't have to tell you any of this. I could've packed my bags and left your homophobic cracker ass in a sling, wonderin' which direction was up."

"I apologize. I'm just trying to . . . to . . . lighten the conversation. Jeez. So I can fuck with you about being black, but gay pride is off limits?"

Custis was growing irate. "Problem bein' the gay stuff is serious and true, the race stuff is just for sport."

"It's not my fault you're gay and embarrassed to tell anyone. Nor is it a shortcoming I'm not keen on humping other men."

"Kiss my black ass, Mason."

"You're my best friend, Custis. I can't put it any plainer. I doubt we'll be roomies again in San Juan, but other than that, you and I are still good to go. Still Custis and Mason, all right? Seriously, I want to put this aside and not dwell on it. I try to take people as I find them, and I try to treat them exactly like they treat me. By that standard, nothing's changed—we've got too deep a history, too much goodwill, and you've done so much for me I could never repay the debt."

"It'll be different, believe me. Your attitude's already adjusted."

"Don't be stupid and paranoid," Mason said.

"Answer me this: What do Elton John, George Michael and Boy George have in common?"

"They're all gay." Mason caught himself. Chagrined, he exhaled and stared down and traced his thumb along a scratch on the table. "And British . . . and musicians, very good ones. Whose friends and fans have stuck by them and made them successful and don't notice their sexual orientation."

"Proves my point, doesn't it? Grammys, Oscars, gold records, knighthood. Hell, Elton could discover a cure for sickle cell and it wouldn't matter—the first thought everyone has is they're homo-sexual. Nothing can overshadow it. Your whole identity is tied to bein' queer. Everything kicks off there, and it will with you and me from this minute forward. Used to be, if you heard my name, you'd think, 'my best friend, my law partner, my six-foot-seven wingman,' and now it'll be 'the butt pirate.'"

"You may be right in some sense, Custis. It was a very effective parlor trick and I took the bait, but I swear to you I will do every-thing I can to be a reliable and admirable friend, just like I always have. At least I'm honest about how it affects me."

"I appreciate it, too," Custis answered in a hopeful tone that left room for compromise. "You've certainly been good as gold up till now. Treated me like kin. I hope we can stay solid."

"Thanks. You are kin."

"So we're cool, you and me? Cool as can be expected with your affliction?"

"We are."

Mason turned the picture facedown and slid it toward Custis. He waited for Custis to collect it before speaking. "So Dylan threatens to let the cat out of the bag unless you persuade me to vote for his grant. How'd they discover the photo? Your, uh, stint as Roy Rogers?"

"Hudgens came up with *Le*Roy Rogers when he was tryin' to humiliate me. You're a beat behind the rest of the orchestra. Need to keep your material fresher."

"Not a bad line, I have to admit."

"I've been around the gay scene in D.C. forever," Custis said. "A few whispers here, even."

"No kidding? I've never heard a peep."

"Best bet is they followed me for a week or two, and I led them where they needed to go. Herman Dylan is rich and powerful, and this is pretty basic detective work. I want you to understand I've been with the same partner for almost a decade, Mason. Monogamous except for an unfortunate split a few years ago. While we were apart, I fell in with some unsavory people, didn't protect my interests like I should've, and this guy I was with for maybe a month—a mistake—took some shots while we were together. I'm responsible for my own idiocy—it was a time in the wilderness for yours truly, too much alcohol, too many clubs."

"Happens," Mason said sympathetically, battling to keep the visuals suppressed.

"After Hudgens threatened me, I called my D.C. friend and he's basically a crack whore these days, blubberin' how sorry he is, sniffin' and cryin' like a schoolgirl. Sold 'em for five hundred pathetic dollars. Who knew, huh? I never thought the pics would surface like this. Never. Hudgens blindsided my ass."

"So that's why you were so hateful around here?"

"Yeah, I was mad at myself for the compromisin' mess I'd cooked up. Mad 'cause I was in a spot and resigning seemed the only option. Rather than come beggin' you to save me and vote against your best judgment, rather than attemptin' to persuade you for the wrong reasons, I called my boy Hudgens's bluff and told him to let it rip, make 'em into posters and billboards for all I care, won't hurt me 'cause I'm leavin' anyhow. And, yeah, sure, it wasn't totally noble. Part of it was I didn't want you or anybody else to discover my adventures in other venues. 'Course, bein' the prince he is, Hudgens says he'll send his package to Atlanta *and* embarrass me here for good measure—Godfather shit—so the next Herman Dylan extortion victim will understand they play for keeps. 'Have to follow through,' Hudgens tells me, 'unless we receive our grant.' Leaves me in a bad way, huh? Shit outta luck both comin' and goin'. I'm Peewee Herman if I stay in Stuart, and I'll be rollin' into snicker-city wherever I go, assuming my new employer doesn't fire me the second he opens the morning mail."

"Who was the cop with you in Richmond?"

"Aw, hell, it was Drew O'Connor, our favorite state trooper. I had him wear the crime-crusher uniform and stop by and say cryptic, boogeyman things to Hudgens, 'cause I anticipated they were goin' to put the arm on me. Figured I'd show a little muscle myself, have Drew tail the dumb shit back to the airport, ride his bumper, flash the blue lights, get under his skin. Problem is, I didn't know I was gonna be flexin' on Godzilla. Turns out I was far too puny. I came with Schlitz; Hudgens was stockin' Hennessy. Thank heavens Drew wasn't there for the main course, if you catch my drift. He'd definitely freak."

"I guess a lawsuit and extortion charges are not on the horizon?"

"My word against his, he was careful how he phrased it, and do I really want a jury and the papers gettin' hold of this? I don't see myself pursuing any legal remedies."

"Well, the upside is now I know, and the leverage from that is gone. We'll put this in the hopper with my problem and sort through it. Stall Hudgens, string him along, give him the rope-a-dope, delay Atlanta but don't burn the bridge in case you need a Plan B. You belong here, Custis, and if push comes to shove, I'll give the people what they want and Herman Dylan can have his cash. I'll tell the commission I've reconsidered. Chip-Tech isn't completely awful, it's just not the best we can do, and you're more important than a thousand grants. I wish we could fuck Dylan and not have you crucified, and I hate to see us get hustled, but no matter what

I'll take care of your interests first, absolutely I will. At least we can solve your dilemma and you're not staring at life in prison—be thankful for the bright side." Mason hesitated, unable to resist, straying past tolerance, a juvenile with spitballs and rubber bands: "Of course, for you, life in prison . . ."

The grand jury foreman, Dewey Lankford, had sent a note asking the judge if the indictment for the county's commonwealth's attorney was "allowable," whatever that meant, and two jury members refused to vote, claiming any evidence against Mason Hunt had to be crooked, but ultimately Leonard Stallings got his wish and on September 8, 2003, Mason was charged with the first-degree murder of Wayne Thompson. Sheila called to tell Mason and Custis the jury had returned, and Custis was in the courtroom when the clerk read the indictments, Mason's last, number 117.

Stallings was a tiny man, not more than five and a half feet tall. He had a mop of red-orange hair, a prizefighter's strut and skin marred by pimples and raw, vulgar bumps. He also was a dandy dresser, always wore a vest and watch chain, French cuffs with his initials embroidered in block letters. A pocket square. After the jury had been discharged, he boldly crossed the courtroom and introduced himself to Custis, offering to shake hands. Custis rebuffed the courtesy, then crouched down like he was addressing a child, hiking his pants at the knees as he lowered himself, his head tilted and framed by a spill of woolly dreadlocks. He glared at Stallings and said, loud enough so everyone could hear, "You better bring your bazooka, you carrot-topped little leprechaun. Better come big. You have Custis Norman's vow you'll be regrettin' this."

Stallings wasn't intimidated. "Leprechaun or not, Mr. Norman, you have my vow Mason Hunt will be found guilty and go to jail."

Stallings had tipped the newspapers and TV stations, and he preened and pontificated for them on the courthouse steps, serving up clichés about justice being blind to office and power. He directed his secretary to distribute a press kit that included his résumé and a color eight-by-ten of himself, his heinous skin retouched in the photo, the blemishes washed away. He claimed to have an airtight case. A slam dunk. Pat Sharpe and Jim Haskins responded the next morning, releasing a nine-page rebuttal document, which included a quote from Sadie Grace Hunt, stating her son Gates was a convicted drug dealer, a serial liar and utterly unworthy of belief, much as she hated to say it. The trial had already begun in earnest, months ahead of its proper arrival before a judge and jury.

People quickly chose sides, and Mason was surprised and heartened by how thoroughly the county supported him. Stallings received his first taste of Mason's popularity when the clerk of court, Susan Gasperini, pretended she couldn't hear him after he politely asked if the order appointing him as special prosecutor had been filed with her and was on record. Sheriff Hubbard and every officer in his employ refused to serve the capias on Mason and take him into custody. "We're too busy," he gruffly informed Stallings, then proceeded to ignore the prosecutor's many telephone calls and a directive from the attorney general himself.

Stallings finally had to recruit a state police sergeant from Charlottesville to enforce the indictment and escort Mason to a magistrate. The officer phoned and declared his business, and Mason agreed to meet him at his law office—noon, sharp—and walk with him to be fingerprinted and processed, and so four days after the grand jury acted, Sergeant Max Lawrence arrived in Stuart prepared to formally arrest Mason, the paperwork in an ordinary off-white folder, the words *Hunt Case* scrawled in Magic Marker letters across the folder's middle.

Lawrence was professional, removing his hat at the threshold and asking Mason if he needed to call anyone or make preparations for bond before seeing the magistrate. "I do have to inform you, sir, you are now under arrest for first-degree murder," he said as he presented Mason with a copy of the indictment. "Commonwealth of Virginia v. Mason L. Hunt" was typed across the top. The policeman had promised Pat Sharpe he wouldn't use cuffs, but he did briefly take hold of Mason's arm and steer him through the door and outside. When the cop released him, the two of them were alone in the bright sun, and Mason, his focus scattershot, nervously noticed the NO PARKING AFTER BUSINESS HOURS sign was missing a fastener and starting to droop from the wall.

When they rounded the corner from the parking lot and began the climb to the ancient courthouse, Mason saw the throng of people, probably four hundred of them, and he initially was petrified, under the impression they were there to witness his shame, rubberneckers and busybodies eager to watch the spectacle of his misfortune, but he soon spotted Sheila and her husband, Roger, and there was Custis and Inez, and Sadie Grace, and he realized they were all assembled, on both sides of the street, occasionally three-deep, to wish him luck and embrace their own. Unsure of the crowd's mood, poor Sergeant Lawrence reflexively groped for his pepper spray and spread his hand over his gun. "It's okay," Mason assured him. "Shouldn't be any problem."

His mother and Custis flanked him, and the sheriff and several deputies fell in behind, and Mason shook hands and took every uphill step with modesty and thanked people for turning out and missing work. Custis informed him that Sheila and Susan Gasperini had called folks and asked them to come, and there would've been a larger group if they'd had more notice. Cecil Priddy was the last in line, and he promised to bring Mason by a bushel of peaches, saying he would've done it earlier but his foot had been stove-up and his wife had been feeling poorly. Like so many others, he never mentioned why he was there or the murder case, carried on like it was any other day and laughed when Mason good-naturedly warned him to keep the peaches away from his uncle's still over in Woolwine.

Mysteriously, three TV crews were waiting near the entrance to the magistrate's office, and the cameramen scampered down the street to videotape the warm send-off. "Not exactly the perp walk our boy Stallings had in mind," Custis said before Mason went inside.

With the sheriff watching and Haskins and Sharpe hovering near the doorway, Sergeant Lawrence inked Mason's fingertips and rolled them across a card, took his picture in front of a height chart and questioned him about his full name, address and Social Security information. It was a degrading state ritual that had greeted every thug, hoodlum, criminal and sociopath for decades, designed to isolate them with a string of numbers and drain their piss and vinegar, flagging them as at least *probably* guilty, giving them a taste of the state's boot heel, and now Mason was an initiate, mug-shotted and listed as a defendant in thousands of police computers, on a par with every thief and rapist he'd prosecuted, never the same no matter the result of his trial, stained. Reduced. He seethed and thought of Gates, how much he despised him.

Next came the magistrate, a lady named Peggy Taylor, and she was apologetic and flustered, but Mason told her not to worry and do her job like he was any other defendant, he understood. She set his bond at five thousand dollars and didn't require any surety, basically freeing him on his signature and bare promise to be in court for his next hearing. As she was completing her forms, Taylor quit typing and peered at Mason and told him again she was so sorry, remarking how terrible it must be to have a brother like Gates. "The worst ever," she suggested.

"Well, he's probably not as bad as Frank Stallone or Billy Carter," Mason cracked, trying to take her off the spot, but she later told her husband she could see the strain in Mason, the weight already aging him.

The trial was scheduled to last three days, beginning February 9, 2004. At the end of September, Jim Haskins and Pat Sharpe visited with Mason at his house on a Saturday morning, and told him they had both good news and bad. "Which you want first?" Sharpe inquired.

"The good, please."

"We have a superb judge. The Supreme Court appointed Andre Melesco from over in Rocky Mount. You acquainted with him?"

"Not really," Mason replied. "I think I ran into him once at a commonwealth's attorneys conference. He was a speaker."

Haskins produced his black comb and whipped it through his

hair. He was dressed in corduroy and tweed and was silent, content to let his colleague carry the conversation.

"I've been in his court," Sharpe continued, "and he's top-notch. Smart as a whip, prepared, fair and he understands reasonable doubt. He'll make the right call, even if it's unpopular. We're fortunate."

"Great," Mason said. "I'm relieved I didn't draw a dud."

"He's a nice guy off the bench, too," Sharpe noted. "A pleasure to work with. We couldn't ask for better. Oh—I know you've already checked—but I did talk with the state bar rep, and he confirmed there's no reason you can't continue to serve as commonwealth's attorney. Like any other accused, you're presumed innocent. He did suggest you might want to obtain some sort of written waiver from everyone concerned if you're prosecuting a crime of violence or a very high-profile case. Or assign it to Custis until we get your matter resolved."

"So what's the bad news?" Mason asked. They were in the kitchen, the breakfast dishes still in the sink, toast crumbs and a streak of Grace's strawberry jelly waiting to be wiped off the table.

"Two items," Sharpe said. "I contacted several lawyers who practice with Stallings, and they all say he's very competent. We shouldn't underestimate him just because he looks like the dwarf spawn of Pippi Longstocking and Alfred E. Neuman. Consensus is the midget can try a case, and he relishes the spotlight. He's no pushover."

"Okay. I wish we had a pigeon, but we don't." Mason was leaning against the counter. "What else?"

Haskins spoke up. "Pat and I filed our discovery motion the day you were indicted and Stallings replied the next week and, to borrow a phrase, there's no smoking gun, Mason. For the life of me, I can't figure what he's holding that's making him so smug. I faxed him and called him and so did Pat, and he simply says he's complied with discovery. Sent me a letter, sort of snide, and told us he knew the law and he'd produced everything we're entitled to. I'm buffaloed. Are we positive he's not posturing?"

"Custis and I have thought and thought and thought, and we're stumped, too," Mason said. "No clue."

"Nothing worse than getting your tail caught in a trap at trial," Sharpe remarked.

"Well," Haskins said, "since he gave us transcripts of your interviews with Bass and Minter, we know it can't be a statement you've made to the cops, and it can't be DNA or fingerprints or blood or other forensics. He'd have to produce it."

"So we're left with a witness, maybe?" Sharpe mused. "You mentioned this hint from Ed Hoffman, maybe surveillance? A bug?"

"There are no witnesses," Mason declared. "It's impossible. Unless someone's lying. It didn't happen, so no one could've seen it. Hell, any witness would've come forward years ago anyway. As for the other, I haven't discussed the case with anyone but you, Jim and Custis."

"We'll stay on it," Haskins promised. "If this is their entire case— Gates Hunt and your ambiguous, perfectly innocent statement to the cops—we'll blow their doors off."

"I'm not counting on it being so simple," Mason said.

In October, the assistant principal at Patrick County High School phoned Mason at work and told him a teacher had discovered Grace smoking cigarettes in the girls' bathroom.

"Grace? Smoking?" Mason was flabbergasted. "My daughter?"

"Yes. She was also giving them to other kids."

"You're sure?"

"Sorry to say, I am. Mrs. Rakes caught her with the butt in her hand and smoke comin' from her nose. Pretty cut and dried unless she's part dragon," he said amiably and gently laughed.

"Well, yeah, thanks for telling me," Mason said. "She's under a lot of stress. I'm not making excuses for her, but with this crazy case against me and her mother passing away, it's been difficult for her. She's a great kid—you and I hear that every day, but it's no exaggeration with her."

"I agree," the principal assured him. "We're going to do an in-house suspension, but we can't give her too much more latitude. In our world, this is fairly serious."

"I understand. I'll sit her down this afternoon and read her the riot act and discipline her at home, too."

"So you're aware, I checked with her teachers, and her grades are falling. She's always been one of our best, but lately, according to her teachers, she's not trying. Very withdrawn, they report. We've also noticed her . . . her appearance is changing, her clothes, makeup, kind of darker than before. We understand how fragile she must be, so we want to be proactive and deal with this before it worsens."

"Definitely. I feel like a fool for not noticing the clothes and whatnot myself. I see her every day, and I try the best I can to parent her correctly. We get together religiously, without fail, and review her assignments and discuss her, you know, her friends and school and whatever else. It . . . I don't know. It must have been incremental. She seemed, how would I put it? Sloppier? Quieter? Tense? But I wasn't aware it was so drastic."

"It's probably only temporary, and I'm not sure I'd call it drastic. She's a wonderful girl, and her small detour is completely understandable. We have counselors here and several other effective options. I'm positive we can nip this in the bud. We'll partner with you and Grace to turn this around. Don't worry, it's what we're here for."

"Yeah. I'm grateful. Thanks." Mason had a thought and rushed to speak before the principal left the line: "Let's not send her to a counselor or cross that line yet. I'd hate to . . . to overreact. I'll try to handle it at home, and you keep me posted on her attitude at school. I'll check back with you in a week or so."

"Absolutely. We'll talk again soon."

Overwhelmed, Mason piled up his arms on his desk and laid his forehead on top of them and shut his eyes. His mind was quarantined, curtained off, a dim, bare stage with scant illumination, and he imagined two words, done in scorching yellow against the black, suspended by taut wires, silently screaming: IF ONLY . . .

Grace was cigarette Gandhi—quiet, level, passive, detached, civil. Mason went to the school and summoned her from her last class ten minutes before the bell. Still in the parking area, yanking on his safety belt, he demanded to know why she was smoking at school and breaking the law by giving tobacco to other underage students.

She shrugged. She wasn't looking at him. He noticed her jeans were ripped and her shirt black. Her mascara did appear different, too pronounced, too vivid.

"Were you smoking?"

"Uh-huh."

"Why? It's dumb and harmful for so many reasons I can't even begin to list them. You want lung cancer? Lizard skin and wrinkles? Want to get expelled from school and have colleges think you're a disaster? Want a crappy job and no future?"

"No," she said, dully, submissively. "I'm sorry." She rolled a strand of hair around her finger, then unrolled it. She was slouching.

"Sorry? That's it?"

"I guess," she said.

"Were you giving cigarettes to other kids?" He left the school and accelerated onto the main highway. A window wasn't completely closed and air whistled through the interior. Mason sealed the glass and ended the noise.

"Just my friends. They wanted them. I didn't sell them or anything."

"I'm very disappointed in you, Grace."

She didn't respond.

"Anything you want to say?"

"No sir."

"So here's the deal: no computer, no phone, no TV, no movies for two weeks. Additionally, you're totally grounded. School and our house will be your entire universe. Understand?"

She nodded.

"Voice, please."

"Yeah," she said, so softly the word evaporated the moment it hit air.

"Okay." He glanced across the seat at her, but she ignored him. "I'm not trying to be an ogre. I realize it's tough for you right now because of bad breaks you can't control. It's wrong you lost your mom, it's wrong you have to fret about me, it's wrong you've been embarrassed by seeing your father falsely accused of murder in the newspaper and it's wrong you have to worry about things most people your age take for granted. You've been a champ so far, and I'm proud of you. Not many fifteen-year-olds could've done as well as you have. You're exceptional, and I love you. But I will not let you use this trumped-up, ridiculous murder charge as a crutch or an excuse or a reason to do as you choose." He relocated his hands on the wheel, brought them both closer to the top of its arc. "I'll admit ninety-nine percent of this is not your fault, but if you quit on yourself, if you think nothing counts anymore, if you fail classes and dress like Morticia Addams and hide in a shell, you're hurting me, too, and hurting people who love you is also wrong. I need you to hold on to yourself. I promise we will lick Leonard Stallings, and nothing will change."

She unspooled a finger full of hair. She slumped against the door, didn't answer, and Mason was scared, stuck, afraid he wouldn't be able to retrieve her. He was distressed, pondering what he could do, and he allowed a tire to drop from the pavement onto the loose gravel shoulder, and the car fishtailed and nearly swapped ends and when he finally steered them back straight on the road, Grace might as well have been asleep, didn't appear alarmed or bothered. She didn't seem to care one way or the other.

Chapter Twenty-two

Three days into Grace's Marlboro Light punishment, Jim Haskins was on the phone, inflamed, Gatling-gunning his sentences, *tat-tat-tat-tat-tat-tat*. "The sonofabitch has the polygraph," he announced to Mason. "I don't know how, but Stallings got hold of the test, and the despicable troll has sent chapter and verse to Judge Melesco. He wants to schedule a damn hearing, so, just as I feared, our well's gonna be poisoned when it comes to the judge. Not to mention the press. It'll be splashed all over the news."

"Whoa, whoa, whoa," Mason stammered. "Say what?" He was leaning on the corner of Custis's desk, Custis standing next to him. They'd been almost to lunch at the Coffee Break, crossing Main Street, and Sheila had come tearing after them, told them it was urgent. "Custis is with me; I'm putting you on speaker so he can hear, too."

"Stallings has the lie-detector results, and he's filed them with the court," Haskins repeated, his voice staccato, crackling from the phone.

"How did he find out?" Custis asked.

"No idea. But it's not too difficult to narrow it down—take you guys, Pat and me from the equation, and it's an extremely limited field."

"I can't believe it," Mason said. "You think Ed Hoffman shang-haied us?"

Custis shook his head. "It'd be off the chart for him. New territory."

Mason sank deeper onto the desk. "Why in the world is Stallings filing the polygraph with the court, Jim? How can he do that? He knows it's absolutely not admissible at trial, completely barred. He's obviously trying to gain a tactical advantage and influence potential jurors. It's blatantly unethical. Clearly misconduct. We need to bust his chops and ask for sanctions or even a dismissal."

"He's clever, Mason, clever. See, he took all the letters we've been whipsawing him with, our inquiries about discovery, and included them with his motion to the court. He's asking the judge to decide whether or not he has to hand over the lie-detector docu-ments." Haskins finally began to brake his speech. "It's angels on pinheads, a ruse, but it gives him perfect cover. He claims he doesn't want his case hamstrung by a technicality, says he's afraid we're setting him up, that we'll appear at trial and complain he didn't release information we were entitled to. In a nutshell, he's asking Judge Melesco for guidance: 'Do I have to give Mr. Hunt the results even though there's an agreement this thing would be buried and can't be used at trial? Does the parties' deal trump the law? Or, if I release the test am I violating the commonwealth's commitment to confidentiality?' Of course, it goes without saying he's manufac-tured the whole brouhaha and doesn't give a tinker's damn how the judge rules—he simply wants to score points by alerting everyone to the unfavorable results. Melesco will see through the smoke and mirrors and realize the motion's a sham, but now he knows more than we'd like for him to. So will your jurors who watch TV and read the paper."

"Wicked," Custis said. "Gotta admit the midget's on his game."

"So who the fuck leaked it?" Mason asked angrily. "It has to be Ed, the AG's office or the examiner. Damn."

"Don't know," Haskins replied.

"Well, I owe you an apology," Mason said. "You were right: I should've avoided the frigging test. I wish I'd taken your advice."

"Could've gone either way," Haskins said graciously. "Let's not dwell on the past. You don't owe me anything. We'll file and ask for sanctions and a dismissal, and Pat and I'll prepare a response for the media. Hell, the polygraph proves you didn't commit the crime you're charged with. Keep your spirits up, Mason. We're still in fine shape. I'll see to it Mr. Stallings has plenty to occupy him for the next few weeks."

After finishing the call, Mason opened the door and flashed his head from Custis's office. "Get Ed Hoffman on the phone," he yelled at Sheila.

The following morning, Mason and Hoffman met at a Hardee's in Bassett Forks, roughly halfway for them both. Hoffman arrived first and was drinking coffee and eating a breakfast biscuit, egg and cheese, its wrapper tucked underneath as a makeshift plate. Mason stalked across the restaurant and stormed into the booth with him. As he hurtled in, Mason bumped his kneecap against a metal support, and a hot tingle rode a nerve up and down his leg. "Hi, Ed," he said sarcastically. "So why the hell does Leonard Stallings have my polygraph test? The test you vowed to take to your grave?" Mason was loud. His neck and cheeks thumped red. His hands were twitchy. He flexed and bounced his leg, trying to jigger away the pain.

"Hello to you, too. I gave it to him. Three days ago." Hoffman gingerly raised the wrapper and its biscuit and moved them to the side, closer to the window. He set his coffee near the food so there was nothing between him and Mason, only empty table. "Sorry. No choice. I was meanin' to call. Soon. I regret you didn't hear it from me."

"Why would you sell me out, Ed? Because you think I failed the test? Is that it? Or did you just mislead me from day one and plan to backstab me regardless?"

"Stallings put the screws to me, Mason. I held with you like I promised until I couldn't hold with you any further. I submitted my written report to Stallings—your test wasn't mentioned. He's interviewed me several times—kept my mouth shut. So did everyone else. The polygraph had vanished. Here's how he works, though. He has a checklist. Thorough as can be. Gives it to me to complete. I've learned he does it with every officer. Very effective device. Catches info and evidence you might've forgotten, and if the case tanks 'cause a cop neglects or forgets and it ain't on the sheet, Stallings can wash his hands. This sheet he gave me specifically asked if there'd been a polygraph. So I don't turn it in. Delayed. Tell him I've given him the whole schmear, maybe he needs to talk to Bass and Minter. Nope, he says. Do the form. So, Mason, I'm not gonna lie, not me, especially to the players on my own team. I leave several boxes empty or put a question mark. He drags me in and drills me on every single blank. I advise him to call the attorney general's office, say this is too complicated for me. I'm a grunt, this needs chain-of-command input. Didn't take him long then. He's filed a complaint against me with the state police. I'll be okay, but he's not happy, no he's not."

Mason didn't respond. Cashiers were shouting orders to the cooks, an older man and woman behind Mason were discussing a recent trip to Niagara Falls and a lanky black kid with flour smudges on his brown company shirt was sweeping the floor, banging and scraping his wooden broom handle whenever he reached beneath a table or booth bench.

"I'm sorry," Hoffman continued. "Unintended consequences. I wish I hadn't offered the deal. I knew the truth before you were hooked up. Hoped I was wrong or you could end-run the exam. Hate it for you. Don't blame you for bein' pissed."

"Not much I can do about it now, huh, Ed? My stock took quite a hit thanks to your not keeping your bargain."

"Didn't see it comin'. Didn't plan to make your situation worse." He reached for his coffee, took several sips and placed it on the table in front of him, keeping both hands around the cup.

"You're not bullshitting me, Ed? You truly concealed this as long as you could? Really?"

"Absolutely. But I can't totally lie for you or anyone else. Not my style. And if you want to be a stickler, I didn't actually tell him. He found out from the higher-ups in Richmond. But I'm acceptin' responsibility."

"Lot of good it does me," Mason complained. "Thanks so much for the late, worthless, facile lip service. I'll recommend you for an ambassador's post at the UN—you'd excel there."

"Appreciate it. Maybe I could do it part-time when I retire from this racket. Get paid to wear those earphones and carry on 'bout embargoes and such." Hoffman gazed at the coffee cup and rotated it a full turn but didn't lift it from the tabletop. "So I'm thinkin' last night, been thinkin' ever since Stallings put the squeeze on me— and, hey, he's a man doing his job, I don't have any gripe with him— been thinkin' how to repair this with you. It's nowise simple. Me, I'm in a bind. Too many masters."

"I'm in a bit of a bind myself, Ed, partially because you promised me something you didn't—or couldn't—deliver." Mason jutted forward and rested both forearms on the table, his stomach flush against its rounded orange edge.

"I'm gonna return what I took as best I can. Put us level."

"How?" Mason asked skeptically. "The damage is done. In spades."

"You pay attention to the magazine I left in Stuart?" Hoffman asked.

"Yeah. I gathered I was under surveillance. Or had been. We've been careful. Thanks." Mason cocked his head. "I hope you're not taping me now, Ed."

Hoffman didn't change his expression. He plowed ahead. "Remember you asked me 'bout people close to you? Remember?"

"Sure."

"You solved it yet? Seemed you was on target."

Mason relaxed, settling into the slope of the bench. "I thought I did, but . . . well, no, I'm not positive. I had some suspicions . . . Nothing's turned up in discovery, so to be honest, we're still confounded."

"Huh."

"In fact, I was probably chasing shadows and too suspicious and obsessing about it—this shit has a way of disorienting you. And this peekaboo show you're doing now isn't helping much. How about you just jump to the nitty-gritty?"

"You spent seven minutes and eleven seconds interviewing a man who'd admitted to a murder. Including the time you spent with your sheriff and Roger Wilson." Hoffman sipped his coffee, peering at Mason over the rim.

"Huh? You mean Allen Roberts? The sting you guys engineered?"

"Yep. I had a watch on it."

"So? Who cares? An experienced detective had spent hours with him and gotten zilch. I'm not a cop, and it's not my job to interrogate people. The fact I went at all speaks volumes. I took the case seriously and had him questioned and did everything I could."

"How many other suspects you, yourself, actually interviewed?"

"I've never given it any thought," Mason dodged.

"I'd bet the ranch the answer is none." Hoffman wasn't cocky, wasn't combative.

"This is meaningless, Ed. Hot air and gibberish. I told Bass and Minter I knew the guy's reputation and had my doubts, serious doubts, but nevertheless I instructed the sheriff to bring him in immediately, and I personally followed through to make certain the case was properly investigated. I've gone over this in my mind and with my lawyers and it merely demonstrates I was doing everything humanly possible to prepare for trial."

"I knew when you wanted to speak to him you was involved," Hoffman said. He sounded almost apologetic.

"Then you need to buy a turban and crystals and mystical bones and set up shop in Atlantic City, because you must have supernatural powers."

Hoffman smiled. He took a folded sheet of paper from his shirt pocket, spread it open on the table and pressed the creases flat with both palms. "Maybe the magazine was too confusing. Instead of hintin', I probably should've had the balls to go full-scale and spell it out clear. Didn't figure I was at liberty to just spill it, but I hated for you to be bushwhacked. Torn between a man I respect and my job and how I felt the case should wind up." Hoffman patted and smoothed out the paper. "Room was wired, Mason. Your sheriff didn't know. We sent an agent with the state computer tech and bugged the place. Days before. Assumed you'd probably interview the suspect. Two reasons: You had to make it look good, plus you could have a gander at what was transpirin'. Try to see where the strings were. You made sure you didn't tape it, too. Left the recorder off."

Mason didn't respond.

"Then you instruct this Roberts boy to dummy up. Tell him not to speak to the police. He's done it, too. Has he ever. Odd you'd give a suspect advice that hinders the investigation."

"I don't remember what I said or didn't say, but knowing Allen like I do, I wasn't convinced. My believing in his integrity and innocence hardly suggests my criminal brother is telling the truth. And if I made him aware he didn't have to incriminate himself, so what? I've been a friend of the guy all my life and had some sympathy for him."

Hoffman put on glasses and bent down over the paper. "Here's what you said. I was listenin'. Wrote it down word for word: 'I know you didn't do this, okay? Don't worry.' " Hoffman stopped and briefly studied Mason. "I'm skippin' a few parts that don't matter." He resumed his reading: " 'As long as I'm the commonwealth's attorney, you will never be charged. You're innocent. You have my word nothin' will happen to you.' " He paused again and fixed Mason with a cop's deadeye, hammerlock stare. "You didn't ask the boy a single question. You're too decent for your own good, Mason. Got busted by your own conscience. Couldn't let Roberts suffer and worry. Sent him home to kiss his wife despite the murder weapon we'd found at his house *and* his confession. Then informed Agent Bass you were prepared to indict—a deceit."

"Roberts didn't confess, and there was never a murder weapon."

" 'Course you was unaware of those niceties when you cut him free." Hoffman refolded his notes and returned them to his pocket.

"I've been doing this for years, Ed, and sometimes you rely on your gut," Mason protested. "We all do. So I sensed the case wasn't up to snuff, and hey, guess what? I was right."

"Ain't here to debate with you, Mason."

"Wait a minute." Mason slapped the table with an open hand, suddenly incensed. "Hang on. Wait. How come Stallings hasn't given us this? He's under an obligation to produce it. It's discoverable as can be."

"Accordin' to Rule 3A:11, it isn't," Hoffman said, his tone self-satisfied for the first time. "Figured this out for myself. Took me twenty-three years. It's held up for me, too, least in other courts, Judge Weckstein's included. Everybody knows how smart he is. Commonwealth has to give you any statement *you* wrote or we recorded. We didn't record you and Allen Roberts, just listened and took notes. Me, Bass and Minter. Three cops heard you. We have to produce any statement or confession you made to the police. Not the situation here. You didn't make the statement *to* us. Little glitch in the rule. A loophole for the good guys. If we're careful, the Hoffman method allows us to keep a surprise sometimes. A derringer in our socks. Ran it by Stallings, he agreed. He was delighted."

"I've *never* read the law to say that. You can't be right."

"Go study it for yourself."

"What nonsense, Ed. The discovery rules are designed to ensure no one is surprised. They're about disclosure and—"

"Listen," Hoffman interrupted. "You guys with the law degrees and English majors truck in this shit, not me. I did two years of night school at Roanoke College. Barely made it through. But as for this one itty-bitty speck of the system which affects me and my job, I'll match my understandin' up against yours or anybody else's."

"I've seen the language a million times," Mason said. "Maybe after so long you start assuming too much or glossing over it, but I'm still convinced you're wrong."

"Don't matter, not really. We have the statements. You're aware now. If your lawyers raise a stink and I'm mistaken, the judge orders us to tell you what you already know. No help to your case in the long term. The evidence is the evidence. I'm gonna let Stallings know, too. Inform him I've spoiled our big finale. Receive my tongue-lashing from him and have another complaint filed with my lieutenant."

"Pretty sinister shit, Ed. You went all out on this, didn't you? The elaborate sting, the rule bending."

"My responsibility to do the best I can toward findin' the truth. Didn't figure you'd just confess to Bass and Minter if they showed their badges and asked politely. Or threatened to haul you into the station for questioning like they do on TV. It'd be wrong if I'd gone half-ass. I've been fair to you, too. Now I've made amends. Don't want to hear no cryin' the blues."

"So Custis and I can remove the cone of silence and stop talking in code? We're not being monitored or listened to? I misunderstood the magazine clue?"

"Our only bug was at the sheriff's office. Nothing else. I thought you might add it up."

"What if Allen Roberts and I have a different recollection?" Mason challenged Hoffman.

"You mean what if you lie and you tamper with a witness? Hard to say. Can't predict who a jury'd believe. Three cops, or you and Mr. Roberts. One thing's set in stone—you went in to see him and you kept the recorder dead. Why?" Hoffman finally broke off a chunk of biscuit and put it in his mouth, began chewing. "It's no foolproof case for us," he remarked through the bread, "but like I told you, if you ask me to handicap it, I'm comfortable the common-wealth will win. You gotta smell trouble, too. With Gates's testimony alone, we're down the tubes. But add the tape of you soundin' so surprised. Blurting to Bass and Minter it's not possible they found the gun at Roberts's house. Jury takes notice. Then stir this last ingredient into the recipe: a commonwealth's attorney who's sittin' on the lab-identified murder weapon and a confession to a poly-graphed witness bebops in and tells the suspect he'll *never* be charged. I'd be losin' sleep if I was you, Mason."

"Who wouldn't?" Mason asked. "Guilty or innocent."

"At any rate, I've done what I came to do. I've salvaged my promise. Actually, there's plenty good in this for you. A trade. You're wounded by the judge and media discoverin' you're not lily-white, but now you'll see Stallings's punch coming. No trapdoors when it counts the most. Good luck, Mason." Hoffman slid to the end of the bench. "I can't cut any slack for you when we go to trial," he said as he was rising. "I'll lay it out true. Have to. Chips probably aren't gonna fall completely the way they should, but you've brought a portion of this hurt on yourself. Brother or not, you were over eighteen and made a choice. Been lyin' ever since, too."

Around the close of October, after the first hard frost had faded the pasture and yard, suffocating the last briar flowers and streaks of clover, Mason was in the barn replacing a lightbulb and he stumbled into an ashtray and butts and matches and a pack of cigs hidden inside a dented metal bucket. His curiosity piqued, he also discovered two wine coolers in the tack room, buried at the bottom of a box of rags. The bottles were clear with snazzy foil labels, the rags were sweatshirt strips, culls from the mill that were ripped lengthwise by a machine and sold in red, yellow, black and green bundles at the downtown outlet store. He put the cigs and ashtray in with the wine coolers and rags and deposited the whole damning collection on Grace's bedroom desk. When he confronted her she lied to him and blamed the hired help, Mo Jenkins, who wore Carhartt, dipped Skoal and drank whatever beer was on sale at the grocery store. He referred to his spouse as "the wife." "I'm sure Mo's a huge fan of room-temperature strawberry wine coolers," Mason said, and she quickly switched the subject, attacking him for not respecting her privacy and entering her room when she wasn't there.

"You forfeit your privacy by breaking rules and lying to me," he told her.

"None of it matters anyway," she replied. "I don't care what you do."

"You are grounded indefinitely," he said firmly. "More for not telling the truth than for the smoking and alcohol."

"It can be forever," she sassed him. "Ground me till I'm a hundred. Might as well." She was snide and flippant in the fashion of someone who felt there was nothing at stake, no jeopardy, no fall past supreme bottom, no state worse than the worst. She lay down on her bed, blue-jeaned legs together, toes rigid toward the ceiling, arms against her sides, her hair fanned on a pastel pillow, her lips thinned and stitched, funereal except for her furious, blinking eyes, the lashes pounding "I hate you" over and over and over.

At the beginning of November, Mason and Custis met again in Martinsville with Jim Haskins and Pat Sharpe. They were at Sharpe's office, on the fourth floor of a bank building, the view of the parking lot and a low-slung, ramshackle furniture store. Sharpe showed them a photo of a twelve-point buck he'd killed with a bow and arrow, and they all briefly talked about Virginia Tech football, and Haskins mentioned an antique trunk he'd purchased at an estate sale. Finally, Sharpe opened a file on his desk to signal the preliminaries were through. "I've received an offer from Stallings," he said, "and we need to discuss it."

It was apparent from Haskins's demeanor that he and Sharpe had already conferred. Resting one leg on top of the other, he casually adjusted his sock to do away with a slight exposure of flesh at the end of his pants cuff.

"Fuck Leonard Stallings and his offer," Custis snorted.

Haskins and Sharpe both smiled.

"Easy for you to say," Mason remarked. "Let's hear it."

"Here's the background," Sharpe said. "I took a chance, just got in my car and drove to Waynesboro and stopped by Stallings's office. Cold. Surprisingly enough, he invited me right in and was reasonably cordial."

"I'm trying to visualize the scene—does he use a booster seat?" Custis cracked. "Fisher-Price desk? Dr. Miguelito Lovelace shrine in the corner?"

The room stayed somber; no one laughed.

"The man's a crusader," Sharpe continued. "A true believer. Craves the spotlight as we all know. But he's no dummy. I told him we're aware the cops listened to the conversation with Allen Roberts and warned him we'll be prepared. He's lost the advantage there, although I'm assuming Ed Hoffman had already given him the news."

"Stallings had to realize we were on to him," Haskins interjected. "And for what it's worth, crazy ol' Hoffman might be right about the discovery issue. Funny how we take things for granted because it's the way we've always done it."

"The rule's ambiguous," Mason said. "I checked, too." He was anxious to reach the payoff, tapping a foot on the carpet. "It's academic now, anyway."

"Stallings is also bright enough to know what we all understand: You didn't shoot anyone, and your brother's an asshole."

"Amen," said Custis.

"But—and I want to phrase this as neutrally as I can—he thinks you were involved. I'm not saying Jim and I do, but because of the polygraph and your interaction with Allen Roberts, Stallings is convinced either you helped your brother or you're covering for him. Unfortunately for us, Stallings is a black-and-white guy, and he feels you committed a crime. Broke the law—years ago and in a minor way, perhaps—but broke it all the same. From high on his soapbox, he also feels it's . . . it's hypocritical of you to prosecute people when your own house isn't in order, so he's not willing simply to let bygones be bygones." Sharpe paused, shifting in his seat. He glanced at the papers in his file, then at Haskins and finally honed in on Mason. An overhead light pinpointed in the centers of his glasses, a tiny bright distraction. "He'll accept a plea to involuntary manslaughter, five years with nine months to serve, a thousand-dollar fine and three years' probation. Additionally, he wants to explore a charge against your brother. You'd be required to assist."

Everyone was silent. Mason could hear, barely, a phone in the adjacent office, more of a pulse than a ring or buzz. "A felony conviction and nine months in prison? I'd lose my law license, too. I mean, hell, I'd be ruined. My daughter, my mom . . . Grace is fifteen years old."

"It's a diabolical offer," Haskins said. "The kind you don't want to take, but you're afraid not to."

"We have a week to decide," Sharpe said. He moved and the reflection was gone from his lenses. "After that, the offer's withdrawn and we go to trial on murder one and take our chances. Could be a not-guilty verdict; theoretically could be life in prison. Or anything in between. I don't have to tell you, of all people, how it works."

"We're ready to fight if we need to," Haskins added. "There won't be any stone unturned, my friend."

Distress in its purest state occasionally cooks up to something approximating sickness, apes the first push of a fever or the raw creep of nausea, and Mason felt his skin spike hot, his stomach pucker, his spine sting and quiver and buckle, and he dipped his head close to his knees and clutched handfuls of hair. His circumstances had finally penetrated him, found a foothold, and for the first time he let down in front of other people. Custis started to attend to his friend, raised from his chair, and then he thought better of it and eased back down, very slow-motion as he sat. Several seconds later, Mason stanched his despair and righted himself. His mouth was dry, his thoughts soupy. "Sorry," he said. "It just hits home after a while. Damn."

"Perfectly normal," Gentleman Jim assured him. "I'd be a wreck myself. It's different if you're on the other side of the table. You're handling it better than I would."

"Truthfully, Pat, how do you see it?" Mason asked. "We all know the best thing you can do for me is give me an honest appraisal."

Sharpe nodded, understood. "You never can tell with a jury, but I rate it fifty-fifty. It's one of those cases where the whole's better than the parts. Ed Hoffman's a strong witness, and your comments to Allen Roberts are difficult to explain away, given what you'd been told by Bass and Minter. There's risk, Mason. Wish I didn't have to say it."

Mason turned to Haskins. "Jim?"

"I don't think it's quite fifty-fifty. I feel we're in better shape than that, but dammit, Mason, it'll go to a jury. Melesco can't help us if your brother sticks to his story, can't strike the commonwealth's case, and once twelve random people start deliberating your future, well, it gets iffy. I'm not telling you anything new, but there's always the possibility of a bad result."

"Okay," Mason said. "Thanks."

"Call me here or at the house as soon as you make up your mind," Sharpe told Mason. "And if you have a counteroffer, I'll certainly communicate it. I sense Stallings has given us his bottom line, but you never know."

As Mason and Custis rode home in the Cadillac, their conversation sporadic, Mason noticed Custis was missing a tooth, had a dark stub at the corner of his mouth. "You break a tooth?" he asked.

"No. Hell no. Damn thousand-dollar veneer popped loose last night."

"No kidding? Huh. Can the dentist glue it on again?"

"Yeah. I called him this morning and told him the news. Problem is, I swallowed the little fucker. I was eating and felt it go down my throat before I figured out what was happening."

"Not good," Mason said.

"Dentist tells me I need to 'recover it.' Right, I tell him. Ain't enough Clorox on the planet for that program to work. It's only been a year since he did the job, so I inform him we'll be starting from scratch, his expense."

"Only fair," Mason agreed.

"He doesn't see it quite the same. Things get tense on the phone. He finally says he'll knock off two hundred dollars, and I advise him he'd better be dustin' off his malpractice policy. Lawsuit's good as filed. Can you believe it? Like we need another headache. What else can happen?"

"We're done, aren't we?" Mason asked, his voice floating, dim.

"Done? Meaning what?"

"There're no more doors to try, no escape routes, no buttons to push. I'm going to wind up tried for murder with beaucoup exposure and my daughter's welfare on the line, and the world's soon going to learn you fancy men instead of women unless I bend a knee to Herman Dylan. Brick walls on every side."

"You could put it like that, I guess," Custis said ruefully. "But there's always hope. I try to stay positive."

"How do you rate my chances?"

"Me? Me, I'd speculate there're definitely some wolves between you and the gingerbread cottage. The kicker is this polygraph in the papers. Popular as you are, a Patrick County jury has been a major mack-daddy advantage for us, and now we might be in a fix."

"Aren't you confusing your stories?"

"Could be. But you get the picture." Custis grinned, revealing his stumpy flaw. "Don't say nothing 'bout my expertise with fairy tales, either. I'll set you and your bad attitude out on the side of the road."

"Amazing," Mason said, and it was apparent he was distracted by his own thoughts, temporarily deaf to what his friend had said. "Amazing." The word was salted with disgust. "How symbolic, huh? Sums it up. Our teeth knocked so far down our throats we're left to pick them out of our own shit. Unbelievable."

"It's a dental problem, Mace. I wouldn't make it into a prophecy or take it as a rooster crowing or burning bush or ring around the moon."

Mason was quiet for the remainder of the trip. The stereo played Teddy Pendergrass songs, and Custis hummed along, joining in on a few refrains. Nearly to Stuart, he asked Mason if he wanted to have a cocktail to soothe their spirits. "Why not?" Mason said. "But first I need you to take me by the office so I can check and see if my mom will watch Grace for me."

"Use my cell," Custis suggested.

"Nah, I need to sign a couple letters, too. Only take a minute."

It was around six o'clock when Custis pulled the Cadillac parallel to the awning at the front of their office, and he waited in the car while Mason went inside, kept the engine running. Mason phoned his mother, who was happy to have supper with her granddaughter, and then he hunted through his desk drawer until he found Ian Hudgens's business card. He dialed Hudgens's number and left a message: "Please have Mr. Dylan get in touch immediately. Not you, but him personally." When he returned to the vehicle, it was growing dark fast, the sun all but exhausted, the fall evenings curtailed, and they traveled through the thickening black to Custis's house and set to drinking.

A few hours later, Mason—for the first time since Allison's death—sidestepped his responsibilities and made arrangements with his mother to keep Grace overnight, and by nine thirty he and

Custis were both blitzed off a bottle of good bourbon Custis had been hoarding. Theirs was a happy, sloppy, obliterating revelry, a soldiers-off-to-battle drunk, a stopgap and artificial joy that had them sloshing toasts to important cases they'd won and Mason's best home run swing ever and the Wu-Tang Clan and San Juan and Custis's several elections to town council. Mason had taken Shoni McClean out several times since their Mount Airy lunch, the last occasion a dinner and visit to a jazz club in Winston-Salem, and it seemed only liquor-appropriate to phone her late on a weeknight and include her in the party, and she was a good sport and came by Custis's at eleven o'clock and pretended to be interested in a bourbon and Sprite, then danced with Mason to an Etta James standard in the living room so he'd quit pestering her about it.

The bourbon finished—killed by Custis and Mason standing shoulder to shoulder and gunning the last shots straight from the bottle—Shoni drove Mason to his farm at two in the morning. She allowed him an inept kiss, but when he slid his hand over her belly and started up for more, she laughed and spun him toward the house and said, "Not tonight, cowboy." Until then, he hadn't tried.

"Why not?" he asked, and before she could answer he apologized, confiding he was smashed.

"Aw, really?" she said playfully.

"Listen," he slurred, facing the house, not her. "Tell Cus I got an idea. Something that might rescue us."

"I definitely will." She was humoring him.

"And don't mention anything to Grace," he said, and staggered around so he could see her. He slapped a weaving index finger across his lips.

"You have my promise," she replied. Earlier that night, he had admitted to her he'd yet to tell his daughter about their friendship, and she'd replied that she understood and wasn't offended. She took his arm and guided him to the door but didn't go inside with him, watching through the window as he stripped off his shirt and stumbled to a couch, collapsing facedown, thank God, so she wouldn't worry over him strangling on his own vomit.

. . .

Mason had experienced very few hangovers since college—it occurred to him the following day that Custis seemed to somehow midwife most of them—and he awakened displaced on his sofa, still clad in his suit pants and socks and shoes, his shirt on the floor, his tie missing, his jacket, with any luck, left behind at his buddy's house. He stood up but was so drained and dizzy he crashed back onto the couch, got to his feet again and wobbled toward the kitchen. He checked the clock, flipped on the radio, started coffee and phoned his mom, who was about to leave with Grace for school. "We're fine, Gates," she said when he asked if they were okay.

"This is Mason," he replied, still woozy.

"Oh. I'm sorry," she said coolly. "Not easy to tell the difference this morning."

"Sorry," he mumbled. "Thanks for helping on such short notice."

As Mason poured a glass of orange juice, Jasper Griffith's hick voice issued from the radio; he was a stalwart on the local call-in show, and he was giving Mason the dickens, citing newspaper accounts of the upcoming murder trial and the failed polygraph and recalling how Mason had high-hatted him at the seafood restaurant. But the final straw was the next yapper, a rational, relatively well-spoken lady from Goose Point Road, who agreed with Jasper, and Mason realized the sea change had begun: He was losing favor in his own county, and in some quarters the disdain would become especially brutal once people began to feel gullible and hornswoggled, their trust perverted. Even worse, Mason understood that in Patrick the heat of the torches and quality of the tar were usually in direct proportion to the size of the pedestal.

He called Sheila at her house and told her he was ill, unplugged the phone, went to bed and never left the farm until late in the day, shaving and showering and hugging a limp, resistant Grace before driving to the courthouse in Stuart.

Chapter Twenty-three

"I need your help, Judge," Mason said straight off, no fooling around, no building up to it, no putting on airs. The request was stark and naked. "I'm in a bad fix. My family and I." He took a seat, but he was restless and the chair seemed small and not to scale with him in it. He looked dreadfully wan and tired, but he was wearing a suit and a jaunty striped tie and his hair was still damp from a shower, full of combed rows. He'd rubbed off a streak of his daughter's makeup onto his lapel when he hugged her at the farm, a foundation smear vivid against deep navy wool. Evidently, he'd failed to notice it during the ride into Stuart.

The man he was addressing, Phil Moore, was a steady, conscientious fellow who'd been blessed with quite the judge's gimmick: Moore absorbed the world through eyeballs that were slightly out of whack with his head, a pair of owlish hazel ovals easily a size or so too big for their confines. His gift in the courtroom was a knack for taming his temper and patiently scrutinizing the daily parade of lies he received from the witness stand—some rank and some intricately wrought—and in most instances arriving pretty close to where the truth was lodged, his curious, active, expansive eyes often appearing to assay and filter the bullshit as it came his way. "If I can, I will," he promised Mason, not knowing what to expect. It was almost quitting time, and he'd had to unlock the security doors when a deputy from the jail's reception desk called to say Mason Hunt was there and hoped to come upstairs for a talk.

"Here's a hypothetical," Mason said. One of the fluorescent over- heads in Moore's chambers was beginning to hum and quiver, becoming more noticeable as the forgettable November day expired outside, cold and drab.

"A hypothetical?" Moore replied, his tentative tone indicating he had no idea where the conversation was going. Like Mason, he was a Patrick County boy, born and raised, and although they weren't the best of pals, they shared the kinship of people who'd been stamped by a place's peculiar ink. Judge Moore could recall the playground's red clay dust staining the canvas uppers of his PF Fly- ers, the smell of woodsmoke infecting shirts and trousers on the drafty school bus and the sight of a skinny seventeen-year-old coun- try girl hoeing a tobacco field in summer weather, clad in cut-off Levi's and a bikini top, sunned dark as a hickory nut, her hair caught by a red bandanna. The two men had seen each other countless times, exchanged thousands of casual words dating as far back as a Cub Scout meeting in the Baptist church's basement.

"Yeah," Mason began doggedly, his features determined but a tick off-beam, "hypothetically a guy has a brother who shoots another man in 1984 . . ." And from there, he confessed everything that had happened, the story of Gates and Wayne Thompson and the echoing .38 shot on Russell Creek Road. It took him fifteen minutes, and twice he backtracked to add details and for a while he tugged and shaped a rubber band he found in his pocket and when he mentioned his daughter's decline and the barn cigarettes, he sort of hunched his shoulders and misfired with his blinking, couldn't keep his voice from rupturing. After he finished, he got up and leaned against the wall.

The judge asked him what anyone would: "Why are you telling me?"

"Because you're the only person who can resolve this."

"Me? How? I don't have anything to do with your case. I recused myself the same day the grand jury handed down its indictment."

"What's the key, Judge?" Mason asked rhetorically. "What stops Stallings?"

"I hate to sound dense, but I'm not following you."

"Gates," he said. "My brother. There's no real evidence against me . . . hypothetically . . . without him. Just some bits and pieces and statements with no context. You agree?"

"I do. Absolutely. If there's no testimony from Gates, the case doesn't even see a jury. It wouldn't survive a motion to strike. And if Stallings is as vainglorious as you're suggesting, I doubt he'd want to be humiliated and would probably dismiss the indictment. A no-brainer."

"So I need to take Gates out of the equation."

"True."

"And you're the only person who can do that." Mason grabbed a chair, dragged it closer to the desk and sat down with purpose.

"I'm still lost."

"Judge Richardson sentenced Gates, but it remains a Patrick County case, and you're the circuit court judge here."

"Yep. Last I checked."

"Gates will tell the truth—or, to state it more accurately, stop lying against me—only if he can get out of the pen."

"Even if I wanted to help him," Moore said, anticipating Mason's pitch, "I don't have any jurisdiction. Twenty-one days came and went years ago. Case is final."

"He can file a writ of *coram vobis* at any time in the sentencing court," Mason said. "You would have jurisdiction to decide the issue."

"Jeez—there's a gem from the archives. I haven't heard *coram vobis* mentioned since law school. It's the king's writ or something, if I'm recalling correctly. To be honest, I don't remember much about it. Never seen one filed."

"It's still on the books, Section 8.01-677. Basically, a prisoner presents new facts to the court that were unknowable at the time of trial and could've affected the verdict."

Moore held up his hand, traffic-cop style. "I don't want to wander too far into a tricky place. If your brother has a legitimate claim, I'll hear it and decide it according to the statute. I'll give him every fairness. But you and I aren't allowed to discuss it here in private. I wish it were different, but I can't ignore the rules."

"Yeah, well, no need to worry about Gates having any legitimate basis for his writ or granting him a fair hearing for that matter. By necessity, any ruling in his favor would have to be . . . extraordinary."

The judge rocked forward in his chair, listening. Like everyone else, he'd suffered right along with the Hunts when Allison died, had gripped Mason's arm at the funeral service and tried to salve the wound they all felt, whispering in a pained, sincere voice, "If I can ever do anything, Mace, anything at all . . ."

Mason drummed his fingers on his side of the desk, a fast, arrhythmic thumping that ended before he spoke again. "You and I both realize there's occasionally a separation, an ugly sulk, between the law and justice. On rare instances, they're at odds. Here's the long view: If I'm convicted, my daughter will suffer profoundly for the second time in her life. She's lost her mother to a damn ridiculous fluke, and now she'll be punished by the loss of her dad. She's had no control over either, and it's eating her alive. Even the prospect of a trial—the *possibility*—is traumatizing for her, regardless of the eventual verdict. She's slipping, giving up, and who can blame her?"

"I can't imagine," the judge said, and meant it.

"My innocent mother, who lived a life of misery not of her own making with Curt Hunt and has since endured the embarrassment and heartache of Gates, gets a second dose of disappointment and the pleasure, at age seventy or so, of raising a buck-wild, heathen granddaughter and probably an illegitimate great-grandkid—"

"Mason," Moore interrupted, "isn't this simply a variant of the defense you and I listen to every day, the type of reasoning I've heard you condemn over and over? You've become the guilty criminal propping up his bawling child or feeble mom as a pity shield. Hell, anytime we send someone to jail, there're ripples and consequences that reach past the courtroom. Nearly every man or woman in prison has a mom or dad or kids or a spouse."

"This is unique," Mason argued. "Here, two innocent people are about to be decimated based on a lie. Three if you count me. A lie—how's that any credit to the system? How's it commendable or appropriate?" Sweat beads were dotting his forehead. He was ashen.

"You okay, Mason?"

"Hungover," he said frankly. "Custis and I last night."

"Can't say I blame you much, given your problems." The judge smiled as best he could.

"Thanks." Mason wiped his brow with his coat sleeve. "At any rate, I admit—hypothetically—I broke the law. But what would you or anyone else have done? Huh? I was twenty-four years old, and I wouldn't have survived my father but for Gates's protection and encouragement. I owed him a debt. There was no real opportunity to think or deliberate. It's not as if I planned and schemed and devoted hours to an elaborate getaway. Plus, that night on Russell Creek Road, I couldn't have possibly predicted the future—I had no idea Gates would become a worthless dope dealer."

"In a certain sense, you're more culpable than most. You were in law school. I'd say you had a better than average feel for right and wrong. You realized what you were doing was corrupt, not to mention illegal." The judge looked at Mason, and Mason held with him, didn't shy from the gaze. "I'd have more sympathy if you'd just kept quiet and refused to tattle on your brother. But you got your hands dirty and helped make it impossible for the police to solve the crime. Wayne Thompson's kid and family have been left in limbo for years. That's not some theoretical, textbook fiddle-faddle; it's a genuine injury you caused. In a certain fashion, it's fair to say Thompson's son has suffered identically to your daughter. *Hypothetically*, of course." The "hypothetically" had plenty of sting in it.

"I don't dispute my guilt. I screwed up. I was wrong. I'm responsible. But please give some thought to any difference it makes. No matter what I decide in 1984, Wayne is dead and Gates shot him. I can't change it or correct it or undo it. I—"

"By the way, how do I know you're telling me the truth?" Moore asked, though he didn't have any doubt Mason was. "Maybe you did shoot Thompson. Maybe Gates is innocent."

"Because you've known me since we were both knee-high to a grasshopper, and because you also know my brother. Because I had no reason or motive to shoot Wayne. Because I passed a polygraph on the money question and Gates didn't. Because Gates has every reason to lie. Because, for a decade, you've seen my character on display in the courtroom. I can probably give you a longer list if you'd care for it."

"Thought I should ask. Go ahead." The jail served dinner at five o'clock, and the heavy smell of cooking oil and fried food began working through the walls and floor, a hint to start, then the room full up. "I'm guessing hamburger steak," the judge remarked. "Can I have them wrap you a plate to take home? It's usually not too bad."

"No, thanks." Mason was anxious to make his point and hardly considered the offer. "So no matter my choice, the crime is done and Wayne is dead. If I'd reported it to the police, what happens? The huge difference is the Thompson family has some peace of mind. I concede as much. As for Gates, he would've actually been better off than he is now. I would've had to testify Wayne was the aggressor. He'd been drinking, and there was dope in his car. He provoked Gates. He had a weapon. Gates catches a manslaughter conviction, a *maximum* of twenty years, though we both know he'd never draw a full sentence. Depending on the timing and who does what later on, perhaps he's not even around to sell drugs at the fairgrounds and earn the forty-four years he's currently pulling."

"You've taken this apart pretty well, haven't you? I've always said if I was facing the very red devil and could pick one person to do my closing argument, it'd be you or Jim Young."

"Here's the shorter version: The coke-distribution charge was worth five years—Tony Black, who's no friend of defendants, no softie—offered it in a plea. The killing's worth ten or so, twenty tops if the commonwealth had miraculously managed to ring the bell. Gates has already satisfied the time he should've received."

"Unfortunately, a jury decided he deserved forty-four years. He elected to not accept Tony's very reasonable offer. We don't get to make this stuff up as we go along. We either have consistency or we have anarchy and star chambers. Law du jour is no law at all."

"Ninety-five percent of the time, I would agree with you. But if that were the case exclusively, we'd hire bean counters, clerks and pointy-heads with computers to run the show. We'd find a drone with a chart and mandatory guidelines to occupy the big chair where you sit. You're the guy who can sign his name to a piece of paper and have a man executed—you didn't get the job to simply pound the rubber stamp."

"I'm always pleased to exercise my discretion," Moore said, "but if I skirt the law, if I cheat or deviate or ignore the rules, then everything I do—and everything I've done—becomes suspect, its legitimacy lost. I go seat-of-the-pants, and I'm just a hack, a fraud with a robe and a pocketful of whims and a sheriff and bailiff to make them come to pass. It's a slippery slope, as they say."

Mason sawed his teeth back and forth across his lower lip.

"I have a bad feeling we're on the verge of your asking me to break the law myself," the judge somberly told him.

Mason was silent. His forehead was glistening. The office smelled of the convicts' dinner.

"I'm sorry," Moore said. "I wish I could be more helpful."

"Here's my take, for what it's worth. Judge Hooker sat in this same office in that same seat and looked out the window, watched the same mountains change seasons, gazed at the same schoolhouse on the knoll, saw the people milling around in front of the drugstore and insurance agency. Then Judge Richardson did the exact same thing. Now they're both dead and gone." Mason stopped making eye contact and bowed his head slightly. "No offense to you, my friend, nothing smart intended, but in a sense it doesn't really matter. See, none of us can gouge too deeply. Calculate for the long haul. Lay the surefire pattern for the distant domino. Either the world is too tightly and infinitesimally tuned for us to crack the code and have any effect, or it's so damn random and disjointed we're spitting in the wind. Point-oh-eight, and I let the kid go who kills my wife. Decimals. One one-hundredth higher, I make a different decision and my life isn't trashed. She sleeps five seconds longer, she clears the intersection. Believe what you will, there're simply too many moving parts."

"So we wish the murders and rapists well and send them on their merry way? We do nothing because we can't do everything? I'm not as pessimistic as you."

"The opposite actually," Mason insisted. "Sometimes we need to choose whatever will cover the most spots on the board—throw a blanket over as much good as we can and quit fretting about the horizon. We have this whole formidable legal apparatus, this dense set of rules and a twenty-nine-volume Virginia Code, and the truth is we can't accomplish any more than right-now justice. You can sit there and talk about this abstract ideal, the integrity of our *system,* worship an idol that's supposed to contemplate the big picture even though we ourselves can't, figure you're keeping the train on the tracks because you have this map that came from the Magna Carta and piles of ancient books, and you can stick to it and never deviate and think you're safe and this will go *A* to *B* to *C,* and I'm here to tell you—I should know better than anyone, huh?—you're mistaken. Allowing my brother to manipulate the courts and damage lives proves nothing. You're in a position to help three people and put an end to a self-serving lie, or you can kowtow to letters on a page at our expense." Mason spoke humbly, was rueful rather than hostile.

Before answering, the judge waited for Mason to raise up and acknowledge him. "So I'll take a stab at it," he said. "Gates is going to file a bogus pleading and you want me to piss on the law and rule in his favor. Set him free before your trial in hopes he'll amend his story. Throw the blanket, as you put it, over you and your mom and Grace?"

"It's what I'm down to, yeah," Mason admitted. "Crumbs and slim reeds. But I've got several pot-sweeteners for you, not the least of which is my own penance." His face pinched with disgust. "Of course, the worst punishment is I'm here helping my brother, a man I hate."

"*Lex ex machina,*" the judge mused, shaking his head. "It'll have to be awfully compelling. Let's hear it." He was skeptical, still far from sold.

Mason visited twice more to encourage the judge's intervention, and the Wednesday court closed at noon for the Thanksgiving holiday,

Gates's typewritten *coram vobis* pleading arrived postmarked from Stuart, not the penitentiary. It was adequately written and decently argued and totally without merit, basically legal bunk, sophistry. The name "Gates Hunt" was typed rather than hand-signed at the conclusion of the paperwork, and there were a few misspellings and a grammatical blunder tossed in for camouflage.

The judge swiveled his chair and peered out the window at the Swails Insurance sign and the austere winter hills and the red-brick elementary school, stuck the pleadings in his briefcase, walked into the empty courtroom and sat there in the gallery, behind the old oak railing, thinking. Struggling. Taking stock of his own empty spot on the bench, built high above everything else. Judge Richardson's portrait hung on the far wall, an oil painting that showed its brush-strokes when the window light hit late in the afternoon. Richardson was holding a law book, and there was a gavel nearby—all the honorable props—and Phil Moore indulged a fanciful thought: He wished he could ask his framed predecessor for advice, quiz him on how the hell to cut the baby.

Chapter Twenty-four

Awakened at midnight by a prison guard and a third-shift deputy from the Patrick County Sheriff's Office, Gates initially was inclined to demand he be allowed to call Bass or Minter or Leonard Stallings, but he thought better of it when the county deputy told him he was being taken to Stuart for a bond determination and a decision on the recent motion to have his sentence set aside, and, heck, it must be pretty darned serious, the cop said, because here he was with a transportation order signed by the circuit judge instead of the clerk and the case was scheduled to be heard in just a few hours. By the time the warden arrived at nine o'clock and notified Bass and Minter, Gates was long gone, so there was nothing they could do except hotfoot it to Stuart and try to discover what was happening with their star witness.

Heeding instructions from Custis Norman to treat the prisoner "liberally," the deputy allowed Gates to ride in the passenger seat without cuffs or restraints, switched the bluegrass station to classic rock, visited a truck stop for three a.m. cheeseburgers and fries, and meandered through the heart of every city and town instead of using the bypasses so Gates could enjoy the storefronts and window displays and the trip would be stretched by several miles. An occasional home already had Christmas decorations burning, roadside Santas and sleighs and candy canes lit by extension cords. "Been almost thirteen years for me," Gates informed the officer.

They arrived in Stuart at four thirty, two hours prior to daybreak, and Gates was placed in the drunk tank alone. Moments later, the lock clunked and in came Custis Norman, a large, flat jail key dangling from a metal ring in his hand. He snugged the door to the frame but didn't allow the lock to catch. The room contained a concrete bench for sleeping and sitting, a metal toilet and a small sink and was fierce with the odor of urine, vomit, underarms and pine-scented disinfectant. Gates was already seated, which left Custis no choice but to stand. There was barely enough space for the two of them.

"Well, well, well," Gates said sarcastically, "if it isn't my little brother's loyal sidekick, Robin. Nice of you to drop by so early in the mornin'. You walkin' the dog and hear I was visiting?"

"Yeah. My pit bull."

"You done your Christmas shoppin' yet? Bought my present?"

"So listen, Gates, here's the deal. You—"

"No, I'm afraid *you* need to listen, my friend." Gates ratcheted a mean-spirited smile. "First, I'm not saying a fuckin' word to you. I don't need Mason sending his lackey to do his bidding. I'll talk to him and him only—you'd think he'd at least have the guts to see me man to man. Second, I'm not stupid. I'm on strike until I'm sure you're not buggin' me, which I figure is occurring right this minute. So you need to make some arrangements." He flicked his wrist several times in Custis's direction. "Hop to it, Boy Wonder. Chop-chop."

"We're not being recorded," Custis said, keeping his anger in check. "And the deal's the deal, whether I tell you or your brother tells you."

"Nope. I'm done." He made a production of reclining on the concrete ledge and refusing to look at Custis.

"Hey, Gates, what kinda bird don't fly?"

Gates yawned.

"Motherfuckin' jailbird, chump, and your wings always gonna be clipped." He left and noisily secured the door, went across the street to their office and fetched Mason. "Has to be you," Custis said. "I tried."

Gates was still in full lounge when Mason entered the cell, the pose an insolent, cocky, infuriating show, like he was a damn emperor receiving his subjects. "Ah," he said, "the hero of Patrick County. I knew you'd somehow find it in your busy schedule to welcome me home."

Nothing would have satisfied Mason more than lifting his leg and stomping the ever-loving shit out of his brother, but he disciplined himself, considered his child and his mother and how this was part of his own punishment, same as a tablespoon of castor oil. "Gates," he said, subdued. "I'd hoped you and Custis could handle this."

"Oh, I'll bet you did. But it ain't goin' to be so easy, whatever it is that brought me here. How's it feel to have your ass in a sling, by the way? For people to learn the truth about you and your crimes? Get knocked off your high horse?"

"We're not being monitored, Gates. You don't have to perform for a tape recorder."

Gates sat upright, picked at his fingernails. "You'll forgive me if I don't believe you. See, I'm gonna be forced to demand we hold our brotherly reunion elsewhere, or I'll be unable to participate." He sliced the final word into four taunting syllables: *par-tic-i-pate.*

"Since you're a convict, our options are limited. Where'd you have in mind?"

"Well, let's see," Gates said. "What wouldn't you think of?"

"This is truly stupid. Why won't you just listen to me? You can keep quiet, and I'll do all the talking."

"Nah." Gates cranked an insincere grin. "I vote for the restroom at W & W Produce. They're open twenty-four-seven, right? Maybe I could snag a cold beer while we're there."

"You can vote until hell freezes over. It's not happening for you. You're a prisoner. Prisoners don't go on field trips. I'm not about to put Sheriff Hubbard at risk, even if I could."

"How fuckin' noble, Mason." Gates stroked his chin. He was

growing a goatee, but it was coming in tatty, needed trimming and thicker whiskers. "Okay. We hike upstairs to the courtroom, the ladies' bathroom, and you find us a radio to hide our discussion."

The jailer was reluctant to relocate Gates, protesting he didn't want to get in the middle of a murder trial; he knew Gates was supposed to testify against his brother and he'd only gone this far because it was Custis doing the asking and the sheriff himself had okayed it before he'd signed off for the day. Custis returned and browbeat him, and they finally phoned the sheriff at home—he was up, dressing to feed his cattle—and he said there wasn't any problem so long as the prisoner remained in custody, instructed the jailer to take him on to the courtroom toilet and sit there next to the door until Gates and Mason finished. "If he wants to see his brother or our assistant commonwealth's attorney, it's his business," the sheriff stated and brusquely ended the connection.

Mason trotted to his office and borrowed Sheila's small black radio while the jailer accompanied Gates to the ladies' bathroom. He stayed with Gates, aimlessly chatting until Mason arrived, then searched the radio, shut the door and left the brothers to themselves.

Gates also gave the radio a good going-over and spent several minutes combing through the bathroom, pouring out the syrupy blue soap from its dispenser, unrolling toilet tissue, upending the trash can, poking and shifting ceiling tiles. "Never can be too careful, huh?" he told Mason. He tuned the radio to mostly loud static, opened both spigots full blast and ran water into the basin. The water struck bottom and splattered up drops onto the cloudy old mirror and the dingy plaster around the sink.

"Satisfied?" Mason asked.

"Well, almost. Never know about you, do I?"

"Feel free to pat me down," Mason said.

Gates laughed. "Don't think so. You feel free to undress, and we'll proceed from there."

Mason glared at his brother, who'd flipped down the commode lid and was sitting on it with his legs arrogantly crossed, one foot on the floor, the other dangling off his knee.

"You too high and mighty for that, Mason?"

"I'm not wired," Mason told him, but he knew it wouldn't matter.

"You can strip, or we can talk about sports and current events. How 'bout them Redskins?"

Mason began with his belt, handing each clothing item to Gates for inspection until he was completely naked, a bare ceiling bulb illuminating him, cold air bleeding into the room. "See? Nothing. Hope you're happy."

"Almost," Gates answered. He discarded the clothes into a haphazard heap on the floor. "Now you can lift your nuts and finish by turnin' around and spreadin' your lovely butt cheeks. Kinda like we do in prison. Kinda like what they did to me before I left this morning and then again when I got here."

"No."

"Have it your way. I don't care. You can save up till you're able to do it for real, after you're convicted. With a prison guard and a larger audience." Gates smirked.

"And you can finish your forty-four-year sentence. Every second of it."

"I'd say you have more to lose than me. Like you've said before, I'll hit mandatory parole in several months, anyway. Thank heaven I was tried before they monkeyed with the rules, huh?"

"You're pathetic, Gates. You truly are."

Gates unfolded his leg and lowered his foot to the tile. "You can do the nut juggle, or I'll call ol' Barney Fife out there and we'll stroll back to my personal suite without you and me ever talkin' brass tacks. Take your pick, big fella."

"Shit like this causes you to seem even more the punk."

"Barney?" Gates yelled, all dare and challenge. "Deputy Fife?"

Mason complied. He cupped and raised his testicles and then turned and spread his legs and reached around and pulled his butt apart.

Gates responded with mock applause. "You'll make somebody a fine bitch. Yessir."

"Can we cut to the chase now, Gates? The less time I spend with you, the happier I am."

"No reason to be so rude."

"May I have my clothes?"

"May I have my clothes, *please,*" Gates chided him.

"Please," Mason said, boiling.

"No, you may not. Let's see how you enjoy bein' humiliated and denied even basic necessities." Gates rested against the commode tank. "So why am I here? What are you plannin' to do for me? And don't waste your breath on any bullshit that doesn't have me waving bye to the penitentiary."

"I could come over there and take them," Mason declared.

"You could, but you won't because you can't afford to upset me."

"At nine sharp, the judge will hold a bond hearing on your writ of *coram vobis.* You stand there and keep your smart mouth shut, and you'll be okay. If anyone asks, you and your jailhouse advisors wrote the motion."

"I didn't file anything, not here, not lately."

"Correct. I did, on your behalf."

Gates cackled, bitter as hell. "I *knew* havin' to save your own precious hide would focus your mind." He cackled again. "So what kind of legal rabbit have you yanked outta your hat for me? The *Koran*? How'd you say it?"

"The specifics don't concern you. Basically, the motion argues your lab report was suspect because they only tested a small sample of the whole cocaine bag. The commonwealth could only prove— beyond a reasonable doubt—a tiny portion was actually dope. Who can say about the remainder? It wasn't analyzed, just weighed. The jury should've only been allowed to consider a penny-ante drug deal and not stick you with the entire ounce."

"Damn, there you go. Now we're cookin' with gas!"

"Today, the judge is very likely to grant you bond pending the final hearing on your motion. I expect you'll be turned loose well before lunch. I have this on excellent authority. Mom is waiting to post your bail with money I've provided her, but she doesn't want you living there. We've made arrangements for an apartment above the flower shop. Rent's paid for six months."

"No walking 'round money, Mason? You probably know this,

being a trained, professional lawyer, but the state really doesn't give you a new suit and a crisp hundred when they're done with you."

"It's negotiable," Mason said.

"I don't come cheap."

"I'll toss in a hundred bucks and the new suit," Mason said sarcastically. "As a bonus, you can keep my jeans and sweater."

"Let me guess—all I have to do is change my testimony. Sing a new tune?"

"All you have to do is tell the damn truth, Gates. We'll have you sign a statement and video you reading it."

Gates gathered his face. "Yeah. Hmmm. And the moment the ink's dry and you have the statement, you bastards revoke my bond and my motion is dismissed and off I go to pull the rest of my forty-four years. You must think I'm a total dumb-ass."

"Yeah, I do think you're a total dumb-ass, but that's not the issue. You need to evaluate what the other side's offering you. Compare your options. They can't save you a single second or pay you one thin dime. There's no reward for being spiteful, other than how great you must feel about yourself."

"They're gonna write the governor and try for a pardon."

"Oh, I'd count on the governor—a politician, mind you— releasing a dope dealer early. You're right: You've got better odds selecting that plan. Yeah, my bad. Hell, Gates, my trial's not till February, and we both realize you're stuck at least that long."

Gates appeared frustrated. "It's worth servin' my whole sentence if it means you'll have to suffer and squirm and get a taste of what you and everybody else has put me through. Fuck it."

"I doubt the judge would grant bond unless he felt your motion had a strong probability of success."

"You're trying to scam me, Mason. Play me for a fool. Look at you standing there with your dick all shriveled up like a bait minnow." Gates snorted. "Well, I'm not fallin' for your bullshit. My testimony changes only if I'm set free and stay free and I have it guaranteed and you drop fifty thousand cash on me. Otherwise, you and Mr. Stallings can settle this."

"I predict you will make bond, I predict the judge will take your motion seriously and strong-arm your court-appointed lawyer and the attorney general's office into a compromise. Moreover, I predict that if you look in the freezer at your new digs, you'll discover five thousand in cash. I'll see to it you receive fifteen more." The radio was popping and cracking and a wispy snatch of an announcer's voice came and went.

"Compromise?" Gates asked.

"I believe the judge will indicate he feels your motion is sound and he plans to grant you a new trial, and he'll note it would be a significant waste of effort and resources to appeal his decision to the Supreme Court or incur the expense of another trial when the dispute concerns the last few crumbs of a forty-four-year sentence. He'll encourage both sides to allow you to serve the remainder of your time by enrolling in the day-reporting center. Basically you'll stop by a couple times a week and attend some classes and piss in a cup. A four- to six-month program. He'll push for that resolution, and I have a friend in the AG's office who'll be sympathetic as well."

"How do I know you won't cut my throat?" Gates asked. He was closer to the edge of the toilet, his hands together and churning, busy, excited, a ball of worms. "I want it in writing."

"Afraid not. Listen. I'm telling you how this will happen for you if you don't screw me. No one is stupid enough to write it down. But you're protected because we want you to disappear. It makes no sense to double-cross you and have you raising hell and whining to the press and returning to Stallings ready to recite your lie again. My goal is to completely put this to rest."

"Once I change, I'm history," Gates said. "My testimony's dead meat after I switch to your side. A moron could see that."

"True, but do you think I want the headache? I'm anxious to tie this off, not have another round with you and Stallings and whoever else." Mason stepped forward and the movement startled his brother, causing him to separate his hands and stand up from the toilet. Mason reached past him and began collecting his clothes, dressing. "Think of it this way, Gates: Even if I do swindle you,

you're no worse off than you were in terms of how long you have to pull, and you'll be twenty thousand richer and the beneficiary of this nice sabbatical."

"You cocksuckers are as rotten as maggots on roadkill. Funny you couldn't make this possible ten years ago."

"My lawyer, Pat Sharpe, will meet you at nine forty-five, before Bass, Minter and Stallings have their shot at you. I've told Pat we anticipate you're prepared to offer a different version of events, but he has no idea your act of conscience is being purchased, so don't spill the beans and cause complications. I'll give you the balance of the money as soon as you recant and we have it on film." Mason pulled his sweater on. His head stuck at the neck opening, then popped through. "Today's the day, Gates. This will come unglued if you don't cooperate right now."

"I want fifty."

"Twenty's the market price. Take the cash and be sprung from jail, or lie and leave empty-handed. We're finished negotiating. Pat will be at your new address. Key's with Marilyn at the register."

"Apologize," Gates demanded.

"Apologize?" Mason repeated, incredulous. "To you? For what? You . . ." He couldn't help himself, couldn't resist the rage, and he grabbed Gates by the throat with both hands and drove him against the wall, but Gates was ready, fought back, clamped down on Mason's wrists and tried to kick him in the groin. Mason twisted and blocked the blow with his shin, and he slammed Gates's head hard as he could into the wall and Gates let loose of his wrist and swung roundhouse, hitting Mason solid on the jaw, and the deputy came busting in and wrapped Mason around the waist and wrestled the two men apart. They stood there panting and glaring at each other, on fire with hate. Above the commode, an unframed cardboard landscape had been jarred crooked.

"Your choice, Gates," Mason said as the jailer was removing his brother from the john.

"Should've said you were sorry," Gates snarled. "Given me my due."

. . .

"I lost my temper," Mason admitted to Custis upon returning to their office, Sheila's radio in his hand, the cord unwound and dragging on the floor. "I promised myself I'd kiss his ass for Grace's sake, and I couldn't do it. It's probably irretrievable now. Totally my fault—we knew what was coming, and I let everyone down."

"Can't blame yourself," Custis said. "We're lucky I didn't go off on him, and I was only in the cell a few minutes."

They sat together and marked time, Mason sipping coffee. There was no sunrise to speak of, only a waxing, uniform gray light that blended in with the mountains and rendered the town sluggish and lackluster, and around nine the sky began to spit snow and plump raindrops, causing Sheila to scurry from the parking lot on the balls of her feet and shake off her umbrella underneath the awning. By nine thirty, Mason and Custis didn't even bother with small talk. Custis took several phone calls and Sheila brought the mail, and at ten fifteen there was still no report from Sharpe. Mason and Custis debated whether Gates had actually made bond, and Custis suggested maybe they should check with Pat's office or try his cell, and they spun their wheels and agonized, Custis twice leaving for the upstairs toilet, mumbling "my stomach" over his shoulder. Mason finally lay back his chair and closed his eyes, a pen-and-ink illustration from a childhood magic primer hogging his thoughts, a sketch of a playing card balanced on its teeny edge, a well-drawn finger coaxing it erect, the king of clubs paralyzed by thin air.

A few minutes before eleven, they heard the phone ring at Sheila's desk, and she quickly appeared to tell them Mr. Sharpe was on the line. All Pat said was "You need to come over here, Mason. Your brother wants to see you." Forgetting his coat, Mason asked Custis to please stay put and watch for the cops and then bolted out of the office, jogging through the raw morning, pelted by rain and sloppy, incomplete snowflakes. He climbed the narrow stairs beside the florist's two at a time and banged on the door, and Sharpe and Gates both shouted for him to come in. Gates was sitting on a sofa, Sharpe standing near a window, the view of an alley and the high brick side of another building. There was a grocery-store fruit basket on a table, a gift from the landlord. The apartment was murky, corners and seams obscure.

"We have some unfinished business, Mason," his brother declared. "You were about to admit how you were sorry for repeatedly fuckin' me over when the deputy interrupted us. We need to tend to that before I go Hollywood with your lawyer." He feigned confusion. "You seem wet. Didn't wear your jacket? Leave suddenly from the office?"

The door wasn't completely closed. A draft pushed in from the stairwell, and Mason heard a tractor-trailer change gears on the steep Main Street grade, the sound of snow chains beating the pavement. He didn't respond.

"Two magic little words: I'm sorry." Gates had his arms spread across the ridge of the sofa. He'd changed into clothes his mother had left at the jail, the pants too small in the waist.

Mason focused on him. "Do you really think I've caused you harm? Wronged you? Seriously?"

"Hell fuckin' yeah," Gates spat. He glanced at Sharpe. "Can you believe this clown?" he asked the lawyer.

Mason went through the same calculus he'd done before, considered his mother and his daughter and how unconditionally he loved them both, but it infuriated him that he'd just been stripped and humiliated and taunted at the restroom. He looked toward Sharpe, who dipped his eyes, wanting no part of this. Gates scooted farther forward, taking down his arms as he moved to the last of the cushion, and the table lamp's sixty watts now illustrated much of his face, white on white, a clear bulb joining mushroom skin. The new light pried him from the dim winter room and sloughed off a warped, elongated shadow onto the wall, and he was suddenly and ferociously every inch his father's sullen son, Curt Hunt writ large in his flesh, reclaimed.

"They say always give the bandit your wallet," Mason sighed. "Don't put up a fight. Not worth your life." He checked on Sharpe again. Felt another chilly draft from behind him. Built the apology in his mind and got ready to pull the lever, let it go. He thought of his father, the rough mechanic's hands, the missing finger joint, the lube and grime in the creases of his palms. He recalled Curt mashing his face into the grass and soil, a grown man's knee set against his nine-year-old spine, and he remembered deciding it didn't matter what he said or how much he begged, because his father would never be satisfied, never relent. "You know what, Gates?" Mason paused, noticing the wet floor around his shoes. "You won't receive another lie from me. I'll leave with my pride and my decency, thank you, two items that must be very foreign to you. You can tell Mr. Sharpe the truth, or you can continue as you are, a cipher and an ingrate, Curt Hunt's only child. His heir. Your account with me is empty."

Mason broke off the words forcefully, briskly, like kindling sticks snapped over a knee, momentarily lingering on his brother when he'd finished. He acknowledged Sharpe with a nod and turned and went into the hall, but he didn't rush or hurry, faced his brother and the room's interior as he was shutting the door, Gates and Sharpe vanishing bit by bit as he pulled the knob, neither of them speaking, a shiny metal 2 swinging into sight, the number glued to the wood. He took the handrail and headed down the steps to his office, never once considered changing direction.

"More of the same," he reported to an anxious Custis when he returned to their building. "It's a hard balance to strike. I'd die for Grace, wouldn't matter how much it hurt or how long it lasted, but I can't—*won't*—let him shit on me like our daddy did. I'll go to trial and take my chances if it comes to that. We'll just have to wait and see if Pat can persuade him."

"Mmmm, damn. I had hopes."

"Yeah."

"Well," Custis said, "a man can't stay down on his knees but for so long."

Thirty minutes later, they heard whooping and hollering in the reception area and jumped to their feet and Pat Sharpe didn't slow up at Sheila's desk or hesitate at Mason's door, entered the room with a resounding "Yes!" his arms raised, a signed statement in one hand, a video in the other. Custis hugged him and hoisted him off the ground, knocking Sharpe's glasses sideways, and they all slapped high fives and yelled and cheered. "Thank you so much," Mason said. "I can have a life again." Sheila came to see what the hubbub was about, and Mason grabbed her by the wrists and flew into a silly jig all around the office, and while they were dancing daft as Dorothy and the Scarecrow, for the first time he could ever recall, Mason felt delivered and altogether loose, finally shed of his loads, no claims against him, no drag, his daddy buried, his brother gelded and behind him, his daughter rescued. He leapt onto the damn desk, yanking Sheila with him, and they bopped, shimmied, reeled and funky-chickened until papers and files covered the floor. There was never a single musical note, only Custis and Sharpe egging them on, but even the expensive pen set engraved with Mason's name was kicked off. "Coming home!" Mason screamed, his arms and legs in a whirlwind. "At last."

"How'd you sell him?" Custis asked Sharpe after Mason and Sheila had finished their gyrations and stepped down, Custis and Sharpe each taking one of Sheila's arms to brace her as she left the desk, her shoes lost from each other on the floor. "Give us the report."

"Oh, man," he said. "I thought we were shit outta luck. Mason comes in and they have a bit of a standoff, and after he leaves, I put on my panhandling rags, and Gates is sittin' there zoning, a million miles away, blowing me off. He keeps checking the freezer and then without any warning he becomes all pleasant and compliant, tells me he's ready to tape. Like someone threw a switch. He skims the statement, signs it, reads it for the camera. I had my secretary waiting in the car, and she notarized it. He admits he made up the murder story, states Mason is innocent, concedes he did it to try and buy himself an early release. Complete exoneration for us."

"The truth, finally," Mason said, his breath quick from the dancing and excitement.

"He made me promise to tell Mason he forgave him. Kept

reiterating it. 'You see who the better brother is,' is how he phrased it. 'Who can forgive who. Who's a child and who's a real man.' "

"A real man in the tradition of Ike Turner and Bobby Brown, maybe," Custis muttered. "Or the Boston Strangler."

"As I'm leaving," Sharpe continued, "after I've recorded him and we're through, he pipes up and says, very cryptically, 'Yeah, so Mason didn't kill anyone, but he's still no Boy Scout, not the man you fools think he is. Mason and me will always know.' He let on like he was doing you a big favor. He's lied and brought you an indictment, and he's acting like he's drinking the hemlock for you. It was bizarre."

"Had to be," Mason remarked, standing on a file folder, its contents scattered. "But you can rest assured Gates Hunt never helps anyone except Gates Hunt. Period."

"You guys figure he's really got a chance at a new trial?" Sharpe asked. "I couldn't believe he was free on bond."

"Not our concern," Custis said emphatically.

"I'm inclined to agree," Sharpe replied. "I've never been a guy to analyze good fortune too scrupulously."

"Before I forget—thanks again, Pat," Mason told his lawyer. "I'm so grateful for everything." The tone of his voice, the sincerity, changed the atmosphere, and the party receded. Sheila stopped in the middle of a shoe strap and peered at the men.

"My pleasure," Sharpe replied.

"Couldn't have done it without you."

"No problem," Sharpe said. "I'm relieved, glad it's over. Whew."

Mason pivoted toward Custis, wanting to confess how appreciative he was, how he valued their ties and connections and years together, how *they* were brothers, how he regretted doubting his partner's allegiance, but he became emotional and got nowhere, his chin and lips in a tremulous kink, his voice tamped down into his throat.

Custis helped him through it, waving him off with a huge brown hand. "No need for all that, Mr. Bojangles."

"I can't even begin to tell you . . ." was all Mason was able to utter.

"You ain't seen my bill yet," Custis kidded him, and the tired old lawyer crack gave everyone an excuse to laugh and be done with the awkwardness, Mason especially.

Custis phoned Jim Haskins. Sharpe hustled to the *Enterprise* office with a press release he'd prepared in advance. Sheila zipped to the courthouse to spread the news. Mason called his mom, who shrieked, "Praise you, Lord!" and drove to inform her minister in person. The instant Grace arrived home from school, Mason explained the video and announced they were redeemed. He was safe.

From the rickety sofa, she watched the tape with her head canted, her neck slightly extended and her lips parted in guileless teenage wonderment, soaking in this man she shared blood with but couldn't recollect meeting, a pale dude with a skuzzy goatee wearing a plain gray sweatshirt, echoes and dribs and drabs of her father in his appearance and mannerisms, the camera jittery in a couple of spots. When Gates admitted lying, she squeaked a soft, satisfied sound and clapped her hands together and left them clenched, then beat the floor with exuberant, girlish feet, running in place, her reaction not so different from her father's. "I love you, baby," Mason exclaimed, and he hooked an arm around her and yanked her closer, her feet still in high gear.

True to form, Gates pointlessly lied to Bass and Minter, promising them nothing had changed. He advised them he'd filed a motion and the judge had released him on bond and scheduled a hearing, but so what, there was no need for them to panic and show up with their panties in a wad. The cops went to the clerk's office and read the *coram vobis* file, called Stallings and warned him there could be a complication. "Awfully suspicious," Minter grumbled to the special prosecutor. "I smell a rat."

Stallings didn't reach Stuart until midafternoon, and he also visited the courthouse to review the *coram vobis* pleading. "This is a farce," he complained to the clerk, who could only shrug and state the obvious, that she wasn't a lawyer. "It's procedurally barred," he fumed. "And nonsense to boot." He called the judge's administrative assistant to request an explanation or a meeting, and was primly rebuked.

376 • MARTIN CLARK

"The judge says it's not your case," she drawled, "and even if it was, he can't talk to you about it ex parte. Meanin' only one side bein' heard."

"I know what it means," he barked.

Custis had convinced Pat Sharpe to let him personally deliver the news of Gates's defection to the special prosecutor, and tipped off by an assistant clerk, he was waiting at the bottom of the court-house steps when Stallings stalked out of the building, a cell phone jammed against his ear. "Yo, Stallings," he yelled. "Over here, my man." Custis was underneath an umbrella, wearing an elegant black wool overcoat. The weather continued to be fussy, with sprinkles of rain and snow. "Got a treat for you."

Stallings folded his cell phone shut and walked to where he was, stood beside Custis instead of in front of him, both of them facing Main Street. Stallings was wet, didn't have a hat or umbrella, and Custis didn't offer him any relief. Stallings put his hands in his pants pockets, hunched forward. "I've been home-cooked, haven't I?"

"Your canary just lost his chirp. Here's his statement." Custis handed him a sheet of paper. "We also videoed him for your viewing pleasure. I'd estimate you now have what we in the trade call a cred-ibility problem."

"Shit."

"Yeah, it's a cruel blow, Leonard."

"He could always change again." Still sideways to Custis, Stallings was watching a pickup loaded with firewood crawl down the street, a layer of slush on its hood and roof.

"I doubt he will, but supposin' he does, he's damaged goods for you. The case is junk."

"Your boss was involved in a murder, Mr. Norman. A criminal sit-ting in judgment of other criminals. You proud to be a part of such?" The smaller man's clothes were wet, his orange hair damp, limp. A snowflake hit his cheek, melted.

"I'm proud of Mason Hunt, yeah." Custis turned and looked down on Stallings. "I'm guessing some turd granted Gates immunity —he's gonna skate, isn't he?"

"Yep," Stallings said tersely. "A man gets shot, we know who was involved, and the guilty go free, unscathed. We didn't lose anything by giving Gates a pass for his cooperation—it's not like he'd ever implicate himself, and there was never a realistic possibility of Mason coming clean and confessing his role, whatever it might've been. I did the best I could with the case I had."

"No," Custis replied, "you didn't. You were too busy puttin' on your pith helmet and scramblin' to bag your trophy to consider anything else. Mason Hunt's no murderer, and you knew that, but you still wanted to bust his ass and hang the trophy on your wall."

"I truly can't believe you guys talked your judge into springing him. The *coram vobis* is total bullshit. Pretty easy to win if the field's tilted and the ref's on your payroll."

"Maybe folks in Patrick tend to look after their own. And maybe around here we're actually willing to make adjustments if need be. Any stupid motherfucker can paint by numbers; it's your freehand work that counts." Custis shifted his weight. " 'Course, as I understand it, this is all righteous. No favors, no skulduggery, no nothing. Just a con finally confessin' his scam."

"Tell that to the Thompson family—they're certainly being well served."

"No need to be a sore loser, Leonard. No need to blame the judge and Mason and me because you coupled your wagon to the word of a rogue and a liar and—big surprise—you wound up in a ditch."

"Every dog has his day, Mr. Norman. You've had yours. Believe you me, I'll be waiting for mine where you and Mason Hunt are concerned."

"Some mighty powerful wisdom, there. I'll write it down so I don't forget: 'Every dog has his day.' Man, that's Oprah-caliber wise. You invent it yourself?"

Chapter Twenty-five

The Saturday following Gates's payoff, there was a party in the rhino room at Mason's farm, a celebration attended by friends and family and Shoni McClean, who kept her distance and left early so as not to seem forward or tacky. Afterward, Mason sat down next to Grace in front of the big-screen TV, and they gabbed and rambled until the wee hours, and she said, yeah, yeah, yeah, oh yeah, it was a humongous relief to be done with the murder trial. As she flitted from topic to topic—boys and school and clothes and people at the party—he noticed her makeup looked less morbidly dark, and in a somber moment, she conceded she actually enjoyed her sessions with the school counselor, Miss Liesfeld, because, no offense, it was nice to have somebody to talk to other than him and Grandma.

Over the next month, she was allowed to rewrite a term paper and do an extra-credit project in world history, rehabilitating her grades so successfully that her report card revealed nothing worse than a solitary B. There was no sign of smoking, no evidence of drinking and far fewer fights, blowups and pouting spells. She and her friend Mary Anne went with Mason and Shoni to the movies, and although it was tense for the four of them during the drive to

Mount Airy, at the start of the feature Shoni offered a tub of popcorn in Grace's direction, and she reached in and took some, volunteering a polite thank-you. Standing around the lobby after the
picture was finished, waiting for Mary Anne to return from the
restroom, Grace inquired about Shoni's bracelet, told the older
woman she thought it was cool, and on the way home they all
agreed the movie had been entertaining, prompting the teenagers
to enthusiastically recount their favorite scenes.

Naturally, Gates held fast to his nature, remained a loafer and a
hoodlum, and within a week of his release he'd moved a druggie
welfare mom and her twelve-year-old son into his one-bedroom
apartment, where the kid slept on the sofa and lived off candy and
cheese sandwiches. Gates clocked just enough temp-agency hours
to keep his day-reporting supervisor satisfied, guzzled beer and
boasted about prison at the Old Dominion and blew through his
twenty grand in less than a month, a used Chrysler ragtop, a state-
of-the-art stereo and a trip to Daytona Beach his main investments.
Drunk and stoned one frigid night in December, he called his
mother and woke her up, pleading to be allowed back into her good
graces. Quickly alert, she told him he was a corpse as far as she was
concerned, gone. "Quit your whimpering," she rebuked him. Days
later, the three hundred dollars in tens and twenties she kept
hidden in her bedroom—stashed in the same place since Gates and
Mason were boys—disappeared, and although she and Mason and
the police all damn well knew Gates had stolen it, there was no
proof, nothing they could do.

The year before, a Christmas tree had seemed like too much
trouble for Sadie Grace, but this season—in much better cheer
despite Gates's intrusion—she found herself a hacksaw in the basement and trekked to the field below her house and cut down a
handsome white pine and dragged it trunk-first back to her house,
smoking a cig as she went. She baked a ham and cooked sweet-
potato casserole and even traveled out of town to buy presents: a
pocketknife key chain for Mason, an Abercrombie gift certificate

for her granddaughter. Christmas morning, as Mason and Grace were stuffing ribbons and wrapping paper into a trash bag and tidying the den, they heard a blunt thump against the window and they turned in unison and a robin—in December, a robin—had flown into the glass, *splat*. The bird had bounced into the holly bush and lay spread there, addled and scared. Grace hurried outside and scooped it up, placed it in a cardboard box with an old pillowcase for a nest and nursed it with bread crumbs and a medicine dropper, but it never recovered, dying two days later, stiff and dry and its eyes filmy, the full-throttle collision simply too much to overcome.

Honoring his end of the *coram vobis* deal, Mason stepped down as commonwealth's attorney. So the resignation wouldn't appear forced or *too* terribly suspicious, he waited until January to inform everyone he'd had a bellyful of public life and needed a respite and was missing his daughter's best years. "Enough is enough," he would say whenever kindly people encouraged him to stay on. The most difficult part of the arrangement was persuading Custis to take over the gig—he steadfastly claimed he was "happy to be Kevin Eubanks forever." Eventually Mason told him a pointed truth, told him he calculated a portion of the reluctance was tied to a fear of being exposed, a desire to stay modest and gray and removed from the spotlight. "I've capitulated to Herman Dylan to save your queer ass," he pushed, "and you're going to repay me by taking the job and making Judge Moore happy. Step up to the plate, or I'll spread the cowboy pics myself. If you're planning to be gay, you need to do it with a little less timidity."

Custis relented and accepted the appointment from the court, became the commonwealth's attorney on March 1, 2004, and one early April weekend at the Château Morrisette wine and jazz festival, Mason and Shoni saw him with a stranger, a slim black man with chic, trendy spectacles and a navy turtleneck. Custis introduced him as Alton, and they visited for a while and Mason invited them to stop by the farm for a nightcap if they were inclined. Not long afterward, Custis's friend appeared to watch him in a local production of

A Funny Thing Happened on the Way to the Forum, and everyone was thrilled with the play and several people got the sense of who this new fellow was, especially with Custis bounding around in his stage makeup. "I'll be damned," some remarked, while others confided it was no surprise.

Custis began to relax, quit sawing himself in half and driving away from his home so frequently, and he brought his partner to Stuart more often, but there were some places they knew to skip, some boundaries they didn't chance, and they never so much as dared to sit too close in public, were always just two guys together, the rest left to your imagination. They even persuaded Inez to travel with them to D.C. for an Al Green concert, and she had three glasses of wine and became tipsy before the show, stood between the men and bumped her hips against theirs in rhythm to the up-tempo numbers.

Mason, meanwhile, hired Larry Cowley, the finest carpenter in the county, to refurbish an old barbershop with hardwood floors and intricate crown molding, and he hung out a shingle there and started a private practice. "From one kinda clip joint to another," Larry ribbed him. The first time he had to appear opposite Custis in general district court, Mason woke up early and slipped on his wing tips using the elaborate shoehorn his friend had given him, sitting in an old Windsor chair and grinning like an idiot as each stocking foot eased down the steel. He completed the routine by buffing the leather with the whirling black cone of a chrome-plated machine he'd purchased on eBay, and his shiny, spiffy shoes set a tone right off, just as Custis had promised they would.

That morning, when Judge Greenwalt commented he didn't know who looked the more uncomfortable in the courtroom, Custis winked and said, "I taught the boy everything he knows, but you don't really think I showed him my whole bag of tricks, do you?" And then they had at it, taking almost an hour to try a shoplifting case. "Don't let my sharp-as-hell, machine-buffed, pimping shoes blind you," Mason whispered as they were walking toward the bench to argue over an exhibit.

By May, the effects of Leonard Stallings and his indictment were waning, and Mason was back to enjoying his porch and rocking chair in the evenings, briefly joined by Grace on the first truly seasonable night of spring, the weather now mild enough that the oil furnace barely fired at all, another cyclical rebirth pouring into the countryside, leaves and bushes and flowers arriving as promised, the dead, scarred world perking up and gaining pace.

Chapter Twenty-six

"Why the hell not?" Custis declared. "Might as well put in an appearance—I'm sure they'll be sportin' free punch and peanuts and the sampler platter from Sam's Club." So both Custis and Mason attended the spring groundbreaking for Chip-Tech at the Patrick County Industrial Park, and all grades of politicians and pooh-bahs showed up to claim credit for the coup and the jobs and the boon to the local economy, and one naïve, self-important speaker lauded Herman Dylan and foolishly proclaimed how much he looked forward to a long and prosperous relationship between the county and the company. "Yeah," Mason whispered to Custis, "a long and prosperous five or six years."

"Reminds me of a celebrity wedding," Custis said. "Where a 'life-time of devotion' lasts about as long as a mediocre sitcom."

Ian Hudgens was there, and he couldn't resist a zinger, a private joke, and in his dull prepared remarks, he noted he wanted to recognize not only Mason Hunt from the Tobacco Commission, but also someone else whose behind-the-scenes involvement had been invaluable, and the smug little weasel asked Custis to stand and the unwitting audience clapped and cheered, the loudest applause of the event, and when all the speeches were done, people crowded around and thanked Custis. Finally, men in suits and women in dresses and heels grabbed brand-spanking-new shovels and posed in a semicircle and Gail Harding snapped a bunch of pictures for the paper.

Herman Dylan had his grant money, Patrick County had its plant, Custis Norman had his reputation and Mason Hunt had his friendship. Yielding to Dylan had been a simple choice for Mason, though he told "The Iceman," after they'd struck a bargain, that by Patrick County standards, his embalmed, blackmailing ass did in fact need a Porsche. A whole damn fleet of them.

Chapter Twenty-seven

"Grace?" Mason shouted her name, and he shouted it louder when he spied the breakfast dishes still in the sink and a black fly buzzing the festering scraps and the cranberry juice sitting on the counter, the lid off. Home from work on a June evening, he dropped his briefcase beside the kitchen table, went to the pantry and shook out a handful of almonds, still irritated. He could see Mo Jenkins out in the pasture, burning brush at the far end. Grace's music was playing, something folky and ethereal he didn't recognize. There were two messages on the machine: a call from his mother about her balky oven and a stream of badly mumbled gibberish from a boy looking for Grace who didn't leave his name. Mason yelled for her again at the top of the stairs and obediently knocked prior to entering her room, always careful of her privacy, though the knock was sharp and he barely waited before pushing open the door.

She was lying there flat on her back underneath a comforter she'd pulled nearly to her chin, pale throughout her face and neck, crying, so limp her arm tumbled off the mattress and bent unnaturally, contrary to the muscles and tendons. Mason hurried in and slid onto the bed and took her hand, correcting the bowed arm. He asked her what was wrong. "Tell me," he said. "It's okay. Did something happen at school? Why're you so upset?"

She sobbed and sniffed and then the bawling spread and jerked her shoulders and convulsed her belly like she was on the verge of vomiting. Mason touched her cheek and smoothed her hair. Acoustic music played, a flute prominent. Her screen saver flashed a head shot of her and her girlfriends, smiles and braces and goofy delight. "It's okay," he said. She caught her breath for an instant and, red-eyed and trembling, told him she was pregnant.

"You?" Mason asked, waylaid. "Seriously? You?"

"Please, please, please, a million pleases, please don't be mad. And please don't tell Grandma Sadie." She wiped snot on her bare arm. "I don't know what I'm going to do," she wailed.

"You're not even sixteen, not till September," Mason blurted. He stood and rubbed his temples with the heels of his hands. He walked in an erratic circle. He thought about Allison, wishing once more she were there to help him. "So who's the father?" he suddenly asked, the moment the question formed in his mind.

She rolled onto her stomach and burrowed up in a pillow, continued crying.

"How in Christ's name did you let this happen? Is there just no end with you, Grace? Do you have any idea how hard I've struggled to take care of you? Worried myself sick? And this is the thanks I get." He kicked a stuffed animal that had spilled from the bed, sending it against the wall. "Dammit." He pressed his temples again. "So who's the father? At least I hope it's not some Goth creep or that Burton kid with the earring."

"You promised me I could tell you anything," she wept, the words curbed by the pillow.

"I did, yeah. I sure did. But as best I can remember, I didn't tell you to get pregnant. Being able to talk to me doesn't give you immunity from irresponsible behavior. You can't do as you want and then tell me about it and expect me to . . . to . . . simply forget it." He sat on the corner of the mattress. "Stop stalling," he said.

She turned sideways so she was able to see him. "Are you gonna tell Grandma?"

"I don't know."

"You're the only person I have to help me and you're just bein' hateful."

Mason couldn't keep still. He stood and snatched her desk chair, turned it backward, straddled it and sat with his forearms balanced on the top wooden slat. "I'm not being hateful."

"I'm so, so sorry," she said.

"I'm sure you are."

"I know you must hate me," she sobbed.

"I don't hate you. You're my daughter and the center of my world. I love you, and that's not easy to say right this moment." He stood. "And I'm going to help you figure this out, and yes, I'm glad you told me. You can count on me. But you can also count on living in a gulag for the rest of the year." He stared down at her. "So who's the father, Grace?"

"Alex," she said meekly.

"The Spanish kid? The boy who did the math project with you?"

"He's not Spanish," she said, suddenly more composed. "He's Filipino. Why do you have to be such an awful redneck?"

"Me? How am I a redneck? I'm not the one fifteen and pregnant, looking at welfare checks and GED classes."

"He's smart and sweet. I suppose you'd rather me be with some dumb jock."

"I'd rather you be worried about the prom and learning to drive a car," he said, "instead of all this." He sighed. "I swear, no matter how you sweat and calculate and bust your butt, it's impossible . . . impossible to . . ." He quit on the thought and became distracted, pensive. He sat on her bed again, but his movements were different, gentle and accommodating, the lathered, bootless energy missing. The three pixilated girls held their smiles, declining sunlight silvered the dust and a cobweb strand in the windowsill, an upturned twig with its solitary shriveled leaf rested in a gutter, a ribbon of smoke from Mo Jenkins's fire curled past the window and dissolved as it went skyward. Thousands of pieces, thousands of arrangements and combinations. "But okay," he said, the words mild, tame.

"Okay what?" she asked, sensing the shift in him.

A series of images strung themselves together in his mind: a frail man standing behind a storm door, his gaze off-kilter, the door's metal scrolls, loops and curlicues running the length of his body like a strange exoskeleton; a roach squirting across a drawer bottom when he was a boy, still living with Curt; the weighted nose of a balsa-wood plane he and Gates had put together and sent sailing across their yard; baby Grace fascinated by her mother's painting, mesmerized by the colors and shapes filling in the canvas; trotting around third base at James Madison, Sadie Grace glowing in the stands. There was a gap in the music and the room fell silent between tracks, and a sliver of reasoning took root: Then and there he accepted that pell-mell came in infinite variety, from grim to sublime, wrecking ball to salvation, and while he'd always understood he couldn't resist either a sovereign with a Calvinist compass or a gale of random bumps and dips, sitting alone with his pregnant daughter, he recognized—damn—he wasn't even wise enough to distinguish blessing from curse, sweets from poison, gold from flashy pyrite.

"I'm fairly confident," he said in a humbled voice, "that we never understand as much as we think we do." He held her hand in both of his. "You and I will stick together. Come what may."

She looked at him, anxious now, unnerved how he'd so suddenly gone sci-fi on her, all hushed and restrained, like there was a monster in him or a zombie's power gaining sway, and he caught her expression and deciphered it, read her doubt exactly. He assured her he was just fine, and still plenty angry, adding that her punishment was beginning immediately. Then he ceremoniously unplugged her computer monitor and hauled it with him as he left to underscore the point.

Later, hunkered down in his wooden rocker, the porch dark except for some inside light filtering through the windows, contemplating the blank computer screen he'd stupidly deposited on the fieldstone, nothing but empty, inert glass framed by plastic, he phoned Custis on the cordless. "I have a question," he announced, assuming Custis would recognize his voice and probably had caller ID anyway.

"Yeah? Really? 'Bout what?"

"I'm thinking . . . well, maybe, I'm convinced . . . Do you believe it's difficult to be sure, early on, about the true nature of things? The repercussions . . ." He stopped. Froze.

"Mace?"

"Sorry." He was silent again. A moth, mostly silhouette, fluttered against the disconnected monitor. A TV or radio was chattering on Custis's side of the conversation.

"Hello?"

"I need to, uh, tell you something. In confidence."

"Absolutely," Custis said.

"But not now, I guess. Probably some other time."

"What the hell's wrong with you, huh? You been samplin' the methadone clinic? Watchin' *Cannonball Run*? You gonna make me drive over there?"

"Nah. I'm okay. Just learning new shit, Custis. Getting schooled. Again. Sorry to bother you."

Chapter Twenty-eight

The man in his mid-twenties was sitting at a food-court table on the second floor of Tanglewood Mall in Roanoke, Virginia, an hour's distance from Patrick County. He was wearing Wrangler jeans, tennis shoes, no belt and a long-sleeve shirt. He'd shaved, but his hair could've used attention. He was compact, intense, fit, and he was eating a slice of cheese pizza, using a plastic fork at first, then his fingers. He was gruff when the dandified man in a suit—a young guy with creases and starch and a peculiar accent—approached him.

"I'm sorry to interrupt your meal," the stranger said. "But I wondered if I might have a few minutes with you?"

"Don't need no credit card. Don't need a time-share. Don't need my family's picture taken. Don't need any more religion."

The stranger laughed, a deep, husky, robust ha-ha-ha. "Good for you. Me either. I agree." He offered to shake. "I'm Dallas Ackerman," he announced, though it was a lie, the name an alias he'd created weeks ago. "And you're Mr. Thompson, correct? Mr. Wayne Thompson, Jr.?"

Thompson slowly, skeptically accepted his hand. "Yeah. Do I know you?"

The man took a seat. He and Ian Hudgens had arrived in Roanoke the day before and followed Thompson until he was alone. Hudgens was keeping watch from another table, dressed casually, piddling around with a plate of lo mein. "You don't, but you'll soon be glad you do."

"How'd you get my name?" Thompson demanded. By trade he was a welder, and the kind of man who had little tolerance for nonsense and tomfoolery, especially today. He pushed away the pizza remains and greasy paper plate. The question he'd just put to Dallas Ackerman translated as "you better not be fucking with me."

"Great, yes, I'd have the same response," Ackerman said confidently. "We got your name from a life insurance policy."

"Oh, damn. I left that off my list. No need for you to waste your breath. I ain't interested in the slightest."

"I'm not a salesman, Mr. Thompson. No, no, not at all. I'm here to give *you* money."

"Sure," Thompson said sarcastically. "There's a first."

"Seriously, Mr. Thompson, I represent Apex-Continental Insurance. Your father, the late Mr. Wayne Thompson, Sr., purchased one of our products years ago. A delayed-benefit, whole-life policy that recently matured. You're the beneficiary."

"Let me guess—he left the cash in a Nigerian bank, and all I have to do is give you a grand so some evil king will release my money. I mean, come on, man, me and you are in a mall and outta the blue you hit me up and expect me to think you're the real deal? What kinda company hunts you down on Saturday afternoon and . . . Hey, how would you even know what I look like?"

"We very much believe in the personal touch, Mr. Thompson. A company hallmark. We phoned your house and your wife said you were here"—this much was true, although they were staring right at him when they dialed the number—"and we obtained your photo from the division of motor vehicles. We have a plane to catch, so we decided to see if we could locate you and save time. Three hundred thousand dollars is a lot of money—you can best bet we do our homework before turning it over."

"Say again? You're gonna give me three hundred thousand dollars?"

"We already have. It was wired into an account yesterday morning. I'm merely here to carry the good news."

"You're kiddin'?" Thompson began to believe there might be something to this. He unconsciously bit a nail.

Dallas Ackerman opened a small briefcase and presented Thompson with a sealed manila envelope. "Here's the paperwork, Mr. Thompson. The money is in the Cayman Islands. We're an international conglomerate, and we try to keep tax consequences at a minimum. I'd probably leave the money there or take it in small cash withdrawals, under ten thousand. The IRS can be very unfair, especially if people become flashy, no matter how legitimate the transaction. If you or your accountant have any inquiries, there's a company card enclosed with my number. It's a switchboard, but they'll connect you immediately or take a message."

"Is this like a TV show? Hidden camera or microphones in the potted plants?" Thompson scanned the mall, flinging his head every which way, his eyes keen.

"Nope."

"So I just got rich?"

"Well, *rich* is a relative term. You just received three hundred thousand dollars."

"No catch?" Thompson asked, his tone more amicable.

"You'll need to sign a receipt."

"Whoa. So . . . wait . . . how do I know the money's where you say it is? I might be signing for somethin' I don't have."

Ackerman nodded. "I'll leave the document with you, and when you're satisfied, you can have it notarized and return it to me. One of our principals is anxious to make certain you've been compensated. He knew your father years ago."

"Knew my dad? How?"

"I'm uncertain, Mr. Thompson. Perhaps he sold him the policy. I'm not in that particular loop. It's not my concern."

"So it's done?" Thompson asked.

"Absolutely. Congratulations."

"This is all legal?"

"I wouldn't be giving you my contact information if it weren't," Ackerman assured him.

"So I can go take out five thousand dollars right now?"

"Yes."

"My daddy fixed this up for me?"

"Indeed," Ackerman smoothly answered, unaware of the irony.

"This is amazing." Thompson beamed. "Last month, after five years at the same job, my factory was closed and I was laid off. Jobs are scarce here. I been lookin' for work and gettin' turned down and we were scrapin' bottom. I got bills to pay. You have no idea what this means to us."

"I'm glad we could help."

"I mean, damn, what did I do to deserve this?"

Ackerman thought for a moment and allowed himself to step briefly out of character. "Nothing, Mr. Thompson. You didn't do anything. It simply came your way. How about that? Blind luck."

"I'm still confused," Ackerman said as he and Hudgens were walking to their rental car. "Who is this Thompson character to Mason Hunt? He's certainly not an intermediary or a shield or a bagman. Definitely not the type. Why's Mr. Dylan giving Hunt's consultant's fee to a welder with no connections or clout?"

"Not for us to understand, Henry," Hudgens replied, using his subordinate's correct name. Hudgens, of course, understood very well the tie between Mason and the Thompsons, and though he and his boss generally kept information very much under wraps, he couldn't resist showing off for Henry, revealing a secret. "The really amazing thing is we only contributed two hundred. Frigging *Hunt* kicked in the other hundred thou. I made the arrangements myself, transferred the cash from his personal account. On his instructions."

"No shit?"

"No shit. It's why I love my job. And why Herman Dylan's flying on his private jet and you and I are coaching it back to the city with no legroom."

"Hell, maybe the welder's working for us."

"Maybe," Hudgens said, toying with Henry. "All I know is it took me forever to scrub the money clean and hide this corporately and conceal our involvement. Let me know if Thompson calls the service with any questions."

"So Hunt lost money on the deal. Go figure."

"Lot of chutes and ladders in our business," Hudgens said gravely. "Always have to watch your step or you might wind up in a rabbit hole."

Chapter Twenty-nine

From his office window, more than two years after Gates's release, Judge Moore spied Mason Hunt trickling up the sidewalk, this large, athletic man wearing a pin-striped suit, and he was moving in dainty half steps, a child at his hip, a little girl, beautiful and exotic and already a spitfire, her skin tinted brown, rangy like the Hunts, set off by Allison Rand's blond hair, a genetic long shot if there ever was one. The tiny girl stopped, tired of walking, and she stretched out her arms for her grandfather to collect her, and she must have said something, because he squatted and laughed and grabbed her with both hands, and right there on Main Street, still laughing, he leaned back and held her aloft and tossed her above his head in the fashion that has caused mothers to scold fathers since the beginning of history, and the girl loved it, her expression close to rapture. "Yeah," the judge said softly to an empty room. "Maybe so."

"Life jigsaws on," Mason had told Moore shortly after Grace gave birth, "but it's okay because the odds are fifty-fifty the very next piece will be my deliverance, just as likely good as bad. The secret is—and here's the sweet part—often we don't really know which is which, especially early in the game. I've added that to the formula—makes it easier to be optimistic even when you've been knocked around a bit. My limitations keep me sane these days. Nearsightedness is my own personal lottery ticket." He smiled the smile of a man who'd learned to offset hardship. "We did pretty well, you and me. Sandbagged the flood. It's certainly not according to our exact design, not the domino I would've tripped, but where would Grace and my grandbaby be if I were in jail?"

"A fine thought," Moore had said, "but I guess I believe in the occasional unpolluted cruelty or dyed-in-the-wool tragedy."

"You can still afford to," Mason quickly replied.

"And reasonable people might disagree on how well we did, given all the laws we chiseled." They'd never mentioned the judge's help with the *coram vobis* decision before then, and they would never speak of it again.

The conversation came while they were eating a late breakfast at the café, and Mary, the owner, had loaded up Mason's meal with extra ham and a second gravy biscuit, free of charge, as she always did for him, and after he left, she allowed as to how the new baby really had changed him, how he was his old self again, the way he used to be when Allison was still with them. Through a rectangle of plate glass, above the stenciled red letters spelling COFFEE BREAK, Judge Moore caught a glimpse of Mason crossing the street to his office, mostly his top half, Atlas's shoulders and flecks of gray hair, and in a sense Moore envied him, a man forged and tempered, all the clay and filler and alloy burned away, someone with tales to recite, advice to give, a place that fit him.

Patrick County being Patrick County, Mary began stacking the dirty dishes from the table and wondered aloud, no malice intended, none at all, "Now is that child Spanish or black? I've heard both."

"Swedish, I think," the judge deadpanned.

Oddly enough, a few minutes later that same day, within a stone's throw of the restaurant, Moore met Wayne Thompson's elderly parents on the sidewalk, in town for errands and to pay their insurance premiums. Mrs. Thompson was carrying two new patterns from the sewing shop and several yards of cloth, her husband a cotter key for the deck of his riding mower. As was the custom, the judge lifted his hand to the bill of an imaginary hat and nodded in Mrs. Thompson's direction, and they passed greetings and commented on how darn dry it was, agreeing a good soaking rain was very much needed. Their exchange was brief and they pushed on in different directions, but the judge soon slowed his pace and peeked over his shoulder as they stepped within inches of the door Mason had recently exited, the shards and fragments from 1984 as close to alignment as they might ever be. The judge tested the scene through his big ol' eyes and registered no regrets, no guilt, no second thoughts. He stopped completely, quarter-turned toward the Thompsons and the Coffee Break and doffed the invisible hat again, this time took it all the way off and brought it to his waist, ending with a tiny bow that would've seemed pure lunacy to anyone watching.

Part Three

My office at the Patrick County courthouse has two curiosities. First, my name is spelled wrong on the fancy brass doorplate the bar association gave me when I began work. Martin Filmore Clark, Jr., it reads. My middle name is actually spelled Fillmore, with two l's, but the lawyers' gesture was so generous and heartfelt I've never complained or asked for a replacement. Better yet is the possum. I'm honestly not certain who gave it to me or when or why, but a stuffed possum sits grinning atop the bookcase in my chambers, guarding the law books and craning its neck so it's visible from the defendant's table all the way out in the courtroom. The creature is a novelty, a child's toy, not a real animal skinned and preserved by a taxidermist, and it has white whiskers and a plastic nose that rattles.

Early one fall morning in 2006, I found it lying on the floor with its polyester paws pointed toward the ceiling, its synthetic gray belly turned skyward. As I was about to pick it up and return it to its spot on the bookcase, Sandra, the newest hire from the clerk's office, knocked on my door and asked if she could come in. Seeing what had happened, she laughed and inquired if the critter was dead.

"Looks like he's been poisoned," I joshed.

"Oh," she replied, playing along. "Think he'll make it?"

"I believe so. He's a tough old cuss. Been through a lot."

"Good," she answered. "Wouldn't want to lose him." She glanced down at an open steno pad. "Susan wanted me to check with you about a file we can't locate. She thinks it might be up here." Sandra ticked off a series of numbers and letters. "It's from 2003, kinda old. Do you have it?"

"I do." I wasn't particularly surprised by the request, neither bothered nor agitated.

"Is it okay if I carry it downstairs? The computer shows the case is concluded. We're just trying to tie off a few loose ends. Locate some strays."

By now I had the possum in my hand, and for a moment I let it dangle, holding it by the tail. "Yeah," I told her. "I'll get it for you. It sort of wound up here and never made it back into the system. More inertia than anything else. One minute a case is as hot as a two-dollar pistol, the next it's collecting dust."

"The index says it's a 'coram vobis,' " she noted, emphasizing the second syllable of each Latin word. "A new term for me. Of course, a lot of this is new for me."

"We don't see very many," I said. "They're definitely rare, thank goodness." I took the file from my drawer and handed it to her, then replaced the possum.

"I sure don't envy you your job," she said sincerely. "I can't believe how much you have to learn and keep up with."

"Can't really argue with you there."

Sandra wished me well and left, carrying the blue cardboard folder with her, a single skinny file about to take its place among thousands of others. I went in the empty courtroom, to where the defendants sit with their lawyers, checking to make sure I'd returned the stuffed animal to plain view. I could see it clearly, no problem. Twelve vacant jury chairs faced in my direction, six in front, six behind, the leather worn and cracked on their arms. Plaster walls, thirty-foot ceilings and dark polished wood vouched that this was a solemn place and not to be trifled with. I considered Sandra's visit and decided, after mulling over the law's majestically stubborn ways and limits, that when they unscrew my misspelled name from the door's ancient panels, I'd tell the new occupant what Judge Richardson told me the day he took me into his confidence back in 1992—I'll offer his wisdom about not being neutered by notions and bloodless statutes, and I'll add a little extra, throw in a mention of how life jigsaws on. Standing by myself, waiting for the attorneys and bailiff and witnesses to arrive for the nine o'clock case, my desk drawers clean and my decision on an obscure writ finally put to rest in a metal cabinet, I was content, convinced it was just fine for me to look through the window at my small town's doings and to walk underneath the line of portraits on the wall, men who'd sat in judgment before I knew much about anything, all of us trying to romance the same haughty, impossible will-o'-the-wisp.

ACKNOWLEDGMENTS

Thanks to: My friend and agent Joe Regal, Liz Van Hoose, the magnificent Gabrielle Brooks, S. Edward Flanagan, Charles Wright, Frank Beverly, Julia Bard, Mrs. Ann Belcher, David "Hollywood" Williams, Edd Martin, Eddie Turner, Nancy Turner, Jan McInroy, Barnie Day and Chris Corbett.

Also, a big tip of the hat to my dad, the venerable Martin F. "Fill" Clark, who—in one way or another—is responsible for just about every page of this book.

As always, I am hugely indebted to Gary Fisketjon, the finest editor on the planet.

Finally, I'm grateful to my sweet wife, Deana, for her help, love, corrections and many trips through the manuscript.

ALSO BY MARTIN CLARK

THE MANY ASPECTS OF MOBILE HOME LIVING

Judge Evers Wheeling is in need of a change on the morning the mysterious and drop-dead gorgeous Ruth Esther English pays him a visit. Hung over, sweltering in the North Carolina sun, bitter toward his estranged wife, and dreading the day's docket of petty criminal cases, Evers allows Ruth Esther to tell him her strange story and suddenly finds himself in wholly uncharted territory. He reluctantly agrees to help Ruth Esther find a cache of stolen money, then recruits his pot-addled brother and a band of merry hangers-on for a transforming adventure that is, to say the least, chock full of the weird, the dangerous and the never-expected. Road trips, infidelity, suspected killers, winning Lotto tickets, and drunken philosophical rants are just a few of the elements that combine to make *The Many Aspects of Mobile Home Living* what it is: one part legal thriller, one part murder mystery, and all parts wild.

Fiction/978-0-375-70709-4

PLAIN HEATHEN MISCHIEF

Moments after finishing a six-month sentence in the Roanoke jail for a crime he might not have committed, Baptist minister Joel King is served some unwelcome papers. His wife wants a divorce, and the teenage vixen everyone believes he seduced is suing him for five million dollars. Holding on to his faith with a white-knuckle grip, Joel accepts a ride out west with Edmund Brooks, a member of his former flock who has some Commandment-challenging ideas about helping Joel find himself. *Plain Heathen Mischief* ranges from the cross to the double cross, from Virginia to Las Vegas, from courtrooms to trout streams, as Martin Clark follows his Job-like hero through dubious choices and high-dollar insurance scams to a redemption no reader could possibly predict.

Fiction/978-1-4000-3411-6

VINTAGE CONTEMPORARIES
Available at your local bookstore, or visit
www.randomhouse.com